THE ZODIAC WARRIORS

TONY MOON

RF
Publishing

THE ZODIAC WARRIORS

Tony Moon
As told by Karen Peradon

Artwork by Ivan Earl Aquila
Published by Red Feather Publishing 2021
karen@redfeather.com.au

ISBN:9780645373905

I would like to dedicate this book to my loving and caring partner, Jo Anne, who has put up with all my highs and lows whilst writing this book and all her encouragement to help getting it completed.
Also special thanks to Karen Peradon my editor/ghost-writer. I couldn't have done it without you.
To all my family and friends—those who edged me on with all your positive words thank you. And to any that have doubted me. Well, huh. I've done it.

First Aries, glorious in his Golden Wool,
Looks back and wonders at the mighty Bull,
Whose back-parts first appear: He bending lies,
With Threat'ning Head, and calls the Twins to rise,
They clasp for fear, and mutually embrace;
And next the Twins with an unsteady pace
Bright Cancer rolls: then Leo shakes his mane:
And following Virgo calms his rage again:
Then Day and Night weigh'd in Libra's Scales,
Equal awhile, at last the Night prevails,
And longer grown the heavier scale inclines
And draws bright Scorpius from the Winter signs:
Him Centaur follows with an aiming Eye
His Bow full drawn and ready to let fly:
Next narrow Horns the twisted Caper shows,
And from Aquarius' Urn a Flood o'erflows.
Near their loved Waves cold Pisces take their seat,
With Aries join and make the round complete.
Next Ophiuchus strides the mighty Snake,
Untwists his winding Folds, and smooths his Back,
Extends its Bulk, and o'er the slippery Scale
His wide stretched hands on either side prevail:
The Snake turns back his head and seems to rage,
That war must last where equal Powers engage.

Marcus Manilius' Astronomica is an astrological poem dating from the 1st century AD. This extract is from a translation by Thomas Creech, 1670 AD.

Hundreds of thousands of light years away, there existed a primeval star system of planets called Horos made up of thirteen planets. The occupants of these planets had many powers, their technology was advanced, their communication faultless, their knowledge great. In evolutionary comparison, if Earth was the hatching egg of a dinosaur, Horos the dying breath of the last man on Earth. The planets of Horos sustained life, fauna, flora, minerals, oxygen and water. Until now.

Prymaw checked off his co-guardians. "Regida, are you clear?"

No response.

"She was right behind me, Prymaw," Plaadio responded.

"OK. I don't have Chime on my..."

"Prymaw? Are you there?" Fyon's voice was unusually wavering. "There's debris coming at me from the surface. We don't have long. The force of the black hole is pulling Horos apart."

"Hold steady, Fyon, we have clearance time."

His radar showed hundreds of flying specks of light. "Castor, come in. I can't make out what is spacecraft and what is space matter."

"We're out at 110 degrees, there's less debris out here," Castor responded.

"Careful Castor, you are on the edge of the trajectory. You could spin off course."

"Relax, Pollux and I know what we're doing."

"Still no word from Regida, she's not on my radar. Or Chime."

There was a crash and Prymaw jerked sideways. A piece of rock smashed his vessel, and he veered towards the gaping blackness that pulled his home, planet Aries, into its chasm.

"Prymaw!" Plaadio yelled, "pull back hard, use your booster!"

There was an unsettling silence. Prymaw breathed deeply as he felt the pull of the black hole on his vessel. He watched as his magnificent planet edged closer to the darkness. Smaller pieces of space debris slipped passed it and disappeared. He could see the swirling red clouds and glimpses of the land below. His family, his friends, his fellow Ariens holding tight, watching the blackness creep closer and closer. He imagined them clutching onto each other. His children sobbing. He felt the urge to travel with it, give in to the pull of oblivion. He watched his planet elongate as it touched the forcefield, resisting its pull and then... it was gone. He cried out, his hands reaching to the window. His chest released a sob of anguish.

"Prymaw, pull back, get out of there!" Plaadio yelled.

Prymaw lifted his head and breathed for a moment. He moved his hand in the space in front of his face. A screen came up. He opened his fingers up wide and waved his right hand to the side. His vessel slowed for a moment and then accelerated away from the hole.

"I'm clear." He breathed a deep ragged breath. "It's gone, my whole planet, sucked into that thing."

"I'm sorry, brother. They're all going the same way," Plaadio said softly. He cleared his throat. "Hastia and Amrez are on my left. Degon is up ahead, naturally."

"Xincon, Teres?" asked Prymaw.

"The idiots are racing," said Plaadio.

"Well, that's dumb, we'll all arrive together." Prymaw shook his head.

"I'm right behind you," Chime came in at last.

"Where were you?"

"Just saying goodbye to my beloved Libra," she replied.

"Talk about cutting it fine."

"It's OK, Regida was on my case."

"For once, I agree with her."

Prymaw ticked off his compadres in his mind. One was missing.

"Where are the Pisceans?" he asked.

"Mequitha and Maroda were the last to take off, this is tough for them. They would have disappeared with their planet if we gave them a choice," said Chime. "I thought for a minute they were going to stay."

"Yeah well, we're all out of our comfort zone," said Prymaw. "At least twelve of us made it. Let's have a minute of silence for Ophiuchus."

"Someone had to be on the edge of the solar system. It's not our fault he didn't jump ship in time," said Fyon.

"Many of us disagreed with him over the years, but he and his kind were still Horoscopians. You will show some respect, Fyon."

There was silence while they thought of Ophiuchus and their own Zodiac kin who had to remain behind, soon to be sucked into the biggest vacuum in the universe.

"We've got thirty seconds before we leave the system. Good luck, Zodiac Warriors, see you on planet Earth."

A wave of energy pulsed through the vessels and the communication was cut. Each Warrior activated their vessels' automatic thrusts, propelling the twelve pods into their extremely long and lonely journey, the only remaining morsels left from a once thriving civilisation. There was no time for them to grieve the disappearance of their entire solar system. Once clear from the atmosphere, the Zodiac Warriors transmuted into each of their vessels to be preserved while travelling the vast universe for thousands of light years, and millions upon millions of miles on course for the only other life-sustaining planet they could find.

At last, the vessels entered the solar system of planet Earth. Dinosaurs crashed through the fertile land, rain drenched the flora of vast forests, and fish flashed through the many oceans. Meteoric debris crashed into the pod of vessels, scattering the pieces into constellations that found an equilibrium in the sky above the blue planet. But the atmosphere drew in the core of each vessel, burning them up, reducing them down to nothing but a small medallion. They scattered apart; the biosphere decimating the force that held them together for so long. As the vessels hit gravity, they plummeted through clouds, clear mountain air, through storms and snow, tearing through the earth's crust of ice, dirt or water.

G iven the look on the faces of the professors in the audience, Lily might as well have been from another galaxy. She was pitching the board for funds to travel to Africa to research the water basins in the savannahs of Africa. Her chest barely reached the wooden podium as she turned her papers, but her voice was clear and sure.

"My thesis asserts that we have a water crisis on our planet. The problem is that my thesis will be in vain if I do not publish in the next six months."

A man in the auditorium sat sideways in his chair, his legs crossed. He sighed and raised his fingers off his legs.

She nodded to the man. "Yes, you have a question?"

"You are aware that there have been over 10000 desalination plants built worldwide in the last ten years? Hydrologists did foresee a water shortage, but everyone knows the NuHydra development has solved that problem. I'm sorry Ms Noor, but your research is a decade out of date."

"Of course I am aware. So why then are water courses contaminated and wars breaking out over water shortages in many fourth-world countries?"

"I'm not sure where you are finding this data. I haven't seen any reports. It is probably a problem with distribution. There are pipes being laid across several oceans. A problem like this does not get solved overnight."

"Distribution is not the problem, sir. Countries have been sending water by ships for decades. For example, the Spanish government has been moving water by barge for years. Wars over water ownership have broken out in many regions of Africa and the Middle East in the last six months. It's just no one reports it. It is unknown how many people have perished through thirst or skirmishes, however according to all media outlets, there is no civil unrest. I have received reports of rioting in India due to waterborne diseases, but this information has been stifled. My assertion is that the water is being stockpiled."

"And you know this how, exactly?"

"I have contacts overseas. I'm active on social media platforms. I talk to people. It's called research."

"Your assertions, or I could call them conspiracy theories, suggest that our governments and world health consortium are dishonest. Yet, you, a young university student seems to be the only one who thinks there may be a problem. I, for one, believe that this, shall we say 'story', will do nothing but besmirch the reputation of Riverside University."

"I have been studying the river systems of Australia, America and the UK. Water basins are reducing. Some are empty. There are droughts in 75% of the Earth. Water quality is falling. The frequency of acid rain is rising. My proposed expedition to Africa will deepen my research in another continent to see what is happening on the ground there."

The man glanced at his associates and raised his eyebrows.

"We will consider your application. Thank you."

Lily collected up her papers and left the podium. Her best friend, Jason Wallace, jumped up from his seat in the front row. He trotted to keep up as she marched out without looking at the small audience of university professors and staff. They passed through the hall and through the sandstone arch that bore the university motto: *Simul discimus, vivimus, supersumus.* Together we learn, we live, we survive.

"Great presentation, you nailed it."

"Oh come on, Jase, he railroaded me!"

"Don't let him get to you Lil, he's just an old fuddy-duddy."

"That old fuddy-duddy is on the board. If I don't get my funding, I can kiss the trip to Africa goodbye. It's so unfair. Universities are merely businesses wanting to make a profit. The only way you get funding is if I agree with the capitalist, greedy idiots who run this place."

"The university or the country?"

"Both!"

"But you've worked on this thesis for years, you can't give up on it!"

"My sweet Jason, you should know me better than that! I'm not letting this go. I can just feel I'm on the cusp of something big. Anyway, I'm starving." She waved her keys in the air. "Want a lift home, get a takeaway?"

They walked to the car park and Lily pressed the button on her keys. The bright blue Mazda MX-5 twinked, and they slid into the leather seats. Jason relaxed back into its comfort.

"Must be nice to have a wealthy dad." He sighed as he admired the sleek lines of the interior.

Lily stamped her foot on the accelerator and Jason jolted forward as she skidded out of the carpark and onto the road.

"Whoa, steady!" he yelped.

"You don't have a clue, Jase. My father is Malaysian, sitting pretty in his massive bloody house in Kuala Lumpur with his pretty new wife and two perfect bloody golden sons. He thinks bank rolling me and Mum means his job is done and conscience clear. But I'm the idiot who has to clean up after her drinking sessions, pay for all the late-night TV shopping sprees. I'd rather have a poor dad who loved me and his wife, not farming her and the mixed-race kid back to Australia when things got messy."

They drove in silence for a few minutes.

"I'm sorry..." they both said together before laughing. "Twins!" they chorused and joined their pinkies together.

The air cleared, Lily asked, "When are you going to quit that dead-end job of yours?"

"When a better one comes along, I guess."

"I can't bear the thought of you packing eggs in that crappy industrial estate."

"It pays. Not that I'd ever afford a beauty like this," he said, stroking the plush interior.

She cocked her eyebrow at him, as if to say, 'don't start down that road again'.

"Why don't you think about doing an exhibition? Those photos you showed me last week are incredible!"

"Where? I don't have the cash to set it up, Lil. Plus, I want to get a few more done. The series just isn't complete without a balance of the animals I'm portraying."

"Excuses, excuses. I swear you'll smash it."

"Yeah, yeah. Hey, shall we go through your funding proposal one last time?" he said.

"Nice dodge, Jase, but yeah, let's go over it one more time."

The funding proposal was ambitious. Lily intended to travel to East Africa where Zakary, an old friend in Kenya, could take her to investigate river systems in the Serengeti.

A week passed while the university board reviewed her proposal. She met up with Jason at the campus bar.

"Heard anything yet, darl?" Jason asked.

"You'll be the first person to know when I do."

"So what's the plan?"

"Leave on the first of next month. I've got my eye on flights. Zakary is on standby. I've packed my bag."

"What about your mum?"

"She'll have to manage. I'm not her babysitter. Part of me just wants this trip so I can have a break from her, to be honest."

Lily had just left her mother, Abigale. They had rowed again; the same argument, the same words, the same outcome. Lily had screamed into her mother's gin-slackened face. But her mother just turned up the TV.

"Must be tough."

"Hmm. Don't wanna talk about it."

Her mobile rang. She looked at the number. "Oh my God, it's them!"

She rushed out of the bar and took the call. Jason watched her through the window. Was that a smile or a slight grimace? She turned her back to the window, and after a minute, ended the call. She stood still for a moment and re-entered the bar.

"Well?" he asked.

Lily swore and shook her head.

"What? You didn't get it? Bugger me!"

"They'll give me $500, that's it."

Lily rubbed the heels of her hands across her forehead and swore again.

"Sorry, Jase. I've got to get out of here. I'm bad company right now."

Jason gave her an awkward hug. "Keep your pecker up, possum. It'll work out."

She ran to her car, holding back her anger until safely in the confines of the Mazda. She put her foot down and screeched out of the university.

"Narrow-minded f-wits! Stupid old stuffed dinosaurs with no vision!"

Swearing and smashing her hand on her steering wheel, she felt her opportunity drain away, like her mother's gin. She drove to her place of sanity, the dojo at her local gym. If there was one thing she thanked her father for, it was how he introduced her to martial arts when she was growing up in Malaysia. She had excelled in kick-boxing and kung fu, gaining black belt as a teenager. When her father had got sick of her mum gallivanting around and embarrassing him, they had returned to her mother's birthplace. But she had kept up her training—more for her mental health than physical.

Lily used the gym to smash out her frustration. The workout cleared her head, but she was still no closer to going to Tanzania. Showered and changed, she drove to her apartment past fast-food joints, car yards and hardware stores. She was sick of being stuck here, in the same old scene, the same old ideas. She felt like the only person on the planet who could see things weren't right. If the university wouldn't support her to finish her thesis and potentially prevent the death of millions of people, she would have to find another way.

Perhaps she could get a loan, but she was a 25-year-old student; banks didn't like those. Perhaps she could ask her father for an advance, but she knew she wouldn't. She couldn't face another 'no', dismissing her as he always did just because she was born a female. She couldn't wait to be free from his money as it was. As she turned her mind around and around, the traffic lights turned from green to red. The car idled at the lights, and she stared out of the dusty windscreen. The state government had outlawed car-washing due to water restrictions. She squirted the windscreen with cleaning liquid to clear it and then right in front of her, as the dust was wiped away, she saw her solution. As soon as the green arrow flashed, she pulled into the car yard on the corner of the junction and turned off her engine. A smiling salesman came to greet her, sliding his fingers wantonly across the bonnet. What is an electric blue sports car worth if it's covered in dirt and stuck at traffic lights every five minutes?

Lily entered her apartment and took a deep breath.

"Mum?"

"Lily, is that you?" Abigale called out.

"Who else would it be, Mum?"

Lily rolled her eyes. At least her mother was awake. She dropped her bag by the door and went into the kitchen. Abigale was sitting at the kitchen table painting. Jars of murky green water, brushes and kitchen towel daubed with swipes of paint littered the table.

"You're up?"

"Mmm hmm. What do you think?"

Abigale held up her painting. Lily tilted her head one way, then the other. She squinted. "It's good."

"It's the cosmos, it's called 'Written in the Stars'."

"I'm glad you are feeling better." Lily put the kettle on. "I've got something to tell you."

Abigale looked at her daughter, wide-eyed. Lily took another deep breath.

"I'm going away."

Abigale put down her paintbrush. "Away? What do you mean?" She scratched her neck.

"I told you, the trip I have planned. To Tanzania."

"No, no. You didn't tell me..."

"Mum, I did."

"Well, you can't go. Not right now. I need... I need..."

"A drink?" Lily flared.

"Yes, no. I'm trying to stop. You know I am."

Lily filled the mug, sloshing water over the counter.

"Please don't go, Lil. I can't manage without you."

"I can't put my life on hold for you anymore. I'm not your slave."

Abigale raised her arm across her body and swept it across the table. The jars smashed onto the floor, the green water staining the floor and kitchen cupboards. The painting of a star-filled sky floated onto the detritus, smudged and distorted. Lily shook her head. She poured the tea down the sink and walked to the doorway.

"I've booked the ticket. I leave next week. I'll find someone to look in on you."

❄

A week later, Lily and Jason boarded the NuDelta airline flight at Perth Airport, headed for the plains of Serengeti.

"Did I thank you for bringing me along, Lil?"

"About a hundred million times! Just get some amazing shots of wild animals, let's show Australia the magical and mysterious things we find there."

"How was your mum when you left?"

"Comatose, but I've organised someone to look in on her. I feel bad for not feeling bad." She gave a shrug.

"So how do you know Zakary?"

Lily laughed, snorting through her nose.

"What?" Jason dragged out the word. He leaned in, resting both hands on one shoulder. "I sense gossip!"

"We used to play poker together, in Malaysia. He's the son of one of my father's friends," she said.

"And?"

Lily squirmed.

"Come on, dish the goss."

"Well, I had a bit of a crush on him when I was twelve."

She winced.

"Go on..."

"I kissed him."

Jason gasped. "You go, girlfriend! Twelve years old?!"

"I know, I know. It was really awkward. He burst out laughing and patted me on the head."

"Aw, sweet cheeks. How old was he?"

"He was about sixteen. He's Kenyan. His parents worked for the Kenyan Embassy in KL. He seemed so grown up, mysterious. Guess I was just too young for him. Gah, I cringe just thinking about. Anyway, we reconnected on Facebook a couple of years ago. I'm just praying he won't remember anything about it." Lily shook her head, ending the conversation.

"Why didn't I know you played poker?"

"I have many hidden talents, plus you're not rich enough to play me!"

"I bet you win all the time."

Lily nodded, "Pretty much!"

The plane coasted into Nairobi's Jomo Kenyatta International Airport at 5.30 am as the morning sun lit the sky a violet red.

"Red sky at night, shepherds' delight, red sky in the morning..." Jason began

"... A new day is dawning and I need coffee!" Lily finished.

"Is poker-boy meeting us? Is he handsome? Single?"

"Yes, yes, and why are you asking?"

"Just checking out my options," he said with a wink. "Maybe it wasn't you but your vajayjay that put him off!"

Lily punched Jason in the arm. "You're so crass! I'm pretty sure he's straight, Jase, and please stay focused on the job in hand!"

"Whatever you say, boss!"

"Come on, can't wait to stretch my legs."

As soon as Lily recognised the face of Zakary Salawudeen, she remembered why she'd dived in with a kiss all those years ago. He had grown into the handsome man his sixteen-year-old self had hinted at. Both Lily and Jason gasped. It had been a dozen years since they had met in person. He was taller than she remembered, his muscular chest just fitting under his crisp white t-shirt tucked into hiking pants. Jason's mouth opened, and he nudged his shoulder into Lily's. She poked her elbow into his ribs and muttered, "Behave!"

Zakary's deep brown eyes locked onto Lily's, and he smiled shyly, holding out his hand.

"Look at you, all grown up!" he said.

She took a breath in and squeaked, "You too!"

Zakary shook Jason's ready hand and ushered them into a taxi to his apartment. He made them drinks and sat them at his kitchen table where maps and supplies laid were out. He showed the newcomers where they would be going.

"Thanks, Zak. I really appreciate you taking the time to guide us. We couldn't do it without you," Lily said.

Zakary smiled his dazzling smile. "This trip has worked out well for me too. Some of the tribe nearby want me to look at some strange soil sediment that's been uncovered by erosion. I've been wanting to check it out."

"Cool. So, what do we need to know?" Lily gathered herself from Zak's captivating good looks.

"It's a bit hairy out there at the moment. A lot of trouble with the Maji Shujaa Mwasi army. They're advancing across the country, and they say the checkpoints are letting them into the national park."

"Is that why there were military at the airport?" asked Jason. "I haven't seen that much hardware since I played Call of Duty!"

"That's normal for us these days. After many years of relative stability, we find ourselves back in war. Many are starving thanks to global warming and the ongoing droughts have driven the people to desperate measures. Water is like gold here. There are numerous militia roaming the country, looking for recruits, money and land. They break out in fighting. The government sends in the army. Many innocent people are caught in the crossfire. No one really knows who is who. It's chaos."

"And you think it's safe to go in?" Jason swallowed.

"I studied anthropology and was born in Kenya. It's like all those bloody great snakes and deadly spiders you have in Australia. You just live with them like they don't exist. The militia—the risks don't translate as dangerous to me. I've lived with and studied many tribes In East Africa, been into the savannah countless times on expeditions and guiding tourists. It's my life. We'll be fine. Don't worry, man! You're in safe hands."

The following morning, the three rose early and headed for the border to Tanzania. Zakary had already organised the 4x4 and gathered all the supplies. They continued to discuss the civil unrest that plagued East Africa.

"It's happening all over the world, not just here. Humans need to band together, not split apart right now," Lily commented.

"Exactly, this planet is heading for disaster, but what can we do?" Zakary asked.

"Knock some sense into us!"

"We need a bloody miracle," Jason said. "Everyone, me included, is so complacent. We think someone else will sort it out, we just wait around doing nothing, hoping someone will come and save us."

They drove for five hours before they approached the border crossing. Zakary asked Jason to pass him the case of water.

"The whole box?" Jason asked.

"This is what gets people over the border these days. Water and shilling."

A guard waved them down, a rifle dangling from his shoulder, a pistol in his halter and a menacing expression etched across his face.

"Papers and passports," he barked.

The three scrambled for their documents and park pass. Zakary handed them over with the bottles of water.

The guard shook his head. "Not good."

"What?" said Lily.

Zakary took a deep breath. "Jason, the other box."

Jason heaved the box through the window. The man tilted his head to one side.

"You pay the fine," the guard said.

"For what? This is crazy!" Lily exclaimed.

Zakary waved at Lily. "It's normal, I got this, shh."

He pulled a wad of cash out of his wallet. "Thank you, sir, this should cover it, sorry for the trouble."

The guard flicked through the notes. He cast his eyes over the interior of the car as if hunting for more prizes. His eyes lingered on Jason's camera, but Zakary broke his train of thought.

"Oh look, here, maybe your friends would like some keja, eh?" Zakary took a carton of cigarettes and passed it through the window.

The man took them and stepped back from the car. He waved them through. The three sighed with relief.

"You're bribing them with water?" Lily asked.

"Like I said, it's more valuable than gold here. The drought has gone on for two years now. People are dying every day. That's what the fighting is all about, not power but water."

The roads soon became rough, but they had to endure another three hours of bumping and tilting before they arrived at the Maasai tribe village. Ragged and road weary, they thankfully stretched out of the jeep and were met by two smiling men. Zak had employed Rasta and Jacob as their guides. The men were Maasai but had left to be educated in Nairobi. They took tourists on safari and knew the land like they knew their own mother. They showed the visitors their hut with camp beds and invited them to the centre of the village to meet the chief. The tribes people, dressed in vibrant shades of red cloth, put on a small feast to welcome them.

"We are happy to have visitors. Our income has gone down with the tourist market. Nobody is coming anymore."

The three sat as honoured guests next to the chief. Lily asked many questions, which Jacob and Rasta translated to and fro. Jason wandered around, taking photos. As the night sky filled the village with darkness, shadows of feet came from the fire and the menfolk danced for their guests, stepping and dipping, singing out their rhythmic song, telling the legends of the land. Afterwards, two elders joined them and told them about a strange patch of ground that had appeared as a result of erosion. With their arms, they told them it looked like something had been dragged along the ground long, long ago. They told a story of the eagle that crash landed from the stars and laid an egg. They described a jewel within the egg.

The next morning, Rasta and Jacob loaded up the vehicles, and they drove 40 km into the bush to the site. It was just as they had been told. There was a long channel carved out of the earth's surface and covered with a black dust. Zakary strode down the channel.

"It must be at least fifty meters. It gets deeper down this end," he yelled.

He crouched down and took samples of the black soil. Lily and Jason walked the stretch of the scarred ground to reach him.

"This is not a normal feature of the savannah. This soil is almost volcanic."

The elder beckoned them to a spot a metre or so beyond the end of the channel. He pointed to a round rock, a little larger than a baseball. Lily and Zakary put their latex gloves on and dusted away the debris. Lily pried it out of the hollow with difficulty.

"It's so heavy."

The two of them struggled, but turned it over. The elders gesticulated and babbled in their language.

"Yeah, yeah. They say the relic is in there. The elders were too scared to move it. They say it's unnatural," said Rasta.

"Should we touch it?" asked Lily.

"The elders say that it is time. They say that too many young men are leaving the tribe. There is a storm on the horizon and that they are no longer the guardian. They say that its power is dormant and must be released."

The rock was cracked on the underside, revealing another layer within.

"Is that gold?" asked Jason.

"Looks like gold or brass. Let's try to get it out."

Zakary fetched a crowbar from the jeep. They prised the crack with effort until the two sides fell apart with a thud. One piece cradled what looked like a medallion. Lily brushed off the earth and smoothed her finger over its surface. She gave it a wiggle, and it came free of the rock.

"Wow, it's beautiful." said Lily. "It's... it feels alive."

A strange vibration thrummed through her mind. The round medallion was thick. It was small enough to sit in her palm, but as heavy as the outer stone was, this seemed as light as a cloud. Yet when she tapped it, it felt dense. It had a raised image on one side and a diamond-like jewel embedded in the middle of the other.

"I can't work out what this metal is, though. It's like stone but has a glow. I've never seen anything like this. The logo looks like the ram's horns of the Aries sign. My sign, actually."

"Maybe. We'll have to examine it. Keep it safe in this," said Zakary, and he handed her a handkerchief to wrap it in. She placed it in the side pocket of her leather satchel. They scouted around the area, taking photos, measuring the channel and taking rock samples. After an hour, they regrouped.

"OK, Jase. It's your turn. Let's get you some money shots! Then we'll head to the river."

They set off into the wilderness of the Serengeti, hoping to track down the migrating wildebeest. Jason pointed to a large herd of gazelle grazing in the distance. A short way down the track were a few giraffes feeding on some trees. They spotted a couple of rhinos with a young one in tow. They drove deeper into the park. The cars slowed down. Jason and Lily scoured the scenery, seeing nothing. Then Zakary put his fingers to his lips and pointed ahead of the lead vehicle. And there was the ultimate picture, a pride of lions and cubs feasting on a carcass of a gazelle. The party inched as close as they dared. Jason's camera whirred and snapped while everyone held their breath so as not to disturb the most majestic creatures on earth.

"This is a once in a lifetime opportunity," said Jason in a low voice.

Lily smiled; the day could not have been more successful.

"OK, onward," said Zakary.

A few more miles down the road was a near-dry watering hole which blessed them with a herd of elephants. The sun now beat down and it was as if the savannah had turned the sound down. They found a tree to sit under and ate the lunch Rasta had packed for them. The air was still, and Lily watched the mirages of heat flicker in the air. She pulled her Akubra down over her face, allowing her jet lag to take command of her eyes.

After an hour, she felt a shadow pass over her and the sound of someone sitting down next to her. She raised her hat and saw Zakary.

"Nice nap?" he asked.

Lily yawned her rosebud mouth and tucked her straight black hair behind her ear. She nodded.

"It's so good to see you again, Lily. I... I was sad when you moved back to Australia."

Lily laughed. "Oh, were you?! I thought I was just an annoying kid to you."

Zak chuckled. "You were a kid, but never annoying. Still play poker?"

"When I find a worthy opponent."

"Not often then?" he winked.

"Have you got a set?"

"Of course. You challenging me to a game?"

Lily pretended to crack her knuckles. "Oh yes, Zakky boy. You better have some skin in the game!"

"Or you could kiss me if you lose?"

Lily closed her eyes and dropped her head. "I really, really hoped you had forgotten that."

Zakary threw his head back and laughed. "Forget it? I've never washed that cheek since!"

Lily groaned and pushed her hat back over her face. "Swallow me up now, please ground!"

"Sorry Lily, I didn't mean to embarrass you. Come on." He leapt up and put a hand out. "I guess we should think about making a move. Let's take you to the water!"

She shifted her Akubra back off her face and put her hands on the earth to push herself up. "What's that? I can feel the ground vibrating."

The elders were already standing, looking off into the distance. They pointed and spoke to Jacob.

"Check that out over there."

She nudged Jason, who was dozing under the shade of the other side of the tree. He opened his eyes and stretched. "What's up?"

"Look."

In the distance, they saw an enormous dust cloud.

"Is that what I think it is?" Jason said, reaching for his camera.

"Uh huh, it's your lucky day! It's the wildebeest," said Zakary. "If we drive east, we could get a closer look as they reach the river. What do you reckon Jacob?"

The guides agreed.

Lily and Jason got into their jeep with Zakary and pulled out behind Rasta, Jacob and the elders.

It was the migration of the wildebeest across the Serengeti to greener pastures. There must have been at least a hundred thousand of these creatures heading toward them, and the dust trail they left rose thirty to forty feet in the air. As the vehicles continued along, they watched as the massive herd slowed up ahead and became more and more congested.

"They've reached the river," said Rasta over the radio, "they cross here but many get eaten by crocodile."

"Poor things!" said Lily.

But the wildebeest had stopped.

"There are too many. Why aren't they moving?" said Zakary.

Rasta had stopped, and they pulled up beside him. The elders looked uneasy. One shouted and shook his head.

"He's saying we should go back," said Rasta, "but we can't, there are more herds coming behind us. The only way out is ahead or we'll be trampled. We'll have to drive through the river. Lucky for us it's the lowest it has ever been."

"What, with crocodiles?" said Jason, alarmed.

Zakary gesticulated to go toward the river. They drove over the embankment and what was left of the Masa River appeared, weaving its dirty brown water through the muddy sand plain. As they cleared the ridge, it became very clear what the problem was and why the beasts were so reluctant to cross. On the opposite side lay an encamp-ment. Dozens of tents were scattered beyond the rise, with guns resting up against them. Hundreds of men—dressed in dusty khakis—sat around smoking and cleaning their weapons. A tattered flag drooped from one of the bigger tents. There were men on sentry watching for crocodiles.

"Shit!" said Zakary. "We need to get out of here. That's the MSM rebel army. They've been attacking villages across the country. They are not friendly."

"I think they've seen us," said Jason as he looked through his camera. "Oh my God, drive!"

A shot fired past them and they flinched.

"Bloody hell!" Lily shrieked.

The rebels were on their feet and leaping into their vehicles. The team and their guides reversed back down the rise out of the firing line.

"Let's get out of here. We should have time if they have to drive through the water."

They turned around, but the horizon of the endless Serengeti was filled with dust. The soldiers were yelling as they cleared the water and revved up the bank after them.

"They're across!"

"There are more herds coming!" yelled Zakary. "We're trapped."

The sound of hoofs got louder as the wildebeest stampeded towards them in a brown cloud of dirt.

"We can drive along the river and try to outrun the herd!"

The jeeps tore off just as a group of rebels appeared over the ridge. Shots tore past the jeep and the passengers ducked and held on tight as the vehicle bumped over rocks and branches. The noise was deafening now as they crashed through bushes and the wildebeest advanced.

"Hold on!" yelled Zakary as he swerved the vehicle up the embankment.

Lily could see the heads of the wildebeest now. She could make out their horns, their great shoulders surging towards them at speeds of 80 km per hour.

The jeeps suddenly lurched down the bank. Lily and Jason pitched forward off their seats as the car entered the water. They screamed. They surged through the current, then slowed down to a crawl. Jason and Lily looked at each other in the brief moment of calm before the jeep sped up and cleared the deep. Behind them, the other jeep was still on the bank. She could see Rasta shaking his head. She looked ahead to see three rebel army vehicles waiting for them, with guns raised.

Jason fiddled with his camera.

"You're kidding me, you're not thinking of taking photos?" said Lily.

"If we get out of this alive, I don't want to lose what I've got," he said as he ejected his memory card, put it in his mouth and swallowed it.

"That's one way of shooting and eating big game!"

"I can't believe you're making jokes at a time like this! Look, you better hide that medallion somewhere."

"Where?"

"Just stick it in your bra."

Lily quickly extracted the wrapped medallion and shoved it under her shirt. She was shaking, but it gave her a feeling of calm somehow. Zakary slowly drove the jeep onto the edge of the river.

"Just stay calm, OK, let me do the talking. We can just pay our way out of this," he said. He swallowed away the dryness in his mouth.

One of the rebels motioned them to get out of the car with the end of his AK 47.

Jason took Lily's hand, more for his benefit than hers. "It'll be OK," she said.

Zakary got out first with his arms in the air. "Hey brother, we're just day-tripping, looking at the animals."

"Tell them, get out of the car!" the rebel said.

Zakary looked at them and nodded. Jason and Lily stepped out onto the muddy bank.

"Walk!" the gunman commanded.

The rebel's mates walked to their side and shoved them along the edge of the river. The talker jumped into his jeep and skidded off. Rasta's jeep was still on the other side and now surrounded with wildebeest, the rebels' jeep also trapped with the herd which were now entering the water.

"If we don't get shot, we're going to get trampled alive," said Lily.

"Or eaten by crocodiles," Jason replied. He was close to tears. He was a suburban boy, used to drive-through meals and his X-Box. This kind of stuff only happened to him in computer games.

"Up!"

The rebel shoved them up the bank and fired at the approaching herd.

"Oh my God!" Lily yelled, "stop it!"

"It's that, or we get trampled," said Zakary.

At the top of the incline, two jeeps were waiting for them. The soldiers ordered them to get in, and they drove furiously along the track back to the army camp. They were pushed out of the jeep and taken into a tent. A soldier took their bags and cameras. Jason glanced at Lily.

"Look, brothers, we can pay you good money, eh? These two are Australians, a rich country, they have cash," Zakary sweet-talked the men.

Jason opened his eyes wide and looked in disbelief. He wasn't able to pay a cent toward this trip.

"Yeah, that's right. Yeah?" Zakary looked at the pair and they nodded vigorously.

The soldier's face was impassive. The tent flap pushed in, and the leader of the army stomped in, flagged by two more soldiers. His left eye was milky, and a scar ran down his face to the corner of his lip, making him look like he was giving a lop-sided grimace. He said nothing but raised his chin at Zakary. His right-hand man lifted his gun and smashed it against Zakary's skull.

"No!" shouted Lily and went to help him, but the soldier stepped in front of her, raising his hands as if she would get the same treatment. Jason whined and swore under his breath.

"He needs help," Lily said in a low, determined voice.

The soldier raised his hand again to strike, but the leader snapped, "No!"

He stepped up to Lily and ran his eyes over her body.

"This one we keep, useful for the men."

The soldiers laughed, and one shimmied up to her rolling his shoulders. He reached out for her breast and without a thought, she blocked his arm and kicked him in the crotch. The other two rebels lunged forward. She elbowed one in the face before the third cracked his gun across her back and she crashed face down to the floor. Jason cried out and fell back, shovelling himself against the canvas with his feet. As Lily fell, the medallion dislodged from her bra and rolled away. She yelped and lurched towards it, grabbing it. But the soldier stamped on her hand. She cried out in pain, a heat radiating through her wrist and up her arm. But the pain disappeared and all she could feel was fire rising into her body. Under her hand, the relic vibrated. Then shards of red light burst through her fingertips. The injured soldiers picked themselves up. Zakary moaned and Jason crawled over to him. The red light increased and like laser beams into the air, they punched out an image. It gathered depth and, like a 3D printer, a shape emerged. The rebel leader spoke in his language, barking orders at his soldiers. But the men couldn't take their eyes off the mirage as it grew. Legs, a torso, it became more solid, arms holding a spear, a mighty head of what looked like a wildebeest.

"What the..." Jason murmured.

The soldier stepped away from Lily, freeing her hand, and she scrabbled onto all fours, holding the medallion in front of her as it built up the form. The monster stood tall on two legs like a man, but had hoofs for feet. She shook her head. Maybe she'd been knocked out. Maybe the wildebeest had trampled the tent. But as she gazed at the image, the beams created a muscled chest, arms and finally the face of a ram with enormous horns that curled back and around and tore a hole in the roof of the tent. On his mid-section he wore a large leather belt with a medallion on it in the centre just like the one Lily was holding in her hand.

The soldiers, terrified, raised their guns and fired at the beast. The medallion instantly retracted its beams, and the monster turned his head and roared. His horns unravelled, flicked out at one of the soldiers, and wound itself around the gun barrel. It picked up the man holding his gun and flung him through the roof of the tent. The other horn dealt with the second soldier. The leader and the third rebel ran out of the tent. Roaring again, the beast snapped his horn towards a blubbering Jason, wrapping it around his waist.

"No!" shouted Lily.

The beast looked at her and went down on one knee. Then, to their amazement, he opened his jaws and spoke.

"You!" it said. "You have my pod. You are born of Aries."

Though Lily shook all over, she managed to nod her head and speak. "Yes, that's my star sign but..."

The creature pressed a spot between his eyes and Lily felt light-headed.

"You have released me. You are my guardian, and I am yours."

"What?"

"You were the first of Aries to touch me. We are now linked."

"Linked?" She looked at the strange artifact in her hand. "Who. Are. You? What are you?" she whispered.

But before he could answer, gunshots rang outside the tent and the beast raised himself to his feet, opened his arms and roared again. His horns twisted in the air and the entire tent lifted up around them and he flung it at the amassed army which aimed their guns at him. He picked up his staff and swept it across the front line. A pulse of heat forced the soldiers to back away in terror and flee. He swept his staff again and a force-field threw the remaining men 20 metres away.

The beast turned back to Lily, Jason and Zakary.

"My name is Prymaw. I am from a galaxy far beyond this one." He pointed his staff to the sky. "Horos. My planet Aries has been destroyed."

"You came from this?" Lily wavered and pointed at the medallion.

"That is correct. It's what you might call a space transporter."

"A spaceship?" she asked.

"Forgive me, I am still downloading your language." Prymaw pressed between his eyes again.

Lily's mouth dropped open and closed again. She had so many questions, she didn't know where to begin. She closed her eyes and shook her head. It felt like a paintbrush had swept through her brain.

"What are you doing?"

"I'm transferring your knowledge to me."

"How? Wait, you now know everything?"

"Everything you know, yes."

"That's super creepy," Jason murmured.

"What do you want from us?" she asked, stepping away. She felt somehow violated.

"We come in peace. Your planet sustains life and we are wishing to stay here."

"We?" Zakary said.

"Yes, where do I find the others?"

"The others?"

"My fellow Horoscopians."

"There are more of you?" she asked.

"Yes, the Zodiac Warriors from my galaxy. We travelled together," he said.

"Believe me, there's no one else like you." Lily shook her head.

"Then you must gather them."

"Me? But..."

"You are of intelligence. You can prochiminate?"

"What?"

"You can see through time and space?"

"Ummmmm, no."

Prymaw pressed between his eyes again and Lily felt fingers probing her mind.

"Stop!" she cried out. She put her hands over her head.

"I see. You are not advanced. But you can find them. Now I will leave you. Keep this medallion safe. This is all of me. Your race will need me and all Horoscopians. Gather the twelve, Arian."

"For what?" Lily asked, but Prymaw had dissolved into beams of light that flowed into the medallion before she finished her question.

"Wait, wait, come back! What do you mean 'gather them'?"

Lily turned to Jason. He stood, wobbling. Tears streamed down his dust-riven face. Zakary was propped on his elbows.

"What just happened? I must be concussed."

A motor revved in the distance. Jason and Lily crouched down behind what was left of the crude furniture, the fear of militant rebels still large.

"Zakary, Lily, Jason!" Rasta zoomed up to the ragged tent.

"What happened?" Jacob jumped out of the car and looked at the destruction and bodies of broken rebels.

Lily ran and hugged him.

"Quick, quick, get in!" Rasta called.

❄

At the village that night, the visitors sat in a hut and stared at each other. Lily held the medallion in her gloved hand, turning it over and over.

"Stop playing with that thing," said Jason. "Can we just go home? I want to forget this whole trip."

"Forget it? How can we possibly forget it! You saw what came out of this, you heard what he..."

"It," interjected Jason.

"Prymaw, what Prymaw said. There are more of his kind and it's up to me to find them!"

"Find them? Are you crazy? We have no idea who or what 'they' are! Lily, we need to take this to the authorities."

"He said he was here to help us, Jase. He's right. The world is heading for extinction. There's not enough water left, but nobody even knows it. They wouldn't have come here if they didn't think they could survive here. It's our only hope."

"We don't know that for sure."

"He saved our lives back there."

Silence hung in the air.

"Zakary?" she pleaded.

"He said he read your mind, Lily. What if he planted something there?"

"What?" Lily slammed her hand on the table. "You don't trust me now?"

"No, of course we do." Zakary and Jason glanced at each other.

"Jason, you saw how closed the university was to my theory. The governments are the same. There's been something going on, I know it. And it's not good. All my research points towards mass water depletion. I reckon we have months left before there won't be any water coming out of our taps and we'll be buying our survival. Zak, you see how bad it is here already. Imagine that ten times worse on a global scale."

Her words hung in the air. Jason shuffled his feet.

"Guys!"

Zakary sighed. "How can you be so calm after seeing that thing?"

"Because I haven't been calm for a long time knowing where we are headed! What happened today was a miracle, our salvation! He said he is my guardian and I am his. Look, if I'm wrong, we'll be the discoverer of alien life and we'll all be rich and famous. If I'm right, then we have a chance to save this planet for our children. Win, win... right?"

Jason groaned. "Don't count on me to be your alien photographer. I'm gonna have trouble developing these as it is." He patted his tummy and winced.

"Come on Jason! It'll be an adventure. Zak, are you in?"

"Once I'm convinced that this is all actually happening, yeah I'm in."

As soon as Lily and Jason got home, she began the search. She typed Zodiac Warriors in search engines. She scoured the net for other locations where similar markings in the earth might hint at other medallions. She searched for images of lions, scorpions, crabs and fish that might give her a lead. After several hours, her eyes dried up, and she wondered if it was all a dream. She promised herself one more page of the current search before going to bed, when something caught her eye. She sat up straight in her chair. A tomb in Egypt showed a goddess who they said was Virgo. The Egyptians had been one of the first civilisations to use the Zodiac constellations, but they usually stuck with gods of Ra and Osiris. That this tomb was dedicated to Virgo made her take note.

Her phone vibrated. It was a text from Zak and her heart gave a little jump.

'Hey. You guys get home OK?'

'Yes. You?'

'Yeah. Still processing what happened. It was really good to see you. You look amazing.'

Was he flirting with her? She hoped so. The goodbye hug at the airport was long, delicious and sincere. There was no denying he was hot, handsome and super smart.

'Cheers. Not so bad yourself ☺'

'Have you found anything? No luck my end.'

'Yeah, a tomb in Egypt. Maybe a lead on Virgo.'

'☺ I have some free time. I could go to Egypt. Send me the info.'

'OMG that's awesome, thank U. Talk soon.'

She emailed him all the information and called Jason.

"How are you feeling?"

"Fed up with looking for my memory card."

"Shit."

"Yeah, you got that right, sister. What are you up to?"

"Looking for more clues. Found something in Egypt. Zak's going to check it out. Either we are the first to release a Zodiac Warrior or all the others ended up in the bottom of the ocean. I think we need a webpage or something, in case someone else finds another one."

"I've got some ideas. Why don't you come over to my place later?"

"Thanks, buddy. See you then."

Lily sat back on her bed and sighed, her mind was full of the Zodiac Warrior she'd found, but a part of her mind kept drifting back to Zakary's soft brown eyes when he told her he hadn't washed away her kiss all those years ago. There was a crash from the kitchen. She jumped up to find her mother bleeding, a broken wine glass in her hand.

"Bloody hell, Mum! What are you doing?"

Abigale pushed Lily's hands away. "Stop fussing," she slurred. "Just getting a drink."

Lily turned the tap on. It shuddered, releasing a stream of rusty water.

"This is crazy! How are we meant to drink this junk?"

Lily ran the tap, but the brown water kept running. She looked in the fridge and pulled out a bottle of sparkling water.

"Here Mum, drink some of this while I get a Band-Aid."

Lily arrived at Jason's flat. He was cleaning his camera lenses, neatly putting them away in special boxes. His flat was a haven of cleanliness compared to her own. She helped herself to a cup of tea, complete with milk, for a change.

"How's Abigale?"

"Bleh, nightmare. Back on the booze. Can I stay with you for a bit? I'm over her."

"Of course you can, darl."

"Thank you, you're a good friend." She gave him a kiss on the cheek. "So will you help me set up a webpage?"

"Yup. But I've done a bit of searching; obscure news sites, UFO sites and even paranormal fan clubs, that sort of thing. Have you heard of 'You saw what?'"

"No, what is it?"

"It's a site where people post UFO sightings, theories about the Yeti, the Loch Ness Monster, that sort of thing."

"Dark web? That sounds scary."

"And an 8-foot half-man half-ram isn't?"

"I get your point. How can I access it?"

"Through a VPN."

"And you accuse *me* of having hidden talents!" she said.

"I'm no one-trick pony, you know!" He smiled. "Anyway sweetie, I have found something interesting," he sang and flipped his head along with his shoulders. Looking smug, he pointed to the screen.

"Continue," she said, smiling.

"Wouldn't you know it, but there is something right here in Oz, up in the Northern Territory."

Lily tilted her head. "Go on."

"Around Katherine Gorge, there have been sightings of something that resembles a goat. Of course, there are feral goats in many parts of the Australian outback but not here." He tapped the map on the screen. "And reports say it stands upright. No one can get close though. It's hard to see and it moves quickly. They say it scales the sheer cliff faces in the region. There's also a local legend about a man who got caught in the jaws of a crocodile. The man was so strong that when the croc sunk his teeth into his head, he pulled his head out with two crocodile teeth stuck in his skull. The teeth grew into horns. But the man's spirit went into the crocodile and so he went mad and roamed the land forever more."

"You think this could be one of them; Capricorn? It sounds kind of familiar."

"There is a very blurry photo that a Scottish backpacker managed to take. He said he and his two friends were camping out near 17 Mile Falls and they got in a spot of bother with a pack of dingoes. He reported that the dingoes went to attack him, and a huge beast leapt into their campsite and took the dogs out. It was dark, only the light of the fire and a small torch, but his girlfriend accidentally took a photo in the scuffle. Look."

Jason enlarged the photo. It was barely possible to make out what was in the frame, but what looked like a small metal medallion just clipped the corner of the photo.

"Oh my God! Yes Jason, yes! You are a genius!"

Lily planted a big kiss on Jason's cheek and hugged him. Jason tried to shrug off the compliment, but glowed inside.

"So what are you going to do?"

"Me? What *we* are going to do is go up there with Prymaw and find him!"

"Oh God, Lil. I can't. My stomach is only just getting over digesting my memory card and the fact that *a great big bloody alien...*" he shouted, "... saved our lives."

"Then I'll go alone, coward."

She said it jokingly, but it stung. Jason, who had been bullied for being weird, for being a freak, for always hiding behind his camera, for being skinny and pale, for being gay, wanted more than anything to be considered brave. At least the monster from out of space seemed to be on his side.

"OK, OK. I'll come," he said, though his stomach churned.

"Correct answer. Now how do I set up this web page on the dark web?"

It didn't take long for Jason to set up thezodiacwarriors.com and embed a no-plan phone number in the pages while Lily booked flights to Darwin.

The land across the centre of North America had been hard hit by years of farming. Soil rendered useless by over-cropping and a shortage of water, chemicals and cattle meant that farms went bust, erosion decimated the land, and many farmhands lost their jobs. Bruce Janson and his best buddy Charlie Winton, from Cheyenne, Wyoming, were two such workers. They weren't particularly unhappy to be released from the hard and dull work of driving heavy machinery, working in the warehouse and being general dogs' bodies. What they did miss was a regular income. There were no jobs anywhere. Many businesses had shut down as the price of petrol increased costs. Most people had no idea the number of everyday items that relied on petrol for their manufacture. The two men sat in their local bar, spending the last of their welfare money, watching the dregs of their beer disappear.

"What the hell are we gonna do now, Charlie?" said Bruce, who had always been content to let his friend do the thinking.

"My neighbour reckons they're hiring at NuDelta, packing boxes, can't be too hard, can it?"

"'Cept you have to apply online. We need to get us access to the inter-web-thingy. Get onto one of those job search apps," Bruce whined. "We ain't got no computer. Besides, I'm too old to start learning 'bout all that new-fangled business."

"We ain't getting any younger, that's for sure. We need to think outside the henhouse, Bruce, need to get entrepreneurial."

"I ain't got no idea what you mean, Charlie, but I could always rely on you to get us out of a crack. What you got in mind?"

"You remember your granpa talking 'bout the goldmines out east?"

"Sure do. But they been closed for years."

"Well, I reckon we should get ourselves down there, see if they left anything behind. They say gold never loses its value. We got enough picks and such to get us started."

"You know, I might still have those ole metal detectors in the back of my brother's shed."

"Go see if you can get 'em fired up. I'll dig out my tent and before you know it, we'll be rich, buddy!"

The following week, they set out in Charlie's old truck along Highway 80, through the dusty fields. They turned off at Rawlins and stopped in Muddy Gap after driving for three hours to stretch their legs and get a bite to eat.

Two hours later, they turned off on a dirt road that led to the Carissa mine. The rusty corrugated buildings were stacked against the hillside with a rickety old wooden bridge that used to carry the ore to the warehouse for processing. They got out and walked around the area. On the rise, they could see the flat lands of Wyoming for miles.

"This place closed down in 1954..."

"Feels like it could be haunted, if you ask me," said Bruce, shivering.

"Firstly, I don't believe in ghosts and secondly, I won't be scared of 'em if they was real."

"What if we get attacked by coyotes?"

"For a 66-year-old man, you're sure acting like a baby. I got my pistol, and you got yours, so we're all set."

They set up their tents and made a cup of tea on their gas burner before turning in for the night.

Once up in the morning, Charlie said, "I reckon we both head off in different directions so as to cover more area."

"Sounds good," Bruce replied, "meet back here around lunch time, hey?"

"And just in case either of us find anything or get lost, or meets a coyote," said Charlie, raising his eyebrows, "take this."

He handed him a walkie talkie, "I think they have a range of 'bout five miles, but just to be safe, check in every hour or so, OK?"

Bruce nodded, looking a little nervous.

They walked off in different directions with metal detectors in hand and swept them across the ground, desperately hoping to hear them go *beep beep beep*. The morning's search was fruitless, and they met up for lunch.

"I ain't heard a peep, Charlie. I reckon we should give up and find a beer in that last town down the road."

"Give up? We've only been here all of five minutes. I ain't heard so much nonsense," Charlie grumbled.

"I don't like the feel of it here, is all. My stomach says so," said Bruce.

"How old are you? That's allays been your problem, Bruce. If it don't come quick 'n easy, you just wanna go home."

"That's bullcrap. I can just feel when things are right or not. You always been so insensitive you can't smell a wet dog."

"Well, if you're such a sensitive new-agey kind of guy, why don't you just feel into that big fat belly of yours and ask it where the goddamn gold is!"

They bickered on for a while until Charlie got sick of it and stomped off with his metal detector. He waved his detector vigorously across his path, which led away from the main site. A faint ping went off in his headset and backed up. He waved his detector, and it pinged again in the farthest reach of the swing. He scrabbled over the rocks that edged the path and swung again. The ping got louder. He focused it and put his toe at the spot. He took his pick out of his belt and struck the earth. The hole deepened, but nothing appeared. He tested the detector again. There was definitely something making it react. Then he saw it. A tiny nugget of gold, no bigger than the size of his fingernail, but gold, nonetheless.

Charlie's heart skipped a beat, and he fought the urge to yell 'Eureka!'.

"Just wait until Bruce sees this, goddamn moaner," he murmured to himself.

As he dug around in the hole to see if there was more, his shovel struck something solid, giving a dull *ting* sound. More digging revealed a piece of flat metal caught under a rock.

"Best call my partner in," he said. He pressed the button on his walkie-talkie. "Come in Bruce, this is Charlie, over."

"Goddamn it, who else would it be?" came the reply.

"Get yourself over here, smart ass. I just proved your wobbling lard belly wrong!"

"On way."

Charlie continued to dig the object out of the stone, but it was securely wedged under it. He stood up and bent down and heaved the rock back. It broke free and he stumbled back. He yelled out in pain as he lay on the ground, and then yelled again, scrabbling to his feet as a scorpion scurried past him.

"Holy shit!"

"What's wrong?" he heard Bruce calling as he came down the path.

"I'm OK," Charlie yelled back.

He leaned down and picked up the small, round object. It felt hot in his hand, like it had come out of an oven. He glanced at the sun, but it was behind a cloud. Then it moved a little in his hand.

"Did that scorpion get a bite of me?" he thought. Before he had time to answer himself, bright rays of deep red flowed out of the medallion.

Bruce appeared on the path and saw an apparition appearing in front of his friend. Beams of light pierced the dusty air.

"Sweet Jesus, I told him this place was haunted!" he stuttered.

A muscular woman took form from the rays of light. Long black hair tumbled down her back and past her bottom. She wore a leather bikini and knee-high boots that looked like scaly armour. Her skin glistened with a rich deep tan. She was fiercely beautiful.

Charlie whistled. "Well, hello! What have we here?"

"I am Fyon of Scorpio. I am a Zodiac Warrior."

"Well, I don't know how you appeared here just like this, but you're a pretty lady. We should get you back to town."

"I am of Scorpio, not 'town'. You have released me because you are of Scorpio. Take me to the others."

"Uh, I'm not sure what planet you are from or what drugs you're on, but I ain't seen your folk around here."

"I told you, my planet is Scorpio. There are twelve of us from Horoscopia."

Fyon closed her eyes. She pressed a spot between them and searched for knowledge in the man's mind.

Bruce stood on the path, staring at the back of the woman. He rubbed his eyes and took another look. Out from under her hair, a tail began to unfurl from the base of her spine.

Charlie's brain seemed to shift under his skull. He took a step toward Fyon and the tail sprang out and hovered above her head.

"Charlie, look out!"

Bruce unholstered his pistol and fired at Fyon once, twice, thr...

Fyon's tail shot out behind her and struck Bruce in the chest. He dropped to the floor.

"NO!" Charlie screamed and ran to his friend.

Fyon collapsed into waves of light and re-entered the medallion, now lying back in the dirt.

Bruce convulsed in Charlie's arms for a few moments before falling back, his eyes in the back of his head leaving the whites eerily gazing at his traumatized friend.

"Bruce, Bruce! Wake up!"

He put his first two fingers to Bruce's throat. Nothing. He moved them to just under his jaw, no pulse. He lay his oldest mate, motionless on the ground, and put his head in his hands.

"What just happened? What just happened?"

He went to the spot where he was standing and pushed the medallion with his foot.

"What just happened?" he repeated over and over.

He took a scrunched-up tissue out of his pocket and smoothed it out. "I'm not touching this thing. This thing is dangerous. I need to turn it in. Bruce is dead. I need to turn it in."

He wrapped it and put it in his bag. Charlie dragged Bruce's body into an old miner's hut and closed the man's eyes. The wound in his chest was a deep red colour, it seemed to glow. He covered the body with an old sack.

"I'll be back for you, buddy."

Charlie hurriedly packed up the gear and drove to the nearest town. His shaky fingers dialled the National Security Agency.

"I need to report an alien landing," he said, still not believing the words that came out of his mouth.

"Yes sir, I got evidence."

It had taken some convincing to find someone to see him. Eventually, Charlie got directed to the NSA facility in Utah. He filled up his tank and set off for the four-hour drive. Once he got to the facility, he went through an hour of identification before being ushered into an office.

"I'm Joseph Schwartz. This is my colleague, Daniel Westerford. Please take a seat, Charles."

"Charlie, no one's called me Charles since I was as big as a flea," he laughed nervously.

"You OK if we record our interview, Charlie?"

"Yes sir."

"OK, recording," said Daniel and gave the date and time.

"You better tell us what brought you here," said Joseph as he leaned back in his chair and crossed his legs.

Charlie told the story, after which he tentatively placed the crusty tissue containing the medallion on the table.

"And you're saying that if you touch this, a woman appears," Joseph confirmed.

"Yes, I told you every which way. You get your people to test it. She said I was Scorpio, so it was me that released her."

"And are you?"

"I was born November 1st 1954. I don't dabble in all that horoscope nonsense."

Daniel poked at his mobile phone and asked it the question, "Yep, he's Scorpio alright."

"So if I asked you to touch this medallion now, you are sure the woman would appear."

"I ain't sure of nothing anymore, but I ain't touching this thing 'less I got some protection."

"OK, thank-you Charlie. We'll take a moment to confer. Would you like a coffee?"

Charlie nodded and the men left the office. He let out a deep breath and looked at the medallion on the table hidden under his tissue.

Half an hour later, the men reappeared with his coffee.

"We got the local sheriff out at South Pass City to check out your story. Your friend has been found and taken in for forensics."

Charlie dropped his head and sighed.

"It seems that the wound you described is a little... unusual. So, we've been given clearance to observe what happens when you hold the medallion in a secure area with armed personnel."

Charlie rubbed his shaky fist across the bristles on his chin. He shook his head.

"Charlie?"

"Oh Lord," he sighed, "OK. I'll do it. I'll do it for Bruce."

They led Charlie through a maze of corridors, down an elevator and into a room. Ten men stood around with rifles in their hands and one wall had a one-way mirrored window. Joseph placed the medallion, now wrapped in a black velvet cloth, on a table.

"These men are here to protect you, and Daniel and I will be observing from in there. OK?"

Charlie nodded. He didn't know what he feared more; the Zodiac woman appearing or not appearing. He swallowed.

"When you're ready then, Charlie. Good luck."

A red light flicked to green to notify they were recording.

Charlie stood by the table. He put his hand out and unfolded the cloth. He stepped back and dropped his arms to his side, his hands opening and closing.

"I ain't gonna be a baby like that darn Bruce."

He stepped forward again and grabbed the medallion. It was hot, like before, and vibrating. The dark red light bled through his fingers into the air on the table. The armed men straightened and put their rifles up to their shoulders.

Charlie wanted to close his eyes, but he couldn't take them off the emerging form on the table. She seemed bigger in this small room. She finished actualizing and stood on the table, looking down on them. Her legs and arms were ripped with deep muscles and her skin shone. Her long black hair rippled around her shoulders. She looked at Charlie and blinked. Her eyes were a deep scarlet. She swept her eyes around the room at the men who focused their crossfires on her. Her spine quivered and her tail released itself and hovered above her head.

"Is that a scorpion tail?" Joseph breathed in the observation room. Both men crept close to the glass, trying to take in what they saw.

"By God, the man was telling the truth."

"You killed my friend," Charlie breathed.

"I mean you no harm unless you mean me harm. That friend of yours fired his weapon, and I see you have more friends with weapons. What is the meaning of this?"

"He, he didn't mean to. He's just a nervous type, see?"

"Where are the Zodiac Warriors? I wish to see my fellows. You will take me to them."

"There are no Zodiac Warriors, ma'am."

Fyon let out a shout of anger. "Then I shall take myself."

She jumped off the table. The men tensed their rifles. She roamed the room.

"Let me out!" she bellowed.

She turned to Charlie and walked up to him. He stepped back.

"Don't hurt me!"

"I told you, I mean you no harm, but you do not want to get in my way."

She put her hand to his face and stroked his cheeks.

"You see, I am peaceful."

"Um, please may we leave now?" Charlie said in a high voice.

"We can't let them go. I've been waiting for an opportunity like this my whole life," said Daniel.

"But look at her, she'd take them all out with one sweep of that tail. Where the hell has she come from? I'm calling the Secretary of the Defense. We can't let her go. She's talking about 'others'. What if extra-terrestrials have arrived? The entire planet could be in mortal danger."

"You gotta let us go now, Mr Schwartz!" Charlie called out.

Joseph picked up the phone.

"Put me through to General of the Army, we have a code red."

"I'm going in," said Daniel, "I'll buy us some time."

Daniel spoke through the intercom. "I'm Daniel Westerford, head of extra-terrestrial research. I'm coming in to talk to you."

Fyon's tail quivered at the interruption. The gunmen tensed again.

The door opened and Daniel slid in. His face twitched with a mixture of glee and fear.

"Lower your weapons," he said to the guards.

They looked at him and reluctantly stood at ease.

"Welcome. You are from Scorpio, I understand."

Fyon cocked her head and looked Daniel up and down.

"We come in peace and we come to help," she said.

"You have a funny way of showing it. You killed a man, and that is not permitted here. We have laws."

"You are in a time of war?"

"No, not here in America."

"Then why are your people carrying weapons?"

The simple question confounded Daniel. There was no easy answer.

"I, we, we carry them for protection."

"From what?"

"What is your name?"

"Fyon."

"Why don't you tell me about your planet? When did you arrive and how?"

"My planet was in the galaxy Horoscopia."

Daniel nodded, his mind going a million miles an hour. "How many of you?" He swallowed.

"There were thirteen planets, and they got taken by a black hole. We came here to find a new home."

"Thirteen planets! A new home? Where are your ships?"

"Here," she pointed at her pod. "You must take me to the other Zodiac Warriors."

"We don't know where they are. You understand that it is highly unusual for us to welcome extra-terrestrial life forms. There is a protocol."

"What do you...?"

Suddenly, more armed men crashed through the door. Fyon's eyes flared and her tail swung out and struck Daniel. The guards fired at her, but she dispersed back into the medallion, and though some bullets hit the walls, at least three caught Charlie in the head, leaving his own scarlet spray on the floor.

"What the hell happened in there?" the Secretary of the Defense yelled at Joseph.

"I, I don't know. That monster decimated half the team and a civilian. How is Daniel?"

"Luckily for him, his bulletproof vest absorbed the venom. He's just got a broken collarbone."

"Thank God."

"Take the medallion thing in for testing. I'm putting Agent Tress on the job to track the other extra-terrestrials down. She's the best at what she does."

Joseph baulked at this news. Everyone had heard about this upcoming intelligence officer. She scared the toughest of agents. Her nickname was 'Woof' because she was like a dog with a bone.

"With all due respect, sir, Daniel and I can handle this."

"You just made a goddamn butchery of the observation room. You'll be in for extensive interviewing for the incident report, and Daniel needs to recover. I need my best people to quell this invasion. Keep the public safe. That's our job."

"Sir."

"I want the lab reports on the venom and what's in the medallion."

"Sir."

❄

Sandra Tress sat at her desk at the CIA headquarters in Tucson, Arizona. Her manicured fingernails were embellished with a little blue crystal. They tap-tapped on her phone as she typed in the web address 'ScopeYourHoro.com' on her phone.

She was going up in the world, it said, and she should look under every stone for opportunity. Open your mind and don't take anything on face value...

She sighed. No love on the horizon then. She was twenty-five at the end of August, considered old in her department, and single. No one had quite hit the mark. Or marks. She had a precise picture of her perfect partner. Neat, serious with a twinkle of humour, outgoing, a lover of quality and fine living. She'd met men who had this on the surface but lacked the X-factor and she'd flicked them after a maximum of three dinner dates. Anyway, her job made it difficult to hold down a relationship, what with all the secrecy, the frequent overseas missions and undercover work. But there had been no assignments for a few weeks, and she was bored.

Her mobile rang, and she closed the tab down.

"Tress?"

"Speaking."

"An assignment has come in. Briefing in my office, now."

Sandra felt a familiar tingle zing up and down her spine. The thrill of a new chase excited her. Usually someone dumped a manila envelope on her desk, and she got on with it. Wheedling out information on the latest technical advances of some new invention in Russia or China. Or tracking down a stray agent. Easy pickings. This time, her boss had summoned her. This must be big. She stood up and straightened out her silk blouse, tucked a stray dreadlock under her

African print headscarf—she always liked to wear something that reminded her of her roots. She slipped her feet back into her heeled boots and slicked on some lip gloss.

Her boss and the Director of the CIA, Grant Sampson, who she had only met once before attended the meeting. Once she had taken the seat offered at the conference table, her boss clicked a button on the phone and an image came up on the screen.

"Sandra, I've invited a colleague into our meeting. He has a special interest in this case. He's been involved in the Pentagon's UFO program for many years."

"UFO?" she echoed.

"Yes, you'll see shortly." He turned to the screen and a man's face appeared.

"Good evening, Mr Focus. You're acquainted with Grant, and let me introduce you to Sandra Tress. We are about to brief her on the outbreak."

Orlando Focus nodded. "What you are about to see is highly confidential, Ms Tress. This is a matter of not only national, but world security."

Sandra knew who Focus was. He was a global name after growing his massive NuDelta corporation. He was always listed as one of the richest men in the world, though he kept a low profile from the public eye. Most would not even recognise his face. She had no idea he was involved in the CIA too. His unusual eyes bore into her. She couldn't quite work out if it was his good looks, well-toned upper body or his charisma that made him so fascinating, yet unsettling. She felt a powerful urge to not let him down, and a flicker of fear if she did.

"Yes, I understand. What exactly are we dealing with here, sir?"

The next few minutes were the most surreal of her life. They played the recording of the carnage in the obs room at Fort George. It showed some sort of mutant woman, who they called an alien, creating havoc and causing the deaths of several good men and a civilian. An hour later, Sandra emerged.

"Don't screw this up, Tress," were her boss's parting words. "We need these aliens brought in. The general public won't cope with it if they come to light. Someone has to be behind all this. Keep me informed."

Sandra headed to her desk. She snorted to herself. Sandra Tress and screw up didn't belong in the same sentence. This was so top secret she had been given a secure office elsewhere in the building. She packed up what she needed and left the open plan office. Once settled, she took a deep breath, wiggled her fingers and opened up her computer. The end of her talons tapped the keys of the computer, causing several screens to flash across the monitor. It didn't take long to find a lead.

"Booya!" she said and smiled.

5 / TAURUS

It was the 65th birthday of Professor John Robertson. He wondered if it was one of those milestones people referred to as 'special'. For some reason, he felt like it was. He decided that it wasn't, because once again he was eating his dinner alone at a restaurant in a city few had heard of, in a country not many westerners visited. John turned the tattered page of a book and tried to concentrate on the story. He had picked it up at his hotel to give himself a break from the usual research papers and online archaeology sites he scoured, looking for evidence of zodiac worship in ancient Eastern civilisations. He sighed, closed the book and looked out into the view. The stunning scenes of Paro in Bhutan did not match John's inner world. He was weary. He had spent his working life as an archaeologist, travelling the world looking for something that would define him. Something that would raise him above the other adventurers, historians and anthropologists who clamoured for a new find, for fresh evidence, for their own holy grail. But no one had ever taken his particular expertise in the Zodiac seriously. His papers had been studiously ignored, his talks attended by plenty of alternative folk but no peers. As long as humans had been looking at the stars, they had made meaning of the constellations. He just needed evidence that his beloved Western Zodiac was also once believed in the Eastern world. He knew the zodiac signs went back as four hundred years before Christ. The Egyptians told the time by the stars using constellations called decans and the dendera zodiac sculpture in the Hathor temple depicted the zodiacs.

The waitress took his bowl away and asked him if he wanted anything else. He ordered a dessert; he couldn't face his hotel room just yet.

John picked up his pen and opened his journal.

'Tomorrow I start the trek to Yak Cave. It is here that Tenzin Rinpoche suggested the myth of the yak originates. The monks say this is where Yagkuk's bones lie. Yagkuk was said to rule over the mountains and plains. He has close similarities to the bull of Taurus. They say he shaped the land and pushed the Himalayas up to protect the Druk civilisation. If my theory is correct, this is where I'll find the artifacts of the lost people of Druk, and finally prove that Western astrology also existed in China. Although the cave is accessible from Bhutan, it actually spreads underground into Tibet, and this is why I believe the Tibetans have buried this story. If Chinese authorities knew that this system overrides the Chinese horoscope, there would be uproar.'

John smiled. He imagined delivering his speech to his peers, who would finally show him some respect. He would have his papers published and his finds displayed at the most prominent museums, and he would finish writing his memoir to much applaud. He ran his hand over the grey stubble on his chin and sighed.

John's kheer arrived, a rice pudding delicately flavoured with cardamon and saffron. Its aroma reminded him of the perfume Jeanette, his late wife, wore. He threw down his spoon and looked out at the view. She would have loved it here; the green slopes of the valley with the magnificent Himalayas as a backdrop. Part of him was glad she wouldn't have to witness the demise of the natural world. Many countries were struggling with the effects of climate change. Drought was common and water scarcity a real threat. He had barely been home to Kent in England since she had died. The house just reminded him of what a difficult husband he had been and the terrible argument with their only child, Timothy, after she died. The loss of his mother affected Tim so badly that he had piled the blame squarely on his father's shoulders. He sighed again and gestured for the bill.

John stepped into the narrow street and breathed in the chilled mountain air. Even though it was May and summer, the nights still cooled to around 15 °C. It cleared his head as he wound his way along the rocky path to his hotel. He was in no mood to exchange pleasantries with the super-friendly hotel owner, but the man called him over, waving a note in the air.

"Good evening, Sangay Wangyel."

"Hello, good evening, sir. I have a message for you."

"For me? Are you sure? No one knows where I am."

"Yes, yes, for you. Here, here."

John took the note and unfolded it.

'Surprise for your birthday. Go to the Paro Sabda hotel.'

John rubbed the back of his neck. "Do you know who gave you this message?"

"No sir, just came through from hotel Paro Sabda on the phone."

"There must be some mistake, another John staying here maybe?"

"No, he said Professor John Robertson, that's you."

John blew air between his lips. He needed an early night for the 5-hour trek the next day. He looked at the ceiling. The people in Paro had been so good to him. They found him a guide, a donkey and supplies. They probably found out it was his birthday and decided to throw him a small celebration. He didn't want to be rude. So he swung around, waved thanks at Sangay, and headed back out into the cold night. The hotel to which he had been summoned was further up the mountainside. He was in good shape for his years, his long, strong legs easily taking the steepness of the hill. It was the best hotel in town, luxurious with a tiled foyer, stunning views into the valley and a top-class restaurant. He didn't suppose he was adequately dressed in his hiking pants and khaki vest, but he still cut a striking figure, his ruddy complexion giving his rugged features a healthy glow. He made a mild attempt to smooth his still dark hair after taking off his battered straw hat before entering the grand entrance.

The hotel was quiet. A couple of guests stood perusing the information stand. Another man trotted down the stairs and passed him. There was a murmuring from a side room, the lounge or restaurant perhaps. There didn't appear to be anyone waiting to give him a birthday cake. He strode to the reception desk.

"Excuse me, I had a message to come here. It's Professor John Robertson."

Before the receptionist had a chance to answer, a voice said, "Yes, that was me."

John turned around.

"Timothy!"

"Hi Dad, happy birthday," he said cautiously.

Timothy held out his hand formally.

John stared at him. He had forgotten what a fine son he had produced. He stood tall. The young man had grown bigger than his own tall stature by the time he was fifteen. Expensive suit, gold cufflinks, his lucrative job was reflected in his attire. A thousand questions screamed through his head. "How did you find me?"

"It wasn't easy!"

They stood awkwardly. but Tim's warm eyes crinkled. "How are you, Dad?"

"What... When... Why are you here?"

Timothy glanced at his outstretched hand. John looked into his son's eyes. He wanted to hug him, but there was still an uneasiness there. He took his hand and shook it.

"I'm here because, well, I want you to meet someone."

"Oh yes, who's that, then? I'm due back in the UK next month though, could have waited."

"Come on."

Timothy led John into the lounge area. They approached a woman sitting in one of the wingback chairs.

"I'd like to introduce you to my fiancée, Jill."

Jill unfolded herself from the seat and stood. She had long hair that cascaded in a smooth reddish-blonde waterfall over her shoulders, wearing a white silk dress that fell over her curves like cream. She caught the corner of her bottom lip in her teeth and held out her hand that carried a huge sapphire ring. He took her cool fingers gently.

"Oh goodness, well, this is a very big, a very special, a happy, yes, a happy surprise," he stammered.

Timothy put his arm around his delicious fiancée and kissed her on the temple.

"Tim wanted your blessing before we set a date."

Jill spoke with a soft accent. John struggled to place it, but it felt rude to interrogate her so soon after meeting.

"Oh gosh, well, I think I need to sit down and have a drink. Timmy, you have some explaining to do!" he said with a wink.

"Dad, I'm sorry."

"Oh, don't be sorry, son. This would have made your mother so happy. We always wondered when you'd settle down."

"No, I'm sorry for the way I spoke to you after she... after the funeral."

"Grief has a way of twisting people in funny directions. Besides, a lot of what you said was true. I should have been there more for your mum. Just too obsessed, you see," he spoke the last words to Jill.

She smiled serenely. "I'm sorry I didn't get to meet her. Tim speaks so highly of her."

"So, how did you two meet? Where? And how did you know where to find me?"

"We met at a presentation I was giving. Jill works as the director for art at the company I was hired to consult for. And as for finding you... well, when you have connections with the top people in

finance, a few credit card payments soon led me to your latest treasure hunt."

John's face fell at his final words. That was the problem with his
wife and son; they never understood the importance of his work.
They laughed at him as if he was some hobbyist looking for old coins
with a metal detector.

"Well, my *investigation*," he emphasised the word, "and years of
research and building relationships with the monks has led me here,
yes. In fact, I'm about to trek into the mountain to where I believe
there is valuable, nay, earth-shattering evidence of zodiac worship in
the east."

Jill cocked her head. "How interesting. What makes you think
there is something up there?"

"There's a myth of the yak..."

John told them the story.

"Fascinating! Oh Timmy, I'd love to see the Himalayas up close."

Tim looked at her, then at his dad.

"Professor Robertson..." she began.

"Call me John, please."

"John, I don't suppose you'd consider taking a couple of helpers
with you?"

John slumped back in his chair. In truth, he preferred solo expeditions. He hated the social dynamics and chit chat of a group. He
found the journey to a place meditative; it allowed him to churn over
his theories, to dream a little. When home, he would even find his
wife's incessant need to talk tiresome. But here was his son, so
recently estranged, sitting with his stunning wife-to-be. There was no
way he could refuse.

He contorted his face into a smile and said, "Of course, I'd love
that!"

❉

They started out later than he expected due to the new members of the expedition. Tim and Jill needed to get some gear and more food before they were ready to make the ascent.

The going was tough. Though John was older, his stocky legs and strong constitution drove him up the incline. Timothy and Jill might have had youth on their side, but he was more used to the altitude and the group kept at a similar pace. Jill seemed to float along, navigating the huge rocks with ease. After two hours, they stopped for a break and some snacks. Once they caught their breath, Jill stood and walked away to take in the views.

"She's quite a catch, Tim."

"I know. I never thought I'd meet anyone, but she just blew my socks off the minute I laid eyes on her. It felt like she knew me straight away, the real me, you know? Felt like we were destined to be together."

"I was beginning to worry you would never find a soul mate. Where is she from?"

"She was born in Egypt, but her parents were Austrian."

"Were?"

"Yeah, they died when she was ten."

John shook his head and glanced at Jill's still back.

"She seems very self-contained, probably explains why. Does she want a family?"

"I... I don't know. She avoids the subject whenever I bring it up. She suffers from terrible migraines. Laid up in bed for days. I think she's afraid of how that will affect a child."

"You've always talked about wanting a child. What if she doesn't, or can't?"

"Dad, I'd do anything for her. I love her." Tim's voice was gravelly. He cleared his throat. "She's smart as well as beautiful. She has three degrees, you know."

"Oh goodness! What in?"

"Astronomy, anthropology and medicine. She trained as a doctor though doesn't practice anymore."

"Woosh! She's probably better qualified than me to make this expedition."

Jill turned. Her hair flowed from her beanie, catching the light and giving her a halo. John had never seen a woman so beautiful. He could see why Tim was enchanted. His son jumped to his feet and strode over, taking her hand and pressing his lips to it. Jill looked at him with equal adoration. John turned towards the path, both teary and embarrassed at their display of affection.

After an hour, their guide pointed to the sky behind the mountain peaks. Grey clouds of the monsoon menaced. He suggested they should press on without a break to get to camp before the rain set in. These days, they couldn't be sure if the rain contained acidic dust particles blown across the globe from industrial countries. Just after 5.00 pm, they reached the camping spot. With little fuss, they erected their tents, and the guide built a fire.

"Look, we've got a couple of hours before the sun goes down. Why don't we have a recce of the cave?"

Tim and Jill agreed. The three left the vegetation and climbed higher into the bare stone of the mountain.

"According to my map, the Yak Cave is directly above our camp." John puffed as he pulled himself up over a granite boulder. "The entrance should be anywhere around... ah!"

He scrambled to his feet and saw a large hole that led into a cave. Tim and Jill joined by his side.

"Has anyone explored this cave before?" Jill asked.

"Not many. As you can see, access is difficult. My contacts in Tibet tell me this is a secret place, so very few are aware of its existence. Of course, the locals here know of it, but they don't like to bring tourists up here because it's too far for many to make the effort without it leading onto another trail, and it can't be done in a day."

John glanced at the sky. "It's going to rain. We should take cover."

"Come on, let's take a look inside," said Tim.

They stepped through the rounded cave entrance and turned on their flashlights. The cave at first sight looked unremarkable. The earth floor was scattered with small rocks, the walls were made up of uneven slabs of jutting granite. As they shone their torches, flashes of lightning filled the space, and then the rumble of thunder sounded outside. The cave mouth dimmed as storm clouds spread across the setting sun.

"Maybe we should have stayed at camp," Tim said, "won't be easy to get back down in the wet."

"Well, we're here now. Might as well look around. Let's go further in," said John.

Jill had already walked ahead, feeling the rock walls with her hands, as if communing with them.

"What exactly are we looking for?" she said.

"Any remains, bones, bundles, artifacts," John replied. "Relics are normally found at the back of the caves, tucked away. Where would you put something precious if you were hiding it?"

"Dad, over here!"

"What have you got, Tim?"

"Was this a man-made cave?"

"I doubt it. Why do you ask?"

"Look at the entrance. It's perfectly round, some of the rock is sheared off until here." He shone the torch at the ceiling. "Then the floor dips away, almost like a channel."

"What are you suggesting?"

Jill crouched down to where the gouge disappeared into the earth.

"Maybe something is buried here?"

John took a small pickaxe from his backpack and knocked it on the floor of the cave gently. Flashes of lightning lit their backs through the cave entrance and more thunder broke out, closer now. John chipped away at the earth. Tim shovelled the soil to the side, while Jill held the flashlight.

"There's nothing," said John. "It's getting late, we should head back."

Another blast of thunder ricocheted through the cave, and torrential rain crashed down.

"Might as well keep going until the rain subsides," said Tim. "Try further along."

John scraped away the earth, ready to give up when he hit something solid.

"Hello!"

He went in again. "Tim, you have a go, my arms are getting tired."

Tim took over with gusto.

"Steady, boy, steady."

Tim dropped the pickaxe and scrabbled through the soil, revealing an egg-shaped black stone. He tried to prise it out.

"It's so heavy!"

"It looks like a meteorite," said Jill.

She took the pickaxe, and the three hauled the rock out of its bed. The flashlight showed a deep crack along the stone. Something within the crack reflected.

"What on earth is in there?" said John.

This was not what he was expecting to find. This was geologist territory. He felt a flash of disappointment and fatigue. "Let's come back in the morning."

"Hang on Dad, let me try to get it out."

"Timothy, this is a very unscientific way to go about this. We are not on some treasure hunt, as you so like to call my work. I need to document this appropriately with photographs, field notes and at least gloves!"

But Tim had bought the pickaxe down onto the meteor with force, and the rock had willingly revealed its bounty. A golden orb rolled free of the rock. Jill gasped and put her hand to her chest.

Another crack of thunder joined a bright flash of lightning, which smashed into the ground outside the cave. They all flinched, and another boom of thunder vibrated the ground beneath their feet. The rocks creaked around them. Dust fell from between the fissures, and suddenly the great boulder that held up the cave mouth crashed down. Rocks and debris tumbled down around them. A piece caught Tim on the temple, and he lurched forward. John grabbed the medallion as a volley of pebbles fell and knocked him down. Jill put her hands over her head and rolled into a ball.

A glow emanated out of John's hand as he lay unconscious. Laser beams of green shot through the dusty air, stamping out an image. Jill raised her head and coughed. She watched with a slight smile on her face as the image grew from 2D to 3D, gaining solidity. Mighty hoofs, a thick body dressed in leather armour, took up almost all the space in the cave. It had huge arms as thick as chimneys, broad shoulders and a massive bull's head with horns. The laser beams retracted, and the beast shook his snout and sneezed. He took in his surroundings. He noticed the two men collapsed on the floor, and then the beautiful woman kneeling before him. The beast blinked a few times and cricked his neck.

"Who are you?" he spoke.

"Don't you know me, Teres?"

She stood and moved toward him. He backed away a step. She reached out and pressed a spot between his eyes.

"You've been asleep a long time. It's time to download."

Teres closed his eyes, then opened them. He smiled, "Regida! My favourite Horoscopian!"

Jill grinned. They stepped towards each other, dipped and bumped their heads, "But you must call me Jill, that is how I'm known here."

"Jill," Teres sounded the word on his lips. "So Jill, you have much to tell."

"Yes, but I must keep it short. These humans need help soon."

"Humans, eh? They look weak."

"Yes and no, you'd be surprised at their resilience. I have grown fond of them, especially this one." She sighed, pointing towards Tim.

"How long have you been actualized?"

"For 125 years."

"That doesn't mean anything to me, explain."

"A human lives for approximately 80 years on average, so nearly two lifetimes."

"Well, you are looking good for your age."

Jill gave a tight smile. "I see you haven't lost your sense of humour on the journey."

"It's probably the only thing I haven't lost," he said quietly, "now, tell me your news."

"The people who I call my parents discovered me in Egypt in the year they call 1895. Anton and Suzannah Mayer, an Egyptologist and his assistant artist who recorded all his findings for him. They were from Austria and worked together. When they were excavating a tomb and spent many weeks cataloguing the main chamber, Anton found a groove in the floor at the base of the sarcophagus. The indentation was a handle to further chambers below. They extricated the stone, and a narrow passage led down to many more chambers which had hieroglyphs carved into the walls. This tomb was dedicated to the goddess Virgo. In the middle of the largest room there sat a gilded throne. The throne held a box made of gold. Anton and Suzannah crept forward and Anton took the lid off the box. My medallion, as they call them, sat within. Suzannah took it out. She was of Virgo. I appeared to them as a small child, for that is what I saw was their souls' desire. I decided to stay, so they adopted me. I allowed myself to grow into a woman. They never told a soul about my true origin."

"But who put you in the burial chamber?"

"I cannot say, but however I got there, I wasn't touched by one of Virgo. I must say, they honoured me well."

"But we were instructed to remain within our pods, not be living in the open."

"By who? Degon? What did he know? Nobody made him the leader. We would have been stuck in this piece of metal forever, Teres. Our mission would have been useless. I was lucky to have the same form as humans. I could go undetected. But we've already been slumbering here for 65 million years. We need to find all the

Warriors. It's taken me this long to find you. And I have seen this beautiful planet ravaged over the last 100 years. There is not much time left. The humans cannot see what is happening in front of them. Earth is drying out and if we don't stop, then it will be dying out too."

"What do you mean 'dying'? This cannot be true, after all we've been through to get here."

"The humans are intelligent. They have advanced well in technology for the time they have been here. But they are flawed."

"How?"

"Greed. They yearn for power, riches, ownership. Not all, but the dominant ones overpower the weaker."

Tim moaned.

"Quick, we must help them. But they must not know who I truly am."

Teres took the matching medallion from his belt and placed it on John's heart. Jill pulled a necklace from under her jacket. Her medallion was a pendant, and she placed it on Tim's chest. The two men's bodies rippled with a strange light. They stirred and sat up.

"Jill, are you OK?" said Tim, clutching the side of his head.

"Oh my God!" John shrieked as he gained focus and saw the mighty bull towering over him.

"It's OK, John!" Jill said. She rose and put her hand on his arm. "It's safe, he is here to help us."

"What the hell..." Tim backed away to the far corner. "What is that thing?"

"He came from the medallion," Jill said.

John looked at his hand and felt the glow.

"My name is Teres. You have freed me from my cage. I am from another galaxy. I come in peace."

"It speaks!" said John, "incredible."

"Jill, Jill, Jill, come here," Tim panted. "Get away from him."

He grabbed the pickaxe.

John stood up. "Extraordinary," he said breathlessly. "Quite extraordinary."

"We're trapped in here with that thing!" yelled Tim.

He threw the puny tool at Teres, who caught it with lightning reflexes.

John crept forward and scanned the beast, smiling. "This is remarkable. Yagkuk has returned."

"My name is Teres, I am from Horoscopia."

Another boom came from outside, and the rocks above them made an ominous grinding sound.

"It's collapsing," John shouted, as dust fell on them.

"We need to get out of here," Tim said under his breath. "There must be a way out."

Teres turned his massive body in the small space and put his shoulder against the rock blocking the exit. "I will free you."

He leaned against the boulder, but the rocks in the roof shifted, releasing more rubble. Teres held his enormous axe up to the unsteady rocks and murmured some strange words. He leaned again and exerted his huge body against the massive stone. His muscles strained, but at last it moved. Teres gave it one last heave, and it rolled away from the mouth of the cave.

"Quick, get out!" he yelled.

Tim picked himself up and grabbed Jill's hand. John followed. Teres came after them and as he lowered his axe, the cave filled itself in with collapsed rock. For a moment, there was silence. Then they all heard a massive crack, and the rocks on the mountainside vibrated.

"You need to get out of here. It's sliding," said Teres.

"What about the town below? It will be buried!" said John. "We have to warn them!"

Behind them, rocks loosened, and the mountain groaned.

"Take them along the path, walk for..." Teres pressed his forehead. "15 minutes. That will clear the landfall. I'll hold it back from here."

They leapt and scrambled down the paths to the camp. The guide stood waiting.

"We need to clear the area," Tim told him. The party walked as fast as possible in the dark. The ground was slippery from the storm. Their faithful guide led them with sure-footedness to a broad plateau that hid them from the view of the campsite and cave above.

Teres ran back to the entrance of the cave. He blew through his ringed nose and stood with legs wide apart. He lifted his battle axe, and in his language commanded for the mountain to settle. It creaked and crumbled as if digesting a banquet. The noises rumbled on through the ground until it ceased. He stayed there for a long time, listening to the mountain that had cocooned him for eons, whispering words of calm to the earth.

Back at the new campsite, John and Tim were arguing.

"We cannot inform the authorities, Tim. We'd have every newspaper, NASA, FBI, CIA, and their bloody aunties up here. We just need to keep this under wraps for the time being."

"That monster is dangerous!"

"He saved our lives and the town. If he was dangerous, we'd be dead by now. Just calm down. Let me think."

"How can I bloody calm down when I've just seen a half man half bull, well more bull than man, my God I don't even know what's happening here. One minute we are in a cave knocked out cold, then we're facing that..."

"Darling, take a breath. I have to say, I agree with your father. Let's talk to Teres and see what he wants to do."

Tim shook his head in disbelief.

"He had bit of a sheltered upbringing I'm afraid; his mother spoilt him," John said jokingly.

"I don't know how you can stay so calm, Dad." He turned to their guide. "You saw that thing. What do you think?"

The guide had remained silent.

"It's the Yak Cave, the yak now free. It's right time." He took out a rolled cigarette and lit it up, inhaling deeply.

"Everyone here is mad," Tim said. "Have you got another one of those?"

The man smiled and nodded. He passed him one with a lighter.

Later, Teres found the party huddled together.

"Thank-you, Teres," Jill said.

"I will return to the medallion. Summon me when you have gathered the others. John, you are my guardian, and I shall be yours."

"Wait, wait!" John cried out. "I want to talk..."

But Teres dissolved into a thousand pins of light that flowed into the medallion in John's jacket pocket.

"Others?" asked Tim.

Around 65 million years ago, one of the Zodiac Warriors landed on a continent that covered half of the planet. The pressurised pod crashed deep into the ground. The young planet was restless. Underground plates shifted and collided and concertinaed into mountains. Others fell apart, allowing the vast ocean to expand between, creating islands large and small. Volcanoes erupted gushing liquid rock—including the vessel from a faraway galaxy—into the valleys. The earth churned and composted and grew wild. Plants cultivated in the rich volcanic humus, they adapted, flowered and died. Trees towered, creating micro-climates and fell after hundreds of years. The roots of a tree exposed from a storm raised the remains of the vessel to the surface.

Eventually an animal so advanced it could move on just two limbs settled on the land. They tamed the countryside to feed themselves. They cut terraces where trees once stood in the hillsides and planted rice fields. A farmer was draining his rice paddy one day, and as he waded through the muddy water, something caught his eye. He stooped down and picked up a tarnished gold medallion. He wiped the mud off it, revealing a glistening moonstone. The other side had a sign in relief. He didn't recognize the symbol. He put the medallion in his pocket, planning to give it to his three-year-old daughter as a toy.

When he returned home, he called Li-mei to sit on his knee.

"Come here, little one. Papa found you something special in the rice paddy today."

She toddled over and smiled at her father. Her mother prepared food nearby in their two-roomed hut. Li-mei climbed up on his lap. He delved into one pocket and brought out a small frog.

"Ooops, not that one, yeesh!" he said.

Li-mei chuckled. "That one!" she pointed to his other pocket.

He pulled out the medallion and handed it to her.

"Mine!" Li-mei said and grabbed the medallion. It made her hands warm, and it wiggled a little, causing her to drop it in alarm.

"Ah, careful, little one. It may be precious. Look at the pretty stone, eh?"

Li-mei slid off his knee and scooped it up. It vibrated again, but this time her curiosity dominated fear, and she put her other hand on top of it. Suddenly, a yellow light shot through her fingers. The rays outlined two figures on either side of her mother. They became two solid people. Her mother dropped a plate and ran to her daughter.

"Look mama! Angels!"

"Husband, am I seeing right?" the woman whispered.

The farmer looked on in a state of shock.

The figures fleshed out. One was a man, the other a woman. They looked at each other and smiled.

"W... Who are you?" the farmer asked.

"I am Castor and this is Pollux. We are from Horoscopia. We are here in peace."

The man opened his mouth, but Pollux spoke before him.

"We were summoned by the girl out of the medallion. She is of Gemini."

The farmer closed his mouth, then took a breath to speak.

"We are not angels, but we are here to help," said Pollux. She turned to her brother, "they are full of questions and fear."

Castor nodded.

"Horoscopia is a galaxy far from here," Castor prompted.

"You know not what a galaxy is?" said Pollux.

"It's like they can read my mind," the farmer said.

"They think we look strange!" said Pollux, looking at the mother.

"I feel strange, now I'm free," Castor said.

"The child wants to play a game!"

Li-Mei held the magic medallion in her hand with wide eyes. She smiled at Pollux and held out her hand. Pollux moved to her and took the outstretched hand. The little girl showed Pollux her collection of butterflies and dried flowers. Pollux stroked her soft hair.

"She is beautiful," said Castor in response to his sister's thoughts.

"You are hungry?" Li-Mei's mother asked.

The twins shrugged. The woman cautiously moved past Castor to her kitchen and put a pot on the fire.

"Can you hear my thoughts?" the man, whose name was Xiang, asked Castor.

"Yes, we can listen to the voice inside."

"Of all of us?"

"Yes, and all creatures."

"All creatures? The bear, the eagle, the locust?"

Castor nodded. Xiang smiled. "All creatures, eh?"

There was a knock at the door.

"We must not tell the village. You must hide!"

Castor and Pollux looked at each other and dissolved back into the medallion. Li-Mei cried.

"Come back!"

Her father opened the door to his neighbour.

"Everything alright here? We saw strange lights and heard a crash."

"Yes, yes, neighbour. My wife is clumsy today."

The man peered through the door. Li-Mei wiped away her tears. Her mother stirred the pot and smiled.

After their daughter was in bed that night, the man picked up the medallion and shook it. He knocked on it, he talked to it, but nothing happened. He tucked it under his daughter's pillow and went to bed.

The man tossed and turned in his bed that night, questioning, imagining and wondering what had occurred in his house that day.

The next morning, he woke to the voices of strangers. He dressed and stepped into the kitchen to find his daughter sitting in her corner playing with the twins.

"Greetings!" Castor said without turning around. "You wish to speak with us."

"You know, it's considered rude to speak before you are spoken to in my house," Xiang said.

"You are thinking how we can be of assistance to you."

"Yes, I am very poor. I want to be a successful man."

"Very well, if Li-Mei says yes, we will help you."

"Daughter, say 'yes' to the strangers," Xiang commanded.

A girl child, or woman for that matter, never disobeyed the man of the house, and Li-Mei said, "Yes, yes, yes!"

From that day on, the twins helped Xiang plant and harvest by listening to the birds and the insects. He dressed them in local clothes and took them to read the minds of local merchants, and used them to discover what was happening in nearby villages. He used this knowledge to make sound business decisions, and he amassed more and more money. But it was never enough.

Pollux and Castor loved Li-Mei and played with her. They taught her many things and made sure she was safe. The farmer became a merchant and took the family to the town, where he bought a wooden house with three stories. The family grew with the addition of two sons. But Li-Mei was always the favourite despite her being a girl and her brothers were resentful. As she grew into a young woman, her father kept a close eye on her. It was only she who held the power to the Zodiac Warriors. Her brothers worked hard and Li-Mei was a lady of leisure. Li-Mei loved the Gemini twins more than her brothers, more even than her parents. One day, in the markets, she saw an old woman selling trinkets. A delicate pearl ring caught her attention. It looked like the pearl in the medallion, and she bought it and slipped it on her finger. She wished she could disappear into it like her friends did every evening.

One morning, when she was out walking by the river, Li-Mei met a young man reading a book. Although she was not allowed to be formally educated, the twins had taught her to read. She bade her mother that they might stop and ask about the book. Li-Mei fell in love with the young man and he with her. Once a week, they met by the river in secret until one day Xiang passed by and saw his daughter unchaperoned.

He stopped and dragged her away in fury.

"You are risking our fortune!" he yelled, "you must never see him again and you must never breathe a word of our helpers to a single soul."

He locked her on the top floor of the house and only released her when she was to summon the twins.

One day, with her heart broken, she refused to hold the medallion, and Xiang made his brothers beat her. Each day, he and his sons visited her in her room, and she refused to summon Pollux and Castor. He raged and beat her as her brothers looked on in smug satisfaction, but still she refused to touch the medallion.

The next morning, her father brought her a lock of hair.

"It is from the head of that scoundrel you fling yourself at."

"I do not believe you!" Li-mei cried. Her father nodded gravely.

The next morning, he gave her a piece of cloth. She unwrapped it to find an ear lying bloody in her hand. She recognised it immediately.

"You are not the only one who can bring them to me. I will find another May born to summon them. I will bring them out and I will destroy that dratted medallion so the twins are with me forever."

That night, she quietly summoned the twins and told them they were in danger. She slipped the pearl ring off her finger and onto Castor's.

"So you won't forget me." Li-Mei smiled sadly and hugged her guardians.

"We will not leave!" Pollux declared.

"You must. My father will kill you if you do not do as he asks. He will kill my love. I beg you! You must go!"

The pair stood fast, but Li-Mei ordered them to return to their medallion. To her astonishment, they dissolved into the familiar yellow light and into the medallion.

She wrapped the medallion in a silk box and begged her mother to deliver a message to her lover. She instructed him to take the medallion and leave the town.

The next day, Xiang came to her room and demanded the medallion. He tore her room apart and beat her while her mother begged and pleaded for her husband to stop.

"I will punish you for this, you spiteful, selfish child."

"And I will punish you, father," Li-Mei sobbed.

That night, she took the belt from her robe and threw it over the beam and then around her neck.

The whole neighbourhood heard the scream of her mother the next morning. The merchant Xiang slowly lost his money. His wife died of a broken heart and he and his sons ended up as beggars on the street outside his grand house.

The young man that had captured Li-Mei's heart rode on a rickshaw out of the village. He didn't know what the trinket was, only that he was to throw it in the sea, which he did. And there the medallion rested for another 500 years.

In modern times, the river was dredged to build a massive port. Huge ships with deep hulls arrived at the city. The silt and sand were dumped on the shore. A worker saw something catch the sun as he moved the sand in his digger. He turned off the engine and jumped out of the cab. He lit a cigarette and climbed the pile of sand he had just made. The moonstone glowed. He smiled and put it in his pocket. The man sold the medallion the following week, and it passed from hand to hand until it came into the ownership of Shen Ng. Shen was a student who had worked hard to be sent to America to study. He packed his possessions, including his father's box, which had been handed down through the generations. He put his most valuable treasures in the box, said goodbye to his mother and left.

When Shen arrived in New York, he put his carved box in his safe where it sat until his son reached the age of 21. It was time to give him his inheritance. But the son was not hardworking or honest. He like to drink and gamble. He tried to chip the moonstone out, but it would not budge. Thinking it worthless, he gambled it away. Now tarnished and battered, the medallion ended up in a shop in China Town.

Tammy Rutherford stood up and stretched her aching back. She had harvested her organic tomatoes and beans, which were plump and juicy thanks to the inventive reticulation system she had set up a few years ago. She left the peace of the poly-tunnel and paused at the Black Ash tree she'd planted when her husband, Bill, passed away ten years ago. Tammy had finished the job of raising their daughter and son into adults. Salina had always been the ambitious one. She had a zest for life that would never have kept her in Newton Falls. Now twenty-three, she had gone to New York City to make the world a better place. A chip off the old block, she was studying a degree in sustainability and communications and supported herself by a job in the NuDelta marketing department.

Tammy brushed the soil off her hands. She shook her head, thinking about the boy though. Steven was turning twenty-one on the weekend, and she was beginning to think of him as a no-hoper. Nothing stuck with this kid. He changed jobs more frequently than his underwear. It was frustrating to see her once bright and bouncy son grow into a petulant and dysfunctional young man.

Tammy's mobile rung. It took her a minute to locate which

pocket in her dungarees and then another minute to find her glasses. She punched her stubby, soil-encrusted finger on the answer button.

"Hello, Tammy Rutherford."

"Hey there Tammy, it's Sheriff Crawford. Got your boy here. Gonna need you to come down here, I'm afraid."

"Gosh darn it, what's he done now?"

"Caught him and his buddies climbing the old paper mill chimney. Been drinking again."

Tammy blew out a long breath. "OK Sam, I'll be there in ten."

Tammy ran her hands over her face and looked at the sky. She didn't know what to do about Steven. She couldn't figure out how two kids could turn out so differently. Maybe it was because Steven was just eleven when his Pa passed away.

Newton Falls was a small place. There wasn't much for its youth to do. Steven had excelled at school; he was on his way to start university two years ago. He was a whiz with computers. But he fell in with a crowd of teenagers that chose weed and beer over college and exams. Tammy got into her pickup and headed to the Sheriff's office.

"This time it's trespassing and disorderly conduct. We can't keep letting him off, Tammy. This is his last warning."

"Thanks, Sam. I appreciate it. I'll have another word with him, but he just doesn't listen to me."

Steven sat sheepishly in the cell. His leg bounced up and down and his hair was dishevelled. He stank of stale beer and smokes.

"Ma."

"What's that on your neck? Another tattoo?"

Steven gave her a sideways glance of defiance.

"Come on," Tammy sighed. Every week her son seemed to cram more holes in his body—be it piercings or tattoos, she felt like there were more holes in him than a sponge cake these days.

They walked out in silence and drove home. Steven kept his face away from his mother, staring at the familiar shops, homes, fields whizzing past the window. Whenever Tammy thought about saying something, she changed her mind. She was lost for words. Her son might as well be on another planet, speaking another language. Bill would have known what to say, but he was even further away.

"Early birthday celebration, was it?" she settled on at last.

"Something like that." Steven pulled a squashed packet of cigarettes out of his pocket and lit one.

Tammy wound down her window in protest.

"That's what killed your father."

"Yup."

"Son..."

"Don't Ma."

"Don't 'don't Ma' me, Steven. You're running out of chances. Next time Sheriff Crawford says he'll press charges and you'll end up in prison. Is that what you want? To break my heart. I hate to think what your Pa would think of you."

Steven bit his lip.

"Yeah well, maybe I should go where Pa is. That'd make life easier for you. No more worryin' what some dickhead sheriff or folk will think." He flicked his cigarette out of the window.

"Steven, don't you dare talk like that! Just get a job and make yourself useful. It's not that hard to live a good life. Stay off the liquor and whatever else you put in your body."

"And do what, hey? I'm not shovelling dirt around like you, or working in some shitty factory."

They pulled up in front of the house and Tammy turned off the engine.

"Well, go get trained in something, like your sister."

"Oh, there we go. That's right, rub my nose in it. I'll never live up to Sal in your eyes." He flung the door of the pickup open and stormed out.

"That's bullcrap! For someone who's not stupid, you're acting mighty stupid," Tammy yelled.

"Get stuffed, Ma. Perhaps if I'd had a dad around, I might not have turned out such a dud."

He stomped off. And there it was; the old familiar feeling of guilt and grief. Tammy gripped the steering wheel and forced the tears to stay behind her eyes. She pushed her anger deep down and took in deep breaths. Inside the house, Steven had shut himself in his room, playing his computer games. She figured that was better than climbing chimneys and getting hammered. She hoped that Salina's visit for his birthday on the weekend would clear the air.

The following morning Tammy rose at 5.00 am to make her delivery of organic produce to the three restaurants in New York that bought from her. She was getting a good price for her labour these days, as so many farms had closed down, unable to irrigate their vast crops.

Tammy listened to the radio for the 5-hour drive into New York City. The news was mostly grim. Forest fires, droughts, more civil scuffles breaking out in countries all over the world. Cows were dying of thirst on the farms and veganism was hitting an all-time high. The sleepy hamlet of Newton Falls didn't know how lucky it was dealing with a few unruly youngsters.

Despite their troubles, she wanted to get Steven a present. Maybe they could start afresh on his twenty-first birthday, with Salina there.

Big department stores just made her uncomfortable; she preferred smaller shops. As she made her final delivery in China-town, she noticed a sign to an antique-looking knickknack store. The shop was dim inside and the clanging bell on the door seemed to send dust into the air. An old Asian man sat behind a counter, writing in a ledger. Tammy glanced around the shop. Strange and eclectic items were crammed on shelves: a pewter tankard, a feathered helmet, plastic crabs, horns, and a pair of vases shaped like fish. A glass case held beaded necklaces and medals.

"Can I help you?" the old man asked.

"Any idea what to give a twenty-one-year-old bad boy?"

"His birthday tomorrow?"

"Why, yes it is. How did you know?"

"People always buy last minute!"

"Ha, you're not wrong. What do you suggest?"

"Bling."

"Pardon?"

"These youngsters, they like shiney shiney. See?" He grabbed a handful of gold chains out of a bowl.

"Mmm, he's not really the jewelry type."

"Ah, what about this? He wears pants, yes? For holding the jeans up."

The shopkeeper held a leather belt with an unusual brass buckle holding some sort of stone.

"It has Gemini sign, see? Like your son."

"That's perfect! How much?"

"For you ma'am $50. Here—I put in nice box."

A bit steep, Tammy thought, but time was ticking on, and she had to pick up Salina in half an hour. She handed over a note and thanked the man for his help.

At first, Tammy didn't recognise her daughter as she bounded out of her apartment block door. She had dyed her long hair blue from the pink it had been when they last got together, and it was scraped up in a messy top knot. She wore a denim dungaree dress with a bright yellow top.

"Blue hair?" Tammy said in mock exasperation.

"Yep, to match my new Docs!" Sal said, stomping her two feet on the dashboard.

Driving for five hours with her daughter was a dream compared to ten minutes with her son. They chatted easily the whole way.

"So how's your job going?"

"It's OK. You know how it is with big corporations. Profit over people, profit over planet. I'm trying to make changes from the inside." She gave a sideways grin.

"That's my girl!"

"Did you hear they are branching into communications? They're rolling out the NuDelta 'NuPhone' at the moment."

"I heard. You can't go five minutes without passing a NuDelta truck delivering Lord knows what, or seeing a billboard offering holidays or credit cards or groceries. That Orlando Focus has got his finger in a lotta pies."

"They reckon he's the richest man in the world now. But he pays well, that's all I care. It's not cheap getting a degree these days. Anyway, NuDelta staff have got a pretty neat deal for a NuPhone and plan."

Sal flashed her new mobile and snapped a selfie.

When Tammy and Salina arrived back in Newton Falls, it was late. After a cup of tea and a piece of toast, Tammy gave her daughter a peck on the cheek and turned in. She noticed the bluish light of Steven's PC flickering around his door frame.

The following morning, Tammy stepped into the kitchen to the smell of coffee and baking. Salina had been up early to make Steven's birthday cake and bring some flowers to decorate the table.

"You beat me to it!" said Tammy.

Salina smiled.

"What time will the lazy ass get out of bed?"

"When I drag him out!"

"Go easy on him, Ma. It's his birthday."

"I reckon I've been way too easy on him. Got in trouble again the other day."

"Shit. I'll see if I can get some sense into him."

"Steven!" Tammy yelled. "Get up! It's your birthday!"

After fifteen minutes, they heard his door open and then the toilet flush. Steven scuffed into the kitchen.

"Stevie! Happy birthday, bro!"

"Hey Sal, Ma." He nodded to Tammy and gave his sister a perfunctory fist pump.

"Coffee?"

Steven nodded after a cursory glance of acknowledgment of Sal's latest look. He sat at the kitchen table but wasn't in the mood for forced talk and flowers. He just wanted the sanctuary of his room. But he loved his sister enough to stay put for now. He tightened his jaw.

"Well now, shall we find some presents?" said Tammy, breaking the silence.

"Aw Ma, please no..."

"Come on Stevie, it's your twenty-first, after all," said Salina. "Here."

She passed him a gift-wrapped box. He took off the paper.

"Deathstar Rebel III, thanks."

"It's the new one, fighting the alien invasion."

"Yeah, cool. Thanks Sal."

"And this is from me." Tammy gave him the wooden box.

Steven let it sit in front of him for a moment.

"Open it then."

"I can't do this. I can't sit here and pretend everything is fine and dandy. I'm messed up. This family is messed up. This whole damn planet is screwed." He pushed his chair back, and grabbing the keys to the pickup, left the house.

Steven sat in a bar until dusk. When the barman refused him anymore drinks, he staggered outside. It was spring, but the nights were still cold. He breathed in the chill air and looked at the sky. Gazing at the pillow of stars scattered across the black canvas was one of the few things that brought him relief. Its vastness seemed to create space in his mind, but tonight it made his whisky-filled head dizzy. He drove home despite the alcohol in his system. His familiar home, where he had lived all his life, was illuminated by the single porch light. Ma had left it on. For him. He sighed. He tried to tread softly past Ma's room, her snoring reassuring. There was no sign of Sal. She must have caught the bus back to New York once they realized he wasn't coming home.

Steven sat down and turned on his computer. His mother's gift and sister's game sat on his desk. He ignored them and took out a fat reefer his friends had given him for his birthday and lit it up. He inhaled deeply. He picked up the Deathstar Rebel III and loaded the disc. Balancing the reefer in his lips, he flicked the lid of the box his Ma had given him. A leather belt was curled within. It was old, nice and worn looking. He took another toke and laid the joint in the ashtray. The belt had an unusual buckle. As he exhaled thick ribbons of smoke, he lifted it out of the box and held it up. He stood, a little wobbly and threaded the belt in his jeans. When he grasped the buckle, a surge of heat shot through his hand. Surprised, he released the buckle, then gingerly touched it again. He took up the smouldering joint and took another draw, but stumbled and fell onto his single bed, giggling at his unsteadiness.

As he lay on the bed, he took the buckle one more time to fasten the belt and as he clasped it, heat shot up his arm again. This time, light poured through his hand, turning it bright yellow. The beams rushed into the middle of his smoky room, shaping into two bodies. Steven could not release his hand from the buckle as the light flashed out. He blinked at the brightness, and as suddenly as it had started, it stopped. The joint dropped from his lips. He quickly picked it up and looked at it. What the hell did the boys lace this thing with? He stubbed it out in the glass on his bedside table and rubbed his eyes.

There were two people standing in his cramped bedroom. He dug the heels of his hands into his eyes and shook his head, but there were indeed a man and a woman standing before him. The woman wore a red skin-tight body suit and at her throat a similar medallion to Stevie's buckle. The man was dressed the same in blue. Though their faces were human, their bodies looked more powerful than the wrestlers he watched on TV late at night. But what terrified him most was that his mind felt inhabited, that his secrets and shames were exposed. He curled up on his bed, holding his arms over his head.

"What the...? Take what you want, just don't hurt me," he whimpered.

"Where is Li-Mei?" the female asked.

"This place looks different, Pollux."

"Where is my little girl?"

"This human is terrified."

"He seems to be leaking," she said.

Though he was used to the image of alien beings, they were firmly encased in his computer screen. Steven had indeed wet himself.

"Tell us, what province are we in?" Pollux asked.

"Province?"

"Where are we? You see, we were separated from a very dear friend and we are keen to locate her," Castor explained.

"Er, what..."

"He doesn't understand."

"He is too afraid. He has darkness, the mind is not clear," said Castor.

"What year is this?"

"Er 2025."

"2025? That can't be right, brother!"

"We need to download."

They pressed a finger between their closed eyes.

"Forgive my sister, Steven. We have now updated. Let's start again. My name is Castor and this is Pollux. You have summoned us. You are of Gemini."

"How, how do you know my name?"

"We can read your mind."

"We are too late!" Pollux cried. "Why did it take so long to be summoned?"

"Where the *hell* are you from?" Steven asked.

"We are from the star system of Horoscopia. We came here after our planets went into a black hole."

"Whoa!" Steven breathed. "A black hole? You mean they really exist?"

"Do you know where the other Zodiac Warriors are?"

"Others?"

"Yes, there are twelve representatives. We must gather."

"Er, no. I can try Google it?"

"Yes, do this and summon them here."

"It's a pretty powerful search engine, but it's not that good."

Steven got up from his bed timidly, still unsure of the two muscled beings in his bedroom. "Um, I'll just sit over there on my chair. Who are you looking for exactly?"

"The Zodiac Warriors, from Horoscopia."

He typed 'zodiac warriors' in the search bar and pressed return. A jewelry site came up, a tarot reader and a site displaying souped-up cars. Nothing to do with aliens. He thought for a moment and toggled to the dark web. This was a more appropriate place to reach out. Lily's website came up immediately.

He clicked on the site but then clicked out of it straight away. What if this was some sort of scam? What if these people were dangerous? Or the CIA was involved? He had read too many conspiracy theorists' blogs to jump into anything blindly.

"Because we are who we say you are and will do you no harm," said Castor, just as Steven was about to ask, 'how do I know I can trust you?'.

"It would be kinda nice if you wait for me to ask the question, you know."

The floorboard outside his bedroom creaked.

"That you home, son?" Tammy called outside the door.

"Yeah, Ma. Go back to bed now."

"You got company?"

"Er, yeah. Friend staying over."

"Ah, OK, well goodnight."

"Yep."

He heard his mother creep back to bed.

"Keep your voices down, OK?" Steven said to the twins.

With shaking hands, he pressed a series of keys and logged on via his VPN. This way, he could do a bit of digging anonymously. He scrabbled for his cigarettes and inhaled deeply, hoping for the nicotine to calm his fractured nerves. He looked at the Zodiac Warriors website again. It had one black page with an icon shaped just like the buckle on his belt.

"Booya!"

The icon flickered, telling him it was waiting to download. Then the screen went blank.

"What the hell...?"

"How is this machine helping us?" Pollux asked.

"This machine rules the world, lady. There ain't nothing this machine can't do," Stevie murmured.

Pollux frowned. "It is rudimentary. I cannot believe you still use your fingers to command it."

Steven looked at her with wide eyes.

Castor roamed around the room, picking up the various paraphernalia scattered around.

"Whoa, whoa, put that down!" Steven said, taking the joint out of Castor's fingers.

Steven scrolled down, the black screen reamed past. Then something caught his eye. A number, in small font in the top right-hand corner. Zero. He rummaged around for a pen and found a pencil stub under several food-crusted plates and dog-eared magazines.

He wrote it down and continued scrolling.

"Tedious," he sighed.

"What are you doing?" Castor leaned over his shoulder while this time Pollux poked around Stevie's bedroom.

"I've got a lead. Some numbers, maybe a phone number."

Another number appeared, and pages later another. This whole situation was so surreal, he was worried he had missed some of the tiny digits. At last, he had 11 numbers, and the pages stopped with a white line.

"Now what?" he whispered.

"Yes, what now?" Pollux echoed.

"I guess I make a call. Does anyone know about you? You said you were here before with someone?"

"Yes, four hundred years ago."

Steven's eyes bulged. "Four hundred? This is some weird shit."

He shook his head and took a deep breath. The twins glared at him as he took his phone out of his back pocket and dialled the number.

L ily and Jason boarded the flight to Darwin. After they had settled in their seats, Lily said, "When we put our bags through security at the airport, I looked at the image on the scanner. The medallion in my bag didn't show up. Weird, hey?"

"It must be made of something other than metal, then. Probably a good job it's undetectable."

"Did I tell you the soil samples results came back from Zakary? He said the samples date back to over sixty-five million years ago."

"Wow! If the Zodiac medallions have been here for millions of years, they must be pretty strong to withstand crashing on to earth, then being buried or frozen or whatever else the planet did all that time ago," Jason said.

"What I don't understand is if it is Capricorn, why is he wandering around and not in his medallion."

"Good question."

"Talking of the hunky Zakary..." Jason nudged Lily in her ribs.

"Were we?"

"Come on. I know you want to talk about him. Don't think I didn't notice that loooooong hug at the airport!"

Lily grinned and nudged him back.

"Spill the beans. I'm your best friend."

"Oh are you?!"

"Come on, darl. You like him, don't you?"

"I do. But this whole Zodiac thing..." She shrugged.

Jason cocked his head at her.

"And he lives in Kenya, and I've got my PhD and my mum is a mess..."

"Excuses!"

"Let's just see what happens, hey? I can't think about it now."

They fell into silence, both thinking about the journey ahead and the strange things they had seen. And, at least for Lily, Zakary.

The plane descended over the scorched earth into Darwin. What was once lush with bush was now brittle and dry. Global warming had shrunk islands off the north coast of Australia, creating legions of climate refugees. Rivers and waterfalls had practically ceased to flow and the tourists with them. The silver lining was that Lily and Jason would probably be the only ones out in the bush.

The trail to 17 Mile Falls was around 30 km and the trip would take five days, including the walk out the other side. They packed dried food, water, tents, and extra clothes and set off. The journey began with a short boat trip across the Katherine River. The area was popular because these falls ran all year-round, but today the river looked silty, and the banks showed that it normally sat higher. Their 15 kg loads weighed them down, and they sweated under the biting sun, even so early in the morning. After trekking for four hours, they called it a day and set up camp under a pleasant grove.

"I'm exhausted," said Jason. "Why don't we release Prymaw now and let him search for the goat?"

"I think there is a better chance of finding him further in. Plus, we don't want to lose Prymaw out here."

They trekked on for the next two days. The scenery was breathtaking; orange sandstone cliffs harboured trickles of water, though the pictures on the map showed gushing torrents.

On the third day, at the top of an escarpment, they were

rewarded with a view of 17 Miles Fall. The water fell the great height into a tributary. They reached the campsite at the base of the falls and dropped their packs with relief.

"Let's eat and then have a scour around," Lily suggested.

After a late lunch, they walked to the base of the waterfall.

"Not a bad spot to spend a few million years in," said Jason.

"It's beautiful."

"Do you think there's crocs in there?"

"Nah. Last one in is a sissy!" Lily stripped off her t-shirt and pants and waded into the water. Jason didn't know where to put his eyes.

"Come on, it's divine!" she yelled.

Jason shrugged, dropped his pants and dived into the water.

"It's cold!" he shrieked.

"It's perfect," Lily said as she swam up to him.

They treaded water, basking in the peace. A noise made them both look up at the waterfall. The sun was sinking, leaving the cliff in shadow, but there was a movement on the face of the cliff at the edge of the water.

"Did you see something?" Jason asked.

"Yes, quick let's get the binoculars before it gets too dark."

They waded out of the water and tried to stem the drips with their t-shirts. Jason crawled into his tent and dragged his camera from his pack. Lily was already searching the wall of the cliff through the binoculars.

"Anything?"

"Nah, I can't see much. The light's fading. Whatever it was is gone. Let's get some sleep and summon Prymaw in the morning."

Lily and Jason were awake at sun break. The squawks of dozens of birds prevented them from sleeping longer. They made tea and ate a muesli bar for breakfast.

"Come on then, let's do it," said Jason. "Let's release the beast," he said, trying to fake some bravado.

"Jason, I'm scared," said Lily quietly.

Jason was chucking his dregs of tea into the bushes and looked up sharply at her words.

"You? You are the bravest person I know. You're so confident and outgoing!"

Lily chewed her bottom lip.

"Sometimes it's a front, Jase. Inside I get wobbly."

"I'm right here, you know I've got your back."

He put an arm around her. She rested her head on his shoulder for a moment. She took a deep breath and kissed Jason on the cheek.

"You're a good mate. Come on, let's get this goat!"

Lily took the medallion out of her pocket and held it in her hand.

"Do I say something?" she asked Jason.

"I dunno," he shrugged. "What happened last time? Can you feel anything?"

"It feels a bit hot." She cleared her throat. "I summon you, Prymaw, Zodiac Warrior of Aries!"

Jason stifled a laugh. Nothing happened.

"God, I feel stupid!"

"I summon thee Prymaw!" Jason said in an imitating, deep voice.

They laughed. The medallion remained impassive in her hand.

"Bloody hell! Are we crazy, Jase? Did all that really happen in Tanzania?"

Jason blew out and shook his head, which contained no answers.

The flies buzzed around, the cicadas revved up, and the sound of the waterfall drew them to the water's edge.

"Zodiac Warrior Capricorn!" Jason shouted at the cliff face, and his voice echoed around them.

"Show yourself!" Lily yelled.

"Let's swim," she said after her echoes were followed by the sounds of the bush.

They dived into the water and splashed around, laughing and squirting water at each other. Jason spotted a frill-neck lizard basking on the rocks and went to get his camera. Lily floated on her back, scanning the rocks where they'd seen the movement the day before.

The sun dried the water on her forehead, making it itch. She rolled over and went to glide back to the bank when she saw a shape breaking the surface of the water.

"What the...?"

Two eyes smoothly rose above the water and surged toward her. She screamed and flailed as she tried to orient herself to the bank.

"Jason! Help!"

Jason ran to the water's edge and saw the crocodile advancing on Lily.

"Oh Jesus."

He bent down, grabbed the medallion and stepped into the water.

"Lil, catch it!"

"I can't, Jason, I can't, ahhhh!" she screamed again as she felt the crocodile scrape against her foot.

"Catch it, he'll come!"

"No! No don't, I can't..."

She went under. Jason bellowed, "Lily!"

He hovered in the shallows, terrified to stay where he was and lose his friend, and equally as scared to go into the water with the crocodile. He called her name again, "Lily! No, no, no!"

Suddenly, there was an almighty crash. The water broiled and churned; splashes erupted from the surface. Jason went in up to his knees and threw futile stones. He yelled at the medallion to help. The water thrashed, and the crocodile's tail broke the surface before disappearing. Then the water stilled. Blood coloured tendrils floated towards him. Jason dropped to his knees and sobbed.

"Lily, no, don't leave me..."

He picked up the medallion and threw it into the bushes, rage and tears fighting for supremacy.

Then he heard her breathless voice, "Jase, Jase, I'm OK."

He looked up and smeared a muddy hand across his face. Lily stumbled out of the water to his left. She was bleeding from her arm, but she was alive.

"Oh my God, I'm sorry, I'm so sorry, Lil."

He paddled into the water and hugged her, apologising relentlessly.

"You tried Jason. Did you see what happened?"

"There was an almighty splash, and the water was churning and rolling. I thought you were dead." He broke down again.

"Something saved me. I went under then I was flung out of the way."

They heard the water erupt again and a pair of horns exploded above the surface.

"Is it Prymaw?" said Jason.

The figure strode out of the water toward them. He had the torso of a human and the head and legs of a goat. He dragged the dead salt-water crocodile by the tail.

Lily gave a hysterical laugh, "No, this must be our friend from Capricorn."

The goat-man arrived on dry land and, after dropping the croc, he walked toward them. He cocked his head and circled them. He came back around and spoke.

"You must be human 'cos you're bleeding. But why didn't you run from me?"

"We have come for you," Lily said simply.

"Betta stop that, missus," he pointed to her arm, "or them crocs will smell the blood and their mates'll come too."

The half-man, half-goat gathered leaves from the bushes and some twine, which he shredded with his teeth and gently dressed her wound. He gave the leaves names in the local dialect and spoke like the indigenous people.

"I don't know how you mad humans have survived on this planet for so long," he said as he tightened the twine around her arm.

Lily winced at both the pain and his reprimand.

"Why'd you come here?"

"We're looking for the Zodiac Warriors," said Lily. "Jason, where's the medallion?"

Jason skirted the dead croc nervously and retrieved the medallion from where he had tossed it.

"This is Prymaw of Aries." She showed him the medallion. "Are you Capricorn?"

He cocked his head and gazed at it.

"Yeah, I'm Plaadio of Capricorn. How d'you know?"

Then he spoke in a language so strange that the birds and insects ceased their chatter, and the bush went silent. Laser beams of red shot out of the medallion in Lily's palm and the gigantic form of Prymaw materialised.

Plaadio reared his head back and whooped, and as Prymaw solidified, he did the same. The two Warriors smashed their chests into each other, then stepped back and bowed heads until their horns met.

Lily and Jason watched on in disbelief.

"Double trouble," said Jason.

Prymaw glanced at Lily and nodded.

"We meet again. What happened to you this time?" he said.

"Attacked by a crocodile. Your friend saved my life."

Plaadio clapped Prymaw on the back. "Come on, bro, we have much to yarn. I'll make a fire and cook the croc meat."

They went back to the campsite and Plaadio skilfully built a fire, then skinned the crocodile as if it was a bunny rabbit and speared it over the fire.

"How long have you been here, brother?" Prymaw asked as they ate.

"What sort of question is that? I have nothing to measure. I came with the land."

"Where is your medallion?" Lily asked.

"Lost it, been both my downfall and my learning."

"We saw a photo. It was the medallion that led us here. How did you lose it? Is that even possible?" asked Jason.

"When I was summoned by a Jawoyn man, he dropped my medallion into a deep gorge. The water was deep, and we couldn't reclaim it. Every dry season, I plunged into the shallow water, but it was gone. Swept away, eaten by the great goanna, or crocs. The medallion you speak of is my buckle, not my vehicle."

"What did you do without the medallion?"

"I lived with the Jawoyn people. Then the light skins came, and I had to hide. I was too different to stay with my adopted tribe. I live this simple life, helping out crazy humans who walk the path here."

"How will we transport you?"

"Transport me, bro? Why do you speak of this?"

"It is time for the Zodiac Warriors to gather. If we want to survive our own apocalypse, then we have to save this planet from theirs," said Prymaw.

"Did he say apocalypse?" said Jason in a high voice. "Did we know about this?"

"Don't you watch the news, Jase? You saw that rebel army in Tanzania. You saw the erosion in the Serengeti."

"Yes, that is in Africa, but not here in Australia!"

"This waterfall is a titchy trickle today. Where we are sitting now was once underwater all year long," said Plaadio. "You're wrong, mate. This land is dying of thirst."

They sat in silence.

"How many are actualized?" Plaadio broke the silence.

"As far as we know, just the two of you. We're searching everywhere for the rest," said Lily. "I have no idea where to look. The world is a big place, and these medallions are so small."

"We need to find Amrez," said Plaadio.

"Amrez?" Jason asked.

"Amrez of Sagittarius. He is the archer. His bow and arrow can find anything," Prymaw explained.

"There is only one problem," said Plaadio.

"And that is?" Jason asked.

"Amrez doesn't stay in one place for very long," Plaadio said.

"If he's actualized, then all we need to do is find the biggest party!"

The Zodiac Warriors laughed at some shared memory.

"One thing I know is, we need as many of us searching for him as we can," said Prymaw.

"So, the mob is finally coming back together. Problem is mate, I've come across a few humans in my time and they don't like the look of me. I can't travel in my Zodiac form."

"You will have to piggyback with me," said Prymaw.

"You can do that?" asked Lily.

"Let's hope we don't merge in the medallion," said Plaadio.

"Ew," said Jason, pulling a face.

They laughed, and for a moment, life felt normal. The fire crackled. Lily looked up at the swathe of sparkles in the Milky Way.

"I can't believe you came from way way beyond those stars," Lily said.

"So many of them," Jason breathed.

"Our spaceships broke apart in your galaxy and formed the Zodiac constellations you have read in the sky for all time."

"So, our fate is written in the stars?" Lily said. "Huh."

Jason yawned. "I'm going to bed, I'm bushed."

"You look it!" Lily laughed and messed Jason's matted hair. "Me too. Good night, Zodiac Warriors."

The Zodiacs nodded. Plaadio poked the fire and threw a log onto it. They sat in silence until the gentle snores of the humans vibrated from the tents.

"Good to see you, bro."

"And you, Plaad. So what do you make of the planet? Does it have potential?"

Plaadio blew air through his nostrils. "You fellas are leaving it a bit late. This place used to be beautiful. These waterfalls flowed year-round, the plants and food were plentiful. It was a rich time. But the whitefellas came and messed with it. Ever since they came, my tribe got smaller, sicker. The land is crying."

"We came here because the planet had enough moisture to regenerate the DNA in the pods. And what about the other resources we need to rebuild?"

"The people of this planet are not advanced. Gemini will need to bring their knowledge of technology. Aquarius to design. Taurus to build. We need to find 'em all first. Look, I just know what's happening here, mate. Maybe other parts of it are OK."

"Let's hope so brother, let's hope so."

The next morning, they packed up the tents and made sure the fire was doused. The two Zodiacs had talked long into the night but appeared as alert as ever.

"Are you ready to say goodbye, Plaadio?" asked Lily. "You've been living here a long time."

Plaadio cast his eyes around the glade. Swooping down, he placed a hand on the ground and closed his eyes. "I am. It is time," he replied. "Are you ready for me to share your bed with you, Prymaw?" he said, laughing.

"Let's get it over with. Don't squash me though!" joked Prymaw, shaking his horns in mock threat.

Lily and Jason stood by as the Zodiacs prepared to de-actualize back into the medallion. After a few moments of nothing happening, the Warriors glanced at each other.

"At the same time?" asked Plaadio.

Prymaw shrugged.

"After three," said Lily helpfully. "One, two... three!"

The Zodiac Warriors remained standing.

"OK, me first, then you," said Plaadio.

Plaadio closed his eyes, and a light shimmered through him, but he solidified again. "Maybe I'm a bit rustic," he said.

Lily and Jason burst out laughing. "You mean rusty, like out of practice?" said Jason.

"Yes, that's what I said," Plaadio huffed.

"OK, I'll go first and then you," Prymaw suggested.

Prymaw's body shuddered, and sharp blades of light focused into the medallion and he was gone.

"Plaadio?" prompted Lily.

"I'm trying!"

Plaadio spoke in his language and Prymaw reappeared.

"It's not working," he said.

Plaadio paced up and down. "The medallion is rejecting me. It is built to accommodate an Aries, not a Capricorn."

"What's the difference if you're all from the same planet?" asked Lily.

"Same planet? We're not from the same planet. We are all from the galaxy of Horoscopia, but our planets were all very different. Our bodies are all very different. The medallion material was mined on Aries, the technology was developed on Gemini."

"The Sagittarians discovered earth. The idea to leave and come here was the Leos' drive. It was Virgo who alerted us to the black hole," Prymaw added.

"An entire galaxy?" Jason whistled through his teeth. "What was your planet like? Was it like earth?"

Lily looked at her watch. "We need to get going. We have a taxi collecting us at the end of the trail at 5.00 pm tomorrow."

"Let us walk and talk, and work out how to transport Capricorn on the way," Prymaw suggested.

As they trekked on, the Zodiacs tried to describe the places they came from, but the humans could not grasp the images they were conjuring, and the language of earth did not have the words to help. It was like trying to imagine a new colour. They fell into silence until Prymaw stopped them.

"Halt. I hear something."

They listened. A man's voice drifted on the air.

"Someone is coming. We need to hide you!" Lily said.

The voice got louder, a woman's voice also spoke. Lily grabbed the Aries medallion out of her bag.

"Try now!" she said. The voices were getting closer. A large boulder obscured the path ahead. "Now!"

Prymaw dissolved into a blaze of laser beams and was gone. Plaadio shimmered, but still stood tall.

"Look at the flowers on that bush, Wendy, they smell divine." They could hear the words of the trekkers now.

"Plaadio, climb a tree or something!" Jason urged.

Plaadio looked at him, closed his eyes and trembled. A deep brown mist enshrouded him. The mist twirled around him, then swirled and boiled, its movement growing faster and faster. It gathered and vibrated and peaked. It concentrated itself into a tight ball and then shot itself towards Jason. Jason opened his mouth and the grenade of mist entered. Jason took a deep breath in, his chest expanded.

"So pretty. I reckon we've got another couple of hours... oh hello!"

Jason opened his eyes wide, his head jigged back slightly. He looked like he was about to sneeze. He shuddered and his button popped off his pants, his shirt stretched across his back.

"Ow, ow, owwww!" he yelled.

"Good morning!" said Lily brightly. "Bee sting, watch out for them, it's the time of the year."

She fixed a smile on her face and realised she was still holding the medallion out in front of her. She slid it into her pocket.

"Enjoy your trek. And, uh, watch out for the crocodiles!"

The couple moved past them with a wave.

"What the hell just happened there?" she said to Jason.

"No, no, no, no, no!" Jason wailed. "Get out of me!"

"Wait, what? Plaadio is in *you?*"

"*It's a bit bloody cramped in here,*" a different voice came out of Jason's mouth.

"Oh my God, is that you, Plaadio?" Lily asked, looking at Jason queerly.

"Get out of..."

"*Yeah, I'm here. This'll have to do for now.*"

"No, it won't!" Jason managed to say. "I can't have you inside of me, I feel, I feel... wrong!"

"You should feel like a strong fella! Go climb that boulder!"

"Would you stop speaking out of me!"

"Here, I'll show you."

Without trying, Jason's legs moved under him and he found himself scaling the rock like a monkey.

"Woo hoo! Go Jase! That's amazing!" Lily clapped.

"I don't want to... whoooaaa!"

Jason took off and leapt into the branches of a gumtree, then climbed down its trunk.

"Stop, I feel sick!" he said.

"Need a bit of training, but I can work with it," Plaadio said.

"We? We? WE? I don't want to be a 'we'! Lily, help me! Get him out, please."

"OK, OK, calm down Jase. Plaadio, can you exit for a moment? Jason needs to consent to this, to this, um... alliance."

"Are you born of Capricorn?" Plaadio's deep voice asked Lily.

Jason rolled his eyes, unable to control which voice spoke.

"No, I'm Aries, that's how I activated Prymaw. But Jason, you are, aren't you? The 18th of January! See, I remembered!"

Jason nodded.

"Then I'll stay put until we're alone again."

"No, no, no! I can't believe this is happening!" Jason's voice rose to a shout.

"You look kind of hunky, Jase. Muscled up a bit," said Lily as she looked him up and down appreciatively.

"Gah!" He raked his hands through his hair. "It doesn't look like I've got much choice. Just let me do the talking... whoa!" Jason involuntarily leapt forward. "And walking, OK?"

"Just relax, Plaadio, enjoy the ride," Lily added.

"OK, OK, missus, I'll try."

Jason leapt forward again like a gazelle. "A, a, a!" yelled Jason and he gingerly stepped forward in his own way. "That's the way, OK. Nice and easy," he crooned.

Jason nodded to Lily, and they shouldered their packs and walked along the trail in an awkward silence, neither of them knowing if Plaadio was awake or inert.

P rofessor John Robertson, Timothy and Jill arrived back in the UK from Bhutan and settled themselves in the family house in Kent. The men talked in depth about their experience; Jill interjected occasionally, answering their questions about what occurred when they were knocked out. After days of examining the medallion, telling and retelling what happened, Jill suggested that they put their energy into finding the other Zodiac Warriors that Teres talked about. John had access to many catalogues of archaeological finds over the decades, and he and Tim thumbed through old copies. They went to the local library and scrolled through microfiche and Internet archives, looking for other medallions. A week went by and they found no leads. Tim and Jill went back to work in London.

John pored through the small print of ancient research with his magnifying glass and looked at the photo of every artifact discovered. Nothing. Not one piece of evidence that could explain the massive bull-man they had unearthed in Bhutan. He tore his glasses off and tossed them on his desk. He rubbed his hands over his mouth and stubbled chin. This was the greatest discovery of his life, but if he couldn't prove it to his peers, if he couldn't back up the paper he planned to write, it was all for nought. He would be laughed out of his faculty. He couldn't bear that humiliation again.

The medallion sat on a small cushion in front of him. Deep in thought, he stared at it. His phone pinged, and he read a message from Tim. Something had come up. He wouldn't be home for dinner. John scrolled through the photos of Bhutan. An idea that had haunted him since that trip flashed through his mind again. He turned the camera onto video recorder, propped it against the back of his laptop and pressed record. He picked up the medallion and held it in front of him. A green light bled out of his fingers. John shook his head as he watched the lights beam in front of his desk and the beast materialize before him.

"John, I am at your service."

"Teres, hello, er welcome."

Teres looked around him. He took a step to the window and gazed out at the rose bushes in full bloom and the green trees at the bottom of John's garden.

"This is your home?"

"Yes."

"It's a fine place."

He crouched down and put his great fists on the floor.

"Teres, I thought it would be wise, er, pleasant to get to know each other a little."

"Yes, we have much to learn from each other."

"Please, take a seat. Can I offer you a refreshment?"

Teres blew air through his nose and sat down in the chair opposite John.

"So, you came from a solar system in another galaxy?..."

That weekend, Tim and Jill came home.

"Are you going to tell him?" Tim said, as he poured their wine at the dinner table.

"A wedding date?"

"No, not a date, Dad."

"Actually, I've been thinking," said John, "I should move out of the master suite so you can move in there. It seems ridiculous that you two stay in the single rooms. You're practically married, after all."

An unsettling silence followed.

"We, uh, are holding off on a date. Both very busy with work," Tim said eventually.

Jill looked upset. She placed her hand on Tim's.

"Darling," she said to him, then turned to John. "The truth is, John, it's me who's delayed it. I haven't been able to think about anything else other than what happened in that cave. We need to find the other Zodiacs, or we won't have a world worth living in."

"I don't see how the Zodiac Warriors can have any effect the state of the world. The government is sorting it all out, you'll see."

"With respect, John, the governments have done nothing but expedite global warming. They simply bow and scrape to the big corporations like NuDelta."

"Jill, NuDelta are the ones saving this planet by paying for the desalination plants!" John patted her on her hand.

Jill shook her head. "Just because I'm a woman, you think I don't know what's going on! Don't underestimate me. I have been around a long... I have visited many countries and studied many civilisations. I have researched history and politics. Believe me when I tell you we need more than money hungry businesses and politicians to change the course of this planet. We're running out of time and the only thing that will make people listen is someone from another galaxy, other beings who have not only knowledge but strength."

She stood, a slight blush on her cheekbones.

"Darling, calm down. He didn't mean to diminish you, did you, Dad?" Tim turned and glared at his father. "He can forget that women are educated these days. He's been called a dinosaur more than once."

"Well, I'm sure it'll all work out... between you two, I mean," John mumbled. "So, what was it you were going to tell me then?"

"I think I may have found a lead," Jill said as she took a seat again. There was an edge of excitement in her usual calm demeanour.

"Really? Where?"

"I was looking through the new Sotheby's catalogue for work and it looks like there's a medallion up for auction." She pulled the book from her bag and opened it to the bookmarked page.

The image showed the familiar oval with the sign of Leo engraved on it.

"Bravo!" John exclaimed, glad to have moved on to jollier news.

"It's next week. Would you come with us?"

"I wouldn't miss it for the world."

The three met an hour before the auction and Jill showed them the catalogue. The medallion was unmistakably another one of the Zodiac medallions, just like Teres' one, but with a pale green stone and the sign of a lion's head.

"How much do you think it will go for?" Tim asked.

"It's hard to say. The reserve is 1000 pounds. Hopefully no one will be interested, and we can get it for a few thousand."

"Let's hope so," said John. "Do you know where it's come from?"

"All I know is that it's come from an estate in Scotland. It's time we went in. We need to register."

They took seats in the middle of the auction room. The auctioneer stood on his podium. There was a bank of telephone operators on either side of him. People came and went. Pieces of antique furniture sold or got passed on. They watched as paintings, crystal bowls, dinner sets and other odd assortments that had seen dozens of lives own them, clean them, fall in love over them, die on them—all start a new life with a bang of the hammer. At last lot 12816 appeared. A gloved man wearing an apron gently held the medallion in his hands, turning it around so the peridot jewel sparkled. He placed it on a spinning plinth and its large image projected on to the screen.

"This artifact is said to have been discovered by the explorer Reinhart McClusky in 1901 on the plains of Saskatchewan in Canada. McClusky's estate in Edinburgh has recently been liquidated. This piece was found in a trunk in the loft of Tryggle Hall. His notes reveal a muddled story of a lion that appeared when he entered a cave. His family say he was often delirious after prolonged explorations due to tropical diseases and lack of food."

"Know how he feels," John muttered.

"Nevertheless, this incredible piece of metal is said to be crafted by the native Indians of the region."

"This is it," Jill said.

"Bidding is now open, ladies and gentleman," the auctioneer called. "Starting at one thousand pounds, who will give me one thousand pounds?"

Jill raised her paddle.

"Thank you madam, I have one thousand pounds. One thousand one hundred?"

A woman from the phone bank stood and nodded. Tim and John glanced at each other.

"We have two thousand pounds via a remote bid. Do I have two thousand, two hundred?"

Jill nodded and raised the paddle.

"Three thousand, thank you," the auctioneer said to the proxy bidder.

"Damn it!" said Tim.

Jill raised her paddle for a five hundred raise. She looked calm, though Tim noticed a slight tightening of her jaw.

"Four thousand," came the opposing bid. "Five, madam?"

Jill nodded.

"Jill, how far are you going?" Tim hissed.

She ignored him, intent on the remote bidder and the auctioneer.

Suddenly the remote bidder jumped to ten thousand. Jill placed a bid with two fingers.

"Twelve thousand? Thank you."

"This is insane, darling!"

"We have fifteen."

"Stop this now, Jill!"

"Twenty, thank you, madam."

"Jill, I think you should listen to Tim. How will you pay for this?"

"I have funds," she stated.

Tim and John looked at each other, not knowing what to do or say.

"Twenty-five."

"Someone knows about the Zodiacs," said Tim.

"Thirty thousand, thank you, madam."

"We can just find them; we don't need to pay for the thing!"

"Fifty."

"Jill, this is madness. I order you to stop right now!"

Jill turned and looked into her fiancé's eyes. "I will be ordered by no man!" she hissed.

Her emerald eyes flickered a pearlescent light and Tim felt a hot pain sear through him. He jumped up, his chair falling back, and rushed out of the room. John half raised but sat down again, confused.

"One hundred thousand."

Jill paused. She looked towards the exit her partner had just dashed through, hesitated for a moment, then raised her paddle.

"Five hundred thousand!" she stated.

The audience hummed and chattered at the excitement. The woman on the phone put one finger in the air.

"Ladies and gentlemen, I have a bid of one million pounds. That's one million sterling."

The auctioneer looked at Jill eagerly. John clasped his chin in his hand. The audience looked on expectantly.

"One million one hundred?" the auctioneer suggested.

Jill sat still. She spun the handle of the paddle in her hand. The room was silent. The woman on the phone held her mouth open.

"Can I take a bid of one million and fifty?"

She allowed the paddle to raise a little in her lap. John muttered "Oh my God!" under his breath.

"One more chance, madam?" the man with the gavel said.

She looked down and shook her head minutely.

"Going once, going twice..." he paused and glanced at Jill one more time. Jill looked at the woman on the phone to the remote bidder, who held her breath and looked back. She penetrated her gaze, and the woman leaned forward a little. Jill closed her eyes and let her senses go through the woman, into the phone, along the vibration of sound waves and out into the ether. She cast her senses through the space between countries and into a receiver on a roof, through the wires and into the hands of the man holding a telephone in South America.

"Gone! Lot 12816 sold to remote bidder 579 for one million pounds." He banged the hammer and Jill released the woman's attention and her own.

"Sorry Jill," John said and patted her hand, still clutching the paddle.

She gave him a small smile. "I'd better go and find Tim."

Tim had rushed into the toilet. He felt raw and off-kilter, as if something had knocked his internal compass and reality was no longer how he expected it to be. He splashed water on his face and drank out of his cupped hands. Jill's reckless bidding was one thing, but the way she spoke to him—looked at him—was what had thrown him. He had felt her pulling away since their return from Bhutan. She had thrown herself into her work, yet when they spent time together, he felt as if he was the only person on the planet. He felt such love from her. His body fizzed, and he wanted nothing else but to wrap himself around her. But her religious upbringing commanded that they not consummate their union until married. Now she was pushing the marriage date back, and he was in a world of longing, love and loneliness.

He stepped into the foyer and wondered if she had squandered her money (so much money!) on the medallion.

"Tim."

"What was going on in there, Jill?" he couldn't tell if he felt angry or concerned or confused.

She went to him and took his hands. "I'm sorry, this is so important to me. It's personal, you see. There is something I should tell you."

They sat in the modern chairs dotted around the grand foyer. Jill swallowed and looked through the doors that went out onto Bond Street.

"Tim, I told you my grandparents were Egyptologists."

He nodded.

"When they were exploring a new tomb, they came across a vault dedicated to Virgo. They found the Virgo medallion in a box in there. When my grandmother touched it, the Zodiac Warrior Virgo appeared."

"Where is it? The medallion?"

Jill put a hand to her throat, and he noticed a fine golden chain that she hooked with a finger. On the end of the chain, hidden beneath her blouse, was the Virgo medallion.

"Why didn't you ever tell me? Why not after we found Teres?"

"I... I don't know. It's a secret I have kept for so long, I couldn't bring myself to say it. Even to you, my darling."

"Have you seen it? The Virgo Zodiac Warrior?"

"It's a she and no. I've never dared find someone to bring her out. It's too dangerous until we find the rest of them."

Tim gazed at her beautiful face and felt his body tingle for her, losing sensation in his limbs and feeling his heart reach for her. He brought her hands to his mouth and kissed them, allowing her skin to linger on his lips as he closed his eyes.

"We will find them, my darling."

John, who had appeared a few moments ago, coughed. The couple saw him and rose.

"Well, that was a close call! Tell me, my girl, have you really got a million pounds?" He raised an eyebrow.

"A MILLION?" Tim shouted, "It was fifty thousand when I left."

"I have funds," she confirmed. "But that's not important right now. We have to travel to Ecuador."

"Ecuador?" Tim and John both chorused.

"The buyer is in Ecuador, Quito to be precise."

"How do you know?" asked Tim.

"I asked," she replied enigmatically and walked out of the auction house.

On the train trip home, John looked at the images of Teres on his phone. They had spoken for over an hour earlier that week. John had asked him about his home planet, about how they managed to get to Earth in one piece. His mind, though sharp and deeply intelligent, could not grasp the technology Teres described. He asked about the other Warriors, could they bleed, die? How did his people live—in cities, communities? Teres asked him many questions about the planet, his life, his beliefs. This video could bring him the fame and distinction he had endeavoured to attain. He composed an email to some of his peers and associates and attached a clip of the video he had edited. His finger hovered over the send icon. The train headed for a tunnel and its horn blasted loudly. John startled and turned off his phone.

Jill had paid a lot less than a million pounds to pay the courier who the auction house hired to pass on the addresses of all the packages leaving the premises. As soon as they gave her an address in Ecuador, she ceased payments. Needless to say, the man's family would have a very merry Christmas, which was what his soul had yearned for. A week later, they boarded a plane to South America.

"It's one of the few places I've never been," said John excitedly. "The museum has artifacts from 800 CE, evidence of the Quitu who they thought there were no remains. Fascinating."

"Did you know Quito is the closest city to the equator?" Tim said, reading the in-flight magazine, "we are literally going to the middle of the earth," he added.

"The temperature is pretty much the same all year round, should be a nice change from England," Jill said.

"So, how are we going to approach this?" Tim asked. "I mean, we can't just stroll up to his front door and ask him to give us the medallion, can we?"

"I have made an appointment to see him," Jill said casually.

"Under what pretext?" John asked.

"He makes art and I acquire art. I'm sure we'll have a lot in common."

Casa de la Luna nestled into the mountainside overlooking the capital city of Quito. Due to the fact that the mansion had been there since the Spanish colonization, and by clever modern landscaping, one would be entirely unaware of its existence. Just for good measure, however, a security guard stood by the gate. His chunky belt holstered a gun, flashlight and pepper spray.

"I have an appointment with Señor Pintado. My name is Jillena Mayer, and these are my associates, Timothy and Professor John Robertson.

The security guard spoke into his two-way radio in Spanish. A crackle and a reply gained them entry through the heavy bronze gates. A driveway wound through lush vegetation. Trees with enormous leaves brushed the roof of the car. A cracked fountain filled with green water and overgrown with plants sat in front of a hacienda-style house. The grand house was a salmon pink, but the facade was crumbling, and the arched window frames were peeling. Two wings spanned out from the grand entrance, flanked by steps. Someone stood at the top of the steps. They were small with short hair but looked neither male nor female. Tim parked the car and they approached.

"Look at this place," said John with glee.

"Do you get excited by anything that's ancient, Dad?" Tim joked.

"Must be centuries old."

The person nodded to them, "Hablas Español?"

"Si," said Jill.

"She's a marvel," muttered John to his son. Tim nodded.

The person spoke to Jill in a rolling Spanish and opened the door to the house, leading them into a vast atrium. Huge pot plants stood either side of the wide staircase. Classical music floated on the air.

"Sígueme."

They followed the person who had introduced themselves to Jill.

"This is Astro, Señor Pintado's assistant," Jill explained. "They use the pronoun they/them."

Astro led them to the right, down an airy corridor flanked by arched windows overlooking the dense bush of the garden. On the other wall, huge paintings were hung. Jill stopped and looked at one.

"They're exquisite."

She reached out and hovered her hand over the abstract forms and kaleidoscope of flowing colours. She breathed in, as if smelling the image.

"His paintings, it's all the wealthy want on their walls these days. Tim, I acquired one for your company last year."

"Yes, they are quite unusual, other-worldly. They seem to transport one to another realm."

They carried on. Jill's heels echoed on the polished terracotta tiles, matching the floating strains of music coming from one of the rooms. The piano reached a crescendo just as they reached a large wooden double door on which Astro tapped.

"Si, adelante."

"Señor Pedro Pintado," Astro announced.

They stepped into a grand room. The walls were washed with watery hues of pink and blue. Light, sheer white drapes hung down the bank of windows. In the centre of the room, a huge armchair faced the windows. An easel was tilted towards it and all they could see was a hand holding a paintbrush that conducted the dying notes of Schubert's *Du Bist die Ruh*.

Once the final notes hung in the air, the enormous chair swung around to face them. John and Tim stifled gasps. Señor Pintado filled the chair. His gigantic feet were stuffed into a pair of silk slippers. An apricot pink kaftan followed the contours of mountains of fat, which rippled onto the arms of the chair. His head was wedged into a concertina of chins. A white Panama hat shadowed his face.

"Bienvenido. Astro, bring some mint tea."

The servant left quietly.

"Please, take a seat."

They settled themselves into a large wooden sofa, which was a good distance from their host.

"We really appreciate you seeing us," said Jill in Spanish.

"Rara vez recibo invitados," he spoke in a lazy drawl.

"Do you speak English, for my friends?" Jill asked.

"Si, si. I don't take guests usually. People upset me. But something you wrote piqued my interest, Señorita Mayer."

"We seem to have a mutual interest in the medallion," she said.

"Medallions, I think you mean?" he replied.

Jill smiled. "Then we are even."

Astro arrived with a tray of tea, served in a silver teapot. They poured the fragrant liquid into the teacups and withdrew.

"It's a beautiful place you have here," John said, his polite British small talk filling the awkward silence.

"It is old and crumbling like me. But it is home and has been in my family for over four hundred years."

"The upkeep must be hard," said Tim, wondering why someone would spend a million pounds on a medallion but not his own house.

"Like I say, I am, what do you call it..." he searched for a word, "allergic to people. I am an empath. I can feel every angst, every fear, every little emotion in those around me."

John and Tim suddenly felt exposed.

"Well, we're pretty even-natured," John said with a laugh.

"Then you are lying to yourself, Señor Robertson. I could feel your fear of obscurity before you entered my front door. And you Timothy, you reek of loneliness and heartache."

The men opened and closed their mouths.

"You see, it makes me a most disagreeable host. But you, Señorita Mayer, you are like my first medallion. You are calm and empty somehow," he trailed off and stared off into the distance.

Tim and John looked at each other with raised eyebrows.

"We'd love to see your medallions and hear about how you came by them," Jill said gently.

Pedro snapped out of his dream state and pressed a button on an intercom by his easel. Astro appeared.

"Tráeme los medallones," he commanded. "How many do you have?" he asked Jill.

"We have two. One was discovered by my grandparents in Egypt, the second we found in Bhutan."

Astro appeared, holding a carved wooden box in white-gloved hands and placed it next to Pedro. He opened it to reveal a cushion holding the medallion. An opal was embedded within.

"Ah, mi pequeña bebe, my baby," Pedro crooned as he lifted the glowing medallion. He closed his eyes in bliss. He held the medallion to his heart and breathed in deeply. "She is the only thing, the only thing."

"May I see?" Jill asked in a whisper.

Pedro stroked the medallion, kissed it with his blubbery lips, and gently handed it to Jill. She took a breath in and turned it over. The Libra symbol was carved into its curved side.

"She was here on this land when my ancestors cleared the forest for the hacienda. The legend says she appeared as an exotic woman—half her skin was white, the other black. She was the epitome of equanimity, of hope. All nonsense, of course. I have no belief in these voodoo stories. But this jewel is the only thing that brings me peace."

"So you haven't..." Tim said.

"So you haven't had it valued?" Jill intercepted. She shot Tim a look and imperceptibly shook her head.

"Its monetary value is of no importance to me. It's how it makes me feel. But this other one, the Leo, this one has a power. It makes me tremble. I do not want it near me."

"Can we see it?"

"Yes, but I am weary now. Please, I invite you to stay in the west wing this evening. I will have Astro make up the rooms for you. We will meet again tomorrow. I must sleep now." Pedro pressed the buzzer again and gave Astro instructions in Spanish. Astro arrived and held the door open for the party to leave.

The flight from Darwin back to Perth was tense. Jason was terrified to open his mouth, terrified he no longer looked like his passport photo, terrified he would suddenly climb the nearest telegraph pole. He slept fitfully on the plane. He seemed exhausted yet his body twitched and spasmed as if Plaadio was trying to escape.

They gratefully made it back to Jason's apartment. Lily dumped her backpack on the sofa and put the kettle on. She turned on the old mobile phone she had used for the Zodiac Warrior web page.

"Hey Jase!" she called out.

Jason emerged from the shower with a towel tucked around his waist. His usually sunken chest was filled out with a pair of hairy pecs, his shoulders just a little broader. He was tanned from the days trekking through the bush. Lily blinked for a moment, her train of thought lost.

"Yeah, what's up?" he said.

"Uh, yeah. Look, I just turned the phone on and someone has called."

"The Zodiac Warrior number? You think someone has found another medallion?" Jason picked up Lily's bag and hung it on the hook by the door. He sat down. "When did they call? Did they leave a message?"

He sat beside her on the couch.

"Only a text message, it just says Gemini."

"You gonna call them?"

"I guess so."

She dialled the number. It rang for a while.

"Hello?" The voice was cautious.

"Hi," Lily said. She wasn't sure how to broach the subject. No one gives you training on how to discuss an extra-terrestrial phenomenon with a complete stranger over the phone.

"You called me," she ventured.

"Did I?"

"You mentioned Gemini."

"Shit, am I crazy or is this a thing?"

"Pretty sure it's a thing." She glanced at the new Jason, he was roaming her apartment picking up her ornaments, sniffing the apples in her fruit bowl, opening the doors onto the balcony. "Where are you?"

"United States, not saying where. Gotta be careful. Download Qriptonite, only communicate through there."

"We need to meet, what state?"

"New York."

"OK, I'll make arrangements."

He hung up. She fired up her laptop and searched for flights. "Looks like I'm going to America, Jase."

He came back through the doors and stretched, allowing the towel to drop to the floor. Lily blushed at the eyeful of manhood and put her hands over her face.

"Put your towel on Jase! Plaadio, if you can hear me, please let Jason be in charge, you are making me very uncomfortable."

"Sorry Lil."

Jason was mortified, he quickly swept up the towel and covered himself. "I think I dozed off for a minute. You've no idea how weird this is."

His face crumpled, he looked teary but then composed himself. "What did they say?"

"It was a guy. He sounded shaken and suspicious. I'm going to New York. Can you stay here, lay low and answer the phone in case anyone else finds us?"

Jason blew out a puff of air in relief. "Happy to."

Lily had sent the flight number and time to the caller who she now knew as Victor and endured the three flights to JFK airport. She couldn't settle to read or watch a movie. Her mind ran over the events of the last few weeks. She wondered how she would find all the Warriors and who she could tell. What would happen to her PhD in which she was falling behind. And how she would remember her pseudonym—Allie. She dozed off but had a nightmare that everyone in the airport was called Allie. Los Angeles airport was a blur but she made it onto the final leg to New York.

There was a growing sense of desperation in the air in America. Every day security became tighter. People broke out in fights in unexpected places as water was eked out and the price of petrol rose. Newspaper headlines told of a gang that had taken over a petrol station. Another screamed about the extortionate price of bottled water on the black market. A third led with 'Farmers Hiring Guards to Protect their Water Tanks'. It took over an hour for Lily to finally emerge. Steven stood at the barriers. He held a piece of cardboard with ALLY scrawled across it.

"Hi, I'm Allie. Are you Victor?"

"Yup."

She put out her hand. He returned a clammy and limp shake.

"How do I know you're legit?"

Lily retrieved the medallion from her bag and flashed it at him. He lifted his chin.

"Best get on the road," he said, casting his eyes around the arrivals lounge.

Lily looked around. Suddenly she felt people were eyeing her. But then a passenger would run into their arms, or they'd turn away and take a call, or walk straight past her for the door. She gave her head a small shake. Stevie pointed to the direction of the exit. She shouldered her bag and followed him.

Once in the pick-up, she spoke.

"My real name is Lily."

"Stevie."

"How did you find it?"

"The medallion? It was on a belt my Ma gave me." He pointed to the belt. Lily gasped at the sight of the medallion, so similar to her own.

"Must be interesting when you have to take a pee," she laughed but Stevie didn't seem to be the joking kind.

"There's two of 'em in it," he said.

"Two?"

"Twins, Castor and Pollux. Who'd you find?"

"Aries, Prymaw first. We just found Capricorn."

"We?"

"My best friend, Jason, he's sort of looking after him back in Australia."

"So that's three."

"What are we going to do?" she asked.

Steven shrugged. "Find the others, I guess. That's what they say we gotta do."

"Have you told anyone else?"

"Got no one who'd care if I did."

"Oh... I'm sorry." She paused. "What about your parents?"

"Pa's long dead."

Lily stopped talking. She didn't know what was worse; a father who didn't care about you, or a dead one who had.

"What about your mum?"

"Ma already thinks I'm trouble, no use upsettin' her anymore."

She thought best not to pry any further. He seemed pretty closed, wounded even. She wondered if she was wounded too. Her thoughts were overcome by fatigue. She dozed off.

After a five-hour drive, they arrived at Newton Falls. It was late, and Lily couldn't make out the house. Stevie showed her inside.

"Shall we bring them out?" she said.

"Better had."

"Is there a shed or something? Prymaw is pretty big."

"Sure, out back."

Stevie hauled open the door of the shed. He switched on the fluorescent light. An old tractor gathered dust at the end, and there were tools and farming gear scattered around the walls. A pile of hay bales was stacked in the centre.

"OK, let's do it," Stevie said.

Lily took the Aries medallion out of the soft pouch and placed her hand on it. It hadn't worked for her at 17 Miles Fall. She felt nervous. She closed her eyes and took a deep breath. The medallion warmed her palm, faint vibrations tickled her skin and to her relief Prymaw emerged through the rays of light.

Stevie took a couple of steps back and mouthed 'whoa'. He swore under his breath and placed his shaking hands on his buckle. Pollux and Castor appeared through their yellow rays. The Warriors laughed and greeted each other head to head as Lily had witnessed with Prymaw and Plaadio.

Then Pollux saw Lily and gasped, "Li-Mei?" She rushed to Lily and took her face in her cool hands, "Li-Mei! My sweet child, you found us. Castor, she's here. My love, how we have missed you!"

Castor came towards Lily. He looked into her eyes. Lily backed away.

"My name's Lily, not Li-mei."

"No, it is you my sweet, don't you remember us?" said Pollux grabbing Lily's hands.

"I... no... I've never met you."

"She tells the truth," Castor said.

Pollux let Lily's hands go. "I'm sorry. Maybe I am mistaken, but there is something in you that I know."

Lily felt as if someone was poking around in her psyche, pulling up images in her mind that were strange. She rubbed the back of her neck and moved away to perch on a hay bale.

"So now we have three of us from Horoscopia," said Prymaw after introductions had been made.

"I have a friend looking into a place in Egypt where I believe Virgo can be found," said Lily.

"I fear we are running out of time. Plaadio brought us worrying news about the planet," said Prymaw. "The humans have caused too much heat and the balance has been destroyed."

"Running out of time for what?" Stevie asked. "What exactly are you doing here?"

"We come in peace," Prymaw said.

"The fact you are saying that makes me think you are not."

"Stevie!" Lily jumped up.

"I don't trust them."

"He thinks we are dangerous to his kind," Castor said.

"Calm yourself, Steven. Let us explain," Pollux pleaded.

Stevie backed to the bench that held tools and plant pots. He felt behind him and pulled out a rifle. "I'm not gonna let some weird ass aliens take over!"

"Stevie!" Lily yelled. "Put the gun down!"

"How do we know we won't all end up dead or slaves to you? How do I even know who you are?"

"I'm just another person who has stumbled upon beings from outer space!"

"They seemed to know you."

"I've never seen them before. Look, I'm freaked out too, but this isn't the right way to handle it."

Stevie burst out laughing. "Freaked out? Freaked out! I have the biggest goddamn freak show on earth in my barn!" He waved the gun at the three Warriors.

"Please, Stevie, put the gun down," Lily implored.

"We swore we would do no harm," Prymaw said.

Lily could see his horns slowly moving at the tips.

"You call yourself Warriors!" Stevie was sweating. He used his shoulder to wipe his face and for a moment the gun pointed to the roof. Prymaw took his chance and a horn shot out and grasped the barrel of the gun, whipping it out of Stevie's hands. He bent the gun in half and tossed it to the side.

Stevie swore and steadied himself, vulnerable, shaking. Lily ran to him.

"It's OK. Calm down. Let's hear what they have to say."

"Yes, you are correct. We are Warriors. Our kind have fought many wars on our planets, amongst our own kind and with each other. But we couldn't fight the black hole. So, we came together, here to Earth and we need your help," said Prymaw,

"You have the power to actualize us," Pollux said.

"And you have the power to keep us imprisoned in our pods," Castor finished.

"Look, we will all go back into our pods right now. Then it's up to you. You can never see us again if you choose. OK?" Prymaw suggested.

"OK, go on then. I need to think this through."

The Warriors glanced at each other.

"We need them to trust us," Prymaw added. "Let's go."

The Warriors disappeared back into their medallions.

Stevie raked his hands through his hair.

"Are you OK?" Lily asked.

"No! How can we know? They could just be here to take over the planet."

"You've been playing too many games. If they were going to kill us, they would have wiped us out by now!"

"I'm just flipping out, OK."

"Yeah, I know, I know. Look, I think we need to find these other Warriors. They're right about the state of the planet. This is what I've been studying for the last three years. This place isn't going to be habitable for any of us at this rate. The governments aren't listening, the people feel powerless. There are wars in Africa, islands are disappearing under the ocean, rivers are running dry. I've seen it. I think these guys..." Stevie looked at her incredulously. "...Aliens might be the only thing that will get us out of it. If they can travel here from another galaxy, imagine what they could teach us?"

Stevie rubbed his face. "OK, OK."

"And besides, the other nine Warriors could already be somewhere here."

Lily pointed at the medallion and tilted her head at Stevie. He nodded and she actualized Prymaw.

"Go on, bring Gemini back."

He hesitated, his hands hovering over his belt. He took a deep breath and actualized the twins once more.

"Thank you, Steven," the twins chorused. "We won't let you down or harm you, we promise."

Prymaw nodded to the two humans. "What is the plan?"

"I'll keep looking online. We found each other after all, and there could be more looking," said Stevie.

"I'm flying home tomorrow night. I'll take a look in the natural history museum while I'm in New York. There could be a clue there."

"You are leaving so soon!" Pollux said.

"Yes, I have to get back to my mother and my studies."

Pollux took a thin band inset with a tiny pearl from her finger.

"Please, wear this Lily. Li-mei gave it to me. If you wear it, we will be able to keep of track you in our minds."

"Who is Li-mei?"

"She was very special to us."

There was a noise outside the barn. The Warriors dissipated into the medallions. Lily slid the ring on to her finger.

The following morning, Lily was up before daybreak; Australian time still coursing through her veins. She was starving but only found coffee and tomatoes in the kitchen. She took a bite of one and rolled her eyes at the fresh, rich flavour.

"I can fry some up for you, if ya hungry?" Tammy had entered the kitchen.

"Oh, I'm sorry," she stammered.

"No, no, don't worry. I'm Stevie's ma, Tammy Rutherford, nice to meet you."

"Lily." She took her outstretched hand. "I've never tasted a tomato so good."

"Thank you ma'am, grown organically in my little patch of dirt." She smiled. Her kindly lined face seemed to light up for a moment. "You don't sound like you're from round these parts."

"No, I'm from Australia."

"And what brings you here?" Tammy asked as she put a skillet on the stove and added a good hunk of butter.

"Um," she scooted around in her jet-lagged brain for an answer. "We met online... and I was passing through."

"So nothing to do with what was going on in my barn last night?"

"Oh, shit, Ma!" Stevie came into the kitchen. "You spying on me? I was just showing her around."

Lily looked at Stevie. Stevie screwed up his eyes and shook his head.

"Well I sure as hell know I ain't got a ram, and there was a lot of talking from voices I don't know. Now are you gonna tell me what's going on or do I need to call Sheriff Crawford and tell him I have trespassers?"

"Ma, you wouldn't understand, it's complicated ..." Stevie glanced at Lily for help.

"It's... we're..."

"Before you enter into any grand lies son, I need to tell you that I've seen the people you been entertaining in your room, and I can tell they come from further away than any Australian."

"We need to tell her," Lily said to Stevie.

"It was that buckle you got me..."

After they explained all they knew, Tammy said, "Well, I say we hand it over to the authorities."

"See Lily, this is exactly why I didn't want to tell her. Goddamn old people just defer to the goddamn government. Those politicians know jack shit about what's happening in the real world. They'd just hide the Warriors or make money out of them.

Tammy thought for a moment and breathed out heavily. "Or kill 'em."

"Mrs Rutherford, can I ask that we find one more Warrior before we do anything. I've got a lead in Egypt. I read about a tomb that was dedicated to Virgo. I'm sure there's another medallion there. My friend is in Africa and he's already on his way. Then let's talk to the Warriors and decide."

Tammy put her knuckles to her bottom lip and sighed. If she betrayed Stevie and called the sheriff, their relationship would be over. Maybe God had sent this situation to mend things. She looked at Steven and nodded her agreement.

"OK. Where do we start? When do I get to meet these Zodiac beings?"

"I'm going to check out the natural history museum while I'm in New York today. I'll see if Jason has got any leads and wait to hear from Zakary. Stevie will continue searching online with Castor and Pollux."

❄

After an hour's work, Sandra organised a video call to speak with Joseph.

"Tell me everything."

Joseph relayed what she had already seen in the obs room.

"What have you got so far?"

"Nothing."

"The lab results?"

"The venom has never-seen-before proteins that break apart all the cells walls of the body. It just turns you to mush, as we saw with Bruce Janson. These pictures show he is basically a pool of flesh."

He shared his screen, expecting her to flinch at the photos of the gruesome melted man. She coolly looked at each one.

"Nasty. What about the medallion?"

"The lab has heated it, frozen it, scraped it, filed it, swabbed it, gassed it, compressed it. It's not giving anything up. The jewel has the structure of topaz."

"Forensics been to the mine site it was found?"

"Yup, nothing."

"Any other Zodiac Warriors coming up on the search engines?"

"No."

"OK, I'll tell you what I got."

"Really? *You* got something?"

Sandra gave a small sideways tilt of the head. It never ceased to amaze her how little credit a woman of colour was allowed. She typed in a phone number in the chat.

"It's a phone number I'd guess. I'll get the comms guys onto it," Joseph said.

Sandra sighed. "Yes, it's a phone number, genius. I did my own searching. It belongs to an Australian female, Lily Noor. She arrived in America yesterday morning. I can tell you exactly where she is, my friend."

Joseph gave a tight smile.

"Want me to go get her for you too?" she asked half-sarcastically.

"No. I'll get a team together and bring her in." He clenched his teeth. "Good work, Tress"

Lily spent most of the bus ride back to New York City texting Jason (at least she assumed it was Jason and not Plaadio). Then Zakary emailed.

'Hey Lily,

Been digging around the pyramids and found that burial chamber you'd heard about. The whole place is a shrine to Virgo and there are no others of its kind. Scientists and archaeologists have always been puzzled and so have kept it pretty quiet. It was discovered by a man called Anton Mayer. He had a daughter called Jillena Mayer. They lived in Vienna. Do you reckon I should go there and track down some relatives?

Hope all is going OK on your end.

Zak'

Lily shot him an email back, 'Yes, go for it.'

It was lunchtime when she arrived at the museum. She scrutinised every exhibit that might hold a clue, looking for the familiar shape of the medallion in the ancient jewelry or stories alluding to the zodiac signs. As she trailed around, she noticed the other tourists. It was like catching a plane, becoming familiar with the faces of those you travel with for fifteen or twenty hours then never seeing them again. And then there were the faces of the past, like Pollux and Castor who were convinced she was someone else. Lily shivered. A man stood close behind her—too close. She could feel his breath on her neck as she tried to concentrate on the display cabinet. She turned and stared at him. He glared back, as if she was in the wrong, and she moved away, feeling uneasy. In each gallery, she noticed him. She thought he was staring at her but every time she looked, he was gazing into a display, or looking at his phone. She again felt the paranoia she experienced at the airport. She shifted her backpack to her front and checked for the bulge of the medallion sitting at the bottom of her bag. There was an announcement over the pa system that the museum would be closing in twenty minutes.

Lily was hot and thirsty. Her legs were aching and it was time to head to the airport. She searched for the toilet sign. Again, she saw the same man out of the corner of her eye and hurried toward the bathrooms. Wanting to get some distance from him once and for all, she jogged down the wide stairs to the level below. The man headed down too, not in a hurry, casually gazing around the museum. She took a deep breath and told herself to calm down.

The modern toilets were cool and bright. She washed her face with water and took a drink. She wanted to text Jason, but it was the middle of the night in Perth now. Instead, she decided to get out of the museum and call Stevie to see if had come up with anything.

Lily swung open the door feeling steadier, but the door gave way in her hands and two men crashed into her and pushed her back into the bathroom. She screamed. The man she'd seen earlier put a hand across her mouth. She struggled to pull his hand away so kicked out hard. He fell away swearing. The other man came towards her, but she kicked with the other foot then swung a karate chop that caught him under his nose. He crashed into a cubicle. She scrabbled for the door, panting hard. The first man grabbed her sweater as she took hold of the door handle, and she swung her elbow back hard. Lily might have been built like a twelve-year-old girl, but her hours of training meant she had speed and power. She ran out of the bathroom yelling for security. Two guards ran over and she breathlessly told them about the men. She wasn't about to hang around and face her attackers and she ran for the exit. She sprinted into Central Park as far as her lungs would take her. She leaned against a tree and drew in great gasps of breath. She peaked around from the direction she came, and all looked tranquil.

Lily was shaken badly. Who was that? Could this be something to do with the medallions? She took her phone out to call Stevie to let him know what happened, when she heard footsteps. Before she had a chance to look, a bag closed over her head. She felt a pain pierce her arm and the light went out.

Lily woke up in a bed in a white-walled and windowless room. She opened her eyes. She felt dizzy, dry-mouthed. Her body ached. She looked around, trying to remember. Pushing the white sheet off her, she was relieved to be fully clothed. There was nothing else in the room except for a chair and a camera in the corner, and no sign of her bag. Frantically, she stepped out of the bed and wobbled. Her head spun. The door was locked, and she banged on it.

"Hey!" she yelled, though her voice was cracked. "Where am I?" She waited, listened. "Hey!"

She swore and banged on the door again and again. A sense of claustrophobia brought panic and she screamed, "Let me out of here!"

Footsteps clicked outside the room and the door opened. Two men entered.

"Hi Lily..."

Before he could finish Lily went for the door. "Who the hell do you think you are? Let me out of here. Where's my bag?"

"Whoa, calm down, come back in here," the man said, blocking her way.

"Who are you people? You can't keep me here."

"Just take a seat, Lily. My name is Joseph Schwartz, this is my colleague Daniel Westerford. You are at the Washington state National Security Agency, at Fort George Meade. We just need to ask you a few questions."

"Washington? How did I get here? Why didn't you ask me in New York? Is it you who attacked me in the museum?" She was trying to make sense of it all.

"I think you know that this is a matter of national security, Lily."

"How do you know my name? I'm an Australian citizen, you have no right to hold me here."

"Why don't you just tell us what you know about the Zodiac Warriors? And you'll be free to leave."

A wave of tingles went through her. "I don't know what you're talking about."

Joseph sighed. "I was imagining you would cooperate with us, Lily. You want to protect your country, don't you? Protect the world?"

Lily's mind was racing. What did they know about the Warriors? Why did they feel threatened? Still, she thought best to act naïve.

"Where is my bag? I need to call my friends."

"Would that be Steven Rutherford or Jason Wallace. I'm not surprised you don't want to talk to your mother Abigale, she probably wouldn't hear the phone, would she?"

Chills went down Lily's spine. "Who are you people? How dare you! You have no right to do this. Let me out of here, now!" Lily stood up shakily. She could feel her blood boil with indignation.

"As my colleague just mentioned," Daniel, whose arm was in a sling, spoke for the first time, "you are free to leave after we have interviewed you. Now I'm sure you would like a cup of tea, some toast and, what is it you Australians love? Ah, Vegemite. Perhaps that's the secret to the powerful kicks and punches you threw!" Daniel chuckled.

"Fine, ask away. I don't know what you think I know."

"Where did you get the medallion we found in your bag?"

Lily never imagined she'd be in a position to say this, "No comment."

Lily had dropped off the SnapMap at Central Park. Stevie had been monitoring her movements and an hour had passed. He began to worry. She should have left the medallion with him. He waited another hour. Stevie summoned Castor and Pollux.

"Lily's gone out of contact, her phone has gone dead or broken."

Pollux wrung her hands and paced. "I cannot lose her again, brother."

"Sister, she is not Li-Mei."

"She is the closest thing to her. I want her to be safe."

"Do not fret, we will find her," Castor said. "Come, let us join and we will listen for her. If she wears the ring, we will hear."

"From here to New York, or wherever she may be?" Stevie was incredulous, but then he remembered he had two beings from another galaxy in his kitchen.

The twins faced each other and joined hands but then their arms merged together, and their bodies melted into one another and the two beings became one. Stevie swore he could see a trail of light emanate from their glassy eyes into the ether.

The kitchen clock ticked gently, the fridge hummed and Stevie tried not to breathe. The faint growl of a truck, the warble of a bird, the creak of the chair filled the passing minutes. The Gemini union suddenly separated and Pollux and Castor returned.

"Well?"

Castor shook his head. "We could not hear her."

"What? Why? Oh my God." Stevie's gut contracted.

"She may be unconscious," Castor said.

"Or asleep?" Stevie asked, trying to keep desperation out of his voice.

"Or she may not be wearing the ring," Pollux said. "We need to cast for other Warriors. Remember Castor, we could sometimes to tune into Librans or Aquarians?"

"Or a Virgo, they have an aligned power."

"Yes. And we will keep trying to locate Lily."

They joined together again and went back into the trance.

While Stevie waited for the Gemini to find a signal, he texted Jason.

'Download Qriptonite, we need to talk. S'

Jason had been pacing the flat. Lily had gone quiet and he couldn't see her on the SnapMap. He tried to sleep but couldn't. At 5.00 am the phone buzzed on the table and he snatched it up.

"Please be Lily," he murmured.

He read Stevie's message and went cold. He downloaded the encrypted communication app and added Stevie.

'What's happening over there?'

'Lily gone missing. Last saw her at Central Park at 4.00 pm. Phone dead.'

'What? Where is she?'

'The Gemini twins have tried to read her but there is nothing.'

'What are you thinking?'

'My guess is government. We could all be at risk.'

'Shit.'

A rapid beat of knocks thumped on the door of the apartment.

'Someone at door.'

'Get out of there!'

'You got to be kidding.'

'Man, get the hell out. They got L, they'll get you.'

The banging intensified, "Police, open up!"

"What the...?" Jason muttered.

He messaged one word back to Stevie, 'police'. A pang of adrenaline coursed through him. There was no way to get out except through the front door. He went to the door but backed away as the pounding continued. The only other option was the small balcony which overlooked six lower floors. Jason shook his head and went back inside. The men outside were now bashing the door with what sounded like a battering ram. The door rattled on its hinges. Jason grabbed his backpack, stuffed in his phone and Lily's laptop and went onto the balcony. He hopped over the railing, his heart beating. He heard the door crash into the apartment, and he leapt to the balcony below. Though his mind reeled, his body was in total control. He reached for the drainpipe and leapt effortlessly from windowsill to windowsill and swung down to the ground. Jason never thought he would be so happy to be housing a Zodiac Warrior.

"OK, Plaadio, I'm all yours!" he said.

Without a moment's hesitation, his legs took off and he raced down the road.

A stro showed them to a lounge, once grand but now peeling and dusty.

"I will get your accommodation ready and will bring you some supper. I'm sorry for Senor Pintado's, how do you say, abruptness. He is a sick man, and he fares better with no excitement."

"No need to apologise, Astro. We feel very honoured to be invited to stay," John said

Astro nodded and left them alone.

"Pedro has no idea about the medallions," Tim said.

"Could he be bluffing? He's quite a character, not exactly lucid all the time," John said.

"I think he feels the balance of Libra but has not seen her. It may be difficult to get it away from him," Jill said.

"Get it away? Are you planning on stealing it?" Tim said.

"Well, he's very attached. I don't imagine he'd sell it to us," she replied.

"Why don't we bring her, Libra, out? Show him?"

"Because none of us are Librans," Jill said.

"But I'm a Leo," Tim said. "If we, I could get a hold of the Leo medallion tomorrow then maybe we could convince him of the true power of them."

"If it doesn't kill him, you saw how sensitive he is," John said.

They discussed their avenues for some time before Astro returned with three bowls of steaming sopa de queso and mugs of spicy canelazo. When Astro came back to collect the empty plates, they stacked them up on the sideboard and lingered before speaking.

"May I ask, what is your interest in the medallions?"

The three stopped their own conversation. The men deferred to Jill who had seemed to take on the role as spokesperson.

"My research has shown that they are prehistoric artifacts which may have come from another galaxy. There are believed to be several in existence." Jill hesitated. "We believe that they hold some sort of power."

"What kind of power? A nuclear power?"

"No, not exactly. If they are in the right hands, they... they may have the power to solve some of the world's problems."

Astro nodded. "I have something to show you, please follow me."

They trailed along a corridor in the east wing and then down a set of ancient steps into a cellar. The air was drier in there, a humidifier whirred quietly. The walls were painted a light grey and on the carpeted floor sat two plinths. On one plinth was the box that Astro had brought Libra in, and on the other, a similar wooden box.

Astro stepped lightly to the plinth and opened the Libra box. This time gloveless, they reached in and picked up the medallion. They held it out and a soft pink light emanated from the opal. Slowly a vision of a woman appeared. John and Tim watched in wonder.

"I have been discoursing with her for many years. She is called Chime," Astro said.

They waited as Chime fully actualized. She was as the myth told; her skin divided into black and white. She balanced a set of scales in her two hands which were joined in prayer pose. She bowed to Astro who returned the gesture.

"Este es un evento raro, Astro, has comprado visitantes," she said, casting an eye over the three.

"Si, por favore, puedes hablar en inglés."

Chime pressed a finger to her forehead. "This is the first time I have had visitors. I am very happy to meet you. I assume you have news of the Zodiac Warriors?"

"Yes, we are in possession of Teres of Taurus and our search for Leo brought us here," said Jill.

"And?" Chime smiled at Jill, she raised her scales which tinkled and she stepped towards her.

"And I am in possession of Virgo, though we haven't found a human to release her."

Jill looked uneasy, she bored her eyes into Chime's and hoped she would understand her silent message.

"We are here to help gather all the Zodiac Warriors as Teres asked," Tim spoke.

"Astro and I have been searching for a long time. Leo was our first find. The time is right. Yes, we must gather."

"May I venture to suggest I try to bring out Leo?" Tim said.

Astro opened the other wooden box. They took out the medallion and held it towards Tim. He tentatively touched the medallion. It fizzed under his fingertips. Astro lifted it for him to take fully. As the medallion sat in the palm of his hand, he felt a power surge through his body. A feeling he remembered from his youth, of pure strength and invincibility. This time a glowing golden light rushed into the room. The humans had to shield their eyes from its brightness as the figure of a lion came forth. There was not much of the human form in this Warrior. He towered over them on two solid hind legs and his finger like paws held a sword. He shook his mane which glowed and flickered like fire. Muscles rippled through his body; he emanated power. The humans stepped back in the small space, wide eyed.

"Degon, welcome!" Chime said.

He took her in. He bared his teeth. The humans stumbled back.

"Och! My faimly!" he exclaimed. He dipped his head and gently touched the top of Chime's bowed head. "Where are we?" he looked around at the room and at the humans.

"We are in a country called Ecuador. These humans have unearthed us," Chime explained.

"Where are the others?"

"John," Jill said, "bring out Teres." She pulled out the second medallion that hung around her neck.

John held it in his fist and watched in wonder as the green lights brought Teres to life.

"Brother, sister!" Teres said when he was formed. They greeted each other in the same way and turned to acknowledge the humans.

Degon noticed the medallion in Tim's hand. He lowered his head at Tim. Tim let out the breath he was unaware he held. He tentatively lowered his head. Degon let out a roar-tinged laugh and touched his head to Tim's.

"I am your guardian and you are mine," he said, clapping a huge arm around Tim. "Do ya ken how long I've bin inside that thing? It feels good to be out of it, ay!"

"It's 2025, Degon."

"A hunner years!"

"Try 65 billion, brother!" Teres said.

"We will tell our tales another time. The news is not good, Zodiacs. This planet is not in balance. There is great danger here, the fall is quickening," Chime spoke.

"Is it the same fate as Horos?" Degon asked, now serious.

"No, the land is being drained, starved," said Teres. "There is movement deep inside that puts life on this planet in peril."

"How can we stop it?" John asked.

"If it's not too late, the Zodiac Warriors have powers that are unique here, powers that can cease the momentum," said Chime.

"But only if we work together; our powers will be amplified by our unity," said Degon.

"Yes, we must rally," said Teres, "and for that we need the help of the humans."

"Humans! How can they help? I saw weakness and ignorance when I was adventuring with McClusky. It is one thing to have a galaxy sucked into a black hole, but it is another to make the black hole yourself," Degon said with derision.

He shook his mane and a lasso of heat spilled around the cellar. "Let's rally now and find the others, come!"

"Degon, halt!" said Chime. "There are forces here that you do not know of."

"What forces, lass?"

"It is called fear," said Chime calmly. "It is a dark force within humans that is as strong as the black hole. It consumes them and makes them dangerous."

"Ay, I saw it," Degon said.

"We must work with the humans, with the ones we can trust, like these people." Chime's scales tinkled as she drew her arm towards John, Tim, Jill and Astro. "They know the ways of this world and from what I have learned from Astro, they will not accept our forms kindly. They will fear us and with fear activated, we are all lost."

"What is this fear you speak of? What weapons does it carry? What form does it take?" Teres said.

"Its power is its invisibility, its weapon is the unknown and it can creep in and seize any human to do its bidding. It cannot die. It *is* a black hole, Teres."

"So we are to remain immobile, doing nothing again until we are all together? It is a poor plan. How can I be sure I will see ye again," Degon said to the humans. "I dinnae like being within another's power."

"We may look weak, we may not have the powers of the Zodiac Warriors but we have dwelled on this planet, we are of this planet and we can save this planet," Tim spoke. He felt shame for his own contribution to the burning depleted planet. It was time to step up, to be a man worthy of the woman he loved.

"It looks like we have nay choice," said Degon.

Astro's pocket buzzed.

"It is the señor; I need to go to him."

"We will talk again soon." Chime bowed and disappeared into the medallion. Teres did the same. Degon looked Tim in the eye.

"I will see ye again soon, I trust."

"You will," Tim replied. "You have my word." He disappeared, leaving a bubble of heat wafting over the humans.

Astro led the humans out of the cellar and locked the door behind them. None spoke as they headed back up to the main house. At last, back in the lounge Astro said, "I will be back soon to show you to your rooms."

Jill leaned against the wall, frowning. She turned her head to one side, her face crumpled as if a shooting pain coursed through her.

"Are you alright, darling?"

Tim held Jill gently by her shoulders. Her pale skin seemed almost blue. She scrunched up her eyes and put a hand to her temple.

"Another migraine. I need to lie down."

Tim helped her to a sofa, poured her some water and closed the door behind him and John.

"Is she OK, old chap?"

"I think so. She just needs to rest. It's been a long day."

"Let's leave her in peace then. How about a look at the garden?" John suggested.

John managed to jimmy open the French doors. They meandered through the overgrown and glossy leaves.

"What do you make of all this?" John asked.

Tim blew through his lips and shook his head. "Feels like I'm in a movie."

"It does. Let's hope it has a happy ending."

They walked side by side.

"Everything alright between you and Jill? What's this headache business all about?"

Tim sighed. He hadn't shared his troubles with anyone, and he wasn't sure his father was the right person.

"I don't know, Dad. It's complicated. We've never... you know, made love. I'm beginning to wonder if the headaches are an excuse to not sleep together."

John wished he hadn't asked. He'd always left it to Tim's mother to have the delicate, difficult conversations. He had never even asked her if she had spoken to their son about the good old birds and bees. He felt shame. Perhaps now was the time to make amends.

"Well, all in good time, all in good time. You can't rush a woman. You know your mother and I waited until our wedding night."

Tim winced at the intimacy of this. "But times have changed, Dad. I mean, what if it isn't, you know... good when we do it? And then we're married and then stuck with each other?"

"Marriage isn't just about sex, Tim, you should know that. Ultimately, it's about friendship, shared values, love, support. The sex won't last, mark my words."

"But she can't really give me a good reason why. She says she's religious but I never see her pray or go to church. She changes the subject when we talk about children. She won't even sleep in the same bed as me. And I can't get her to commit to a date. It's terribly frustrating and I'm getting pretty tired of it."

Tim's voice rose, his long-suppressed anger erupting with his words. "What's a man supposed to do?"

"Calm down, son. From what I know of Jill, she is an extraordinary woman. She's probably got her reasons. Are you thinking of finishing it?"

"God, no! She's amazing, I love her, can't imagine life without her."

John put his hand on Tim's shoulder. "It'll work out, Tim. It'll all work out."

Astro knocked on Jill's door with aspirin and a cup of tea.

"Tim told me you were not feeling well."

"Thanks Astro."

Astro put the tray on the bedside table and went to the door, but before they left Jill spoke.

"Astro, how long have you been working for Señor Pintado?"

"For around six years. My grandmother was the housekeeper here. When I came back to visit her before she died, the señor offered me the position."

"And has he been here all his life?"

"Si, I believe so."

"Do you know anything about his parents?"

Astro snorted. "Only a few pieces, he is often not making sense. He has dreams which he then paints. Some days he is not so lucid. You are lucky you caught him in a good mood. He can be a very difficult man. I would not like to be in his skin."

"Why do you think he is so obsessed with the Libra medallion?"

"I do not know. Why are you asking me these questions? The señor is a very private man."

"Yes, I understand." Jill paused. "So he knows nothing of the true nature of the medallions?"

"I do not think. He is not stable. I think it might push him too far."

"Astro, I am a little like Señor Pintado in that I can see things that others cannot. I can see inside people sometimes. I..." Jill wrung her hands. "I think that Señor Pintado might be a Zodiac Warrior himself."

Astro opened their eyes wide and looked at Jill.

"This is impossible! How could that be?"

"I have been told that some Warriors can live on earth in a human form. I think that your boss is the Zodiac Warrior of Cancer."

"And he does not know this?"

"I would say he's forgotten, buried it. His paintings speak of another world. If I'm correct, our problem is how do we bring him back?"

❄

John lay in the narrow bed in the largely empty room he had been given by Astro. He marvelled at the beings he had met that afternoon. His own Teres with the fiery Degon, the balanced and wise Chime. He re-watched the recording of his conversation with Teres. He had spoken of his planet, its colours, shapes and customs. He had described the journey they had made to Earth, the technology they had developed. It had made John's mind reel. He had discovered alien life. He could change so much with the knowledge of these beings. With the press of a couple of keystrokes, he could become famous, a hero. At last he would gain the hard-won recognition for his life's exploring, for his numerous papers. He could look his peers in the face with rectitude, those who had teased him for mistakenly choosing astrology over astronomy. What harm could it do? He logged onto his email pulled up the draft of his message. He typed in his colleagues' email addresses. He remembered his wife's advice to 'sleep on it'. He would send it off tomorrow. It was what he deserved, after all. The cave was his discovery, he was Teres' guardian. As his eyelids closed, the word 'guardian' echoed through his mind.

When Astro checked on Pedro that evening, they saw how the visitors had unsettled him. Pedro's blood pressure was high, and he was agitated and fearful that he had shared too much. Astro administered extra medication to calm him. He interrogated Astro on the trustworthiness of the guests and told them to lock Libra away carefully. He ate even more sweet treats than normal and fell into a fitful sleep on his day bed.

Finally in bed, Astro thought about Señor Pintado. All that Jill said made sense now. The mystery of his past, his strange habits, his teetering on the edge of sanity. Astro had never seen another medallion, but the señor's attachment to Libra showed that he had some sort of unconscious affinity with it. His extravagance in buying the Leo medallion further proved the theory.

Pedro called Astro in the early hours of the morning complaining he couldn't sleep, that he wanted the medallion by his side. Astro had retrieved Libra and at last Pedro dozed off. The only time Pedro was calm was when he had taken anti-depressants and had the Libra medallion close by. If they actualized Libra in front of Pedro, he would surely go mad, clinically insane. But—Astro thought—if Pedro had an excuse to witness any visions, it could carve a path to his true being.

After a sleepless night, Astro knocked on Jill's door. "Can I talk to you. I think I have an idea."

Jill waved for Astro to come in and they perched on the end of the bed.

"There is a P'aqo, a shaman in the mountains. He conducts ancient Ecuadorian ceremonies with *la purga*. I can get him here, and he can give Señor Pintado the tea. We can bring out Chime, and she can talk to him when his mind and spirit are open."

Jill thought about the idea, it was perfect. Using ayahuasca was the safest way to make Pedro remember his true being—the shapeshifter Xincon of Cancer.

Astro prepared them all breakfast and Jill relayed the plan to John and Tim.

"Why on earth do you think he could be a Zodiac Warrior?" John asked in bafflement.

"I can see it in his eyes."

"His eyes?"

"I don't know. A hunch. His art. His lack of history. It just all seems to add up."

Neither John nor Tim could find a reason not to explore the idea.

The arranging of a shaman does not happen overnight, and a week went by before Astro was able to secure a date and time. Meanwhile, Tim brought himself up to date with what was happening to the planet, something he had been careful to avoid since his financial advice to his clients was rarely earth friendly. He discovered that 95% of the Amazonian rainforest had been cut down and burnt. He saw how over 15 million hectares of Indonesia were palm plantations, destroying the ecosystem due to the death of wild animals and soil erosion. He read about climate refugees and wars breaking out over the ownership of water basins. When he saw that pollution had changed the climate of over 90% of the planet, he slammed his laptop shut. He felt shame at his contribution to the greed that had caused the downfall of the earth. He wondered why he hadn't woken up before, and why humankind had let it go on for so long.

John scoured the local museums, trying to absorb the local history and culture of Ecuador. But all he could think about was Teres and his own dwindling reputation. He sat in a bar in Quito drinking shots of aguardiente. He drunkenly told some men in the bar in broken Spanish about his friend Teres. They laughed at him, clapping him on the back. They thought he was talking about a bullfighting movie. John waved them off and took his phone out of his jacket pocket. He rubbed his eyes to mitigate his blurred vision and open his email. The draft came up, and without hesitating a moment more, he pressed send.

Don Arturo arrived at the hacienda late in the afternoon with an old, bashed leather satchel. Astro had told Pedro that a doctor was coming to check him out and to give him some herbs to calm his anxiety. Don Arturo slipped quietly into the room and sat with Pedro for a long time before speaking. Pedro engrossed in his painting and listening to his classical music, was seemingly unaware of the shaman. Astro brought the tea which this time was the ayahuasca brew. As Pedro drank the tea he winced at its bitterness. Astro apologised for forgetting the honey.

Don Arturo gently hummed. Half an hour went past with no action. Then Pedro dropped his paintbrush and looked intently out the window. Don Arturo changed from humming to singing a song and shook a rattle. Pedro looked at him queerly but Don Arturo simply nodded at him and continued with his low monotonous song.

"Astro!" called Pedro.

"Yes señor?"

"Come, come. My medication, I feel a funny turn coming on."

Pedro retched. Don Arturo held out a bowl and Pedro vomited into it, his vast body quivering from the propulsion. "Astro! Help me!" Astro cleaned his face with a damp cloth.

"You are OK now, señor, you will feel better now. This doctor, he has given you medicine. I will bring you water."

Astro scurried out of the room. Outside, Jill, John and Tim had the box containing Chime.

"He is ready."

Astro actualized the Libran Warrior and led her in. Pedro was slumped in his chair with his hands on his temples as if trying to hold his head in place. Don Arturo circled him, blowing on different parts of his body and shaking the rattle gently.

"Astro, come, come. Something strange is happening, I feel most unwell. Give me water, yes water." He guzzled the glass of water and suddenly became aware of Chime. "Who is this? Who? No more visitors!"

"It is I, Chime from Libra."

She floated towards him, gently tinkling her scales.

"No, no!" Pedro waved his hands in the air as if to erase the image.

"There is no need to fear, señor, I am here to help you remember."

"Remember?" he shook his head.

"You have been here for a long time, is that so?"

"Long time? Long time," Pedro looked at his feet, lost in a thought.

"You came from far away."

"From my dreams, from my dreams."

"From Cancer. Do you remember?"

Pedro's eyes flitted around the room. The shaman intensified his chanting.

"Xincon, you are from Cancer."

Chime stepped closer to Pedro. She took his face in her hands and his body relaxed at her cool grip. "You are Xincon, I am Chime."

Pedro's body melted away for a second. It flashed into a muscled torso, giant claws of a crab rested on the arms of the chair. Then the humongous form of Pedro flickered back.

"No, what is happening here? Astro! Astro!"

"Shhh, you have forgotten, that is all. The Zodiac Warriors are gathering. We need you Xincon," said Chime.

The Cancer Warrior appeared again briefly but Pedro fought for his human form and his body reverted.

"I... I am dreaming. Astro!"

Don Arturo sung and intoned around Pedro. Astro stood behind Pedro and massaged his head.

Chime took the ottoman at Pedro's feet. "Tell me of your journey."

"My journey?" Tears fell over Pedro's cheeks. "Yes, my journey." He took a deep breath and a different, deeper voice told the story.

"They told me it was June 1756. A ship called Leon sailed to a rugged piece of land, only sighted once before. They call it Isla San Pedro because it was the day of St Peter when they arrived. The crew needed fresh water and ice. A party rowed ashore. A man called Nicholas found my medallion as he dug under the snow. He quickly put it in his pocket and returned on board. When the ship arrived in Peru, Nicholas fell in love with a girl and made her pregnant. The girl's father banished his sullied daughter and the couple ended up here in Quito. Their first son was born in the dry season, the star sign of Cancer.

"They called him Pedro. When he was ten, he found me in his mother's drawer and I came out of the medallion. They were terrified, they called the shaman and he sliced off my claws and buried the medallion deep in the rainforest. The shaman came every day to heal me. But when they cut me, I changed my own shape to look like the boy and I grew like him. Then the boy got bitten by a snake and he died." Pedro stood. "They took me in and cared for me like a son.

Eventually they couldn't remember from where I came, and they forgot their real son died and I was Pedro Pintado."

Pedro lay down on the day bed. Astro wiped the sweat drenched face of Pedro, the shaman intoned and swayed.

"I had many hard times in this body, many times I wanted to lose it, but I forgot how to come out. Then it was easier to stay inside, exiled from within."

The voice changed back to Pedro's. "My own words are not making sense to me."

Pedro looked questioningly at Chime.

"It will take time, Xincon. I will introduce you to others from Horos and you will remember more."

Pedro fell in a doze. The shaman's chanting petered out. It was silent.

Astro motioned Chime to leave the room.

"Did he remember?" Jill asked as soon as they emerged.

"Yes, he remembered how he came to be here, but we will need more sessions."

"We will see how he is on waking," said Astro. "We could have made things better or worse."

"When can the shaman do another?" asked Tim.

"Usually in a day's time."

Pedro was quiet when he came to the following morning. His usual bolshiness had subsided, he was contemplative. Astro tidied the room, pottering around him, waiting for him to speak.

"Am I crazy, Astro?"

"No señor, no more than any of us."

"Then why do I believe I am from another planet?"

"Because you are. What you saw yesterday was no illusion. Chime is real and so is Xincon."

"What am I to do?"

"You must uncover your true form, señor"

"But when I did that before, I was feared, abused. This body holds fear."

"But it also holds strength and courage."

"Bring me the medallions."

Astro fetched the medallions along with Jill, Tim and John. They entered Pedro's chamber.

Señor Pintado quivered in his throne. His body wanted to repel them all, to retreat to the world of paint and music, but there was an irresistible impulse within him that promised sweet relief, that harboured a memory of youth and potential. Astro picked the Libra medallion up. The light flowed into Chime, materializing into the air in front of Pedro.

"Please, bring out Degon of Leo," she said.

Tim stepped forward with the medallion in his hand and the mighty lion emerged.

Pedro gasped, tears streamed down his face. He held out his hands to the warriors.

"I remember you!"

"Who is this?" Degon boomed.

Tim winced. Everything about the Warrior was bold, his magnificent mane, his rich voice, his upright stance. Tim remembered being forthright and confident, he'd had big ideas when he was a young man, ready to sacrifice almost anything to make the most money, to make the biggest deal. He was bold and brash, his potential shining bright. But at some point he had shrunk. His flame had gone out. He had folded under the confines of boardrooms and a computer screen. He had bent himself to dress in the finest tailored suit, to own the most expensive car, wear the designer watch. He had exchanged his burning flame of passion for a fancy fireplace.

"This is Xincon of Cancer, Degon. He has lost himself in the confines of a human body. We are trying to help him find his true form," Chime said.

"Xincon! You were always good at hiding. Do you remember when we visited you on Cancer? You showed me your country and you kept changing shape, tricking me. Your family took your power away because you were not using it for good," Degon said.

"Bring out Taurus, John."

John stepped forward and unwrapped his medallion. Teres emerged filling the space with his enormous body. He looked at the others and nodded in greeting.

"Back so soon! What's new?"

"We have found Xincon but he has lost himself. We are here to help him come back, Teres."

"My old friend, you are amongst your kin, come show us your true shape. You must be tired of that old body, eh?"

Pedro blinked. Another body appeared momentarily, then Pedro's enormous bulk returned.

"Do you remember how your people invited all Horoscopians to Cancer. It was a moment of triumph in our galaxy when we were all united. No other Horoscopians could put on a celebration like Cancerians; your food, music and generosity were unmatched," Teres said.

Pedro shook his head. Snippets of his planet were flitting through his mind, but he was unable to cling onto them for long. "Where is Amrez?" he said, a memory staying for a moment. His Sagittarian friend had been like a brother to him despite them being as different as cayenne pepper and a cold cucumber.

"We haven't found him yet," Chime said.

"But you could help us, Xincon. If anyone can keep him in one place, it will be you," said Teres.

They shared memories and each time Xincon's original form returned a little fuller.

"I have my claws back," Xincon said, as he waved a huge pair of pincers across his body. "They cut them from me but now they are back."

He snapped the pincer but the noise startled him, and the human form of Pedro returned. "I don't understand what is happening to me. Astro, help me, bring me my pills."

"Xincon, stay with us a while. Remember us. It is OK for you to retreat into the human form," Chime said evenly. "In fact, it is wise and safe, as you are without a medallion. We will visit you daily and help you remember."

Xincon returned, his powerful body rose from the chair that had accommodated Pedro for so many years. He picked it up in his claws and threw it out of the French doors into the garden. The humans winced as glass shattered.

"I am sick of this body," he yelled but suddenly retreated back to Pedro.

"He has had enough for today," Astro stepped in. "Leave him now, please."

The humans and Warriors looked at each other and left the room as Astro settled Pedro on his daybed.

"Going to be a process then," said John.

"Yes," said Chime, "but we have made progress. We will visit him and talk with him daily. Xincon will return, Pedro will come to understand he is a disguise, not a human."

"Five down, seven to go," said Jill, "we still have work to do."

As Jill tried to rest that night, she looked out of the open window. The drapes blew in from the breeze. The damp smell of the earth, the round disc of the full moon reminded her of Virgo. Her planet was serene and cool. The stories Degon, Chime and Teres told that afternoon made her homesick. She had wanted to join in. All she wanted was to be with them all again, with the familiar and yet even now she couldn't reveal to them her true being. She couldn't even converse with Teres—the only one who knew her true identity—because it was John who held the medallion. But she pushed her desires to the back and concentrated once again on her search. As she had done a million times, she wondered where the other Warriors could be. She needed the communication skills of Castor and Pollux. Geminis were the masters of connection. Maybe they could help plot out where the others had landed. She listened to an owl that hooted into the night.

She listened to the wind rustling the giant palm leaves. She listened and listened, and then she heard something new.

Next door John could not sleep either. He had turned his phone on after the long day and opened to a string of emails in his inbox.

'Professor Robertson,

Thank you for your hilarious video. However, these memes are more appropriate for social media platforms rather than clogging up the in-boxes of busy professionals.'

'John, love that you have a mechanical bull at your place. When's the party!'

'Dear John, I think you've been hacked.'

'Professor Robertson,

The association of professional archaeologists' board wishes to let you know that your membership has been revoked. Our professional body of working archaeologists and anthropologists do not take your attempts of levity or possibly delusional reports lightly. We are sorry to see this outcome.'

John put his head in his aging hands and sobbed.

Sandra had flown to Washington the next day. She was in her hotel room working when she came across a video on social media. She chuckled out loud at the comments of the video. Sandra watched the interview carefully a second and third time. The alien, Teres of Taurus did not seem dangerous. He seemed quite charming and intelligent. Something about his eyes reminded her of someone, though she couldn't quite think who it was. Her bejewelled nails hit the keys as she searched the Internet. A few phone calls confirmed the name of the man who had sent the video to colleagues around the world. One of those colleagues had posted it on social media. Most people declared it a hoax. It took a few hours for her to find that Professor Robertson had recently arrived in Ecuador. She was about to book a flight to Quito when her boss called.

"Tress, there's been a development at Fort George Meade, a break out. You need to get there immediately."

Sandra sighed. She had quite fancied Ecuador but instead ordered a taxi to the headquarters.

When Castor and Pollux came apart Stevie was bursting to speak with them. Tammy sat at her kitchen table, unable to take her eyes off the merged twins.

"There's someone after Jason in Australia. The police just went to his apartment. I hope he's managed to escape. The government must have got wind of the Warriors. We're not safe. They've probably got Lily. We need to find her."

"We still couldn't hear her, said Pollux.

"But we connected with Regida of Virgo. She is coming," Castor finished.

"From where?"

"From the south."

Stevie pulled his hand over his mouth and chin and breathed deeply.

"It's too dangerous to stay here. We need to hide."

"Hide where, Stevie?" Tammy asked.

"Where I always hide, Ma, the old chimney. 'Cept this time you're coming with me."

"That's crazy talk. I'm not crawling up there!"

"You got to Ma. It ain't safe here. They've got Lily and they're knocking her door down in Australia."

"I'm not leaving this house, Steven. That's final."

Stevie sighed but he knew better to argue with Tammy when she had that tone of voice.

A million bright lights flashed and flickered against the navy-blue sky. They reflected on water that licked a beach so white it gleamed in the moonlight. A sea of semi-naked bodies under the lights sweated and thrashed to a heavy beat. The rhythm rose and rose and rose, the notes squeezing out until they could go no higher and merged into one continuous note that managed to go higher, pulsating, teetering on the edge. It stopped for a nanosecond. Then the beat dropped, the bass kicked in, and the crowd cheered and threw themselves in the air together. In the middle of the dancefloor a curious man towered above the rest. His muscular torso gleamed, sweat gathering in the crevices of his abdominals, his massive arms pumping the air. He ran his fingers across his widow's peak and black spiky hair. He gestured to his friend he was getting a drink and weaved his way to the bar.

"Rez! What can I get you?" the barman yelled over the music.

"Water, then bourbon on ice."

A girl sidled up to him and slid into his arms.

"Hey, Irena!" He kissed her full on the lips. He turned back to the barman, winked and skulled his drink before corralling the girl away.

An hour later, Rez's closest friend and manager, Marko, asked the barman if he'd seen Rez. The barman flicked his thumb in the direction of the chill out tent. Marko pulled aside the flap. The interior was dark, there was a musty smell of smoke and incense. A mish mash of rugs lined the floor, and the draped silks gave it the air of the middle east. Party people lounged on cushions in groups smoking, laughing, talking. Marko noticed the unmistakable boots of Rez who was sprawled across Irena.

He nudged it with his toe. Rez grunted.

"Hey man, get up. You're on in twenty."

Rez stirred, "Wait, what?" He winced at Marko.

"Your set is up next."

DJ Rez lifted the girl off him as if she was as light as an arrow feather and jumped up. He grabbed his sunglasses and placed them on his eyes.

"OK, let's really get this party started," he said and slapped Marko on the back. He had to duck low to get his tall frame through the opening of the tent. Dancers were still thrashing in front of the stage. Rez leapt up and jigged next to the DJ as he played the last tunes of his set. He took his headphones out of his bag stashed at the side of the stage and lit up a cigarette.

Then he was on. The crowd cheered. He didn't bother acknowledging the DJ, though he respected the guy. These people just wanted tunes and it was now his job to deliver. These punks wouldn't know what had hit them. Shame they didn't have dancing hooves like him.

In the village of Podhom, Slovenia in 1605 a young peasant girl called Ana found an unusual metal pebble in the Radovna river while washing her family's clothes. It was a tarnished gold colour and had a blue glassy jewel embedded in it. A hieroglyph was etched in the other side. When she touched it, purple light splayed through her fingers and an image appeared. She screamed and prayed to God. The villagers heard and ran down to the river and saw a beast in the water. He stood firm in the strong current, with four legs of a horse and the torso of a man. He raised his head and breathed in the cool air. He carried a bow and quiver across his back. The women wailed. The men grabbed them and shuffled them back, keeping their eyes on the apparition. One man whispered to a boy to go fetch the duke and his men.

The beast stepped towards the people, they flinched but Ana was mesmerised. She felt sad she had screamed. She saw in the eyes of the beast a friendliness, an innocence. She moved towards him, her bare feet not feeling the chill of the water. Ana took the bread from her pocket and handed it to him. She could hear her mother calling her name, to come back. Ana smiled at him and he smiled back.

"I am Amrez from Sagittarius," he said. "Do you want to get away?"

She nodded.

"What is it they call you?" he asked.

"Ana," she croaked.

"Take my hand, Ana."

In a daze, she took his outstretched hand and before she knew it, she was straddled across his back. The villagers screamed as they fidgeted on the riverbank, weaponless and terrified.

"Hold on, Ana," he said.

Amrez waved and took off across the river to the other side and galloped off into the wooded country. That night Amrez and Ana camped out in the woods. Amrez caught a rabbit and cooked it over a fire. He told Ana about his home, though she understood little, and he did not learn much from this young girl. The next morning he told her he would deliver her back to her village. But as the settlement came into sight, a loud shot rang out and Ana fell onto the ground, as dead as the rabbit she had eaten the day before. Amrez took his bow and arrow and shot in the direction of the gunfire. Within a second, he loomed above the men holding muskets aimed at him. The men quaked in fear and shot point blank at Amrez. Amrez roared and kicked his front legs up, flooring the men. He escaped, angry, injured and bewildered. His medallion was still nestled in the dead girl's apron. He watched from afar as the parents of the girl lifted her body, sobbing and distraught.

Every day, after he had washed his wounds and dressed them as best he could, he returned to the outskirts of the village and saw people go to the house where Ana's body lay. He saw a man dressed in robes visit and leave some hours later and finally, he watched as they carried the body in a cart and buried her on the outskirts of the village with no marking for the grave. He understood that she was gone, and he was horrified he had been the reason.

Amrez now took caution when he came across humans, he hid and waited for them to pass. He retreated to the forest and cried for the young girl who had freed him. He approached horses he found in the wild, but found them without a language. He saw that humans were all built the same as he and he saw that horses were all built the same as he, and he saw that he did not fit.

One day he came across an old woman in the forest. Though he made himself barely visible or heard, the woman looked straight at him.

"So, there you are. I was waiting to catch a glimpse of you."

Amrez slowly emerged from the bushes that hid him.

"You are not afraid?"

"Hah, I've seen a darn sight worse than you! Come, let us talk and get warm."

She gestured him to follow. With a basket stuffed with plants, she led him through the trees to a lean-to near a stream. She filled a kettle from the water and poked at the fire pit outside her hut. She dropped some of the leaves in the water and settled it over the fire. Amrez lay on the ground, his body propped against a log.

"I'm Ksenija."

"Amrez of Sagittarius."

"Where did you come from?" she asked.

Amrez told her his story. He explained that until he got the medallion back, he was exposed. He told her there were others from his galaxy.

"The priest took your medallion. Ana's family are lucky to be alive, they say you are the devil. There are men searching for you. You are in danger."

"I cannot stay like this." He waved his arm across his rump. "I need to look all human."

"I am a healer; I work with the plants to cure ills but the church has banished me. They call me a witch, a hag who casts spells and jinxes people." She sighed. "When I was a young girl, my mother sent me out into the world to learn and fend for myself. She said that standing on my own feet would teach me about life. I worked for a man in the town. He was a healer too and he fixed up men who had fought in the war and had injuries that were very bad. He knew how to remove dead arms and legs. I would watch him and clean up after. Lucky I have a good stomach."

"Are you saying you could..." Amrez sliced his hand across the rippling horse torso that lay beside him.

Ksenija nodded.

They spent the next two days sharpening her largest blade and preparing her tinctures. She examined his body and made incantations. She fed him with broths and herbs that would speed up recovery. Finally when all was ready, she fed him some bright red berries. These drugged him, and once he lay on the operating table in her one-room hut, she fed him more until he fell into a coma.

Amrez awoke face down. He saw the earth, floor through the hole on the table. His mouth was dry. He lifted his head and looked around him. Dried herbs hung from the ceiling. The room was barely furnished. Wood was stacked against a wall. Ksenija came and placed a hand on his head and spooned a red juice into his mouth. He fell asleep again and so it went for many weeks. Then one day, he awoke with a start. He could hear a familiar sound, the beat of horse hooves. He pushed himself up onto his elbow and looked down the side of his body. Half of him was gone—though he still felt his tail swishing. A man's voice outside hailed Ksenija. He heard the whinnying of horses driven hard and the clanking of weaponry. Amrez sat himself up, wincing. His back felt tight and tender. He put his two hoofed feet on the floor and tried to stand but crashed to the ground, his balance thrown. He could hear Ksenija answering the men. Amrez dragged himself to a small stool by the hearth. The hide covering the entrance was thrown aside and two men squeezed into the space. Amrez reached for a blanket and dragged it over his legs. As the men's eyes became accustomed to the darkness, Amrez said, "greetings."

The men stepped closer. "You the traveller the hag mentioned?"

"Aye, just stopping for a brew."

"You seen any strange sightings on the road?"

"What do you mean by strange?"

The men glanced at each other.

"You just report anything seeming odd, alright?"

Amrez poked the fire and nodded.

The men looked around the hut and left.

After a good time had passed, Ksenija came into the hut.

"You are healing well. Time to get you walking again, then you must leave."

Amrez agreed and he set about learning to walk with two legs. He fashioned boots from horse hide to cover his hooves and the woman found him clothes to wear. She taught him some of the world and finally, after the moon had turned six times, he was ready to go.

Once Amrez met humans who saw him as one of their own, he realised that they were not all bad. Quick to learn and a master with his bow and arrow, he soon gathered wealth. He became loved by the royal house of Habsburg and gained titles and land. He fought in their wars and made heroic acts. He delayed finding his medallion because he had no urge to return to its encasement. He loved planet

Earth; its smells, tastes and delicacies, its women (and sometimes men), the air, the greenness, the highs of alcohol and opium and the sweet nights of dancing and revelry. It all suppressed the sadness he felt for poor Ana. Amrez never aged. He travelled the world and experienced all that was on offer. He gathered friends and lovers, he grew his money and business interests. He was a man of the world with a deep secret, and he always kept his boots on.

When the priest had entered the house of Ana's family, he noticed the medallion on the table. Ana's father told the priest it was in his daughter's pocket when they recovered her body. The priest looked at them with suspicion, but he took the medallion after banishing the devil from the house. It was a rare piece. The jewel shone like those he had heard about in Vatican in Rome. The duke would be very happy, and it would pave the way for a clear path to promotion within the clergy. Indeed, the duke took the medallion and had it set in a crown and the priest was duly rewarded.

The crown ended up in the house of Habsburg and was lucky to survive fallen dynasties and wars. Centuries later it gathers dust in the Habsburg-Lorraine Household Treasure and once in a purple moon it got featured for display in the Imperial Treasury of Vienna.

The beats peaked and the dancers, pumped with narcotics that gave them energy to party all night heaved themselves in the air. DJ Rez raised one fist in the air, the other on his headphones and smiled. Another girl stood at the front of the decks and gave him a slight raise of the eyebrow. He nodded and brought the house down with one more tune. Battered and bashed bodies trailed away to swim in the sea and watch the sunrise. Marko and Rez drove back to the villa they rented with the girls and a few revellers. They lounged around, slept had sex and swam in the pool while staff brought food and drinks.

Rez looked over at Marko. "Where to next, bro?"

"Vienna, my man. The Donauinselfest, the biggest open-air festival in Europe. You got a two-day break, then we leave."

"Cool."

A couple of girls came and sat on the end of his sun lounger, and he was absorbed once again in the human form.

The strength of Plaadio's power seemed endless, but Jason could not have kept running. His muscles were not used to such exertion.

"Stop!" he panted. His body slowed down to a halt, and he bent forward with his hands on his thighs and puffed. "We need a plan. I can't just keep moving."

"*I am getting weaker too, bro,*" Plaadio said. "*The further I am away from my pod, the less power I have. I need Amrez's bow and arrow to locate it.*"

"Good, my body won't survive at this rate."

There was a small park across the road. Jason looked around him and jogged onto the grass and crouched down among a group of grass trees. He took his phone out of his back pocket and messaged Stevie.

'Any news?' he typed.

'The Geminis have just picked up something. Another Warrior, Virgo. They are trying to read her mind, but it is a harder when the person is not present.' Jason let out a deep sigh of relief.

'Thank God.'

'You need to get out of Australia.'

'Where?'

'What about the guy from Africa?'

'Zakary?'

'Yeh, find him.'

'OK.'

Stevie's suggestion wasn't bad. Zakary had been snooping around Egypt, looking for the Virgo medallion. It was far enough away to escape the Federal Police or whoever was after him. He opened up Lily's laptop and searched for an email from Zakary. He sent him a message to get onto Qriptonite, too paranoid to put any more details about the situation.

Within minutes, Jason got a notification.

'What's up, man?'

Jason filled him in. 'Where are you?'

'I'm at the airport in Cairo. I got a lead on Virgo and I'm headed to Vienna. Why don't you head over too?'

'No cash mate.'

'I'll transfer you some now.'

'Thanks. I'll pay you back. Will let you know when on flight.'

When Jill joined the men at breakfast the next morning, she announced her departure.

"I am making a short trip to America."

"Why my darling?" Tim asked.

"I received a message from some old friends. I haven't seen them for a long, long time."

"I'll come with you, we both will." Tim looked at his father for affirmation.

"No, you both need to stay here to actualize Teres and Degon so they can continue to work with Chime and bring Xincon back fully. I'll only be gone a few days."

"Are you sure, my love?" Tim felt a strange angst about her travelling alone when the world was so unstable.

"Of course, I'm perfectly capable of catching a plane across the border."

Jill smoothed his face with her hand and dazzled his heart with a smile. She kissed him lightly but lingeringly on his temple.

The information from Gemini was not anything concrete, like an address. It would be like the game 'hot and cold'. She sensed that they were on the east coast, so New York was an obvious place to start. At JFK airport, she found a quiet spot in an end cubicle of the washrooms and sent her feelers out into the ether. She waited for a recognisable signal. A long time passed by before she picked up the twins' vibration. She exited the airport and flagged a taxi.

"Where to, ma'am?" the driver asked.

"South," she said and looked into the man's inner being. He wanted to retire by a lake. She would make sure the man was well on his way to do that by the time she found the Gemini twins. The signal was strong until Philadelphia. They'd been on the road for two hours, and so she instructed the driver to stop for a break.

After half an hour, she picked up the trail. They set off and reached Baltimore. It was getting stronger. She had a metallic taste on the roof of her mouth. They bypassed the city and continued south. After half an hour, they pulled up outside a gate. The National Security Agency, Fort George G Meade. The taxi driver turned to Jill.

"Is this where you want me to drop you, ma'am? It's nearly midnight." He yawned.

"Yes, but we can get some sleep at a motel. I'll need you to drop me here in the morning and wait for me."

He looked doubtful. She pulled out her wallet and counted two thousand dollars, more than double the fare. His eyes widened.

"Yes, ma'am."

The next morning, he dropped her at the gate. Jill approached the guard.

"I need to see the head of security," she said.

The guard consulted his computer.

"Do you have an appointment? I'm not expecting anyone." He looked at her with suspicion, but her demeanour ensured his respect.

"I have something he will be interested in."

"And what might that be?"

"Tell him it is connected to the Zodiac Warriors."

The man raised an eyebrow in disbelief. Another UFO nut trying to get in. He went into his hut to make a call. Jill had made a quick assessment of the place she had been led. If Gemini were in here, it meant the US government had got wind of the Warriors and she had to play her trump card. She fingered the medallion under her sweater.

The guard came back out and nodded for her to follow him. The large security gates opened, and he led them to the front door of the looming black glass building. Inside the foyer, a man stood waiting.

"Joseph Schwartz. I understand you have some intelligence for us."

He held out his hand. Jill shook it.

"Jillena Mayer. Yes, I believe I do."

"Before we go into an interview room, we need to search you, if you don't mind."

Jill relented to being patted down by an armed guard and walking through a scanner. They searched her bag and gave her approval to continue. Joseph scanned the images and nodded.

He led her to a room and introduced Daniel, who had joined them.

"So Miss Mayer, tell us what you know about the Zodiac Warriors?"

She smiled and hooked the medallion from under her clothes. The men glanced at each other.

"It didn't show up on the scanner?" asked Daniel.

"No, like the others," said Joseph.

"Others?" Jill asked. She felt a thrill run through her, but she had to remain impassive.

"Er, yes, we have come across other examples of this phenomenon. May I?" Joseph held out his hand.

"I'm sorry, I can't give this to you. It has been in my family for many generations."

"We have reason to believe this is a dangerous weapon, Miss Mayer. For your safety, I urge you to hand it over."

Jill smiled. "I am perfectly safe, Mr Schwartz. It is you who is in danger, I fear."

The men looked uneasy. They felt for their holsters, making sure Jill could see they were armed.

"Then why don't you tell us why you are here, Miss Mayer?"

She didn't answer immediately. She tucked the medallion back inside her sweater.

"For you to tell me what you know about the Zodiac Warriors, and what you intend to do about them."

The men laughed. "You should work for the CIA, Miss Mayer."

"You know these Zodiac Warriors are alien beings who intend to take over planet earth?" said Joseph, now serious.

"And you know this from where exactly?" she asked.

"One of the aliens has killed a civilian and badly hurt Daniel here."

Joseph waved his hand to the sling holding Daniel's shoulder in place. "Now, please cooperate with us Miss Mayer and surrender the medallion where we can secure it."

"Which Zodiac Warrior?"

"That's classified. Unless you want us to use force, I'll ask you one more time, as a matter of global security, the medallion please."

Jill put her hand over the medallion at her chest. "As I said, I cannot hand over the medallion."

The men stood, giving a fake look of dismay.

"Look at me, gentlemen. Surely you don't think my simple necklace is of any danger?"

Jill looked into Joseph Schwartz's eyes, and his expression

changed for a moment. She turned her attention to Daniel, whose smile also vanished.

Jill took a deep breath. She felt a surge of guilty power. What she was doing was forbidden on her planet, yet it gave her a rush. The men sat back down heavily in their chairs and sighed deeply.

"Woah," Joseph gasped.

"Man, what is going on?" Daniel gazed dreamily at Jill.

"You're going on a little trip," she said gently. "You are feeling good?"

"I feel like I'm floating!" Daniel laughed.

Joseph put his hands in the air and wriggled his fingers, watching in amazement. He stroked the back of one of his hands and sighed.

"Now, gentlemen. Tell me what you know about the Zodiac Warriors."

The men animatedly relayed how they found Scorpio. Intelligence had led them to Lily, who was here in the headquarters.

"And what about Gemini?"

Joseph had stood up and was swaying around the room as if he had some music playing in his ears.

"Not yet!" Joseph giggled. He walked behind Daniel and massaged his head. Daniel groaned in ecstasy.

"Have you found any others anywhere?" she asked.

"We have..." Daniel began.

"Shhh, it's a sec... a sec... a secwet!" Joseph said and both the men cracked up laughing, repeating the word 'secwet' over and over.

Jill watched them coolly. They would be intoxicated like this for twenty-four hours and once the neurotransmitters drained out of their system, they would hit a low few recovered from. Not only a deep depression, but physical pain accompanied the comedown which no amount of medication could disrupt.

"It would be fun to take me to see the other medallions," she suggested.

"Fun, yes. This place needs to lighten up. Come on Dan!"

Joseph leaned on the door handle and Dan burst out laughing when it wouldn't open.

"Your card... you need to scan your security key! What is going on with you, man?"

"With me? You're the one acting all... secwet!" Joseph burst out, clutching his knees, wheezing with laughter. Dan waved his good hand in the air, trying to regain control.

"OK, OK, I don't know what you put in my coffee, Jo, but I've never felt this good at work!"

The men cleared their throats and tried to look serious. After several bouts of giggles they pulled themselves together and led Jill out into the corridor. The slick and sombre interior of the National Security headquarters dulled their exuberance for long enough to get them to the secure room three floors down, which now housed not only Scorpio but the Aries medallions. They were enclosed in a separate glass cases.

"Where is the young woman?"

"She is in interview room 205." Joseph looked at Dan who went "oops!" and both men chorused "it's a secwet!" before collapsing against each other in fits of giggles.

"How about we make it a foursome and you bring her down here?" Jill said flirtatiously.

Daniel licked his lips and Joseph nodded his assent.

"Go get her, Dan."

Jill walked around the cases.

"Wanna see something wild?" Joseph leered. "You wanna see the video footage of that thing?" He pointed at the Scorpio medallion. She nodded.

He pressed a keypad embedded in the wall, which caused a screen to drop down. He selected a file and played it. It showed Charlie holding the medallion and Fyon actualizing on the table. She watched Daniel enter the room and Fyon lash out. The gunfire followed and she disappeared.

"Why were there so many armed men in the room?" Jill asked.

"Did you see that thing? That is an alien right there, lady. It killed a man. Do you know what's in that thing around your neck?"

The video footage had sobered him. He paced the length of the room, knocking his fingers against his head. "Why am I here? What's happening to me?"

"Never mind all that now," she crooned. "We're here to have fun, right?"

As he made his way back to where she was standing, she took him by the shoulders and looked into his eyes. She took his hand and let it graze her breast. He shuddered, half closing his eyes. Jill willed for Daniel to return with the girl, but Joseph put his hand behind Jill's neck and scrunched her hair in his hand, pulling her body towards him roughly.

"Shhh, steady," she whispered. She undid his top button and slid her fingers gently against the skin of his chest. Joseph moaned, every nerve of his body alive thanks to the surge of serotonin coursing through him.

At last, the door opened and Daniel let Lily into the room. She looked bewildered. Jill pulled away from Joseph.

"What the hell is going on?" Lily asked.

"Hi, my name is Jill Mayer. And you are?" Jill held out her hand.

The name rang a bell, but Lily couldn't place it.

"Lily Noor and I'm being held here illegally for no reason."

"Joseph, Daniel. Why don't you go and find us some drinks?" Jill smiled and winked at them. They left like eager puppies.

"What the hell is going on?" Lily asked. She noticed the glass case which housed Prymaw and tried to open it.

"I'm here to help," Jill whispered. "Are you the guardian of Aries?"

Lily hesitated. "Who are you? Are you with the government? And what the hell has got into those two?" Lily gestured toward the door.

"Let us speak quietly—they could be recording. In answer to your first question, I am the guardian of Virgo," she said and brought out the medallion.

Lily gave a wide-eyed nod of recognition.

"Secondly, no I'm not with the government and thirdly, I have just given them a feel-good drug. They will be pliable."

"But why did you come here? How come they didn't take the medallion off you?" Lily was feeling more suspicious, she didn't know who she could trust. Yet this woman had a purity and a directness about her.

"Because I'm here to get you, Aries and Scorpio out of here."

"Really?" Lily swore with relief. She tried again to lift the glass case off the medallion. "They're locked in."

Jill stood next to Lily and spoke fast and low. "When they come back, I'll persuade them to open them up. You must get hold of Aries and bring him out. I'll actualize Scorpio. They will have the strength to get us out of here. Once we are clear, they will go back into the medallions. I have a car waiting."

"But how can you actualize..." Lily began.

The door opened and the men shimmied in with a bottle of bourbon and four glasses.

"Ladies!"

"Just play along," Jill whispered to Lily.

She swung around and pierced Joseph with a smouldering look. She approached him and slid her hands around his hips.

"What a big... gun you have!" she grabbed a hold of the handle and pulled it out of its holster. She swung away to the centre of the room.

Daniel poured Lily a drink. She took it, her hand shaking.

"So..." he backed her up to the wall and leant in to kiss her. She could smell a mixture of coffee and bourbon on his breath. "You're a hot little Aussie girl. Always been curious about your... country," he leered.

Lily felt the bile rise in her throat. She'd 'played along' all her life. Without a second thought, she hoicked her knee into his crotch and extracted the gun from his holster. Daniel recoiled onto the floor, curled up like a woodlouse.

"I'll show you what a hot little Aussie girl can do!" Before Jill had a chance to react, Lily shot at the glass case that held Prymaw. She reached into the shattered glass as alarms went off.

Jill shoved Joseph away and shot at the other glass case which exploded.

"Not quite what I had in mind," she declared.

The alarms screeched, and the lights switched to a florescent blue hue. As Jill went to pluck the Scorpio medallion out of the pieces, Joseph bounced off the wall. The serotonin coursing through his body was boosted by adrenalin, and his reflexes were sharp. He caught Jill around the neck with his arm before she could grab the medallion.

Lily prayed that Prymaw would emerge. She held the medallion tightly, blood dripping through her fingers she'd slashed on the shards. The alarm was deafening, and she couldn't make out where Jill was through the flashing blue light.

"Jill!"

Lily could see bodies moving on the other side of the cases.

"Come on Prymaw!" she yelled. "Jill! Where are you?"

"Dan, secure the girl, don't let her get the medallion!" Joseph shouted.

Suddenly something hit Lily across the back of her head and the medallion tumbled out of her hand. She fell onto the floor and felt glass pieces pierce her cheek. She saw Daniel's feet jump over her and reach for the medallion.

Jill struggled to loosen Joseph's grip. His training meant he knew exactly how to immobilise someone. But Jill wasn't someone; she was a Zodiac Warrior. She let her body relax completely and it slipped out of his grip like a piece of silk.

"Dammit!" he lurched towards her, but she had already reached the Scorpion medallion. She grabbed it, but Daniel appeared to her left. He lashed out, and she ducked out of the way. He fell forward into the empty space, and she kicked the Aries medallion out of his hand.

"Lily! Catch!"

Lily was bleeding from her face and arms. She couldn't see a thing, but she reached out and somehow the medallion landed in her hand. The blood stung her eyes and the blue light disoriented her, but she felt it vibrate and another presence filling the room.

"Prymaw? Are you here?"

"Fighting again, I see! Trouble seems to follow you, Lily."

"Thank God. They captured us. We need to get out of here."

Joseph and Daniel scrabbled to their feet and moved back from the warrior.

"Open the door, Jo, open the door!" Daniel shrieked.

Jill spoke a strange language. Lily recognised it from the words Plaadio used at 17 Mile Falls. She swiftly fixed the medallion onto her chain next to her own.

Fyon emerged, her tail flashed around, ready to strike.

"Fyon! It is good to see you, sister!" Prymaw yelled.

"Is it? This planet has proven unfriendly."

Joseph swiped the door with his card and the men fell into the corridor, shouting for help.

"We need to get out of here," Jill yelled over the din.

Prymaw ducked his head and squeezed through the door. Fyon gestured for Jill and Lily to go next. Two armed men were already racing down the corridor, their guns ready to fire. Prymaw unfurled his horns and flicked them over effortlessly. They tumbled over each other. More men came from the other direction. Fyon turned and held her tail up high, quivering and ready to strike. They backed off. The group fled along the corridors, looking for the way out. A fire exit sign led them to a stairwell.

"We have to go up to the ground floor," Jill said.

The three Warriors raced up the steps. But Lily, who hadn't eaten for hours and was only human, trailed behind. Her face was dripping with blood from the broken glass and her arms stung from the gashes. After only a flight of stairs up, the guards bashed through the door and advanced on Lily.

"Help!" she shouted to the Warriors who had forgotten her in their haste.

One of the guards shot at Lily and she flung herself against the wall. Fyon turned and came back to fetch Lily. She shot her tail down the stairwell, sending the guards down like dominoes. She reached Lily who was holding onto her cheek. With her muscled arms, she swept Lily onto her back and ran up to the others. A door led to the ground floor foyer. Men were already charged with weapons.

The alarms suddenly went silent. The four stood together. The doors to freedom were on the other side of an army.

"What is it with these people?" Fyon raged.

"Don't move!" said a man dressed in military fatigues.

"Regida..." said Prymaw in a low voice.

Jill looked sharply at him.

"You have not changed that much, sister," he said quickly.

"Surrender and come peacefully!" the man shouted.

"You take the front line," Prymaw whispered to Regida. "Fyon, you take the middle, I'll tackle the back line and clear the doors."

"I need my bag," Jill murmured.

"Put your hands in the air!"

"Lily, get the bag and hide behind the reception desk. This could get messy," Prymaw said as he raised his hands.

"Gold padded, designer," Jill said as she raised her arms and gazed deeply into the eyes of the nearest soldier.

The man's face went slack, and he dropped his gun. Jill went to the next man who said, "sweet Jesus!" and turned to the man behind him, grinning madly. As Jill sent messages into the brains of the men, they each became a slushy mess of emotion and ecstasy.

"Hold your weapons!" their leader screeched.

Jill turned her gaze to him. His will was strong, but eventually his brain gave way and released a flood of serotonin. He rolled his eyes in the back of his head and a huge smile spread across his face. The other soldiers looked uneasy. Fyon stepped forward and raised her staff towards the diminishing group.

"Sir?" one of the men said. "They are advancing. What are our orders?"

But their sergeant was looking vacantly in the air.

"Stand aside!" Prymaw said, his deep voice resonating across the foyer.

Fyon strode forward again, but the men panicked at the sight of her tail quivering over her head and fired. Fyon roared and swept her tail across the men. Prymaw leapt forward, his horns catching the ends of rifle and tossing them away from the terrified soldiers.

Lily took her chance and ran close to the edge of the foyer to the reception desk. She realised she was still holding the medallion in her hand. She shoved it in her pocket and catapulted herself over the desk, leaving blood smeared on its surface. Scanning the office, she saw Jill's bag in a pigeonhole. Shots rang out in the foyer. She looked around for her own backpack, but it was not there. It sounded like the foyer was being ripped apart. As Lily turned to get back out there, she stumbled. She felt dizzy and tried to orient herself. The room was spinning. Her face throbbed and in that instant, she blacked out.

Prymaw and Fyon fought their way to the glass doors, but the security system had locked them. Fyon swiped at the last brave soldiers. Prymaw raised his staff and with his horns he drilled a hole in the glass, pushing it out with his staff. Jill scoured the reception area, looking for Lily.

She called out. "Where's the girl?"

"I saw her go over the desk," said Fyon. "We need to get out of here before more arrive."

"Lily!" called Prymaw. "That girl is always in some sort of trouble! I'll find her."

Prymaw leapt through the mess of bodies and jumped behind the desk. He saw Lily sprawled on the floor and lifted her gently in his arms. Jill's bag hung from her shoulder. Her skin was pale, her face covered in blood oozing from the gash, and her body limp. A shot of concern went through him. He scooted over the desk.

"Go, go!" he yelled at Fyon and Jill. They ran across the tarmac. Prymaw only had to growl at the two men guarding the gate, and they opened it for them. The taxi was parked where Jill left him. The driver's mouth dropped open as they approached the car.

"What about Gemini?" said Jill. "I followed their signal here."

"Gemini? They are in a place called Newton Falls, New York state," Prymaw said.

"I don't understand."

"Lily made contact with the one who guards the Gemini medallion. The twins were especially fond of Lily. Perhaps you picked up on their signal to her?"

He glanced at the girl in his arms. "Look, I need to help her."

They heard the sound of cars approaching.

"We don't have time. You two must both retreat."

"She will die, she has lost too much blood."

"Take her with you. I will go to Gemini and bring you out there. Quick!"

Sirens sounded louder and louder.

Fyon dematerialized without a second thought, her beams of light concentrating at Jill's chest. Prymaw hesitated. He wasn't even sure he could bring a human with him. He closed his eyes and in a few seconds, he and Lily were gone. The medallion, along with Jill's bag, dropped out of the air to the ground. Jill picked them up and slid into the car. The driver's shaking hands started the engine.

"Where to, ma'am?" he said in a wavering voice.

S andra Tress walked into the smashed foyer of Fort George G. Meade and took in the armed forces who had been reduced to jelly. Despite the carnage and several dead bodies, the men were giggling and wandering around like wide-eyed two-year-olds caught inside a Disney movie. Some were stroking the suede of the upturned chairs, others were hugging each other.

"What the hell just happened here?"

Her black patent high-heeled boots stepped over the debris, and she headed to the security control room. She gazed into the facial recognition panel, her brightly patterned head wrap reflected back at her. She admired how it matched the ruffled yellow blouse. The door slid open, and four faces turned to see the tall African American woman who had entered. The men sat at the monitors in shock, speechless.

"Hey, fellas. Wake up."

The men roused themselves.

"Who are you?"

"Agent Sandra Tress CIA, I'm managing this case now." She flicked her badge at them. "Want to tell me how you managed to let two people escape the American Security headquarters?"

"I couldn't have imagined it in my wildest nightmares," one of the men said, shaking his head.

"I need to see all the footage. But hurry, whoever did this is getting away."

A man approached Sandra to report.

"We've located Schwartz and Westerford. They're not making much sense. We're getting a psych in to assess them."

"I want to talk to them. Set up an incident room. You guys..." she addressed the men, who still looked dumbfounded. "I want all the footage from the last 24 hours."

They didn't respond.

"Now!" she snapped her fingers.

Half an hour later, Sandra was watching the videos showing the extraordinary behaviour of Schwartz and Westerford after interviewing Jillena Mayer. She scrutinized the breakout over and over, looking for a clue. Something strange happened to Jillena's eyes before the men started to act strangely. She had blinked and a milky film covered her eyes for a moment. She zoomed in and noticed something else unusual about them. The detail was barely visible but her iris contained a thin silver coloured circle. From a distance, it just looked as if she had startlingly blue eyes. She pulled up the video of Teres and zoomed in. He had the same circle, though his eyes were dark brown. It was hard to get a visual of Scorpio and Aries in the breakout room due to the flashing lights, but the earlier footage of the Scorpio in the obs room proved her theory. In addition, Jillena did not seem surprised to see the scorpion creature or the giant ram. Could Jillena be one of them? She went back to the control room.

"How did she get in the building?" Sandra asked.

The man clicked through and viewed the footage of Jill showing the security guard her medallion. Sandra immediately recognised its likeness to the Scorpio piece. A quick search found sapphire was associated with Virgo.

"Alert all airport authorities to apprehend Jillena Mayer if she tries to leave the country."

What about the girl? Sandra had led them to her and now she was gone again. She didn't give up anything in the interview. Was she an alien, too?

"Bring me Lily Noor's phone. I assume they already traced all calls and contacts? I want the report. Also, put a watch on all borders for Professor John Robertson."

In the report, Sandra read how the police had found no one at the apartment of Jason Wallace in Australia. Lily's phone, passport and belongings were all left behind at Fort George, but she did discover she had recently been to Tanzania. Interestingly, close to her own birthplace in Nairobi.

Sandra stood at the whiteboard in her office. She drew twelve circles and put a zodiac in each one. She added information on Scorpio, Aries, Virgo and Taurus. She began by looking for a link between the humans, the places they were found, their appearance, anything that might give her a clue. She figured that since Jillena Mayer had a name, a human body and identity, that she would be the best one to hunt down.

"Now, Jillena Mayer. Where did you come from and where did you go?" Sandra's talons would not stop tapping until she found out.

Jason chewed his fingernails as he waited to get through customs at Vienna Airport. He attempted to breathe slowly as he passed by airport security. His passport had raised no red flags for authorities, which made him believe that they—whoever *they* were—were only after Lily and not him. But he had no news from Stevie about her, and his stomach and chest felt caught in a vice. Ragged and bleary eyed, he fell into Zak's arms.

"Hey, it's OK, man, it's OK."

"That's easy for you to say, mate. I've got a bloody alien living inside me."

"Come on, let's get you some breakfast and tell me everything."

"Any news from Lily?" Zak asked.

"Nothing, man. I'm so worried."

"Me too. But she's tough."

Jason grunted. He's been over every possible scenario on the plane. He'd sent Stevie a message the minute he could start up his phone, hoping like a lottery ticket holder beyond hope. But there was no news.

Zak took him to a café and ordered espressos and croissants for breakfast. The strong coffee and fresh pastries calmed Jason's nervous system, and he took in the grandiose architecture. His fingers itched for the safety of his camera. Zakary listened to how Jason and Lily found Plaadio. He then brought Jason up to speed on his inquiries in Egypt.

"So the Mayers discovered the tomb in Egypt in 1895. Suzannah Mayer sketched and catalogued all their finds in meticulous detail. When they returned to Vienna after that expedition, they had a child.

"That doesn't sound too strange."

"The girl suddenly appears at around the age of ten and there are no records of adoption."

"They might have adopted an orphan in Egypt. I don't suppose there was much red tape in those days."

"I thought that at first, but when I tracked down Suzannah's journals, which are very detailed, the account of gaining a child is very vague. She literally just appears out of nowhere."

"And what's this got to do with the Virgo Warrior?"

"The girl's name was Jillena. There is no record of her birth or her death. But there is evidence of a Jillena Mayer, living in England today."

"Mate, I still don't understand what you're saying. Perhaps it's a granddaughter of the Mayers."

"My theory, Jason, is that the girl is the Zodiac Warrior of Virgo, and that same girl is still living today over 125 years later."

"Whoa! You think we've found her... Virgo?"

"Yes, perhaps, but we don't know where she is now. I tracked an address in London but got no reply from the telephone number."

"So we hit a dead end?"

"For now, but as one end dies, another beginning is born. Look what I saw in the paper this morning," Zakary said as he slapped the Vienna Times on the café table.

The leading story claimed, 'A Million Lives Lost to Thirst'.

"Bloody hell, a million! So Plaadio is right, the planet really is in trouble."

"Yes it is, but that's not the article I meant."

"What am I looking at?"

"Here."

Zakary pointed to a piece at the bottom of the page. The headline read 'Habsburg Crown in All its Glory'. A black-and-white photo of an ornate crown sitting on a velvet cushion had the caption, 'The Hyacinth Sterne, the Habsburg's most unique and priceless crown has been put on display from the Treasury for the first time in 100 years.'

Zakary tapped the photo. "Look man, look at the crown!"

Jason's eyes widened as he recognised the jewel set in a familiar looking medallion at the centrepiece of the crown. He could feel Plaadio fidgeting inside him.

"It's a medallion! Whose though?"

"I don't know, but let's go and see it in real life. We might get a clue."

"I think Plaadio will know," said Jason as he felt the strength of the Warrior rising inside him.

"Come on, let's go."

Zak paid the over-priced bill, thanks to the extortionate price of the bottled water. They walked down the cobbled streets towards the museum. Zak went quiet. He went to start talking, but then stopped. He chewed on his lip.

"How is Lily?"

Jason looked incredulous.

"I mean, how was she after Tanzania?"

"Busy, we went straight off to the Northern Territory, then she went to the States. Things have been crazy."

Zak nodded. "Yeah, yeah." He paused. "Did she, did she talk about me?"

The motivation for Zak's questions dawned on Jason.

"Ah, yeah. I see. I mean, you two go back a long way. I think she really likes you."

"She does?"

Jason stopped and turned to Zak.

"Look, normally I wouldn't betray my best friend's trust. But since... since we don't know where she is right now. Yes, she does like you, Zak. A lot."

Zakary's face lit up, and he gave a deep sigh.

"Thanks, bro."

Jason had never seen a building so grand as the Hofburg Palace, except on TV. Its pale façade was in perfect symmetry with dozens of arched windows and columns holding up a roof crowned with three green domes. Inside, the Imperial Treasury housed royal jewels, religious regalia, many Habsburg treasures and an assortment of other items, some of which dated back a thousand years.

They trailed around the galleries, gazing at dazzling orbs, sceptres and crowns, crucifixes and an ornate baby's crib. The special exhibition of the Hyacinth Sterne was housed in its own gallery, a darkened room with a glass case at its centre. The crown was made of shining gold, studded with purple jewels. Inside, a deep purple velvet set the backdrop for the medallion, its bright zircon jewel on the front diadem of the crown. It was elegant, simple and breathtaking. Jason photographed it, blowing it up on his camera to see the detail.

"Let's see if we can look at the back of the medallion," Jason suggested.

They moved around and crouched down low to see if they could make out the insignia on it.

"It looks like a cross," said Zakary.

Jason searched up the zodiac symbols on his phone. "There are no crosses," he said, "unless... look Zak, the Sagittarius one is an arrow with a line through it. Is there an arrow above the cross?"

"I can't see. It's hidden from view. But I guess that's who it must be."

Two more men entered the room. One was tall and looked like he had stepped off the cover of a magazine, dressed in designer jeans and an aged leather jacket. His black hair spiked up and to one side. The other man wore a white suit and had sunglasses on, much shorter than his friend. They stood out from the mainly older and foreign tourists looking through the museum. Zakary and Jason were still on their knees examining the crown.

"Let me shine my phone torch on it, we might be able to see," said Jason.

The tall man put his fingers on the glass case and stared deeply at the crown.

The shorter man shuddered. "Hey, man, let's get outta here. This place creeps me out. All this old stuff." His phone rang, and he pulled it out of his pocket. "Hey, bambolina! Where did you end up last night? Crazy party, eh?"

He left the room. The tall man stood impassively, breathing deeply.

"Nah, can't make out the rest of the symbol," said Jason as he and Zakary stood up on the opposite side of the crown.

The man looked at them, a little startled. Jason's head pulled back a little.

"*Amrez?*" Plaadio spoke.

The man frowned. He took a step back.

"*Amrez of Sagittarius? It is you!*"

No one had called him Amrez in a century. He was confused. He had DJ'd for thousands of people all over the world and often got recognised, but not by that name. He was DJ Rez, and that's what everyone called him. But this man said 'Amrez', if he heard right...

"*Amrez, it's Plaadio!*"

Rez shook his head. How was this happening? He had lost his medallion for over 400 years and here it was, along with Plaadio?

Over the centuries, he had barely allowed himself to recall his fellow travellers. Being a Zodiac Warrior only reminded him of the young girl who had died at his fingertips. He wasn't interested in hanging onto his painful past, losing first his home and people and then the blood of an innocent on his hands. He had been given a second chance, and he was going to make the most of it. Turning on his well-heeled boots, he fled out of the exhibit room, yelling at Marko, who was lounged on one of the security staff's chairs, talking into his phone. Rez weaved around the display cases, knocking tourists and their guides sideways.

"Hey Rez! What's the hurry?" Marko said.

Marko chased him through the dimly lit rooms. Jason, driven by Plaadio, didn't miss a beat and ran after him. Zakary, trying to catch up on events, joined the chase.

Rez raced through the obstacles of exhibits and people, watched by the robes of popes and knights he once knew, his reflection glinting off century-old swords. He blasted through the exit door into a light-filled walkway with stairs leading to the main palace. He flew down the steps and heard the door bang open behind him, with Marko calling his name. Rez looked behind him briefly but carried on, his long legs speeding him ahead. Marko leant on his knees, bewildered and puffed from a lifestyle of too much good food and wine. Jason and Zakary burst through the door and crashed into him.

"*Talk to him, I'll go after Amrez,*" Plaadio yelled to Zakary and took off with a gait equally fast as Amrez.

"Hey, why you upsetting my friend? Who the hell are you?" Marko stood as tall as he could against the lithe Nigerian.

"We just want to talk to him, man. They go back a long, long way."

"Oh yeah? How long? I've known Rez since he was... since I was a kid. There isn't anyone worth knowing if I haven't come across them. I'm his manager and closest friend. So tell me again..." Marko jabbed Zakary in the chest three times with his first two fingers, "who —are—you?"

Zakary grabbed Marko's fingers and twisted them back. "I'm a peaceful man, Mr. Manager, but I don't like people who act hostile. Now why don't you take me to your house in case my fast-footed friend doesn't manage to catch up with his old, old, old before-your-time friend."

Rez knew exactly where he was in the vast palace. He'd spent countless months revelling here with the Habsburgs and their courtiers back in the mid-1800s. His taste for music and his thirst for women and wine meant he had trodden these opulent, spacious rooms countless times. They were good days, despite the wars and the lack of creature comforts. He had lived a full and exciting life here. He fast walked along the portrait-filled galleries and easily found his way to the main entrance with its pillars and sweeping staircase. Glancing behind him, he saw a flash of a body moving towards him. Rez picked up his pace and trotted quickly down the stairs and across the polished floors out into the fresh Vienna afternoon. Now he could gallop and lose the ghost from the past that followed him.

But he was rattled. This couldn't mean the Warriors were gathering... finally, could it? When he allowed himself to think about it, he had dreaded this day, more than any battleground, more than any heartbreak, even more than being confined in his medallion again. He wished he had never seen his metal pod again and could continue living his life on this extraordinary planet. He relished its tastes and colours, its music and magic of nature, the human body and the ecstasies it brought. He had no interest in being part of a group who weren't human. Amrez had revelled in his own air of mystery, of exoticism. He enjoyed being special; sharing it with eleven others would dilute it, take it away. He ran in to the Michaelerplatz. He hadn't noticed where Marko had parked the car, but he knew one of the streets, the Kohlmarkt, where his favourite shopping haunts were. He ducked through the welcoming doors of his favourite designer boutique. The shop manager welcomed him, and lead him into the private viewing room, offered him champagne, then brought out a rail of the latest designs for him to choose.

Jason exited the palace and looked around. Tourists milled around the plaza, which joined four roads. He glanced along each in turn, to no avail. He turned and looked up at the baroque palace. Within seconds, he was scrambling up the statue of Hercules. From his head, he pulled himself over the pillars and onto the roof. Jason felt heavy. There was none of the spring he had in his step back in Australia. He climbed the copper roof of the central dome. Jason tried to close his eyes, but Plaadio was back in command, scouring the streets.

"Why is this so hard?" said Jason, pulling in lungfuls of air.

"*I am far from my pod. My strength is going.*"

"Great, so now I'm doing the grunt work!"

He looked up. "Whoa, look at the view!" Jason snapped away and spun his camera for a panoramic shot.

"*Typical! Always had to go his own way,*" Plaadio growled.

A shout from below caught his ear.

"Hey, you! Come down, you are not allowed up there!"

A security guard stood with his hands on his hips. Another one spoke into a walkie-talkie.

"We need to get out of here," Jason said as Plaadio, a beat ahead of him, clambered down the dome and raced across the roof in the opposite direction. Once down the other side, he walked across the courtyard and into the chapel. There was a choir singing the most celestial song Jason had ever heard. He took off his jacket and sat in a pew, calming his breathing, tuning into the music. After ten minutes, his phone vibrated in his pocket. It was Zakary. A text came through.

'Where are you? I had to let the guy go. He was kicking up a stink. But I got an address.'

Jason texted back.

'Chapel.'

Jason went to the door and peered out. All seemed to be quiet. He waited for Zakary, who arrived soon after.

"What happened?" he said.

"We lost him."

"OK, well, that sleazy friend of his gave me an address. Let's check it out before they can get away."

It was forty-five minutes later by the time they had located the house and a taxi to get them there. It was set in the magnificent Austrian countryside, nestled among the dense trees. A long driveway took them to a mansion that looked fit for a prince. They got out of the taxi, the only car to be seen.

Jason asked the taxi driver to wait, and he and Zakary cupped their hands and looked through the window.

A cleaner suddenly loomed, and both she and the men jumped.

"No one here," she said in broken English through the glass. "All gone."

"When?" Zak asked.

"Now, now, they leave, all gone."

"Did they leave an address?" asked Jason.

Zak gave him a sideways glance and raised his eyes.

"You never know," Jason argued back.

They got back into the car and directed the driver back to the city.

"I don't understand why he is running from us," said Zakary.

"*Because he puts independence and freedom above all else. Being part of the Zodiac Warrior mob means commitment. He never was a team player,*" Plaadio explained.

"So why not let him be?" asked Zak, "Do you need him? Does he not have a choice?"

"*Amrez's power is in his bow and arrow. He can find whatever he is looking for. Without him we might not even find the other Warriors, or my pod."*

"But without the other Warriors, we may not find him. You saw how fast he ran, and now he knows we are here," said Zak.

"I'll text Stevie. Perhaps he can bring Gemini here to help," Jason suggested.

After many long hours later, the taxi pulled up outside the modest home of Tammy Rutherford. It was evening and birds were fluttering to their roosts. Jill pressed an enormous wad of cash into the driver's hand. With a searching look into his soul, she asked that he not repeat what he saw at the NSA headquarters.

Jill knocked at the door. A dishevelled Stevie opened it up a crack.

"Hello?" he said warily.

"I'm Jill Mayer. I'm here to see the Gemini twins."

Stevie's mouth formed an 'O'. He poked his head out and scanning the front yard.

"Who sent you?"

"No one, I... I received a message from Castor and Pollux."

"They said Regida would come. Who are you?"

"I am Regida, that's my Horoscopian name," Jill said as she brought out the medallions.

Stevie opened the door wide and let her in.

"You're a Zodiac Warrior?"

"Yes, but please, we must keep it quiet. I am acting as human. Where are Gemini?"

Stevie touched his belt, and the duo emerged. They smiled at the sight of Jill and they bowed and touched heads.

"Something terrible has happened. My friend Lily, who has the Aries medallion, has disappeared..." Stevie began.

Jill held up her hand.

"I know, she is with me..."

"What the hell! Where is she then?"

Stevie went to the door, but Jill put a hand on his arm.

"She is with Prymaw. We broke out of the facility..."

Stevie interrupted, "What facility? What are you talking about? Where is Lily?"

"Your friend is hurt, and she will need some medical attention. She went into the medallion with Prymaw, but we must be ready when they actualize."

"Oh my God!" Stevie said, at once relieved and worried.

Ma walked into the hallway.

"More visitors, Steven? You are becoming quite the entertainer!"

"Ma, this is Jill, she's a... she has some of the Zodiac Warriors with her. Lily is with them but hurt. Can you fetch the first aid kit?"

Tammy nodded. "You better come and sit in the front room. What sort of injuries are we talking about?"

"Glass, she has lost blood."

Stevie raked his fingers through his hair. He paced back and forth across the room. All he really wanted was to smoke some weed and forget about all this.

Once Tammy had returned with hot water, bandages, glue stitches and antiseptic, Jill placed the medallions of Aries and Scorpio on the coffee table. She spoke in her language, and Prymaw and Fyon appeared. Stevie and Tammy looked at the two new Warriors with open mouths. Prymaw held a limp Lily in his arms. He laid her gently on the sofa, she moaned.

"Lily, Lily? It's Stevie, are you OK?"

"Mind out the way Stevie, let me take a look at her." Tammy placed a hand on her son's shoulder.

She bent down on her stiff knees and cleaned the wound on Lily's face, gently placing glue stitches across the gash on her cheek. She bandaged her arms and asked Stevie to get her some water. She crushed painkillers and mixed them in the water and helped Lily sip it.

The Zodiac Warriors took up all the space in the living room. They listened to Regida. She told them of her life living on earth as a human, called Jillena Mayer, and how she had found the others one by one.

Stevie sat by Lily and looked at her beautiful smooth skin, now shattered by the glass wounds. She looked pale, and she groaned as his mother cleaned her up.

"She could have concussion. She's got a couple of lumps on her head. What the hell happened to you guys?" Tammy asked.

"We had to break out of the national security facility." Regida briefly relayed the escape. "She must have fallen when we were running away."

A vibration in Stevie's pocket broke his gazing. He pulled out his phone and his eyes opened wide.

"Guys, hey guys!"

Stevie jumped up and ran to the Warriors holding his phone out.

"Look! Jason has sent a message. They've found Amrez of Sagittarius! But he ran away."

"Jason?" Lily murmured.

"Typical! Where are they?" Prymaw asked.

"They're in Vienna. He wants us to go over there."

"Once we have Amrez, then we can locate the missing Warriors with his arrow. It's about time he pulled his weight," said Fyon.

Tammy had been listening. "And how do you suppose you're going to get this one out of the country? You've just broken out of a National Security facility, plus she's in no state to travel."

"But they're not after *me*, Ma. If all the Warriors travel in their medallions with Lily, I can get us all out of America."

"Then I'm coming with you, Stevie," said Tammy.

"Ma... you don't have to..."

"I want to."

"Then it's decided. I'll contact the others to meet us there," said Jill.

"Others?" said Stevie and Tammy together.

"Yes, Leo, Libra and Cancer. I have been looking for the Zodiac Warriors for many years. They are in Ecuador. The time has come for us to help the planet."

Jill organised everything. She arranged for her housekeeper in Vienna to air the house, Villa Saphir, her family home on the banks of the Danube. It was a grand mansion in the countryside outside the city. She called the Pintado house. It had only been around thirty hours since she had left them, but Astro, who had answered the phone, told her Pedro had been talking to Chime, Teres and Degon for many hours. She gave them the address in Vienna and sent it to Jason and Zak via Qriptonite.

It had taken a dedicated level of bargaining to persuade Pedro to leave his home. Another anxiety attack setback their progress, however, he agreed on hiring a private jet and flying under heavy sedation.

Tammy and Stevie set off in the pickup to New York. Stevie's bag sat between his feet, the medallions of Virgo, Aries and Scorpio cushioned inside his clothes. It freaked him out, knowing that Lily was in there too. She had responded well to his mother's ministrations, and Prymaw had also performed some sort of energetic healing. Though she was drowsy, they explained to her that they were going to Vienna to meet up with Jason and Zakary. A slight smile had caused a wince of pain in her cheek.

Once in New York, they parked the truck in Salina's building car park. They had argued over what they were going to tell her. Stevie suggested they had won a competition to Vienna, but Tammy wanted to tell her they were going on a mother and son bonding retreat. The final story was far-fetched, but at least more believable than the truth, and it reflected the current stand-off between them.

"I told him he was out of chances, told him he needed a reality check," Ma said to Salina. "I put a pin in the map of the world and said I'd take him and leave him there. Then to find his own way home."

"Jeez, Ma. That's a bit extreme. Couldn't you just have flown him up to Alaska?"

"Nah, too easy Sal. I want him to experience a new culture, a new language. See how his privileged ass manages when he hasn't got his home comforts around him."

"Still, Vienna, that's not the worst place in the world. I'd love to go to Vienna!"

"It's what the map said," Tammy affirmed. She didn't like lying to her daughter. "Anyway, thanks for letting us use your parking. I'll be back in a week or two."

"I thought you said you're leaving him there?"

"I am, but might be nice for me to see a bit of the world too."

"That's great Ma, I'm happy for you. Wish I was coming with you!"

She turned to Stevie, who had kept his mouth shut. "Are you OK, bro?"

Stevie nodded. Sal gave him a hug and whispered in his ear, "just call me if you need anything." She kissed him on the cheek.

At the doors to the airport, Tammy and Stevie simultaneously took a deep breath before entering.

"Any luggage?" the check-in girl asked brightly.

"Only carry on," Ma replied, "travelling light."

Stevie felt his backpack weigh heavily on his shoulders, yet he was loath to place it on the conveyor at security. As he went through the body-scanner, an alarm went off. He felt sweat prickle his forehead and upper lip, a shot of adrenalin swept through his heart, which beat frantically.

The security woman pulled him to one side. She tapped down his body and felt around his waist, pausing at the belt.

"Fancy belt sir, but I'm afraid you need to take it off and put it through the x-ray."

Stevie's throat was dry. He glanced at his mom who was waiting on the other side. A security screener watched and waited, his hands resting on Stevie's backpack. He walked back through the scanner. It went off again.

"You got any coins in your pockets? Watch?"

Stevie shook his head. Then he remembered the ring he had put through his nipple as a dare one drunken night. He sheepishly lifted his t-shirt, hoping Tammy wouldn't be able to see. The guard nodded. Stevie smiled at her, though his insides had turned to sludge. Once through, the screener asked him to open his bag. Stevie undid the zip. The man poked around inside and waved his drug-detector wand over everything. He put the swab in a machine. The seconds ticked by. Tammy's fingers twitched; she knew her son smoked cannabis. Stevie held his jaw tight. The machine pinged and a green light prompted the security guard to wave him off. He gave Stevie back his bag. Stevie shoved his belt in it and they moved off.

"Got time for a drink, Ma?"

"This time I think I'll join you, son," Tammy said.

The taxi dropped Tammy and Stevie at the entrance of a huge villa. They had never seen such grandeur. Two men emerged from the enormous front door and quickly hopped down the stairs.

"I'm Zakary Salawudeen, this is Jason Wallace..." he held out a hand but looked into the taxi.

"Tammy Rutherford, and this is my son Stevie."

"Where's Lily?" Jason said, echoing Zak's thoughts.

"Ah, well..."

"What's happened?" Zakary's voice quivered. He had chewed his nails to the bone, worrying about her. He couldn't wait to see her and now...

"She's OK, she's OK." Tammy saw the panic in the man's eyes.

"She's with Prymaw," Stevie said, holding up his backpack.

Zakary put his hands to his face.

"It's OK, she'll be alright," said Tammy. "Come on, let's get inside and sort her out."

The well-furnished lounge room looked out onto the rear gardens through enormous windows. The back gardens swept down to the river. The three men and Tammy sat on the luxurious sofa, unaware of its comfort. They gazed at the medallions on the marble topped coffee table. Stevie retrieved the belt from his bag and put it next to the others.

"This is a strange business we find ourselves in," said Tammy.

"Should we bring them out?" Zakary asked.

"Yes," Plaadio answered through Jason.

Stevie held the buckle of the belt in his hands and yellow beams of light built the shapes of the twins.

Then, unbidden and unbeknownst to Jason, a thick brown fog emanated from his body and shrouded him. He shivered deeply, and Plaadio stepped forth, leaving Jason like a limp rag as he collapsed onto the sofa next to him.

"You could have warned me!" Jason gasped.

Plaadio greeted the twins in turn before grasping Jason's hand and helping him to stand again.

"I'm sorry, mate. I've been a shocking guest in your body." He cricked his neck and stretched his arms above his head. "It feels good to be out."

Plaadio looked around the room, then eyed up the trees in the garden through the window. Jason sighed and shook his head.

"Please, can we get Lily out?" Zakary implored.

Castor and Pollux agreed. They spoke to the Aries medallion, and Prymaw appeared with Lily in his arms. She flickered open her eyes and looked at the familiar faces.

"Jase! Zak!"

"Oh my God, what happened?" Jason asked.

"It's my own fault, I shouldn't have fired that gun."

"Gun! Where the hell were you?" Zakary said.

"At the American National Security facility. They had already seized Scorpio."

With that Prymaw actualized Fyon, who quivered into being. She greeted her fellow Warriors, then stalked the perimeter of the room as if checking for danger.

"Where's Jill?" Lily said.

The gravel in the driveway crunched as limousine slowly ground to a halt.

"Better bring her back before her boyfriend comes in. Apparently, she hasn't been altogether honest with him," said Tammy, pointing at the medallion.

"Jason, can you let them in," said Zakary. "I'm gonna help Lily get to her room."

Zakary swept Lily up in his arms and he carried her upstairs to her room to rest.

Lily clung to his neck and looked into his face. It was etched with concern. She smiled.

"Lighten up, Romeo!"

Zak smiled. "That makes you Juliette. I was so worried about you. What happened?"

She told him what she could remember of being kidnapped and the break out, though it felt like she was grasping at the tail end of a dream.

"So Prymaw took you into the medallion? What was in there?"

There were no words to describe the feelings she was left with. They were even harder than describing a dream, and she was not sure she wanted too.

"I don't remember. It's like I was under anaesthetic, I guess."

"It was weird, you not being here. I didn't like it. I always want you to be here, Lily."

Lily's heart did a flip. She smiled and reached her hands to his face. He gently stroked the wound on her cheek and leaned over, brushing his lips on it. At last, his lips made it to hers. After a lingering kiss, Lily patted the bed next to her. She curled up in his arms and fell asleep.

Castor and Pollux turned their attention to the Virgo medallion. An aqua green light-show flickered from the medallion, casting their faces in a bath of light that made them look alien. The light disappeared just as Tim and John entered the room. Jill sat down on the sofa.

"Jill, darling."

Tim went down on his knees. He took her in his arms and whispered, "God, I've missed you," in her ear. He looked into her deep green eyes. "Are you OK my love? You look different?"

Jill smiled and kissed him. "I'm fine."

Astro wheeled Pedro in behind them. His Panama hat was pulled down as far as possible over his eyes, and sweat ran down the creases in his face. John and Tim rolled their eyes.

"I never want to be in the air again! I need more medication. Astro, get my pills!"

"Remember who you are, señor. Remember what we talked about? With the Zodiac Warriors? You are Xincon of Cancer."

For a moment, a flash of the powerful crab-like body took the place of the man. But the massive form of Pedro returned, and he wiped his face with a towel supplied by Astro. Jason, Tammy and Stevie gawked at the huge man, unsure if he was human or Horoscopian.

"I don't know what you are talking about. You are wicked, evil. This is a trick. I want to go home. I want to go home now!" Pedro yelled, spit foaming at the corners of his mouth.

"Insufferable," John muttered.

Astro shook three pills from a bottle and Pedro greedily knocked them back and closed his eyes.

"I am Prymaw of Aries, this is Plaadio of Capricorn and the Gemini twins Castor and Pollux."

The humans then introduced themselves.

"Please, let us bring out our comrades!" Prymaw said.

Tim opened his briefcase and took out the medallions of Leo, Libra and Taurus. One by one, the Warriors emerged until they outnumbered the humans in the room.

Jason was astonished at the different forms and quietly took photos of the Zodiac Warriors as they emerged.

After the customary greeting and more introductions had been made, Degon spoke.

"Tell me what has happened. I have been absent fae too long."

"We have all been absent, Degon," Prymaw said. "We will all speak one by one..."

"That will take too long. Tell me, who is yet to be found?" Degon growled.

"Amrez, Haastia of Aquarius and the Piscean sisters," Pollux listed.

"But we know Amrez is in Vienna," Plaadio added, "we saw him two days ago."

"How can you be sure it was he? His form is not one that fits with this world."

"Yes, Degon. I am sure. Besides, he was gazing at his medallion. I do not know how he has managed to be in the shape of a human, but I know it was he."

"Two days ago, you say? That over-indulging idiot will be long gone by now," Degon roared.

"Keep your mane on Degon. We need to come up with a plan to catch him. I'll make him see sense," Fyon said.

"And we have no idea where Aquarius and Pisces are?" Chime asked.

"No, but with Amrez's arrow, we can find them both," said Plaadio.

"Not necessarily." Stevie spoke for the first time. "We can make an estimate of where their medallions landed based on the locations of all yours."

Stevie unzipped his backpack and pulled out his laptop. He fired it up and pulled up a map on the screen.

"I've input the locations of Gemini, Virgo, Scorpio, Capricorn and Aries. If I put in the other five, I can run an algorithm to discover where the last two are."

"Or we could just catch Amrez," said Degon, who was standing in the middle of the room.

"Give the boy a chance, Degon. He knows what he's talking about," Castor said.

"I don't trust these humans," Fyon said as she paced backwards and forwards past the floor to ceiling windows. "They are a dangerous mix of fearful and armed."

"Whatevs," Stevie said and snapped his laptop shut.

"We are all in it together, humans and Horoscopians," Chime broke in. "We can help each other."

Fyon pffted at Chime's remark.

"Let's work this out in a logical order. If we find Amrez..." said Plaadio.

"If, if! That self-centred peacock will give us the run around until the black hole comes. We can't expect to wait for him," Teres added. "I say give the boy a chance."

Stevie hiked his bag on his bag and left the room, shaking his head.

"Thank God that toxic little wretch has gone," Pedro sighed, "he's like a dark cloud of acid rain."

"Now look here, mister. I don't know who or what the hell you are, but you done nothing but complain since you got wheeled into this room. Then you go ahead and insult my boy like he's a maggot. And you others..." Tammy turned to the Warriors scattered around the room, "dismissing him like he's a dim-witted nobody. I'm done with you too."

She left, leaving John, Tim, Jason and Astro.

"Astro, give me my pills!"

"But Señor, you have already taken too many. I think it wise to rest..."

"Stupid imbecile! I said pills, now!"

Pedro grabbed Astro's wrist and pulled them close to his sweating face.

"I pay you to do as I ask, you pathetic little idiot!"

Astro breathed in and set their lips in a tight line. "Then I quit, Señor. I will not be your slave anymore. You get your own pills."

They wrenched their arm from Pedro's grip and left the room.

"This race is emotional," Chime said as the door slammed for the second time. "We need to understand that."

"They are weak," Degon said.

"And they disguise it with their weapons," Fyon added. "Regida, you are very quiet. What say you, sister?"

The room went silent. Tim glanced from Jill to Fyon and back to Jill.

"Regida?" Tim asked. "Who is Regida?"

But he knew the answer in his heart. Everything about his fiancée suddenly made sense. He swallowed, "Jill? Are you...?"

Regida was motionless. Inside she felt a piece of her heart fall away, yet her face showed no emotion, for the Virgo race do not cry.

"Timmy, I wanted to tell you, the time was never right. It's complicated..."

"You're a Zodiac? You've used me! You tricked me and my father so you could find this... this freak show!" he waved his hands at the Warriors.

"Timmy..."

"Don't, Jill, or whatever your name is. I... I can't stay here."

Tim, white faced, stalked from the room. John looked around

them, giving a long blast of air through his nose. He shook his head and followed his son.

Fyon stood at the window. The light beams shone onto her skin that radiated a deep chestnut hue. Jason snapped a photo.

Suddenly, Fyon's tail snapped the camera out of his hands.

"Stop shooting that thing!"

She tossed the camera, Jason's prized possession, into the corner.

"NO!" Jason fell to his knees and picked up the shattered pieces. "No, no, no! Not my camera! You bitch!" he yelled. "They should have kept you locked in that facility. You accuse us of being dangerous! You were the first to kill a man. I should just call the American embassy and tell them where you all are."

Fyon, Degon and Prymaw stood over Jason.

"Leave him be," Plaadio said, "he will not."

"And who the hell do you think you are?" Jason stood and pushed past the three Warriors. He faced Plaadio.

"You inhabit my body and suddenly think you know me? If you'd even just listened to Stevie, or let me get a word in, we could have helped you. Zak and I know exactly where Amrez will be tomorrow. But no, you are a bunch of self-absorbed narcissists. For superpowered aliens with all your muscles and clever tricks, you are no better than us."

Jason pulled a flyer out of his pocket and threw it on the table. He stomped out of the room, leaving the Zodiac Warriors gazing at the words 'The Donauinselfest. DJ Rez headlining!'.

Stevie stormed into the grand hall and punched the wall. All he wanted was to light up a big reefer and forget about everything. He took the duty-free bottle of whisky he'd bought out of his bag, cracked the lid and took a swig. The front door was open. He could hear the raised Warriors' voices. He didn't feel much hope for the planet if they were to be its saviours. Not for the first time, he felt a wave of fatigue pass over him. Life felt pointless. Like it needed too much of his energy to push on, and for what?

The summer afternoon drew him out. The villa looked over fields and hills, yellowing in the dry summer sun, yet still picturesque, peaceful. He wandered into the garden. An oak tree offered a wide trunk, and he flopped down under its branches and took another swig. The hum of insects calmed him. He inhaled the unfamiliar scent of a different country and closed his eyes.

"Mind if I join you?"

The accented voice of Astro startled him.

Stevie took them in for a moment. Astro's cheeks were red, and they had tears in their eyes. Stevie shrugged his assent. Astro sat next to him and he offered them the bottle.

"Gracia," they took the bottle and slugged.

"How come you're not with... what's his name? Pigro?"

"Ha! I just quit."

"Good on you. He doesn't seem the greatest of bosses."

"No, I put up with him for too long."

They sat in silence, sharing the whisky.

"I think you should look at your computer and work out where the others might be."

"What's the point. No one gonna listen to a punk-headed stoner."

"Maybe, maybe not." Astro shrugged. "Maybe we can show them we have our own skills?"

"I don't even know why I'm here. This is all crazy."

Astro unzipped their bum bag and extracted a lighter, then a skinny joint. They put it to their lips, lit it up and took a drag.

"You want?"

Stevie's face broke into a rare smile. He took the joint and relished the fragrant smoke.

"Didn't pick you as a smoker," Stevie commented.

"I needed something to keep me sane in that house. The only reason I stayed was because of Chime. She's a good one, you know?"

Stevie looked sceptical.

"She told me about all the Warriors. She said they are out of balance until they are altogether. Aquarius and Pisces are women. They need all of them."

"So?"

"We could find them, you and me."

"Find what?" Ma had walked over.

"The last two Warriors. I asked Stevie to run his check. Maybe we could find them."

Stevie coughed and stubbed the joint out by his side. Tammy ignored him, trying to cover up. She smiled.

"Do it, son."

"But do you know where the other medallions were found?" Stevie asked Astro.

"Si."

Stevie took a drink and wiped his mouth with the back of his hand. He looked at Astro, who held his gaze.

"Alright."

He handed them the bottle and took his laptop out of his backpack.

"Tell me."

Astro gave Stevie the areas where Libra, Cancer, Taurus and Leo were found. They knew that Lily discovered Aries in Tanzania, Virgo originated from Egypt, Capricorn in the north of Australia. They guessed Sagittarius was in or close to Vienna. Stevie knew the twins had been somewhere in north China before they wound up in New York.

"Where was Fyon?"

"I don't know."

"Shit, the internet is patchy. I need some power to generate the algorithm."

"What are you up to? Why are you out here?" A voice said.

Zakary had seen the three of them under the tree from Lily's bedroom window.

"Those muy stupido Zodiac Warriors. We quit them," Astro said.

"How is Lily?" Stevie asked.

"She's sleeping. We talked a while. She will be fine. So, what's going on? Why did you quit?" Zak asked, looking toward the house at the moment Tim and John launched themselves through the front door. Tim held his hands to his head, his father talking to him seriously.

"What on earth is going on?" Zak asked.

Tammy approached them and called them over. "What happened in there now?"

"She's one of them... Jill. She's a goddamn Zodiac."

"I'm sorry, Tim. We only found out before we left. She made us swear not to say anything," said Tammy, holding her old gardener's hands in the air.

A roar of rage reverberated from the house and a door slammed. Jason stormed out and roared again, swearing.

"Hey, Jase, man! Calm down!" Zakary said. "What happened?"

Jason stalked to the group. "That fricking bitch smashed my camera!"

"Who, Jill?" Tim asked.

"No, that scorpion mutant." Tears of frustration wet Jason's eyes.

"Ah man, I'm sorry."

Lily appeared at the top of the steps. "What's all this racket, you guys. Can't you let a chick sleep?"

Zakary trotted over to her.

"I'm sorry, Lily. Things have gone a bit pear-shaped down here. Come and sit down with us."

Jason gave Lily a hug. "You haven't met these guys yet. Astro, John and Tim, this is Lily."

They shook hands. "How and where did you all find them?" she asked.

"Well, we've just found out that my girlfriend is one of them. She must have been searching for... God knows how long. Oh my God, Dad, she must have got to you through me. The conniving..."

"What do you mean, Tim?"

"Dad, you've been on this Zodiac mission forever. You published research, it's not like people don't know about you."

"Lily, do you know where Scorpio was discovered?"

Lily pulled away from John. "Wyoming, why?"

"We're going to find the other Warriors. Stevie has his programme running right now," Astro explained.

Stevie typed in the final co-ordinate and hit enter.

The group was silent, waiting. They could hear the voices of the arguing Zodiac Warriors in the distance. Stevie's computer beeped, and he zoomed into a spot on the map.

"Booya! I've got one."

They all leaned over his shoulder and looked at his screen.

"Alaska," they all said together.

Sandra knew the men and women she worked with called her Woof. She preferred to liken herself to a salmon swimming upriver. There was no doubt in her mind she would reach her destination and no way she could stop in that pursuit. It just meant she had to keep on swimming and be smart about it. Which is why she watched the CCTV footage of every car that arrived and left the vicinity of Fort George Meade the night of the break out. She was lucky it was late in the evening, still there were a lot of license plates to run through the system and follow up. She was also curious as to where Lily Noor had stayed the night before Schwartz and his team had apprehended her. Surely Lily Noor wouldn't have come all the way from Australia to the United States with the medallion if it wasn't something to do with the so-called Zodiac Warriors. When she got bored with searching for people in the Fort Meade area, she swapped to getting footage from the JFK airport and searching for Lily. Cleverly, Lily had made up a false name, but Sandra soon matched the passport photo with the slight Asian woman who arrived in New York that day. Sandra punched the air when she saw Lily had flashed her gold medallion at the young man. It was harder working out where she went, as the cameras were not so helpful in the car parking area. When she hit a dead end, she returned to Fort Meade. Slowly but surely, she eliminated person by person until she thought she identified a New York registered taxi. She waded through hours of footage, following the car until the trail went cold.

The next day, Sandra left the digital world of her laptop to visit to the taxi driver in the real world. As she drove into the city, cars were leaving laden down with supplies. New York was in a state of panic. There was even a police cordon around Central Park where people were trying to collect the water from the Reservoir. She eventually made it to the address of the taxi driver. With rather too much persuasion, he finally gave up the address. Once she had let him out of the headlock, he shook his head and said, "I wouldn't go there, miss. I'd leave them well alone. You have no idea what you're dealing with."

"And you, my man, have no idea who they are dealing with. Have a nice day."

It was a long and boring drive to Newton Falls on the New York State Thruway. Sandra adored civilisation. City life was her oxygen and she never really dug the colour green. She shared the road with cars and caravans as people escaped the dry city for places where they hope they could access fresh water. She drove slowly past the address in Newton Falls and parked her car under some trees a way down the road. Though it did nothing for the rest of her outfit, she changed into sneakers. A pickup truck was parked outside the modest house. The engine was crackling under the bonnet, and she felt the heat of it with her hand. Someone was home. She took a photo of the license plate and pulled a little box from the handbag slung across her body. Sandra placed a battery-powered GPS tracker under the car, and it attached with a satisfying magnetic thud. She crept to the side of the house, edging her head around the window. The kitchen was empty. Cups and crockery had been left unwashed in the sink. She heard a door close in the house and ducked down. She took in the backyard of the house. A lush and extensive garden spread out the back. A large barn adjoined it. Sandra took another peek into the window and dashed across to the barn. She squeezed in the door. It smelt of hay and dried cow manure. She sneezed. It was dim in the barn, so she lit up her phone torch and scanned it across the ground. The fine dust on the ground showed footprints. She followed the boot prints and found not more footprints but hoofprints, enormous ones. She checked for others and the prints were in pairs, not four for a bull or cow. Placing a dime by the prints, she took photos to show the size. A quick search on the net showed these were super-size cattle hoofs. A car door slammed. She got up and left the barn, turning the GPS tracker on.

"Alaska! Where in Alaska? That's not the easiest place to find something," Tammy said.

"The co-ordinate is actually off the coast, in the Bering Sea," Stevie replied. "I don't know if that makes it harder or easier."

"I propose we go and find it," John said, relishing an opportunity to explore.

"All of us?" Zakary said.

"I'm more than happy to get out of here," Tim said and sighed.

"I will have to stay. I lost my passport in the US National Security facility," Lily said. "Plus, they'll be looking for me."

"Someone has to stay to look after these numb nuts," said Tammy.

"I'll stay with you," Zakary said. "You're not strong enough to be here on your own."

"I'm fine!"

"Jason, John, Tammy?" Astro asked.

They nodded. Tim was already on his phone to book flights.

"Do we tell the Zodiac Warriors?"

"Nah, they are too self-absorbed to care," Jason said.

"They'll need our help to find Amrez anyway," said Zakary.

"Just make sure they don't do anything stupid," said John. "If they start running around Vienna, the whole world will want a piece of them."

"And the Americans will come swooping in and it will be the end of them."

"Suits me," said Jason.

"Come on, Jase. They are our only hope to bring our planet back from the brink."

"Are they? They don't seem to be able to organise a comeback in a rubber band factory."

"How many seats am I booking?" Tim asked.

They counted and Stevie confirmed, "Five."

Thirty hours later, the group landed in Anchorage, Alaska. It was late in the evening, but the sky was light. They waited an hour for the daily plane to the small town of Nome on the Seward Peninsula coast of the Bering Sea.

Tim had booked the motel ahead of time and the party shivered in their European summer clothes and entered the basic accommodation.

"Talk about riches to rags!" Tim commented.

"With Stevie's co-ordinates, it shouldn't take us too long to find the medallion," Tammy said.

"At over 50 metres in the freezing Bering Sea. God knows where it could be now! If they landed over six million years ago, it could be anywhere."

Everyone was quiet, the futility of their impulsive decision sinking in.

"Well, we can but try," John said. "I've come across some wonders in my time and unless modern humans have interfered, relics and remains stay pretty close to where they originated. Question is, how do we get to the exact location if it's in the water?"

"Look!" Astro said.

They were looking out to the ocean and the silhouettes and bobbing lights of fishermen's boats could be easily seen in the dusk.

"Those guys must know the Bering Sea like the back of their hands, and if there has been any strange activity around here in the past," they said.

"Let's get some sleep and ask around in the morning," Tammy said, yawning.

They all woke early, the daylight intruding on their sleep-deprived eyes at an unearthly hour.

"How the hell do people sleep around here?" Tammy said grumpily.

"Eye masks," said Jason, waving a silky padded piece of material in the air.

The server came to their table in the little restaurant and poured coffee in each cup without asking. No one objected. The waft of bacon and toast improved their moods, and they breakfasted quietly.

Stevie's phone beeped, and he retrieved it from his jean's pocket. "Sal!"

Tammy looked up. "Put her on speaker."

"Hi Stevie, where are you guys? I've been trying to call you both."

"Hey kiddo, sorry we should have let you know..." Tammy said.

"Know what? Are you OK?"

"Yes, there's been bit of a change of plan. We're in Alaska," Stevie said.

"What? Wait... Alaska? Alaska USA?"

"Er, yeah."

"But you were going to Vienna..."

"It's a long story, honey," Tammy said.

"OK, well, never mind. It's probably good actually..." Sal's voice wavered.

"What's wrong, Sal?" Stevie said.

The others had stopped eating, hearing the tension in her voice.

"Things have gone ass up here. Haven't you seen the news?"

"What's happened, honey? Are you OK?"

"Something's going down," Tim scrolled through news sites on his phone.

"What?"

"They've run out of water in New York. People are rioting. It's going crazy."

"How can the city run out of water?"

"Listen Sal. Just get the hell out of there. Come to Alaska. There's some major shit happening here too," Stevie said.

"Get on a plane to Anchorage. There's a daily flight from there to Nome. We've got some powerful allies on our side. I promise you nothing bad will happen," Tammy added.

"What are you talking about?"

"We're looking for someone. Something."

"Ma, you're being weird."

"Just get out of there, Sal," Stevie put in. "You can help us."

"OOOkay, I'll let you know when I leave." She hung up.

"Let's go and find some fisherman," said John.

"And maybe some scuba divers?" said Jason. "I'm sure as hell not getting into that water."

It was still early enough for the returning fishermen to be washing down their decks and carting their haul to freezers. The party layered up and made their way through the small town to the jetty.

"Any shipwrecks out there?" John asked one of the fishermen.

"There sure is," the man answered gruffly.

"Does anyone go diving out there?"

"One or two crazy mothers, yeah."

"Where do I find one of these mothers?" John asked.

"Bering Bell. You'll find Mad-eye Mack propped up in the corner."

Stevie and Jason walked to the end of the jetty and looked out to sea. Stevie lit a rolled cigarette under his windcheater and inhaled deeply.

"So where do your coordinates lie?" Jason asked.

Stevie looked at the sun and orientated himself. Finding north, he stuck his arms out towards the left of the jetty. "Out there about 25 miles."

"Should be pretty easy to locate."

"Hmm, doesn't mean that the medallion is there. They say the currents aren't that strong out there, but let's face it, could be anywhere."

"I'm not giving up till we do, mate. Show those so-called Warriors what us humans are made of."

"How'd it feel having one inside you?"

"You make it sound dirty!"

"Ew! You know what I mean, man!" Stevie punched Jason in the arm.

"Bloody strange. I never knew when he was going to arc up. But strong too. I mean, you should see how he scales a tree, a building. I felt like I was high and stone-cold sober at the same time."

Jason took some photos with the new camera Tim had bought him at the airport.

"How's the whizz bang new camera?"

"A. Mazing. Way better than that the piece of crap I was using. That Scorpio thing did me a favour."

"Funny how things work out, hey?"

They heard a whistle and turned to see Tammy motioning them over. They walked towards her and Astro.

"What you got, Ma?"

"Just been chatting to the skipper of that trawler over there. He told us about an area they call the Fisherman's Foe."

"What's that?"

"He said there is a rip or something about twenty miles due south east where many fishing boats have sunk. He reckons there are dozens of wrecks down there. The fishermen avoid it at all costs," Astro explained.

"Do they know what causes it?"

"No, no one has been interested in investigating it. They just steer clear. It's under ice for most of the year, they don't have time."

"That's got to be it, hasn't it?" Jason said.

"Can he show us on a chart where it is?" Stevie asked.

"I'll go and ask him," Tammy offered.

The group reconvened at the Bering Bell and ordered fish and chips and pints of beer. They looked at the map on Stevie's laptop. The fisherman had shown Tammy on the chart, and it fell within a kilometre of Stevie's coordinate.

"So, let's say that's where the medallion is... why is it causing boats to go down?" Tim asked.

"Good question. Perhaps an Aquarian hasn't got their hands on it?" Astro said.

"Are there any stories in the area of strange sightings? For example, there were local stories that told of Plaadio in the Northern Territory. There could be some clues."

"I can check out the library," Tammy said.

"Yeah, there's a museum up the road too," John added.

"I'll do some online research," Jason said.

"See that man over there?" Tim said, nodding his head to the end of the bar.

They all surreptitiously glanced at the grisly looking man, cradling a pint.

"That must be Mad-eye Mack. They told us about him at the jetty. He's a diver, and might be mad enough to help us out."

"Do you want to talk to him, Tim?" Tammy said.

Tim shrugged and agreed.

"There's one thing I've been thinking," Tammy said. "Salina, she's an Aquarius, you know. Maybe we should wait for her to arrive. Then we can get her to actualize the medallion."

"Well, I'll never forget her birthday again," Stevie said. "She texted me to say she'll be here tomorrow morning. So sounds good."

"Meet back here at around six?"

"Sorry, we're late," said John to the assembled group. "How did everyone go? Astro and I had a fascinating chat with Dorothy, who works at the museum. Did you know that the Iñupiat people originally came from the Thule culture and migrated from islands in the Bering Sea around 300 BC?"

"Well, we do now, Dad." Tim rolled his eyes. "But did she tell you anything that might give us some clues to what we're dealing with out there?" Tim pointed towards the sea.

"Ah, yes, forgive my digression. There is a local legend that on the longest day of the year in the middle of June, the sun's beams become gold dust. There is gold in certain areas of the Bering Sea, you know. In fact, right at the beginning of the twentieth century, little old Nome was awash with over 10,000 people all looking for gold..."

"Dad, please!"

"Oh sorry!" John knocked his head with his knuckles. "So, the story goes that a sea creature, not a mermaid, but some force, gathered up the gold dust in a whirlpool. Some believe there is a huge nugget of gold in the ocean there. But the sea creature jealously guards it and so whenever anyone gets close, it dashes the boats to pieces."

"That ties in with what Mad-eye Mack told me," Tim said. "He's been obsessed with that story and has tried to find this sea creature three times. Lost his sight in one eye thanks to the last attempt. But get this. He told me he found a nugget of gold down there on one dive. He said the sea and sand had shaped it into a pebble. When he picked it up and brought it up to his vessel, it gained so much weight that they had to hoist it up to the boat. After they released it out of the net, it dropped clean through the deck, out the bottom of the boat and back into the sea. A splinter from the deck flicked up and stabbed him in the eye."

They all shook their heads in disbelief.

"It must be the medallion; smooth like a pebble, a gold colour."

"But why can't they bring it to air?" Jason asked.

"Aquarius is an air sign, actually," Astro spoke up. "It is the water bearer. It holds the vessel of water, which relates to the emotions. This world is full, so full, of emotions. You all saw how Pedro suffered. He is also sensitive to the internal landscape of those around him."

"So, are you saying that whenever it comes up to the air, the sorrows of the world become too much for it to bear?" Tammy asked.

"Si, sorrows and joys! It is a world overflowing with humans and our emotions."

"Perhaps if the Aquarius Warrior is brought out, then she can carry it without it being too heavy," Tammy suggested.

"Tim, do you think Mad-eye Mack is up for one final attempt? And can we trust him with the Warrior?" John asked.

"Look, why don't we invite him over for a chat?"

"I'm not sure he'll be able to talk much. He's been sitting there all day trying to find the bottom of his glass," Tammy said.

They all went silent.

"What else can we do, Ma? We have a pretty good idea the medallion is out there, and he knows the sea better than any of us. He must have contacts."

"Gotta say he has a point, Tammy," Jason said. "I don't see any friendly scuba diving tours in town."

"It's dangerous out there. Around thirty fishermen lose their lives on the Bering Sea every year. I reckon that sea creature is a ferocious force through the whole strait," Tim added. "I'm going to talk to him."

Tim pushed his chair back and went over to Mad-eye Mack, whose head was now nodding over his pint. He spoke to him and gestured towards the table. Mad-eye cast the group an uninterested look, but Tim persisted, and the huge body of Mad-eye Mack finally dislodged itself from his stool. Tim pulled up a chair and introduced him to everyone. Mack wore a thick jumper over his barrel chest, holes and frayed edges peppering the sleeves. His long black hair was tied back with wide grey strands scattered throughout. An uneven yellowing beard matched his milky eye, which he cast around the table. Tim bought Mack another drink with a whisky chaser.

"Thanks for joining us, Mack," John said. "As I think my son Tim here explained, we're needing to find an artifact which we believe to be in the area known as the Fisherman's Foe. We'd like to accompany you on what we can almost certainly say will be your last and successful quest to find the gold you've been looking for all these years. Tammy's daughter will join us tomorrow and I'm sure she'll agree to diving with you to retrieve it."

"We should also tell you that the medallion is extremely power-ful. But it's not something that can be exchanged for money," Tammy said. "There is a responsibility that comes with it."

"I have accurate coordinates of where it should be. With your knowledge, we can probably locate it pretty quickly," Stevie put in.

"And at this time of the year, I'm guessing it's pretty calm out there?" Jason asked, already feeling green at the thought of it.

Mad-eye Mack put his hands on the table, as if to steady himself. His good eye peered at each one, then he put his head back and let out a rumbling laugh. The rumble grew into a roar, and he slapped the table with his enormous fingers. Tears dripped from his good eye.

Once he caught his breath, and his laughter fully discharged, he said, "You pale-faced pack of fine talking lilywhites would'na last a minute on a boat moored in a bath. That's even if I could find a rig to take us out. But thank y'all for the entertainment. I haven't had a laugh like that for ten years!"

He scraped the chair back, stood up and downed the whisky.

"Best of luck to ya."

Mack stumbled to his stool and retrieved his parka. He left the pub chuckling to himself, leaving the table of outsiders in silence.

"There must be something that can persuade him," Astro said. "Everyone has a weak spot."

"I'll go after him," Tammy said. "One oldie to another."

"No, Ma! He's drunk and looks like a nut job."

"I'm fine, Stevie. Don't fuss over me, I've wrangled more than a drunk old goat with one eye before."

Tammy left the pub, shrugging on her jacket before stepping into the cold night.

Sandra sipped her third coffee at Ogdensburg International Airport. She would have to make it last since three were her self-imposed limit per day. As she was waiting for the plane to leave for Anchorage, she had continued the most intense search she had ever made. Jillena Mayer had certainly been a master at covering her tracks. Sandra wasn't entirely sure if she was onto the right person. She had been taken down several rabbit holes that resulted in a dead end. And she had got lost several times trying to find her way back. She was almost certain that an address outside Vienna belonged to this woman, or alien, but she needed to go there herself. As soon as she had apprehended the people in Alaska, she would go on a trip to Europe. It was times like this she really loved her job.

"Hey, hold up Mack!" she called to his disappearing hulk. She walked fast to catch up. "Hey, hey, Mack!"

He stopped and turned around. She bustled up to him.

"Can I talk to you? Just for a minute."

She was out of breath.

"Look lady, I'm not taking anyone out on some hopeless quest. My diving days are over."

"But you know there's something out there, right?"

"There's helluva lot out there, don't mean I have to go chasing after it."

Tammy paused for a moment.

"What happened on that last trip?"

"I'm also not interested in dredging up the past. Good night to you."

He made to walk off.

"Did you lose someone out there, Mack?"

He stopped.

"I can tell," she said to his back. "I know the look of that weight of grief, gnawing away at your life force. Churning events over and over, wishing something had gone different."

Mack turned around and faced her.

"I've never told anyone, but I believe I was responsible for the death of my husband."

Mack looked up at the stars in the sky and sighed.

"You can tell me what you gotta tell me, lady, but I ain't taking you out there."

Tammy forged on. Truth was she needed to tell someone. A drunk stranger living on the edge of existence would do.

"It was me who got him smoking, when we first met, my Bill. We were just teenage sweethearts experimenting, and I dared him to smoke a ciggie. I got him to start but could never get him to stop. He died of lung cancer 10 years ago. I miss him every day. Tried to raise my kids right, but then Stevie went off the rails. They needed their Pa. I've spent every minute since regretting that day. And now something's come into my life that's given it meaning again. Something bigger than me, bigger than all of us, pulled me out of that stinking hole of regret, and that's what I'm offering to you."

She took her phone out of her bag and, squinting without her glasses, pulled up a photo she'd taken of the Gemini medallion.

"Does this look like that nugget you found?"

"Bugger me!"

"There are twelve altogether, Mack. And they're not gold."

She paused, aware that this could send him on his way.

"Well?"

"I've seen what comes out of these medallions and I swear on my children's life, and Bill's memory, God rest his soul, they are much, much more valuable than gold."

"There ain't nothing more valuable than gold, lady."

"The name's Tammy. And these 'nuggets' are from another galaxy; they hold the life forms from the planets that were in it. We reckon it's what's caused the boats to go down around there."

Mad-eye Mack looked at Tammy's face.

"I know you've spent your life looking for that gold and I'm guessing you lost more than your eye on one of those trips."

Mack looked beyond Tammy's shoulder.

"I lost my boy out there. He was as crazy as I was for the gold, and we knew no one else would go near Fishermen's Foe. I was old and stubborn, and he was young and reckless. Made a good pair. He went back down after the gold dropped through the deck. Said he'd catch it. The boat was taking in water. I waited as long as I could with a splinter of wood sticking out of my eye, but he never came back up. I should've drowned with him that day. Drowning myself here anyway."

Tammy took a deep breath. She reached out a hand and touched the top of his arm.

"Nothing I can say will help you, I know that. But taking us out there to find this medallion will help all of us. It might not feel like it out here in the back of beyond, but this planet is dying, Mack. The Warriors that live in these medallions can help us save it. I know it sounds like a tall story, but I seen it with my own eyes."

"My grandma was Iñupiat. She told me every story has a bone of truth in it. She showed me how to gauge a person. I do believe you, Tammy, but there ain't a boat from Anchorage to Barrow that would take you there. Too many's been lost."

"What about your boat?"

"Ha! That piece of junk barely made it back to the port. It's just a rotting carcass."

"Will you try, Mack? We won't leave here until we find a way to get that medallion."

Mack shook his head and grasped his beard, pulling it down his chin.

"I'll ask around."

Tammy squeezed his shoulder. Mack nodded and left her standing under the pale glow of the night sky.

❄

The next morning, Tammy waited anxiously at the tiny airport, watching the sky for Salina's plane. Eventually it drifted in, and her daughter emerged onto the tarmac looking washed out.

"Hey honey!"

"Ma, it's so good to see you. New York is going nuts. You can only turn the water on for two hours a day. People are rioting and others are getting out of the city. The roads are packed, airports full of security. And that's not all..."

"Hush now, you're here now. Let's get to the motel. I was worried about you. Stevie's looking forward to seeing you. I have so much to tell you and it's pretty out there. Now, how are your scuba diving skills?"

"Diving? I did a brief course about three years ago in Hawaii, remember? I got pretty good at holding my breath, but I wouldn't count it as a skill though. Why?"

Tammy drove Sal back to the motel where the others were waiting at the reception. After brotherly hugs and introductions, Tammy sat Sal down. They all got a coffee from the vending machine and sat down on the threadbare sofas in the reception.

"So, what's going on, Sal?" Tammy asked.

"Everything in New York has gone crazy. There's no water, people are panicking. Everyone was leaving, heading for the lakes. I left. Called you guys. I drove your truck back to Newton Falls. I wanted to pick up some warm clothes for Alaska. I got to the house and," she paused.

"What, Sal," Stevie said.

"Someone was snooping around the house."

"Who?"

"It was a woman, a black woman. I was in the cellar looking for my ski jacket. When I came back up the stairs, I saw her looking into the kitchen window."

"Did she see you?"

"No. She went into the barn. I was scared. I just got into the car and drove. Flew straight out of Ogdensburg International Airport."

"They found Lily. They're on to us too."

"Who is onto us? Who is Lily?"

"Probably CIA."

"CIA? What the hell is going on here?"

Tim and John wondered if their homes were also being turned over. It felt like a line in the sand, that there was no going back to their old lives, that maybe there was nowhere safe for them to go back to. No one spoke.

"Hey!" Sal snapped her fingers. "What's going on? Why are you all here and why is someone searching our house?"

And together, they told her about the Zodiac Warriors. Sal looked at her brother, expecting him to burst out laughing, that it was all a joke, but she had never seen him look so serious. They explained how they needed her on the dive to find the Aquarius medallion.

"Why didn't you tell me earlier?"

"I didn't tell anyone, Sal. Ma overheard us talking with them. Then a bunch turned up on the doorstep and, well, I guess you woulda thought I was hallucinating or something."

"And so, you want me to dive down and get this medallion thing because I was born in February?"

Everyone nodded.

A cool blast of air swept in as someone entered the motel door. Mad-eye Mack looked a little fresher than the night before. Though he was approaching sixty-five, his cheeks were smooth, punctuated by wrinkles on the edge of his eyes.

"I found a boat. Had to buy it, mind. I hope you people know what you're talking about. I just spent the last of my savings."

John jumped up and pumped Mack's hand.

"Mr Mack, I knew you'd come through!"

Tammy smiled.

"This is my girl, Salina. She's done some scuba diving, so we have an expert on crew."

"Ma!" Salina was about to protest, but Tammy nudged her in the ribs.

✳

The boat, *Sedna's Return*, was a shambles. John suggested that the owner should have paid Mack to take it off his hands. There were repairs, cleaning and an engine overhaul that needed to happen before they set off. The only plus side was that the boat was in the water and so at least watertight. It so happened that Astro knew about boat engines and was soon covered in grease, half their body above deck, the other half dangling into the bowels of the craft.

Tammy and Stevie scrubbed the salt-encrusted decks and wheelhouse. John and Tim headed to the chandler with a shopping list. Mack threw a dry suit at Salina and asked her to try it on and then made sure the oxygen bottles and scuba gear were in good order.

Jason ran from person to person carrying out instructions and fetching tools, cleaning supplies, brooms, tea and sandwiches.

As the clock clicked round to dinnertime, Astro flicked the key in the ignition and the engine rumbled into life. The crew let off a tired cheer and decided to call it a day. They crawled into the Bering Bell for beers and dinner.

Six hours later, they were back on board. Salina carried on the dry suit and fiddled with the gear. Jason provided food and flasks of hot chocolate. Mack was at the helm. Tammy fussed around Salina. Astro showed Stevie a thing or two about the engine. John and Tim were rugged up and stood at the bow looking out to the choppy seas of Bering.

Mack turned the key and the decks vibrated. He increased the throttle. Astro smiled. Tim unhooked the ropes from the narrow jetty and the rig chugged out to sea. Tammy, Sal and Stevie had their heads together, looking at the chart and the printout of the co-ordinates. The large bulk of Mack took up most of the wheelhouse. Jason wedged himself in a corner and wondered how he managed to end up on a boat in Alaskan waters. Not knowing where to look to minimise seasickness, he settled for his camera lens and clicked at the grey seas.

After they'd cleared the port, John stooped into the wheelhouse. "How long till we get to the zone?"

"It's pretty good weather, about two hours," Mack grunted.

The craft dipped and rose with the waves. Jason blew a long breath through his lips and resolutely pointed his camera at the crew huddled in the cramped wheelhouse.

"How are you feeling, Salina?" Tim asked.

"Pretty scared, to be honest. I don't really understand what's going on here. My world has just turned upside down."

"Yeah, I know that feeling," he said morosely, and turned his face to the ocean.

After an hour and a half, they could no longer see the land. The waves swelled in hypnotic rhythm. Conversation had dwindled. In the distance, Jason noticed a softening on the horizon. Slowly, a mist curled along the surface of the ocean until it blanketed them.

Only the blip of the radar showed where they were.

"We're approaching Fisherman's Foe," Mack said. "About another 3 miles west."

"Come on, Sal, I'll help you get into your suit," Tammy said.

"I don't even know what we're looking for, Ma. This is crazy. I don't want to do it."

"Do you think I'd ask you to do this if it wasn't important?" Tammy said. "Come on! Where's that spirited fighting girl?"

Sal fixed her mouth and nodded. Her Ma was right, she could do this.

"OK," Stevie said, "I reckon it's about here."

Mack cut the engine. He undressed to his shorts and pulled his worn-out suit over his beer belly. He groaned as he pulled it up, and moving his long ponytail to one side, motioned Tammy to zip him up.

They tested the oxygen tank and pulled the masks over their heads. Tammy squeezed her lips together tightly, holding in the fear for her daughter.

"I don't like this fog, Mack," she said. "What if we can't see you when you come back up?"

"We're attached to this rope, see? You can't get rid of me that easy."

He winked his good eye.

"Flashlights?" John asked.

"Check."

"How far down is it?" Jason asked.

"It's only 50–60 metres deep. Walk in the park. Ready?" he asked Sal.

She nodded. He reminded her how to control the air in the dry suit, checked her tank and waddled to the stern of the boat. Mack leapt into the water. Sal stared through the mist into the choppy grey waves. She opened and closed her fists, then jumped. The others breathed in the fog that hid even the ripples from their entry.

Mack and Sal left the movement of the surface and fell through the water. Sal kept her eyes on Mack to follow any instructions. They sank down through water speckled with plankton and fish. Sal felt her feet softly land on the seabed, throwing up sandy silt around them. She felt like she was standing on the moon, weightless in a strange world. She glanced around at the rocky floor of the ocean and wondered how on earth they would find a medallion that would fit in the palm of her hand. They had about forty-five minutes of oxygen to find a needle in a haystack.

Mack placed a flashlight at their feet and gestured for her to move in a semi-circle, as they'd discussed earlier. They turned and scoured the sea floor, moving pebbles and rocks. After fifteen minutes, Sal saw something glint in her torch beam. She kicked her feet and saw a piece of metal wedged under a rock. She pushed the rock to one side to reveal what she thought was a coin. But it was too big, unless she'd chanced upon an old shipwreck that had sunk with old coins from a bygone era. She picked it up, and a chain slithered through a hole in it. It was a necklace. Sal put it in her pouch. She felt a tug on her waist and turned to look at the rope that connected her to Mack. It tugged again. She turned herself back toward him and swam in the direction of the rope.

Mack hovered above the seafloor. He motioned for her to look ahead. She saw what he was showing her and shook her head, not knowing what she witnessed. The water looked like it was boiling. Bubbles coursed around in a whirlpool sphere as tall as her. She could feel it vibrating. Swimming closer, she put her hand up to the edge of the current. It forced her hand away. Sal shook her head at Mack. He gestured for her to go in underneath. Sal opened her hands out, questioning his suggestion. She touched the force field again and her hand rebounded.

He was crazy. He didn't really expect her to go inside this furious mass of current? Mack pointed to the base of the vortex. She paddled down to the seabed and peered into the eddy. She could see a gold mound at the centre. Sal inched towards the powerful mass that seemed to be protecting what was in the centre, or possibly signalling its position. If it was a Zodiac Warrior, perhaps it wanted to be found as much as they wanted to find it.

Sal snaked her arm along the sand into the force field. Her whole body shook. She stretched her arm but couldn't reach the gold. She took a deep breath and pulled herself closer, using the rocks to lever her way in. A roar coursed through her ears, making her teeth rattle. The interior of the current was like being in the engine of a jumbo jet. She could barely listen to her mind. Her fingers opened and closed, trying to grasp the gold. She pushed herself in further. The oxygen tank knocked against her back violently and she felt a pop. At last, her fingers reached the medallion. She tried to pick it up, but it felt attached to the sea floor. She remembered that she had to hold the medallion in her bare hand. She forced her other hand to pull off her glove. The icy water made her gasp. But as her lungs tried to breathe in, she choked. Her chest heaved again. Her head buzzed, and she felt adrenalin rush to her heart, making her want to breathe more, but nothing came through her tube. She made a final push and her hands curled around the medallion. Her lungs heaved in vain, her body convulsing. There was a rushing sound in her ears. Then silence. Blessed silence. Salina lost consciousness.

Mack saw Salina's legs quiver and kick unnervingly. He grabbed her legs and as he pulled her out, a bright turquoise light beamed through the water. Suddenly the ball of broiling water moved, its edges morphing and flowing, until lit with the blue light, a form of a woman emerged. She looked at Mack for a moment, then she swept up the limp body of Salina and shot upwards. Mack took in deep breaths of his oxygen then kicked his legs upwards, following the trail of bubbles the Zodiac Warrior of Aquarius left behind her.

While the humans planned their rescue of Aquarius, the Zodiac Warriors continued bickering in Regida's mansion.

"Warriors! We need the humans to help us," Chime implored.

"What for?" said Teres. "We are strong enough to gather what we need to create our new planets in this galaxy."

"If we don't hurry, there will be no more resources left. They are destroying this world," Regida added.

"Well, we can't stay here and make this our home," said Fyon.

Prymaw shrugged. "We could. It has enough water, resources, food, a good climate for us all."

"There is no room. If we want our kin to regenerate, we need more space. We had our own planets in Horoscopia. And I can't live with these pathetic humans," Degon argued.

"They don't have the mechanical and technological advances for us to inhabit any new planets, or they would be doing so themselves."

Pollux felt defensive about the humans she had spent so much time with. "We have the knowledge. We can teach them."

"They are not evolved enough, muy stupido!" Pedro said bitterly.

Plaadio looked at the ceiling. His mob in Australia argued less than this. In the Jawoyn tribe, they sat in a circle and each man or woman spoke. This was futile. "So, what do you suggest? Go back into our pods until they are ready? Some of us have no choice but to live on this planet. Some of us respect this race even though a few of them are destroying the country. There are good people, Degon. Anyway, without the humans to free you, you are just trapped inside a piece of metal. We have to work with them."

"Work! That's an understatement," Fyon said.

"One of us could stay out of their pod, keep an eye on things. Amrez seems to like it here," Teres suggested.

"No!"

"No way!"

"Trust Amrez? Pah!"

"Silence!" Degon yelled.

"Stop ordering us around, Degon!"

"I can't hear myself think with you all yelling."

"Well, you're yelling now."

"Are you going to stop me, Prymaw? Last time I recall you not faring so well when you told me what to do."

"I'm not scared of you, Degon, and I will not be bossed around by you."

"I'll bring you both down if you don't stop!"

"Shut up, Fyon!" Degon and Prymaw said together.

Pedro put his hands over his ears and blubbered. Chime and Regida shook their heads in dismay.

"This is getting us nowhere. We need a plan," said Plaadio.

"We agree," the twins said.

"Yes, a plan but a subtle one, not go in all blazing like Degon wants to."

"You think pussy footing around these humans will get results? Look, Prymaw, look Plaadio!" Degon cast his muscled arm around the room. "Where are your precious humans now, eh? They're gone. Given up."

"Not quite," said Castor.

He opened the door. Lily and Zakary were standing outside, listening to the squabbling Warriors.

They all stopped speaking and looked at the two humans. If they felt embarrassment, they didn't show it, but left space for Lily to speak as she stepped into their midst.

"How dare you! This is our home. You have landed here expecting us to accommodate you like it's an everyday occurrence. You are visitors here. And we say how things go. We might not have superpowers, super brains or be as strong as oxen but we are part of this incredible planet, made of the same matter. Yes, we have made mistakes, no, we are not perfect, but neither are you. While you are all arguing in here, the others, the 'stupid' humans, have gone to find one of you."

"Humans have never seen anything like this. Fyon, Regida, Prymaw, you all saw what can happen when you show yourselves to people. We will protect our planet until we know it doesn't need protecting."

Fyon let out a derisive laugh. The others also looked sceptical.

"Until we can guarantee your safety, the world must not know about you. You need to find Amrez and the last two Warriors and you can only do that with our help," said Zakary.

"They speak sense," Chime said. "Once we are all gathered, we will have the power to rescue the planet. We will all be saved. I have not travelled a million light years to see our hope of survival destroyed."

"What do you suggest, human?" Fyon asked.

"Your Sagittarian friend is a DJ and is headlining at this festival tonight." Zakary pointed to the flyer Jason had tossed on the table.

"And what exactly does that mean?" Degon growled.

"It means he's playing music to a crowd of thousands of people, and if we are smart about it, we can catch him."

※

They agreed to put their differences aside and their horns and heads together. The plan was a straightforward strategy of positioning the Warriors who looked like humans around the dancefloor and backstage. They each held a medallion ready to actualize, though Teres volunteered to stay back and keep an eye on Pedro, who needed a constant watch. But Amrez was likely to recognize all of them apart from Lily. Though Zak and Prymaw were against the idea, Lily persuaded them she was well enough to be the bait. The reputation of DJ Rez confirmed what the Warriors knew of Amrez; he never could pass up a pretty face. Though Lily's face was stitched and covered in a bandage, she dressed to enthral. Her toned kick-boxing body made Zak's blood pulse when he saw her dressed in skimpy shorts and a midriff top. She put her long sleek hair in quirky top knots, which also served the cover the disconcerting lumps she still had on her head. She smeared fluorescent make up under her eyes and applied neon eyelashes and orange glitter lipstick.

The festival heaved in the balmy summer evening. The island sitting on the famous Danube River buzzed with excitement as bands performed to a sea of music lovers. Signs on the riverbanks stated 'The Danube flowing to you courtesy of NuHydra'.

The team used Regida's boat that had a mooring on the river at the Mayer estate's jetty. The twins set up a microphone for Lily to talk with Fyon, who was manning the comms.

"You need to get into the mosh pit," Zak said. "It's going to be crazy in there, be careful."

"I'll get onto the stage and dance up there. That way I should be able to capture his attention."

"We'll be positioned on either side of the area," Pollux said. "Castor and I can read what's going through your mind. We will also tune into the other Warriors, including Amrez. Try to get him in a place with no other people. When you are in position, say the code words 'piece of cake'. We'll be close by."

"You have Prymaw in your bag, yes?" Regida checked.

"Yes. Oh wow, I love your outfit!" Lily said.

Regida nodded. She wore a white latex jump suit and a pair of Jimmy Choo sneakers. "I'm glad Tim isn't here!" she said, though her usually inexpressive face told a different story.

"So you'll take care of Amrez's right-hand man? Marko, he's very loyal to Amrez, but I don't think he'll be able to escape your enticement. He needs to be out of the scene," said Zakary, looking the Virgo goddess up and down. "Amrez is on stage in half an hour. They are setting up now. His set is one and a half hours long, so pace yourself," he warned.

"I hope he plays some good tunes."

"Well, he's very popular, wouldn't be headlining if people didn't like his stuff."

"Is there anything else I should know about him?" Lily asked.

"He's fast. Don't get him spooked. He'll already be wary after Jason and I chased him in Vienna."

"And he is charming," Chime said, slightly wistfully. "He can lure you in with his eyes alone. Don't get lost."

Zakary shifted on his feet and took a deep breath.

"You don't have to do this Lily. We could just all jump him when he gets off stage."

"It's OK, Zak. I won't get sucked in by his charm, and I won't spook him. Trust me. Piece of cake. Right?"

They checked Lily's mic one more time and ensured Fyon had a handle on the buttons.

Lily gave Zak a kiss on the cheek, and they went through the barriers into the crowd that was already waiting for the DJ to start while a support act played. She let go of Zak's hand and disappeared into the dancing bodies. Castor and Pollux separated and worked their way to the front sides of the stage. The DJ threw a disc on the decks, warming up the crowd. The sun was on its downward descent and a golden glow showered the crowd.

Lily squeezed her way to the front. Girls lined up along the front barrier, dressed in tiny tops and miniskirts, holding glow sticks. The music faded. A man dressed in a thick puffer jacket put the mic to his mouth and yelled, "Yo!"

The crowd cheered back.

"Yo!" the man held the microphone to the crowd who yelled "Yo!" back.

"Yo! Yo! Yo!" they ping-ponged back and forth.

"OK! You ready for dis?"

The crowd cheered.

"I can't hear you! YOU READY FOR DIS!"

The crowd roared back, amplified.

"Yeahhhh! Give it up," he rumbled into the mic, "for my man, the straight shootin', sweet talkin' one and onlyyyyyyy D... J... REZZZZZZZZZZ!"

Amrez appeared behind the decks, lifted up a on platform from under the stage. He wore a Roman warrior's leather skirt and a breastplate, surrounded in dry ice. He had a bow slung over his shoulder and a vinyl record spinning on a finger. The crowd went ballistic. Amrez flung the disc into the audience and with lightning reflexes drew an arrow from his back and shot the arrow straight through the record, shattering it into pieces. At that moment, the music dropped. The crowd dipped as one and threw themselves around to the beat.

The girls next to Lily screamed and flung their arms in the air, moving their bodies to the rhythm. She had to admit, Amrez was impressive. As he moved in front of the deck, he pumped his hands in the air, throwing the crowd into further frenzy. His long muscly legs seemed to catapult his broad chest above the other guys on the stage. His dark hair spiked jauntily in a small mohawk.

Lily had to time her move. Jumping on the stage too early may mean she got bumped off by security, but she had to make sure she got Amrez's attention.

After an hour and fifteen minutes, Amrez brought the set to a close. The audience was pumped, and as Amrez disappeared back under the stage on his platform, Lily swore. She expected another fifteen minutes. The crowd chanted for more, more, more! Lily pushed her way to the end of the barrier and ducked down. The sun had dipped, and dusk made it difficult to see before the night lighting came on and people's eyes adjusted. Lily easily vaulted onto the stage and crouched down. Suddenly, an explosion of fireworks shot out from behind the speakers, and Amrez reappeared to the roar of the audience. He put on a tune and a tone revved up to such a high pitch until bam! The beat dropped, and the fans went crazy. Lily leapt up and jumped up and down on the stage, shaking her head, bum and boobs. She rolled her shoulders and danced her way to the decks, looking directly into Amrez's eyes. A security guard approached. Amrez raised his chin at the guy, telling him to back off. DJ Rez held his hand out to Lily. She took it and he pulled her in, their bodies close, his hands running up and down her back. He let her go with one arm, to adjust the deck, holding her in close with the other. Lily kept gyrating to the music. She could smell Amrez's body, his sweat and sweet cologne. He was even bigger up close, towering over her small frame. He morphed the tune into a new one that managed to get his audience to rave even harder. He pushed Lily in front of him and ducked down, lifting her up on his shoulders. The view was incredible. A sea of writhing humanity cocooned by the river Danube, all pulsing to the same rhythm in ecstasy.

Zakary watched the performance, swearing under his breath. He couldn't bear the thought of Lily getting hurt again. He pushed his way out of the throng, rushing to get backstage.

Amrez bought the set to a close with the same tone winding down to nothing. Suddenly, the platform moved, and he and Lily dropped down. Once the platform hit the ground, Amrez slid Lily off his shoulders.

"That was amazing!" she said breathlessly, meaning it.

Zakary cleared the crowd and heard the audience roaring and clapping as the set ended. He ran to behind the stage, but a security guard put his hand up and pushed him away.

Amrez grabbed her hand and amidst the back claps, fist pumps and "awesome mans!" led her backstage. Darkness had ascended. He guided her through the metal barriers that seemed like a maze into a marquee. Musos and bands were in various stages of pre-performance rehearsal or post-performance inebriation. Guitars were being tuned, racks of clothes rifled through and drinking games happening. Amrez took her to a curtained-off corner. Inside, there was a sofa and a small fridge.

"Take a seat. Drink?"

Lily nodded. He chucked her a can of NuBeer. He slipped the leather skirt off and pulled a pair of baggy jeans over his boots. The breastplate clattered to the ground. Lily watched his pecs and biceps before they disappeared under a metallic gold designer t-shirt.

"Great set, eh?"

He had a Germanic accent, which only added to his charisma.

"It was sick!"

"Where are you from?"

"Australia. I'm Lily."

Amrez flopped down next to her on the sofa and they clinked cans.

"What happened to your face?"

"A little accident with a gun and a glass cabinet."

"Ohh, I like a badass..."

He leant in to kiss her, but her mobile buzzed in her bag.

"Sorry, hang on. Shit, it's my mum. I've got to take this."

Amrez let out a deep sigh. "It's OK I gotta take a piss."

He dodged around the curtain.

"Hi. Mum. Look, it's a bad time..."

"Hey love, where are you?"

"I told you, I'm overseas. Are you OK?"

"Shit. No. I'm so thirsty..."

Lily rolled her eyes. "Look Mum, I'm not around. You're big enough to go get your own booze. I've finished with your..."

"Lil, it's not the booze. I quit, after you left. I know you hate me when I'm on it. I wanna get better. It's the water, there's no water coming out of our taps."

"What do you mean, Mum? Just call a plumber."

"It's not just me, the whole of our suburb is out of water. Everyone is fighting in the supermarket for bottles of water. The toilets aren't flushing. It's disgusting. Haven't you watched the news?"

Zakary fidgeted in the crowd. He grabbed his phone out of his back pocket and dialled Lily's number. "What the...?" he mumbled at the engaged tone and hung up. He saw the security guards were busy with a girl who'd passed out, so he leaped over the barriers towards the green room tent.

Amrez came back in and slid onto the sofa. He nuzzled his face into Lily's neck and licked under the opposite ear her mum was talking into. Lily pushed him away.

"No, I've been caught up with... work. Just a minute, I can't hear you."

Lily stood up. Her handbag fell off the sofa, spilling onto the floor. Prymaw's medallion rolled out, and Amrez and Lily both looked at it at the same time.

"Shit! Mum, I'll call you back." She dropped the phone

"What the?" Amrez looked at Lily and narrowed his eyes. They both lurched for the medallion.

Amrez swore and kicked it out of the way.

"Piece of cake!" she yelled into her mic.

Amrez scooped up his gym back and flung the handles over both shoulders. He yanked the curtain aside and ran through the marquee.

"Piece of cake!" she repeated.

Her head tingled, and she could feel pressure against the pigtails on her scalp. She scrambled across the floor, grabbing the medallion. Through her fingers, red lights zoomed into the focused body of Prymaw. The people in the marquee screamed.

He shook his head at Lily and then laughed. "Another tent? What is it with you and tents?"

"He's over there, get him!" Lily shouted as Amrez flew through the tent opening into the night. The twins and Zakary were already outside. They stepped in front of his barrelling body. He shoved them out of the way. Prymaw fell out of the tent, screams of alarm scattering around him.

"He's going to the west exit!" Pollux yelled, giving her brother a hand up.

"Fyon, get Chime to the west exit," Lily said into her mic.

"On it," Fyon replied.

Prymaw galloped after him, dodging festival goers, food trucks and stilt walkers.

"Dammit, he's fast," Prymaw said. "We need back up."

Castor spoke the words to the Leo medallion. Degon lit up the night. His mane sparked and flamed. He threw his head back and roared. "Amrez!"

"He's heading south!" Castor yelled.

Plaadio sprinted to the south exit. Amrez skidded to a halt at the sight of him and changed direction.

"There are too many people!" Prymaw said, "We're going to lose him."

Zakary looked at Lily. "You OK?"

She nodded, though it was the conversation with her mum she was more shaken about, and the weird sensations on her head.

"Back to west," Fyon said into Lily's ear.

They jogged to the west gate just in time to see Amrez vault over the barrier and suddenly come crashing down to the ground as if he had struck a brick wall. Prymaw reached him. His horns unravelled and bound the squirming body of Amrez. Chime materialized out of the ether, holding her scales up in the air. Plaadio arrived and put his spear to Amrez's chest. At last, Degon ran through the alarmed spectators. He stood over the writhing body of Amrez with clenched fists.

"Good work, team," he said reluctantly and whacked Amrez across the side of his head. Plaadio tied his wrists.

Zakary whistled. "So Chime can be invisible!"

Lily nodded. "Pretty cool. Where's Fyon?"

The boat came roaring along the river. Fyon swung it around at speed, practically capsizing the vessel. She pulled up at the jetty.

"We need to get out of here before the Warriors attract attention. It's been risky enough," said Zak.

"Come on, let's get on board. I have something to tell you," Lily said.

They jogged through the barriers and ran down the jetty. Prymaw picked up Amrez's limp body and climbed aboard.

"Didn't waste any time learning how to drive this thing then, Fyon?"

"Ach, it's a piece of toast!"

"Er, cake, a piece of cake," Zakary corrected.

"Toast, cake, it all the same."

"Hold on, where's Regida?"

"Picking her up on the way." Fyon pulled on the throttle, and they lurched forward.

After a few minutes, Fyon swung the boat around, kicking a lick of water into the air. Everyone tumbled to one side.

Regida was waiting at a small jetty. Her white catsuit gleamed in the night.

"What is she doing?" Zakary asked.

She had a rope in her hand. As they drew closer, they could see a man was at the end of it, on his hands and knees.

Regida lifted her hand and signalled for them to stop.

"Good dog, now stay," she said.

The naked man on the end of the leash was on all fours and had his tongue hanging out. He looked at her and nodded.

"Is that Marko?" Zak asked. "What have you done to him?"

"You didn't turn his brain to mush, did you?" Lily asked.

"No, apparently this is his deepest soul's desire."

They looked at her blankly. "To be a dog," she clarified. "Piece of cake."

Warriors and humans shook their heads and as Regida stepped elegantly onto the boat, Marko barked, whined, then barked again.

"Let's get out of here before Amrez comes around," Regida said to Fyon.

Fyon needed no more prompting and sped away upriver back to the Mayer estate.

Lily scrolled through her phone, looking at news sites. "Oh my God!"

"What's the matter?"

"My mum called, there's no water coming out of mains taps in Perth. News sites report the same in Sydney and Melbourne. In America too. Zak, the water is running out!"

Zak looked at his phone. "It says NuHydra is building and opening desalination plants and dams all over the world. That the future is in these plants."

"So why is the water running out? I need to get Abigale over here."

"Abigale?"

"My mum, Zak. She can't cope with this. She's on her own. I need to get her on a plane out of there."

The boat slowed. Teres was waiting for them and caught the rope Plaadio chucked him.

"Did you get him?"

"Yes, but we need to get him inside before he is fit enough to make a run for it."

"The cellar is ready for him. I'm sure the selection of wine down there will keep him happy."

Prymaw bundled up Amrez in his horns and held him aloft up the lawn and down the steps under the house. He laid him down gently. All the Warriors except Pedro stood around him. Chime poured water on his face. Amrez spluttered and opened his eyes.

"*Ach, Gott verdamme dich!*"

He let a volley of bad language stream from his mouth, struggling against the cloth that bound his wrists.

"Good to see you, comrade," Teres said.

"I see you are still a free spirit, brother," Degon said.

"Untie me, you bastards."

"Only when we can be sure you don't run."

Amrez laughed. "I wouldn't be a Sagittarian if I didn't run, now, would I?"

"I'm surprised you can get around so quickly on only two legs," Plaadio said.

"Now we are matched then brother, but I bet you a thousand euro I could still outrun you."

"Which is why I won't!"

"Boring! Boring! Some things never change."

Amrez jumped up. "Ahh, I can smell a fine vintage or two down here. Come on, let's crack open a bottle. We are celebrating, aren't we? The team back together. A nice, cosy reunion. Except some are missing. Let's see, I can see Degon, of course, taking up all the space, leading the charge. My friend Teres." He made a bow. "Plaadio keeping the rules, Regida, my dear exquisite sister, still impassively beautiful. Chime, ouch, you pack quite a punch and ah, Castor and Pollux still so cool and reading my mind, I'm sure. Fyon, sharp and sassy, how are you girlfriend? So that leaves out my shellmate Xincon, my watery friend Hastia of Aquarius and, of course, always last and often least, those Pisces sirens, Mequitha and Maroda. Where are they?"

"Xincon is indisposed as a rather unstable human, but he is here. As for Hastia, some humans..." Degon began.

"I think you mean our friends and the people who have found you all and brought you back to life," Lily interjected.

"Oh hello, it's you—Lily, I think you said. I never forget the name of a beautiful temptress," Amrez said. "Mmm, feisty."

Zakary put his arm around Lily and shot Amrez a look of warning.

"Not to worry, my friend, my hands are tied!" Amrez said, raising his bound wrists.

"Our human friends have gone to search for Hastia, and we are yet to locate the Piscean sisters. This is where we need you, brother," Plaadio said. "And Xincon and I have lost our pods."

"That's very careless of you, Plaad, not like you," Amrez tutted.

"And where is your pod, Amrez?" Chime asked.

"As safe as the crown jewels, my dear."

"We are going to have to break them out of the museum somehow. We can't use your bow and arrow if you do not have the power of your pod."

"What a shame. I guess you'll have to find someone else to clean up your mess for you then, won't you?"

"AMREZ!" Degon roared. Everyone winced. "While you have been gallivanting around, enjoying this hedonistic lifestyle, you seem to have missed the fact that this planet is dying."

"Yup."

"And that we need to help this planet and its inhabitants."

"It seems I have. Soz. Now, lovely to see you all again. Have a nice life and er, don't keep in touch."

Amrez strode toward the bottom of the steps. Plaadio stepped in front of him.

"Thing is, brother, you don't get a choice."

"Oh yeah, well watch me!"

Amrez scissor-kicked one foot into Plaadio, the other into Chime. He then front-flipped over the twins and back flipped over Teres. Teres lashed out with his trine and caught the back of Amrez's t-shirt, which ripped.

Amrez scowled at the damage to his designer shirt and slid out of it. Regida swung her staff at his ankles, which he hopped over and ran for the steps. Degon roared and gave chase, but Amrez stopped abruptly at the top of the steps. Pedro peered down into the cellar. He was sobbing, tears of blood fell over his cheeks and snot bubbled down his fleshy face.

"Help me," he begged, "help me!"

Amrez turned and walked back down, his head hung low.

"Untie me. I need to help my friend."

Teres slashed his binding, and they carried Pedro down, placing him gently on the ground. He shook and sobbed and quivered, scratching at his arms and face.

"He needs to find his pod and regain his true form. His body is deteriorating. He is dying in this disguise." Regida said. "Will you help him, Zodiac Warrior Amrez?"

The six humans watched the water in silence. John and Stevie scanned the waves with their binoculars, the others squinted through the fog. Half an hour passed and all they could see was the rope attached to the two divers uncoiling off the deck.

"They've only got about 15 minutes of oxygen left," Tim said.

A breeze rippled across the surface of the water, ruffling their hair. It came again, stronger. The boat tipped a little and Jason's knuckles turned white as he grasped the railing. The wind rushed around the boat and the waves kicked the bow up and down.

"What's going on?" he asked.

The sea under them rumbled and flashes of turquoise glimmered under the water. The boat rocked as if in a fierce storm, knocking Jason off his feet and the others clinging onto the nearest solid piece of the boat.

"Look!" shouted Stevie.

The Aquarius Warrior and Salina broke into the choppy waves 500 metres from the boat, which bobbed the row of concerned faces on the bows. They watched the shape of Aquarius rise out of the ocean.

"She's got Sal! Oh my God, what's happened to her?"

"Where's Mack?" John yelled.

Mack burst through the water like a whale and swam frantically after Aquarius, who surfed across the ocean to the boat in seconds.

The Zodiac Warrior arrived at the side of the boat and passed Sal into Tim's arms. He laid her on the deck and felt her pulse.

"It's weak."

Tammy crouched over her daughter, talking to her sternly.

"Wake up, Sal, you hear me? Wake up now, my girl!"

"She needs oxygen," Mack said as he hauled himself aboard. "Her tube came loose with all the ruckus this creature was causing down there."

"I'll get the spare tank. Ma give her CPR!"

Astro crossed herself and put her hands together in prayer. Jason chewed his nails and John hovered around, uncertain what to do.

"We should radio for help," Tim said.

The Aquarius Warrior hovered, a mass of rippling, watery muscles. She pressed the jewel on her wristband. "I can heal her," the Warrior said.

She kneeled at Sal's head and dipped her head downwards. A trickle of water streamed from between her eyes onto Sal's forehead.

Tammy counted one, two, three, one, two, three and pumped her hands on Sal's breastbone. No one said anything.

"One, two, three," Tammy counted.

"She needs medical attention," Tim said.

"She's not going to die," Tammy said firmly. "One, two, three, one, two, three."

"I'm calling SOS," Tim said.

"Come on, Sal. Come on, baby." Tammy compressed Sal's chest and held blew air into her mouth.

Suddenly, Sal's eyes flickered open and she spluttered.

"That's my girl," Tammy breathed, her voice cracking.

They helped Salina sit up. She looked around her, confused, and glanced at the medallion in her hands. The Aquarian shimmered in her watery cloak above her.

"Who are you?"

"I am Hastia of Aquarius. Thank you for freeing me. I have been in my pod for a very long time. It feels good to be out."

"My son died because of you!" Mack approached her angrily. "You've destroyed boats and people's lives!"

Hastia's height grew, and the boat heaved over waves that appeared from nowhere.

"Mack, calm down, take it easy mate." Jason stepped up to him.

"I have no knowledge of what has happened here. Water has power and does not like to be contained. I told the others so when we left Horoscopia, but they did not listen," Hastia said. "I am the water carrier. I am not contained by water."

"Why did the pod sink to the bottom when my son bought it up?"

"My vessel needs to be suspended in water unless in the hands of an Aquarian."

"Let's get you two out of your suits. You need a hot drink," Tammy said.

Astro scooped a bucket over the edge of the boat. "We'll put the medallion in a bucket of water."

They gathered in the wheelhouse, Mack and Salina wrapped in blankets, and drank hot chocolate that Jason handed around. They stared at Hastia. She looked like water, her shape constantly moving, currents flowing through her, yet not a drop was evident on the floor.

John listed the Warriors they had found and where they were.

"I must join them. I can feel trouble with the waters on this planet. I can feel trouble with the people of this planet too."

"What is your power?" Stevie asked.

"I can manipulate water, but I can also feel water. Water exists in all living things, and I can interpret the currents that run through them."

"We should contact Lily and Zak and let them know."

"There's no coverage out here. Let's head back to Nome," Mack said. "Put her back in the gold medallion."

"Friend, I can feel you have much hatred directed at me. I never forced you to take the actions you did. I mean no harm and I am sorry for your loss, but that loss is not for me to carry. Some feelings are painful, some never go away, but shooting them at others is the road to self-destruction."

Mack grunted and stared at the Warrior with disgust.

"I think it's time you went back inside and let us get back to Nome without any further harm. That girl nearly died getting you off the bottom of the ocean floor. I don't want any more trouble from you."

Without saying another word, Hastia's form melted into a vortex that poured back into the medallion in the bucket.

"Take it down below and make sure it doesn't fall out of that bucket," Mack growled.

He turned the key in the engine. The fog was still thick around them. But Astro put their hand over Mack's.

"Wait, listen!"

They could all hear it. The quiet chug of another boat approaching them.

The VHF radio crackled.

"*Sedna's Return*, come in."

"Who knows we are out here?"

"Repeat. *Sedna's Return*, come in. This is the Water Police. We request permission to come on board."

The engine got louder, and they saw the lights through the fog.

"The police?" Tammy said.

Stevie had a look of concern on his face.

"Might not just be the police. If they found out our address, they could have traced us here too."

Everyone hesitated for a moment, then they saw the bulk of the Water Police vessel through the fog.

"We need to get out of here." Stevie yelled. "Now!"

Mack turned the key and *Sedna's Return* burst to life. He turned the wheel and pulled on the throttle.

"We can't go back to Nome," said Mack

"We can't go back to America," said Astro.

"Then where?" Tim said.

"Russia," said Mack. He turned the wheel and put the boat in its highest speed.

The Water Police boat followed, their lights cutting through the fog.

"We have to go faster!" John said, as he looked out over the stern. "They're gaining!"

"It's OK, Russian territory is halfway across the Bering Strait. They'll be out of jurisdiction soon."

But the lightweight police boat zoomed up to their port side.

"This is the police! Cut your engines, I repeat: Cut your engines!" a man's voice yelled through a loudspeaker.

The fog cleared enough for them to see a team of armed police.

"That's not just the Water Police!" Mack shouted over the roar of the engine. "That's the CIA."

"Go faster Mack, they are reaching for their weapons," John yelled.

"Desist or we will shoot!" the voice came again.

Within seconds, a bullet ricocheted off the metal frame of the wheelhouse.

"Go down below!" Mack ordered. "John, get back in here now!"

John stumbled across the deck and another shot was fired. He dived down and bullets hit the middle of the boat. He commando crawled into the wheelhouse.

"I'm not leaving you up here alone."

Another bullet landed on the side of the boat as the police came alongside.

"Don't be a hero, old man, I got this."

Mack swung the boat sharply and everyone down below lurched to one side. The bucket slid across the floor, spilling some of its contents.

"Sal!" Tammy yelled. "Catch it!"

The water police boat accelerated and spun around in the path of *Sedna's Return*.

"Holy shit!" Mack yelled and turned the wheel sharply left to avoid collision.

The crew lurched in the other direction and the bucket cavorted out of Sal's reach, hitting the side. As the boat righted, the bucket flipped over.

"Sal, grab it!" Jason yelled.

Sal launched her body across the wet floor.

As Mack banked the boat away from the police, another police vessel appeared out of the fog in front of him.

Mack swore. "There's more of 'em!"

Sedna's Return was flanked. Mack slowed down. He could see the faces of the police through the window. John could see the same in the other boat.

"Turn off the engine now!" the instruction came. Mack put the engine in reverse and revved the throttle in defiance. One of the men raised his gun, both hands on the firearm. He looked Mack in the eyes.

Sal's fingers touched the medallion just before it skittered across the floor of the cabin, spraying up water droplets like a skimmed stone.

The agent fired. The bullet shot right at Mack. He closed his eyes in the split second he had to move, he suddenly felt a power surge around him, a cool sensation went through his body and every noise was muffled. Water roared in his ears like the day his son was killed by the ocean. He felt the air in his body release. He no longer needed to breathe, and he knew he was at last released from his anger, guilt and sorrow that had plagued him from that day.

But then he was back, breathing and still standing at the wheel. *Sedna's Return* was moving swiftly through the water, almost above the waves, flying along at a speed much faster than the one the engine could have ever achieved.

Mack looked behind him as the heads of Tammy, John, Tim and

Astro emerged from below. They all saw the enormous figure of Hastia surfing the vessel over the waves. The police boats were capsized in their wake. A flare shot from the boats for rescue.

"What the hell just happened there?"

"She saved your life," John said, "I've never seen anything like it."

Mack glanced at his navigational equipment and steered the ship towards the coast of Russia. Hastia pushed them through the Bering Strait, guided by Mack. All the others, except for Salina, came up from the cabin.

"Where are we going?" Tim asked.

"To a town called Lavrentiya, the only place with an airstrip in thousands of miles."

"We can fly out of there?" John asked.

"Yes, to Anadyr and from there to Moscow. I have friends here, distant family, actually. I used to come here as a young 'un. I can call in a couple of favours."

"There's no damn way we'll be allowed to enter Russia like this," John said.

"That is the official line," Mack replied. "I've lived here a long time. I can negotiate anything with enough cash." He'd clocked Tim's expensive watch and designer jacket from the first time he approached him in the Bering Bell.

"How much?" Tim asked.

"Two million rubles should do it."

"That's over $25000!"

"I've got six illegal immigrants and an alien on my vessel. I reckon that's a pretty darn good deal."

John nodded at his son. He had to agree with Mack.

"Give me your watch," Mack said to Tim.

"What! No way. Jill bought me this..." he trailed off. "Fine, take the blasted thing."

He shook it off and dumped it in Mack's hand.

Sedna's Return slowed down as the shoreline came into view. Hastia appeared on the deck.

"I think it wise for me to retreat. Remember, I must be suspended in water while I'm inside."

Mack cleared his throat. "You saved my life back there. Thanks."

Hastia nodded. "Salina, bring me my pod."

Salina's pale face emerged from the hatch.

"Hold on." She went to the skipper.

"Mack." Sal opened her palm and held out the necklace. "I found this when we were down there."

Mack's jaw dropped as he lifted it from her hand.

"This was Jimmy's medallion, my God, I don't believe it." Mack had tears brimming in his eyes. "Thanks, Sal, thank you for finding this."

John coughed. "Well, we'd better see if we can moor up and find a flight out of here. Good job we all have our passports, at least."

Hastia disappeared into the medallion and Sal placed it in the flask that had held the hot chocolate, now filled with water. Mack guided the boat into the small port and everyone else gathered up their gear. The windswept village looked like it was losing its battle against rust. Old sea containers were stacked along the coastline, pieces of scrap metal littered the beach and the large square buildings looked like their colourful paint was the only thing holding them up. A few men stopped what they were doing and watched. One of them approached the boat.

"Not allowed!" he said in Russian.

"*Privet!*" Mack shouted to him. "Hello!"

He jumped onto the jetty and strode towards him. He spoke in Russian to the man, waving his hand back at the boat. After much conversation and the watch passing hands, the man motioned the group to join him. They disembarked with their meagre belongings and walked towards Mack.

"Andrei here has agreed to give us a transit visa. He needs the night to process the paperwork. Tim, there's a phone here to wire the fee through. We can charter a plane to Anadyr tomorrow. I've arranged accommodation with my aunt Okko-n. They'll want to treat us special. They don't get many visitors here. Hope you're willing to eat whale!"

Sal and Jason both winced. John rubbed his hands together. The rest agreed, and the fishermen led them into the village.

Okko-n welcomed them into her house. Her grandchildren raced around them, and she scooted them out of the way. They sat on plastic stools while she served up a hot tea and placed plates of unusual looking titbits on the table.

"Damn, no coverage here either," Jason said. He wanted to contact Lily and Zakary.

"I wonder how they got on with Sagittarius?" Tim asked.

"I'm sure Jill, I mean Regida, managed to work her magic," Tim said bitterly.

"How are you feeling about all that, Tim?" Tammy asked.

"I don't want to think about her, but all I can do is think about her. I just go round in circles. She's from another galaxy. They don't cover that one in the self-help books."

They all gave a sad laugh. Tammy patted Tim on the hand.

"Anyway, enough of my troubles. Sal, how are you feeling now?"

"I think my brain is still trying to catch up on everything. But physically, OK."

"My stomach is still trying to catch up on everything," Jason said as he forked a rubbery looking morsel from the plate.

"You eat, eat!" their host said with a big smile on her face and slapping Jason on the shoulder.

"I... er... was just looking."

"Da, eat, is good, make you strong, da? You too skinny."

Jason swallowed and looked at the others, desperation in his eyes. Okko-n's warm brown eyes urged him on. He delicately placed the grey blob into his mouth. He chewed, trying not to gag. And chewed. The children watched on, waiting for his declaration of deliciousness. He chewed more, his eyes darting to the others for help.

"Delicious," he said to them, weakly, through his mouthful.

All amused eyes remained on him as he was stuck, chewing on

the whale blubber, unwilling to be rude, yet unable to swallow or escape. Salina screwed up her nose, her vegetarian stomach turning at the thought of it. Thankfully, Mack burst through the door.

"Ah, see you've all settled in. You've met my Aunty Okko-n." He gave her a bear hug.

While he spoke to her in Russian, Jason spat the whale meat out and handed it to one of the dogs sniffing around the table. He closed his eyes and wished he was back in Australia eating a sausage sizzle.

That evening, the villagers invited the group to watch them perform their traditional dances. They drank a locally brewed spirit which Jason thought tasted of whale flesh. The others were happy for the warm hospitality and warm liquor to recover from the previous twelve hours. They slept well on mattresses in Okko-n's children's rooms.

Even though he had stayed up drinking into the early hours of the morning, Mack was up first and roused the group.

"Our papers are ready. Andrei stayed up all night making, er securing them for you. You have to catch the flight to Anadyr airport, from there you can fly to Moscow," he announced to the bleary eyes.

"Come on, you shabby bunch," he nudged Stevie with his foot. "Those agents ain't just gonna give up and go home, you know. They'll be onto us in the twitch of a reindeer's nose."

It didn't take long for the group to get themselves into Okko-n's kitchen, where she poured them coffee and a thankfully simple fruit and lichen salad and bread rolls for breakfast.

One of the men who had told stories the night before knocked. He had a jeep with a trailer on the back ready to take them to the airstrip. They thanked her and said their goodbyes to Okko-n and the children who ran after the jeep, then waved them off. In a few minutes, they arrived at the untarmacked strip where a dented plane waited. The jeep joggled over the tundra and pulled up by the steps to the door.

"Great service around here, that's for sure," Jason said.

They jumped out of the jeep and stood in a group, waiting for Mack.

"Well, go on then. Get on board," he said.

"Aren't you coming with us?" Tammy asked.

Mack looked surprised. "No, my home is here."

"But you can't go back to Nome, Mack," John said.

Mack scratched his head. "I'll be OK."

"You saw what we were dealing with out there, man!" Stevie said. "They captured Lily. They found out where we live. They won't stop until they have the Zodiac Warriors safely locked away."

"I'll take my chances. Got places to hide out."

"Mack," Tammy implored.

He shook his head. "It's been good to know you."

"Well, good luck, old fellow." John stuck out his hand. Mack took it.

"Good luck to y'all, it's been a ride, and thanks."

They turned to board the plane. Mack stood on the airstrip, waiting for them to disappear into the cabin. The man who drove them to the airfield gave a shout.

"*Politsiya! Toropit'sya! Toropit'sya!* Hurry! Go, go!"

Mack turned.

"What is he saying?" Stevie said.

"Sounded like police," Astro said, "Is the same in Spanish."

The pilot had pushed the steps away and was about to close the door.

"Wait!" Mack shouted, as the engines of vehicles could be heard.

"Mack, get in quick! Sir, sir, our friend is coming, OK?"

The pilot looked at his watch and shook his head.

"No, he has to come, look he's on the steps!"

"Let him in!" Tammy yelled.

The pilot tipped his head and opened the door. Mack leapt across the gap and fell heavily inside the aircraft. He urgently spoke to the pilot in Russian. The pilot checked everyone was strapped in.

"*Toropit'sya!*" Mack hissed, "*pozhaluysta!* Please!"

The engines rumbled and the wheels began to move. Three jeeps appeared around the hangar.

"Let's hope this pilot can get us up quick."

At that, the plane accelerated, getting faster and faster. The jeeps careered over the grass to get to the plane, but the momentum was fast. The jeeps screeched to a halt as the wheels left the airstrip, narrowly missing them.

"What if they are waiting at Anadyr?" Sal said.

"How long before the flight leaves for Moscow? And then what?" Jason said.

The task of returning to Vienna and to keep dodging the CIA seemed impossible.

Not long after they took off, they began their descent. They could see the contours of the brown tundra below them.

"Oh my God," Tammy said. "Look over here, guys."

They all leaned across and looked out of the window. Cranes, earth movers and thousands of vehicles were building a huge processing plant.

"See the flags over there? It's the NuDelta logo."

"I can't read what it says underneath."

"I'll take a photo," Stevie said. He snapped the banner on his phone and zoomed in on the image.

"What's it say, Mack? It's in Russian."

"*Ledyanoy kombayn. Ledyanoy*, that's ice, anyone knows that. But *kombayn*, let me think. Combine... I think it means 'harvester'. Ice harvester."

"Orlando Focus is harvesting ice in Russia now? He owns ice in Russia?"

"He's everywhere," Sal said. "This is creepy. I don't like it."

No one could argue. The only comfort was that they had Hastia safely cocooned in the flask.

Deep in the heart of Iceland, Lake Höggormur filled the crater of a volcano over 200 metres deep. The top half a metre of the lake was water. Below that it turned to sludge and then solid ice. A man stood at the edge, gazing at the glacial surface of the lake. He turned, the same glassy look of the lake in his eyes.

He was tall, muscular and easily hiked down the brown lava rocks of the mountainside, switching this way and that on the snaked path. The valley opened up before him. A waterfall fell at the end of the gorge. He crossed a bridge towards his house, clinging onto the cliff face on the other side. He paused a moment and took in the crashing water. He would bathe in it later, after he had relaxed in the geothermal springs that bubbled in the sanctuary of his garden. He began the climb up the other side.

The house was an architecturally designed glass box. Though inaccessible by road, the house was built into a ledge so that no errant explorers or hikers would ever see it. Even the helicopter pad was out of sight. The walls and ceiling were made of glass, giving panoramic views of the valley and the volcano.

He removed his jacket and boots in the outer room and swiped his hand across a panel, allowing the glass door to slide across and let him in. There were no walls to separate the space, though a deep alcove that seemed to be carved into the rock held a bed that was scattered with silk sheets and a polar bear pelt. Something stirred within.

He went to his kitchen and opened the fridge. He pulled out a crystal bowl.

"Wakey, wakey Sophia," he whispered. "I've made you breakfast."

He walked over to his bed and placed his hand on the silk sheet, feeling the muscular curve of her. He slid his hand up her body. She stirred again.

"Wake up, my darling," he purred and pulled the sheet away.

"Ahhh, you are so beautiful. Here, my pretty one..."

He pulled Sophia's breakfast out of the bowl by its tail, and gently laid a dead mouse next to the head of the sleeping python. He stroked her head and left her to feast.

From his desk, which looked out over the lower green slopes of the Icelandic summer terrain, a phone peep-peeped. His mobile had been flashing at him all morning.

"No rest for the wicked, eh, my love?"

He went and settled himself in the large leather chair and pressed a button on the phone.

"You have good news?" he said, leaning back, inspecting his manicured fingernails.

"They got away."

His hands came slamming down onto the glass desk.

"Imbeciles!" he hissed. "First, you let them escape a secure government facility and now you can't even track down a bunch of misfits in broad daylight! You told me Tress wouldn't let me down." His voice was low and so cold that shivers went through the man on the other end of the line.

"I'm sorry Mr Focus. We would never have found them in Alaska if it wasn't for her. We sent out two boatloads of police and they still managed to get away. Two of the men were drowned. They must have had help from one of the aliens."

"Do you know where they went?"

"Russia, sir."

Orlando Focus smiled. "Of course."

"The local politsia tried to stop them at the airstrip, but the flight had already left. The Russians and the CIA are not exchanging information. We'll have to wait until they arrive either into Europe or back to the US."

"They know they can't get back into America now with the CIA on their tails. Leave the Russians to me."

"Yes, sir."

"Send me a full report. I want to know exactly where they are going and who they are."

"It's on its way."

He opened his laptop, and an email was already in his inbox.

"Any leads on the other medallions?"

"We've had a report of strange sightings at a festival in Vienna, but not corroborated. No witnesses willing to come forward with photographic evidence."

"And where is Tress right now? Has she traced the girl with the Aries medallion?"

"She's working on it."

"I want a video call with her now."

"Sir."

He pressed the end call button. There was no time to waste. He spun his world globe around and traced his finger across Iceland to east Russia. He drummed his fingers on the spot that the runaway humans were at that moment flying. Another spin and he stopped it at Vienna.

Focus pressed his phone again. "Viktor."

"Da."

"There is a group of Americans, British and Australian arriving in Moscow. They'll be at the airport, possibly heading to Vienna. I'll send you their details. Follow them, but observe only. Understand?"

"Da."

"Let me know as soon as you see anything... strange."

His mobile phone showed dozens of missed calls from Grant Sampson. He picked up.

"Orlando, buddy, we've been trying to contact you. There are riots happening all over the world. I thought you had this water situation under control?"

"My desalination plants are working around the clock. Surely I'm not the only one who has a handle on the water situation?"

"Well, you made it very difficult for other developers to build."

"I merely raised the standards. It's not my problem the investors wouldn't fund the high levels of safety, sanitation and purity of the water. You yourself were on the steering committee."

"But none of us could have foreseen the drought, the dropping of the water tables. All that fracking went and polluted half the good drinking water."

Focus put his hands behind his head and allowed himself a half smile.

"I'm doing all I can, Grant."

Orlando Focus opened a news site on his browser. Reporters around the world stood amid scenes of panic and mayhem. Groups of protesters tried storming desalination plants. He smirked at the security he'd set up and gave a deep, satisfied smile. It had taken a long time, a lot of money and some smart alliances, but now he controlled nearly all the drinking water sources in the world. The human race had had a good run at it. Now he was executing the penultimate part of his plan. He was turning off the tap. And, at last, the final piece—the Zodiac Warriors were being found and he would bring them together again.

His phone beeped.

"Yes."

"Sandra Tress on video call."

"Good day Ms Tress, thank you for updating me."

"No problem, Mr Focus. I traced the address in New York state..."

"Yes, yes. I'm aware of that. What I want to know is how exactly you managed to let them get away?"

"I'm sorry Mr Focus. We were right on top of them."

"Did you see any extra-terrestrial activity like that we witnessed at Fort Meade?"

"I believe their boat was powered with some extra force..."

"So they have uncovered another one. You see our problem, Ms Tress. These people need to be located immediately."

"Yes, sir."

"Am I to assume you are not up for the job? I'm sure Grant can find you a filing job for a few years."

"I am the best person for the job, Mr Focus."

"Good. I assume you have some information about Vienna?"

"Yes. I have an address. I was on my way there when I was diverted to Alaska."

"Good. I await your findings."

Focus sat back in his chair and viewed the magnificent fjord for a moment. He turned to the back wall of the huge room. It was filled with tanks holding snakes from all over the world. He looked at his collection, walking along, gazing lovingly at the reptiles, all kept at the perfect temperature and fed their authentic diet of rodents and insects especially flown in from each country of origin.

"He who wants to be a dragon must eat many little snakes," he crooned to them.

Amrez dropped his head. Xincon had been his closest friend of all the Warriors. He couldn't bear to see him this way.

"Yes, I will help him. You say he was in Ecuador. Is that where his medallion will be?"

"We think so," said Regida. "He said he has been there since he took the shape of a boy, and his medallion was taken into the jungle by a shaman."

"Then I'll need my medallion back," he said.

"Why?" asked Zak.

"Because we can't be far from our pods. They are like our power source. I can't use my incredible pod-finding skills if I am that far away from my own."

"So, we have to fetch it from the museum," said Plaadio. "Zakary, you know where it is. You can fetch it with Lily first thing tomorrow."

"You're kidding, right?" said Zakary with a laugh.

Plaadio shrugged. Amrez laughed. "Where have you been, my friend? Under a rock?"

"We've all been under rocks, Amrez," said Teres, "except you and Regida."

"Good point. You see, brother, my medallion is now part of a crown that belongs to the richest most famous royal dynasty in Europe, the Habsburgs. It's a national treasure and worth a fortune. You can't just go and ask the museum guard to hand it over."

"Then we steal it," said Degon.

Zakary and Lily glanced at each other. "That will be just as hard," Lily said. "We need to know how to get past the security, the layout of the building, the alarm system."

"What do you suggest then, little human?" Fyon said.

Lily's eyes scanned the floor. "We could go to the United Nations headquarters. They will hear about you at some point. And they will be impartial and help you out."

"Impartial? Possibly. Bureaucratic, definitely. I know what they are like. It'll take too long," countered Amrez.

Pedro moaned and shivered on the floor.

"It's late and we need to make him comfortable," Chime said. "Let's get him up to the main house. Meet in the drawing room in half an hour and we will plan a way to get the medallion."

"Fyon, keep your tail on our runaway friend here, just in case," Degon ordered.

Amrez stepped up to Degon. His brown eyes flashed red and his nostrils flared. He brought his face close to the Leo. "I don't need a babysitter, and I don't need you telling me what to do. I told you I will help."

Degon let out a warning roar in Amrez's face, though he flinched not.

"Settle down, brothers," Plaadio said, pushing them apart. "Back off, now!" he spoke harshly as the two Warriors held the other's gaze. Prymaw stepped forward, ready for a fight.

Teres kneeled at the side of Pedro. "Hey, I might be strong but a little help here please!"

Degon finally turned away from Amrez. Prymaw kneeled on the other side of Pedro and together they pulled up the enormous limp body and took the stairs to the garden.

Once Pedro had been settled and sedated, Lily and Zakary met up in the drawing room. Lily and Zak continued to talk about the water crisis.

"They are rationing water in Perth. People are already fighting. We need to get the Warriors together. They are our only help. People will listen to them."

"Not if they are scared of them though."

"It's the governments who are instilling fear by chasing them down and trying to imprison them."

"Who can we go to?"

"The United Nations. Like I said, they'll be impartial and protect the Warriors."

"I hope you're right, Lily."

"The quicker we get Amrez's medallion, the quicker we can get Xincon back. I wonder if the others have found Aquarius?"

"And hopefully Amrez can locate Pisces. It can't be that hard."

Early the next morning, they reconvened. Zakary had found a black-board and chalk. Lily returned from the garden.

"I've had a look at the Treasury website. The Hyacinth Sterne is a temporary exhibit. In two days, it gets taken back to the vaults underneath the museum. We might have a chance to intercept then," Zakary explained.

"I spent a lot of time there in the seventeenth century. Know the place like the back of the queen's arse."

"Can you draw an accurate plan, Amrez? Exits, entries, etc."

"Easy."

Lily passed him some paper out of the bureau.

"Do we know what time the changeover happens?"

"No. I say we stake out the place tomorrow. Get an idea of when the security guards change shifts. Ask some questions. Check out the CCTV points."

"I can stalk the guards under my invisibility, take a look at the security headquarters and find out where the Hyacinth Sterne is stored," Chime suggested.

"What if we replace the medallion rather than take the whole crown?" Lily said.

"How?"

"Look at this pebble." She produced a stone she had found on the riverbank. "It's the same shape and size. We can glue a fake jewel on and just swap them over."

The Warriors and Zakary agreed.

"I have some costume jewellery upstairs. I'm sure I can find something that resembles the garnet," Regida offered.

"We can disable the building's communication and alarm system," the Gemini twins said together.

"Let's get some rest and do a recce at the Treasury tomorrow morning so we know what we are working with," Degon said.

The next morning, Chime, Lily, Zakary, Amrez and the Gemini twins drove into the city. They paid their entry fee into the Imperial Treasury and split up, slowly working their way around the rooms. In its own room, the Hyacinth Sterne took pride of place in the central display cabinet. Lily whistled.

"It's beautiful."

She took photos from each side, scrutinising the medallion.

Amrez called them over to a painting. "Look, that's me! Man, they were wild days! I'm in quite a few of these, actually. The prince used to hate posing, so he'd get me to stand in for him. I must say I was a far prettier subject. See how the artist catches my profile just so."

"Shut up, Amrez!" Zakary hissed. "You'll draw attention to yourself, to us!"

Amrez tutted and moved on to another painting, laughing at memories.

"He's a bloody liability!"

"I'll take care of him," Lily said. She grabbed Amrez by the arm and steered him to a member of staff.

"Excuse me. My aunt and uncle are arriving next week. Uncle Bob is a bit of a history buff and would love to see the Hyacinth Sterne. Will it still be here in the Treasury by then?"

"An incredible piece, isn't it? Unfortunately, it goes back into storage tomorrow. Can't say when it will rotate out again."

"Oh, tomorrow! What time? I'll come back and take some photos for him. My mobile battery has just died, you see."

"I'm sorry ma'am. We reorganise the museum before 8.00 am. This is your last chance. We have some lovely postcards in the shop though."

Lily thanked him and they walked back to Zakary.

Chime went into the washroom and locked herself in a cubicle. She pulled her scales out of her bag and let them settle. She waited until the person next to her had left and listened for anyone approaching. Once all was quiet, she took a breath in and faded away. She opened the door and saw nothing in the mirror. Once out of the toilets, she drifted through the museum. If her scales were only minutely unbalanced, her form would return. She stuck to the walls of the rooms, avoiding the tourists, and looked for a guard on the move.

She observed two guards talking and looking at their watches. One left, giving his colleague a wave. She followed, keeping so close behind him she could smell his cologne. Round his neck he wore a lanyard, and he waved the card across the security pad. He pushed the heavy door and Chime slipped in behind him. In the room, a bank of screens took up one side. A woman was sitting on a chair holding a mug of coffee.

"Guten morgen, Heinrich."

"Hi Ingrid. Any coffee left?"

"Ya, help yourself."

Chime looked at each screen in turn. She saw Lily and Amrez

walk arm in arm to a curator and talk. Zakary was looking at the Hyacinth Sterne. He moved around the room and glanced at the camera. Chime noted the camera numbers at the bottom left-hand corner of the screen. There were cameras in the corridors, shop, and some exhibits had a dedicated security. She noticed a camera on an empty corridor outside the lift in the entrance and another at the lift doors on the basement floor. She could read a sign on a door that said, 'Treasury Store'.

Heinrich poured himself a coffee and flicked open a newspaper. He and Ingrid chatted idly about shift times.

"You on tomorrow?"

"Yeah, early shift with the changeover. Hate it. Gives me the creeps going down to the vault."

"Believe in ghosts, do you?" Ingrid taunted.

"Wanna swap?" he said.

"No, I'm good."

"See, you're scared of it down there too!"

"Blödsinn!"

Chime smiled.

"OK, better go and relieve Johan. You know how grumpy he gets."

"Ya, see you."

Ingrid left the security headquarters with Chime following close behind.

Back at the house, the group reconvened. Lily worked on the fake medallion. Amrez adjusted his drawings and briefed them on how to get in and out. Chime, Degon and Plaadio devised the plan.

"Fyon, how are your stone setting skills?"

"What do you mean?"

"Can your tail remove the medallion and replace it?"

Fyon swished her tail around and banged it on the table.

Everyone flinched a little. She picked up the pointed end and two little pincers opened and closed.

"This little beauty has the fine motor skills of an octopus," she bragged.

"So, we'll smuggle you down in your pod and you can make the switch." Plaadio said.

"How will we distract the staff?" Degon asked.

"Fancy starting a little fire, my friend?" Plaadio suggested.

Degon's eyes lit up and his mane gave a little puff of flames.

"Castor, Pollux, can you cut the cameras to IMPT 7, 8, 11 and 15. These are the main areas."

"I'm not babysitting this time," Teres spoke.

Everyone went quiet.

"Prymaw," Degon announced finally.

"No!"

"We don't need you this time, brother," Plaadio said.

"And what are you doing, Plaadio?"

"I'm planning this thing!"

"We're all planning it! What is Teres going to do?"

"We may need him to move doors or walls," Degon said.

"Don't be ridiculous!"

No one said anything. "Suit yourselves." Prymaw stood and strode out of the room.

Zakary shook his head. "Who knew aliens could be so touchy!" he whispered to Lily, who sniggered.

"I'll check on him."

She went after him.

"Hey, Prymaw!"

"What is it, Lily?"

"You have done so much, don't be angry."

"I don't care. It's just Degon is always trying to outdo me. He's insufferable."

"Nobody seems to like him that much."

"Because the only thing he likes is himself."

"He does seem rather big-headed. Was he always like that?"

"Yes, there were many fights on Leo, each one of them trying to outdo the other."

"Don't let him get to you, Prymaw."

Prymaw harrumphed and walked away.

When Lily returned to the drawing room, Plaadio was running through the final plan on the blackboard.

"Does everybody know what they are doing? Chime, you are integral in this. Any questions?"

"No, all clear."

"Degon, no theatrics, OK? Just a little heat."

"Of course! What do you take me for?"

"OK, just checking. We can't afford to mess this up."

"How is the fake coming along?"

"Lily and I are nearly done. Amrez has confirmed it looks accurate," Regida said.

"OK, good. We'll leave at 6.00 am."

Everyone dispersed to rest and run over their part of the plan.

The next morning, the team arrived in a van. In the end, Regida and Plaadio remained behind with Prymaw. The streets of Vienna were quiet. Only the clanking of the rubbish collectors echoed along the cobbled roads. The sun had already risen, and it shone brightly off the windows.

The twins left first to locate the fuse box.

The others waited for the guard Heinrich to arrive, along with the museum director and another helper. They let themselves into the Treasury and disabled the alarm. Chime, already invisible, slipped in behind them.

Opposite the ticket desk in the hall, an old lift went to the offices on the first floor and to the vaults below where other valuables, paintings, letters and obscure treasures were stored.

The director told Heinrich and the assistant he was fetching the keys and disappeared up in the lift. Heinrich went to put his bag in the security room while the assistant checked the phone messages. Chime remained perfectly still. Then the director appeared out of the lift and walked into the exhibition room, where Heinrich and the assistant were now waiting. He unlocked the case and with gloved hands, the assistant lifted the Hyacinth Sterne off its cushion.

The three walked back to the lift and as it opened, Chime quickly stepped into the far corner. The doors closed. Heinrich breathed heavily through his nose and shivered. He ran his hand through his hair and gave his head a scratch, dislodging a hair. It drifted down, past his collar and headed straight for one of the bowls on Chime's scales. She watched in horror, unable to move in the cramped lift for fear of alerting them to her presence. She lowered her scales as the hair fell. She crouched down and moved the scales across her body, but the hair caught the shift in the current and it followed the scales like a heat-seeking missile. Gently, quietly, Chime blew the hair, and it narrowly missed landing on the scale's bowl.

"Did you feel something?" Heinrich said. He rubbed his hand on the back of his neck. "I hate it down here, I tell you. It gives me the creeps."

The other two laughed. "Don't say boo," the director said, "or Heinrich might pass out." The assistant chuckled.

"I can hear his knees knocking!"

They laughed again and Heinrich scowled.

The lift doors opened, and they all got out except for Chime. As soon as the door closed, she came back and pressed the lift to the ground floor.

"Hey, why is the lift going up?" she heard Heinrich say. "See? Weird stuff is happening."

Chime took the Leo medallion out of her pocket. Saying the words, he appeared in a flash of gold, taking up much of the space.

"OK, Degon, do your thing."

He shook his mane and the temperature in the lift went up. He shook it again and flames dropped to the floor.

"Enough, go back into the medallion."

But Degon couldn't help himself do one more shake and another stream of flames dropped to the small fire already in the lift.

"Degon! Enough!" Chime hissed. He disappeared as the lift went back down, giving Chime a moment to become invisible. The doors opened and Chime stepped around the fire. Smoke was already billowing. Heinrich was hovering by the door. He turned and his eyes grew wide.

"Oh, my God! Fire, fire!" Heinrich shouted.

The store door was open, and the director and assistant were placing the crown back in its place. Chime hovered smoothly into the room just before they ran out, alerted by Heinrich's cries. The director yelled out in alarm and grabbed the fire extinguisher.

"Close the door!" he shouted to the assistant at his heels.

She slammed the door to keep the fire away from the precious and ancient treasures. Chime reappeared. She took the Scorpio medallion out and actualized Fyon.

"What's happening out there?"

"The fire, Degon went too far as usual."

"The fool. He has no subtlety! Where is this thing?"

Chime gave her the fake medallion and retrieved the crown. Fyon quickly got to work. Her pincers deftly peeled back the gold claws holding Amrez's pod and, after dropping it in Chime's hand, she replaced it with the pebble from the Danube.

"Hopefully no one will even look at it," Chime said.

"Nearly done. There. How are you going to get out of here?"

"Walk out, I hope."

Suddenly a blast of water shot out of the sprinklers in the ceiling and a siren began to wail.

"The fire must be out of control. That idiot Degon!" Fyon said.

"Get back into your pod, Fyon. I need to get out of here."

Chime ran to the door and tried to open it. But it was locked. She bashed her shoulder against it, to no avail. She thought for a moment and re-actualized Fyon.

"Can you open the door?"

Fyon put the end of her tail to the lock and, within a second, unlocked it. She gave the door a kick to open it. But flames and smoke from the lift shaft escaped around the edges of the doors. The Warriors retreated to the room and closed the door.

"We're trapped!"

Chime looked around. There were no other doors or windows. But she remembered Amrez's sketch of the palace. He said a tunnel stretched between the chapel cellar to the west to the Treasury as a means of escape in the Middle Ages.

"Teres can break through into the tunnel to the chapel."

She retrieved the final medallion and said the words in her tongue. Soon Teres filled the space between the treasure-filled walls.

"What has happened?"

"Degon's fire got out of control, and we're trapped in this room. Can you break through the wall into the corridor to the chapel? I think it should be about here."

As the water poured down on them and the alarm screeched in their ears, Teres moved a large shelf out of the way with Fyon's help. He stood square to the wall and held his axe against it. It vibrated and plaster dropped from a crack in the ceiling. Then a crack split the wall in two and bricks fell away. Teres wedged his axe in the wall and placed his hands inside the crack and swept the wall aside as if it were a pair of curtains.

"Go, go!"

Chime and Fyon ducked under his arms and he followed into a pitch-black corridor. Teres closed the gap in the wall as neatly as he could. They crept slowly along without a glimmer of light, Teres leading the way. After feeling their way for a quarter of an hour, he stopped.

"A door ahead."

"Can you hear anything?"

"Only those sirens going off in the museum."

The three stopped and listened. Teres gently took the handle of the door and pulled it open. A heavy cloth hung in front of it. Fyon used her tail to pull it to one side. Something moved on the other side and Fyon struck out with lightning reflexes. There was a squeal. She pulled her tail back in, clasping a dead rat in her pincers.

Chime and Teres breathed out.

"Fyon! What if was a human?" Chime reprimanded.

"Don't worry, I can smell the difference between a rat and a human. Just."

They stepped into a dark room, a chink of light only evident around the edges of another door.

"You two better go back into the pods. This should lead up into the chapel."

Alone again, Chime gently opened the door. Old stone steps wound around and around as it got lighter and lighter. She could see daylight brightly now and hurried her steps. An archway appeared. She was nearly out but came to a halt as solid iron bars blocked her exit. Tourists and clergymen were moving around the chapel. She ducked back into the shadow.

Lily, Zak and Amrez watched the entrance to the Treasury from the van. They expected the spectre of Chime to knock on the door at any moment, but instead a sharp siren filled the air.

"Is that the alarm? Castor and Pollux should have disconnected it."

"Something has gone wrong! What do we do now?" Lily said.

"Shit! Do we go in?"

Castor and Pollux appeared from the side of the building.

"What happened? You were meant to cut the alarm system as well as the cameras!" Amrez said angrily.

"We did. That's the fire alarm."

"Degon!" they all said together.

"I knew we shouldn't have trusted that fool!" Amrez banged the dashboard with his fist.

"Where's Chime?"

Castor and Pollux shrugged. "We will try to locate her."

After a few moments, they spoke. "She is below somewhere."

"Underground?" said Lily.

Amrez rubbed his face and pulled his hands through his hair.

"She'll keep her calm. She has Fyon and Teres with her."

"She must have got as far as releasing Degon in the lift, and if she had made it back to the ground floor, she would have got out by now," said Lily.

"Which means she is still in the vault. Is there a way of getting out?"

"There is the passage to the chapel, but that was blocked off a hundred years ago."

"If she has Teres..."

"That explains why she's underground. They're making their way to the chapel!"

They jumped out of the van. Fire engines had screeched to the front of the treasury.

"I hope they save my paintings," Amrez growled.

As they ran through the palace, the staff were directing people to evacuate the building.

"Quick, this way!" Amrez opened a door and rushed them through. "We won't even get access to the chapel if we don't hurry. This will get us to the courtyard."

He raced them through rooms and doors, forcing locks until they were back in the open air. Then through another building and they were at the entrance of the chapel. A man was directing people out into the courtyard as the sirens were wailing.

"We won't all get in," Castor said.

"I'm small, I can sneak in," Lily said. "I'll meet you back at the van."

"Be careful." Zak pecked her on the cheek. They turned and joined the flow back to the muster point.

Lily pressed herself close to the wall and let the crowd flow past as she inched in the other direction. For once, she was grateful for her small stature. She crept around the door and took in the beautiful space. The bright whiteness of the stone walls with a central chandelier oozed with holy opulence. The usher closed the doors and she was alone. She crept along the east wall of the chapel.

"Chime!" she stage whispered. "Are you here?"

Lily heard a footstep. "Chime?"

"I'm here!" In the corner of the chapel, a small opening was blocked with bars. "In here!"

Lily went up to the bars. "You made it!"

"Here are Fyon and Teres." Chime handed the medallions to Lily. "Now, get me out of here. I'll go into my pod and you can reach through."

Chime placed the pod by the bars and disappeared into it. Lily squeezed her hands through and managed to reach it with the tips of her fingers. She heard a sound. The doors were opening and men's voices spoke.

The men came in, checking the chapel for signs of smoke. They walked up the centre aisle and Lily swiftly grabbed the medallion and rolled under the altar, which was hung with a white cloth. She breathed gently, listening to their rising voices, concern and shock at the fire she assumed, and willed them to leave.

Suddenly, the fire alarm stopped. An eerie silence permeated throughout the chapel. This prompted the men to investigate what was happening, and as soon as she heard the door click shut, Lily ran down the aisle. She cautiously peaked through the large doors until it was clear and walked briskly to the waiting van.

"Thank God!" said Zakary.

"I did!" Lily said. "Couldn't have got much closer to him under the altar!"

Zak drove them back to the house in silence. They all hoped that the Treasury hadn't been ruined, and that Chime had succeeded in her mission.

Back at the house, the Warriors were brought out, and the debrief began.

"You idiot!" Amrez shouted. "You and your giant ego almost got Chime and Fyon killed. Humans were in danger. Let alone all that junk in the Treasury that humans care about so much."

"I did what was asked of me!"

"No, you tried to steal the show with your pyromania."

"Calm down, both of you," Regida said.

"No one was hurt. Chime and Fyon made the exchange and we are safe. Chime, give Amrez his pod."

Chime passed him the jewel of the Hyacinth Sterne.

"What's this?"

"Your pod."

Amrez shook his head. "No, this isn't my pod, this is a trinket, a fake!" He tossed it on the floor.

"No, I swapped them over. Chime watched me."

Lily picked it up. "It's not the one we made. Look, the jewel is set better and is a slightly different shade."

"It is not my pod," said Amrez. "Look, feel it." He snatched it out of Lily's hands and tossed it to Plaadio.

Plaadio passed it to Prymaw, Teres, Degon, around to each of the Warriors who turned it over.

"We replaced a fake with a fake," Chime said quietly.

"And nearly burnt down the entire Hofburg Palace," Plaadio added.

"Pedro is deteriorating quickly," Regida said. "We need to find your pod, Amrez, or we will lose one of us and our strength with it."

Zak sank into the sofa. Lily looked at the ceiling. Amrez went to the window and stared out into the garden.

"I'll use my bow and arrow. It will be in the country somewhere."

"And how do we know you'll return?" Degon hissed.

"One more word out of you and I swear you'll never see me again."

"I've had enough of your bickering!" Prymaw shouted. "Go and find your pod, Amrez and be back before dawn."

Amrez's eyes flashed. He turned and stormed out of the house, picking up the gym bag that carried his bow and arrow on the way.

24 / THE FUNERAL

In 1405, the priest, who had visited Ana's family after her death, made his offering of the unusual medallion to the duke. The duke admired it greatly and commanded it to be incorporated into his new crown. His jeweller was called and given the brief. The old jeweller had never seen a specimen so fine. He designed the crown to show off its beauty and polished the metal to make it shine. He crafted one hundred little gold claws to hold it in place. But every time he tried to set the stone, it tumbled out of his fingers or pincers. He crafted a bezel to hold the medallion, but still it slipped out. Whatever he tried from all his years of experience, he could not get the piece to stay in the setting. Terrified of losing not only his reputation but possibly his life, he found a pebble by the river and coated it in burnished gold-leaf. He selected a jewel in colour and size to match and carefully etched the strange symbol on the back. No one but he had carefully examined the original. He easily set the fake piece in the crown. The problem was how to dispose of the original. He wanted it away from him and safely hidden. He asked God for help and opened his bible. The book fell open at Proverbs 21:1. 'The king's heart is in the hand of the Lord, as the rivers of water: he turneth it whithersoever he will.'

In the hands of the Lord. He would hide the medallion in the local church, high in the roof space with the birds and the mice. No one would ever know.

Amrez walked down to the banks of the river. He breathed in the muddy aroma. This was the first thing he smelled when Ana found his pod and had brought him out of it. He sighed and hung his head. He had never wanted to see the pod again after Ana was killed. Now, he was used to Earth, knew the ways of the humans and delighted in its gifts. Being with the Warriors only reminded him of the young buck he once was. Everyone treated him like a child and yet he had lived a thousand lives compared to them. He itched to run, but he had promised them he would return. He pulled his bow out of his bag and plucked an arrow from the case.

Amrez closed his eyes and thought of his pod. He drew a picture in his mind's eye, following the smooth contours and the purple zircon jewel. He envisioned the sign of Sagittarius and pulled back his bow. The arrow flew straight up into the star-filled sky in a trail of sparkles.

Within a second, he was gone.

He landed heavily on a tiled roof. He stood still and listened. His arrow was embedded in the tiles. The darkness in the surrounding land told him he was in the country. A steeple rose up behind him. He was standing on the roof of a church. Amrez walked to the edge and looked down. His way down was either a drainpipe or a tree. He swung into the branches of the tree and gently dropped onto the soft grass.

The door to the church was open and he let himself in. An inner door revealed wooden steps leading him up to the steeple. Halfway up, he found a small hatch in the wall. He pushed the door in with his foot and only just managed to wiggle his body through the opening. It was dark and dusty. Little beasts rustled. He shone his torch and saw the tip of his arrow among the beams. Amrez commando crawled across the boards and reached a small wooden box right below the arrowhead. He opened it and pulled out a leather pouch crusted with age. Inside lay his medallion. He dropped it into his hand. Flashbacks of his home and his family surfaced. He sighed.

"Party's over DJ Rez," he whispered. He pulled the arrow through the ceiling and wiggled back out of the roof space.

Back at the house in Vienna, Amrez swore he heard all the Warriors let out a sigh of relief when they saw him, which irritated him. He had no desire to linger amongst them.

"We've finally heard from the others," Lily said as she entered the kitchen where Regida was making tea. The Warriors sat and stood around the kitchen table.

Though Regida didn't pause, Lily saw her back twitch.

"What news?"

"They are in Moscow, waiting to catch a flight back. They were successful. That's all Stevie said."

"When will they arrive?" Regida tried to control her voice. The thought of seeing Tim filled her with both joy and dread.

"In two days."

"That will be enough time for Amrez to find Xincon and Plaadio's pods," Regida said.

"Yes, he just left."

Later that day, Amrez returned again with the Cancer medallion.

"Where was it?" Teres asked.

"Where no modern man has ever been, by the looks of it. Somewhere in Peru. I found it in an ancient, buried city in the middle of dense jungle. In some sort of shrine. I didn't hang around. Like I promised, I came straight back," he said pointedly.

"Let's gather the others and give it to Pedro."

Amrez tossed the medallion to Teres.

"You take it from here, bro, my day's work is not yet done."

Amrez returned to the garden and put his mind to the Capricorn symbol. He felt weary, forgetting the energy it took to travel with his arrow. He took a deep breath, pulled the bow string and flew.

Chime knocked on Pedro's door and went in. The man was quivering on his bed, dragging in breaths. His face was oozing as lesions broke out and each time he moved, he cried out in pain. Blisters on his arms and legs made him seem even larger. Red tinged discharge leaked from his eyes and nose.

"Pedro, my friend. Amrez has found your medallion, Xincon's pod from Cancer. You remember?"

Pedro moaned.

"Here, hold it Xincon."

Chime gently placed the medallion in Pedro's shaking hand and he yelled out in anger. The Warriors hovered away from the bed. Pedro moaned, murmuring in Spanish.

"Nothing is happening," Fyon said. "We are too late. His body is barely alive."

"Just wait," Regida whispered.

"Xincon! Brother!" said Plaadio.

Pedro coughed a hacking cough, spraying blood droplets across his sheet. His chest heaved, grasping for oxygen, but failing as his mouth fell wide open, his tongue reaching for something his body could use to stay alive. He grunted, his eyes rolled back, and his body went flaccid on the bed. The medallion dropped to the floor. Chime felt his pulse and shook her head.

"No, no, no! Xincon! Come back!" Teres said, grabbing his other hand.

"There is nothing in his mind," Castor said, "all is quiet."

Prymaw let out a cry of rage. Degon dropped his head. A silence hung over the room. Each Warrior trying to make sense of what they witnessed and what it meant. Chime pulled the sheet over Pedro's grey face.

"We will have to bury him," she said quietly.

They left the room. Lily picked up the medallion, turning it over in her hand.

"We were too late," she said. Zakary drew her into his arms, but she pulled away. "And I don't know what this will mean for the Warriors."

The passengers on the plane in Anadyr opted to stay on board while supplies were loaded, and more people boarded. Each scanned the countryside and airport through the small windows, expecting an official vehicle to come careering toward them. But the flight departed within the hour, arriving in Moscow nine hours later. Terrified of leaving the airport or splitting up, they took turns to sleep until the flight for Vienna left in the afternoon.

The party arrived back at the house in Vienna travel weary, feeling a mixture of cautiousness and jubilation. Lily and Zak were especially pleased to see them, but the mood was low. Mack and Sal were introduced. Sal clutched onto Tammy's arm, unable to believe the array of beings gathered in one room. Sal actualized Hastia and the Warriors' spirits lifted as they welcomed her.

Amrez arrived back from Australia soon after. He tossed Plaadio his medallion with the comment, "don't even ask what I had to go through to find it."

He greeted Hastia, then looked at his fellow Horoscopians.

"What's going on?"

"I'm sorry, brother. It's Xincon... he didn't make it."

Amrez closed his eyes. His old friend, the only one he really cared for, was dead. Astro put their hands over their face and let out a sob. Tammy cupped her hands over her mouth. The others sighed. Jason shook his head and Stevie swore. Tim tried not to look at Regida's impassive face. John put his hand on his son's shoulder.

Degon stepped into the middle. "Tonight, we will honour our Cancerian brother. We will eat and remember him in the Horoscopian way. Then we will find Mequitha and Maroda, our Piscean sisters. Thank you, Amrez, for your help."

"Help? My friend is dead because of me. You are all right. I am a self-centred narcissist. I am bad—bad news, bad karma. I will find Mequitha and Maroda. Then I will exile. I will return to my pod, where I am safe from harming another person."

"Amrez, do not take responsibility for Xincon. He put himself there. You did your best," Pollux said.

"If we hadn't had to chase him down, he would have got back in time to save him. Don't try to sugar coat it. Amrez is the one who should be dead, not Xincon," Fyon spat.

"Fyon!" Regida exclaimed.

"As always, she speaks the truth. I cannot be here anymore." Amrez kicked a chair with force and stormed out.

That night, they sat in the garden around a large table. The midsummer air was warm. A feast of dishes had been brought in and wine glasses were filled. The full moon poured her light on what looked like a celebration but was, in fact, a commiseration.

As the Warriors and humans gathered, there was no chatter or laughter. They each took a seat. Degon at one end and Prymaw at the other. Prymaw stood. Xincon's medallion sat upon a plinth in the middle of the table.

"Where is Amrez?" Degon growled.

"In the house, he refuses to join us," Fyon replied.

Degon roared. He shouted Amrez's name and the humans flinched.

"Prymaw, we will fetch him," Castor and Pollux said together. "We'll talk to him."

"There is too much talk. Prymaw, let's go."

The two fire Warriors marched back to the house. Regida sighed.

Chime closed her eyes. Teres shook his head. "Brothers, go easy," he called after them. Degon's mane shook droplets of fire. The humans sat uneasily in the quiet. Then roaring and crashing came from within the house. Degon's anger and Prymaw's determination were palpable.

At last, they emerged. Amrez was bound in Prymaw's horns, his face grazed, and his stylish clothes ripped. Amrez took a seat and folded his arms, fury flashing in his eyes.

Prymaw withdrew his horns and cracked his neck. "This night we say goodbye to a fine Horoscopian. We took a long journey to get here. There was always the risk that one or more of us would not survive. Our friend Xincon was one who loved his home more than any and had no desire to leave it. Let us hope he has returned."

The Warriors each spoke a word in their language and guzzled the contents of their glass down in one. The humans raised their glasses and took a sip.

"Now we will sing him home," Degon said.

He opened his mouth, and a low grumble emanated. Strange words flowed above the tone. One by one, the other Warriors joined in. The humans could detect no tune, yet the resulting sound had a haunting beauty. The song went on and on. Stevie looked at Jason. John gave Tammy a sideways glance. Finally, after a quarter of an hour, Degon's voice faded out and slowly the others until Chime's high tone remained. She brought it to a close and silence filled the air.

"Let us give the final hand."

Fyon put her hand on her fellow water sign's medallion. Each Warrior placed their hand on top.

"You too." Regida invited the humans to place their hand on the pile.

"Travel well, Water-brother," Fyon said and slid her hand out from the bottom of the pile.

"Be happy, Cancerian."

"Journey with love, Xincon."

One by one, the Warriors spoke a word in English or in their own tongue and removed their hand. Then the humans each said their tribute and pulled their hand away.

"Goodbye, boss," said Astro.

"Rest in peace."

"Vale!"

"God speed."

Finally, Tammy's hand dropped onto the medallion. It was warm from the pile of hands. Not warm, but hot. She felt it vibrate under her palm. Her eyes widened, and she looked around the table to see if what she felt was normal.

"It's hot," she stammered. "It's, it feels... alive!"

With that, silver beams of light shot out between her fingers and concentrated in the air above the table. The rays busily worked until a towering form took shape. Everyone pushed back their chairs and stood, watching as the solid mass of Xincon appeared before them.

"Xincon, Xincon!" they all shouted. "He's not dead, he made it!"

"Tammy, you are of Cancer?"

She shrugged, "July 1st, I guess so!"

The Warriors leapt up and down and hugged and banged heads. The humans laughed and watched in awe as the muscular crab-like man waved an enormous claw around the table. Amrez leapt up beside him, his dazzling smile restored to his fine face. Then Fyon jumped up and looked into his eyes before they dipped their heads for the Horoscopian greeting. Prymaw and Degon crashed onto the table, sending plates and dishes flying.

The night turned into one of raucous celebration. They ate and drank and danced. Humans and Warriors together, arm in arm, head to head. Tammy, Mack and the rest told Lily and Zakary about finding Hastia and Zak and Lily described the heist.

Regida approached Tim.

"Can we talk?" she asked.

Tim shrugged. They walked to the bank of the Danube. The noise of the laughter and music faded. They sat on a bench and watched the moonlight scattering in the black water.

"I should have told you. I wanted to, but it seemed such a big thing to say."

"Tell me now."

"I am from Virgo. As far as I can tell, we are built the same as humans. I've never risked going to a hospital or seeing a doctor, but I've studied the human form and it aligns with Virgoans. We have life partners and children, just like you, Tim."

"But you don't want to be with a mere human? Is that what you're saying, Jill? I mean Regida."

"You can call me Jill." She put her hand on his arm. "Tim, I love you. There is nothing I want more than to marry you and have children together."

"Superhuman Virgo children? Is that even possible?"

"I don't know, Tim. But there is something else..."

"You left someone behind?"

"No. I have no family. Just like here. My parents died and I never partnered. That was why I was chosen to come here. I had few attachments."

"What then?"

"Once we consummate, once we make love, we, I would lose my powers."

Tim turned and looked at her.

"And you don't want to lose your powers."

"Not yet, not until..." she trailed off.

"Until what, Jill?"

"Until we have found all the Warriors. They need my powers."

"Not necessarily! We only have the Pisceans to find now. We're so close." He took her face in his hands and breathed in the scent of her skin. "I love you Jill, I love you so much it hurts."

He drew his hands over her chest and caressed her breasts, clothed by her silk blouse. He pulled her in close and kissed her, devouring her mouth. For a moment, she leaned in.

"I can't, Tim, I'm sorry." She pushed him away.

Tim released her and jumped up. He blew out and pulled his hands through his hair.

"You can't keep me hanging on like this." His voice rose. "It's now or never, Jill."

"I can't right now, Tim. I'm sorry."

He sighed and stalked away, unable to look at her.

As the moon receded and dawn approached, all but two of the remaining revellers fell asleep. Most were as unconscious as the last two of their Horoscopian friends who slept alone somewhere else in the world. But Regida and Tim lay in their separate beds in separate rooms and stared at the ceiling.

A man who had not slept for many hours and feared he would never sleep again, sat in a car a little way down the road from the house. He dialled with shaking fingers. Someone picked up his call immediately.

"Visual on twelve Zodiac monsters and ten humans," he said in a thick Russian accent.

"Follow them. Report every hour."

The man finished the call and poured another strong vodka-laced coffee from his flask.

Castor and Pollux looked at each other.

"Did you hear that?"

"Yes, sister. We need to move on."

Castor and Pollux woke the humans one by one in the early hours. "We are being watched, we need to go."

John and Tammy shook their offspring awake. Lily came out of her room yawning.

"What's happening?"

"Castor and Pollux tuned in to something. There is someone watching us. We need to get out of here."

"How will we do that?"

"The warriors will go back into their pods. Amrez will find the Piscean sisters and we will join him."

"But we have to evade the spy, or he'll just follow us."

"Not if we leave by the river."

The rest met in the drawing room with bleary eyes.

"It's probably the government—we've evaded them before and we will now. As far as Castor and Pollux can tell, it is just one man."

"I can make sure he is immobilised long enough for us to get out of here," Teres said.

As everyone charged around the house packing what little they had, Teres left. He crouched into a ball and rolled across the lawn, picking up the grass onto his body. When he bounced back onto his feet, he was cloaked in green. He moved undetectably, despite his bulk, as if he were part of the earth.

A hundred metres along the road, he saw a white car parked on the verge. He crept along until he was an arm's length from the boot. Quietly, he laid his axe on the tarmac and pushed down. The ground gave way like butter, and he commanded it to fall away at each wheel. The car sank down. Inside, the man spilled his hot coffee over his legs as the car lurched into the ground. He yelled out and went to open his door, but already the earth was falling in around him and the door jammed up against the bank created by Teres' power. Within minutes, the car sat in a deep hole, the man trapped inside until someone came along with a crane to winch him out.

Teres ambled back to the house where Regida and the humans were waiting.

"Great job!" John cheered his Warrior.

"Amrez has left and all the others are safely in their pod. Lily has gone with Prymaw," Regida explained, though Zak looked unhappy.

"We'll head to the airport via the river. Then wait for Amrez to get in touch," Tammy explained.

"See you there then," Teres said, and disappeared into the medallion in John's hand.

There was no need to wait, Amrez called Regida as they were racing along the Danube.

"Back to the cold for you guys," Regida said as she came off the phone. "We're heading to Iceland."

Sandra Tress pulled up alongside the hole in the ground. She got out of the rental and looked down onto the roof of a car. A muffled voice yelled for help.

"Son of a bitch," Sandra muttered as she shook her head. She pulled out her phone and rang for emergency services before following the pathway left by Teres. The mansion was empty. Through the kitchen window she could see unwashed cups and plates, empty wine bottles. A table in the garden still held the remnants of the previous night of revelry.

A faint revving of an engine in the distance led her to the river-bank. Splashes of water still dried on the jetty. She put her head in her hands and swore. If she let them get away again, she was in deep trouble. After her video call with Mr Focus, Sandra had felt chills through her body every time she thought about him. If she failed, she was worried about a fate far worse than filing. It was his eyes that gave him away, and she shuddered at the thought of him.

The following lunch time the humans landed in Reykjavik. Amrez wore dark glasses and had the collar of his polo shirt pulled up to his ears. Hungry and eager to hear what Amrez had discovered, they went to get coffee and breakfast. Amrez chose a table at the back of the café.

"Are you all right, old boy?" John asked.

"I got recognized yesterday. I've done dozens of shows here."

"Ah, I see."

"And Marko has listed me as a missing person. He keeps calling me but I've blocked him."

"Just tell him you are taking a holiday," Tammy said.

"I've missed shows. He'll be sued. There'll be investigations. It's better I just disappear."

"Where's the Pisces medallion?" Mack asked as he tucked into his breakfast.

"It's inaccessible. My arrow took me to this whacking great volcano in the middle of the island. It's full of ice. They are in there somewhere, who knows how far down."

"Let's get there and actualize the rest of the Warriors," Tim said. "We should be able to find a way to get them out."

"We'll need a helicopter. There are no roads and it's pretty high up."

A couple of hours later, Regida had chartered two helicopters to Lake Höggormur. The views were breathtaking. Rugged mountains were striped in green and white. Glacial lakes stood out like jewels and waterfalls crashed into ragged fjords. The helicopters dropped them on the top of a mountain filled with water. Regida instructed the pilots to return in two hours.

They stood at the edge of the mountaintop lake. John crouched down and put his fingers in the icy water and winced.

"Let's bring out the Warriors," Amrez said.

Regida spoke the words to the Aries medallion, and Prymaw and Lily arrived.

Tim brought forth Teres. Stevie placed his hands on his buckle and the Gemini twins actualized, alert and tuning in to the air. Tim allowed the quivering Leo to land, sending puffs of steam up from his feet. Tammy held out the Cancer medallion and Xincon appeared, towering above her. Astro brought Chime into being. Mack held Fyon's medallion wondrously and gawked as she formed in the air. Jason unwillingly held Plaadio's medallion, though it was far better than releasing the Warrior from his own body. Salina emptied her flask into the lake and Hastia rose out of the turquoise water. She placed her medallion back in the container and handed it back to Sal.

"Let me dive down and see what's in here," she said.

Her graceful body of rippling water plunged below without as much as a splash. An eagle circled silently miles above them. The humans waited and watched their breath dissipate in the air like ghosts. After a few minutes, Hastia returned.

"The water is shallow, but below is solid ice. I cannot shift it so it must go down a long way."

"Let me see," Teres said. "Come with me, Hastia."

"Be careful brother, you are of earth, not water."

"I will just try to crack it a little."

Teres jumped into the water like a whale. Hastia shook her

ripples and followed him. They emerged much quicker. Teres climbed onto the land, streams of water pouring from his hairy body.

"It's no good. Unless I move the mountain, I can't get into it."

"Then I will melt it," Degon said.

"Even the mighty Degon couldn't melt a mountain," said Prymaw.

Degon roared a flame of fire towards Prymaw, who jumped out of its reach.

"Don't goad me, brother."

"And what? I'll toss you in that ice bath and extinguish your flames once and for all!"

"There is nothing I cannot do!"

"Including messing up," said Fyon, her tail swishing dangerously.

Stevie and Sal exchanged a glance.

"Guys, calm down."

"Only Degon could destroy hundreds of years' worth of history. Subtlety was never your strong suit," said Amrez.

"Bossiness is though," Pollux and Castor both said.

Degon was glowing. His muscles twitched and his nostrils flared as he glared at them.

"And stubborn, you just can't back down, can you?" Plaadio added.

"They speak the truth, Degon. We agreed to work as a team, but you are a one man show," said Regida.

The others agreed.

"What are they doing?" Tim murmured to John.

Tammy and Mack shifted uneasily. Jason chewed on his lip, nervous of the atmosphere.

"Stevie," Pollux said quietly.

He glanced at her and she stared into his eyes. He felt a thought land in his mind.

Chime was talking now, calmly accusing Degon of greed and glory.

Stevie let a laugh of wonder escape through his nose. He had received Pollux's message. "They are stoking his fire," he whispered.

The Warriors continued to rile the mighty Leo Warrior as he turned from one to the other, growling, advancing, lashing out. His mane danced with flames, the ground beneath his huge feet scorched and spat.

"Why?" Sal asked.

"To give him enough power to melt the ice."

The humans joined in. They threw abuse at Degon until he let out a roar so loud it shook their eardrums. He faced the lake and with his sword held high, he took a step in up to his knees. The water boiled around him. He took another step, steam rising.

"I wouldn't do that, if I were you." A loud voice cut across the lake.

Degon lowered his arms. The others looked across to see a muscled man standing on the other side.

"Who the hell is that?" Stevie asked.

The man stepped into the water, but instead of sinking, he glided across the surface. The Warriors stood straight and raised their weapons.

"Are they snakes' heads?" Sal breathed.

"Bloody hell!" Jason said, as the man floated towards them with one foot astride two huge beasts. Their thick heads curled out of the water like figureheads—except these seemed to be alive.

"Stop!" the man commanded.

There was silence on the top of the frozen volcano. The man took in the row of Zodiac Warriors.

"By the God Horos... is that...?" Castor said.

"Ophiuchus?" Pollux finished.

"Ophiuchus?" Prymaw called.

The corners of the man's mouth twitched and then smiled. "I prefer my earthly name, Orlando Focus."

"What?" Sal breathed sharply.

"Ophiuchus?" Plaadio repeated. "Is it really you?"

"Ah, I see you are surprised, Plaadio. I wonder why that might be."

"Your planet, it went first, you..."

"Died?"

"How can this be? Step forward and let us see you," yelled Degon. "This is some sort of trickery," he said to the others.

"Hah! You think a human can travel on a snake raft?"

He spoke a strange word that came from the back of his throat and a green-tinged mist floated from his mouth. The two cobras rose out of the water and lunged towards them, hissing. Tammy, Sal and Jason screamed. They all scurried backwards from the shore.

"Our brother! Is it really you?" Regida said gently. She stepped toward Ophiuchus, whose raft was now a metre away from the black shore of the lake.

"Careful, Reg." Fyon's tail drifted slowly behind her back. She stepped forward next to Regida. "Why are you here?"

"Come now, dear Fyon. Is that a way to greet a long-lost brother? I see you haven't lost your sting."

"He's another Warrior?" Astro murmured to Stevie. They were unsure if they were following correctly. "How many are there?"

"But there's only twelve Zodiac signs," Tammy said.

"No, there is another constellation that everyone ignores," John said. "Ophiuchus."

"Never heard of it," Stevie whispered.

"Me neither," said Tim, "but he and his snakes don't look terribly friendly."

"But he said he was Orlando Focus. He's—was, my boss. He can't be a Zodiac Warrior!" Sal hissed back.

"How did you make it out alive?" Teres asked. "On your own...?"

"No better way to travel, especially when your neighbours leave so late."

"We saw Serpentaria go, we saw it get sucked into the hole. We would have waited, brother."

Orlando raised a hand. "It's all in the past now. They say, 'forgive and forget' here, no?"

"Yes," Plaadio agreed, "what matters is we are here, together again."

Hastia silently rose behind Orlando.

"I know you are there, sister of the sea," Orlando said. "What say you?"

"I say we are not yet all together. My friends are frozen below us, but I assume you are already aware of that."

Orlando gave a wheezy laugh. "Of course, this is too much of a coincidence. Eleven Zodiac Warriors hiking on a remote, inaccessible volcano and happen to bump into their long-dead neighbour. Really, Hastia, nothing escapes you!"

"Where are they?" Hastia demanded.

"Enough! I will get them!" Degon waded into the icy water.

Orlando hissed another command and his snakes reared up and sprayed at Degon. Flames flew back at the snakes and a green vapour swirled in the air.

"Your pets don't scare me!" Degon exuded flames, ignoring the striking cobras. Hastia disappeared under the water and created a wave that swished the snake raft backwards.

"Hold your fire, Degon!" Orlando yelled, his voice echoing around the crater. "If you melt this mountain, you will flood the entire island. And this is pristine water the world needs right now. Anyway, I have this."

He held up his hand. The Pisces medallion's aquamarine jewel caught the sunlight.

"Degon! Pull back!" Prymaw waded in and pulled him by the shoulder. "He has Pisces! Hastia! Cease!"

Hastia rose behind the raft, her internal waves ebbing and flowing.

"They are here, safe and sound. Come, my friends. Come to my home and we will reunite. And celebrate. Come, come. Pod-holders too! Everyone is welcome."

He glided to the western shore and stepped onto the lava beach. The two snakes slipped out of the water and wound around his neck.

"This way," he beckoned them.

Amrez shifted on his feet.

"The arrow took me here," he muttered. "Not to him."

"Hastia, you were closest. Is it the Pisces pod?"

"I believe so."

"Let's go, but with caution," Prymaw said.

"We don't like it," Castor said.

Amrez raised his hands. "See? If anyone can read the situation, it's the Gemini twins."

"Regida, can you see what his soul desires?" Plaadio asked.

"I tried."

"And?"

"I have never experienced it. I see nothing."

"Nothing? Why? Is he protected?"

"No, he was open. It means that he already has what his soul desires."

As the Warriors conversed, the humans attempted to work out what was happening.

"What the hell is going on?" John said.

"We're not going with him," Jason whimpered.

"It's OK bro, the Warriors have got our back."

"I don't like it. It's not safe," Tim said.

"What, we wait here on a freezing mountain for the helicopter?" Mack said.

"We need to stick with them," Lily said. "We need each other."

"We've come this far, guys," Zak added. "We need to do it for the planet."

"There's no way I'm going with that freaking... freak!" Jason blustered. "You seriously thinking of following that snake man? Guys!"

"John?"

"He's a Zodiac, isn't he? He's probably just a bit fearsome, like Fyon. I say go. That's five of us vote we go. Astro?"

Astro bit their lip. "I say we go. It is safer with the Warriors than out here."

"Jason, you have survived a rebel army, a crocodile and a gunfight. Remember, you're brave now, mate?" Lily said. "Come on."

"Tammy, Sal?" Lily looked at the two women, who held hands tightly.

"Whatever we do, we must stay together. Come on Sal."

Sal swallowed and nodded. "I like snakes, anyway."

The Warriors and humans walked around the lake to where Orlando had motioned. They followed the path down to the valley. John and Tammy gasped at the beauty of the waterfall. Hastia, who had flowed down the mountain in a rivulet, dived in, leaping under the crashing water.

"Wow," Sal breathed when they came to the glass house.

Orlando let his guests into the house. The humans gasped at how the glass box seemed to hover over the valley below. The temperate atmosphere felt welcome after the biting cold wind coming off the ice on the mountaintop.

"I don't have many visitors out here, so welcome. Please, take a look at my snake collection."

Sal and Tammy gazed at the array of reptiles. But the wall of snakes made the rest feel uncomfortable.

"Please, sit. I have refreshments."

Orlando motioned to a man who was in the kitchen. He brought a tray of mugs full of steaming hot chocolate.

The Warriors stayed on their feet. Fyon roaming the perimeter and running her finger along the tanks of snakes. Orlando sat on the luxurious sofas with the humans and took a sip from his mug.

"How did you come to be here?" Prymaw asked.

"I escaped in my vessel seconds before Serpentaria was consumed by the void. It was clear to me your timing would not accommodate my survival. It's OK, I had a long time to process. I chose to travel in my form and not scurry into the pod you so elegantly designed on Gemini. It was an interesting journey. I can fill you in another time, if you care to know... which I doubt. I arrived here with a bumpy landing and sunk to the bottom of a sea. The waters thrashed and receded. The earth cracked and groaned and built an island around me. I made my home alone with my snake brethren there in the Atlantic Ocean. I healed and eventually emerged to begin my wait.

"All creatures great and small wandered the earth and I waited. Monsters came and went. Fire and ice battled over the earth. Land broke apart and smashed together. Mountains arose, seas filled, and I waited. And I waited. At last, nature took its evolutionary path to grow beings that walked on two legs and used intelligence to expand, then flourish. I have witnessed the birth of humankind. I have had a hand in shaping their psyche with the help of my serpents.

"They called me many names through the eons. Today I am Orlando Focus but I was the hero in many myths they still tell today. My name was once Odysseus. Yes, that was me! I sailed the world over and over, searching for you all. And it was when I was at sea, trying to return to Ithaca, I found one of our kind at last. When I heard their siren song, I knew it was my Piscean sisters. On my ship that day, listening to my exquisite sisters crying out to me from the depths of the ocean, I found my allies. You see, legend has it I was bound to my mast, but what dear Homer didn't know was that my snakes set me free. I dived down and rescued the so-called sirens, Mequitha and Maroda.

"Sadly, the human race did not recognise me as a Zodiac sign. You see, my constellation cannot be seen like yours. It sits on the periphery of the visible sky and can only be seen here, around the arctic circle in the summer sky. Some things never change, eh? Pushed to the edges, unadmitted, invisible. No matter. I am a Horoscopian with resources. I don't need a human guardian. It was lucky for me I found the Pisceans. They have allowed me to access my pod all these years."

"Where are they, Mequitha and Maroda?"

"They are here, as I said."

"You have been with them all along?"

"Yes, since that day on the Mediterranean Sea."

"He lies. My arrow landed on that ice lake."

Amrez looked at the medallion in Orlando's hand. He spoke in language but nothing happened. Regida spoke the same words. Chime, then Fyon joined in. All the Warriors recited the Horoscopian words that should have released Mequitha and Maroda from their pod. Orlando smiled. Degon could not contain the power that they had riled in him at the lake. He roared and pounced on him, crashing his body to the floor. Orlando shouted a command. A door opened and a well-built man stepped through, then another, followed by two women with huge snakes draped over their muscular shoulders. The four formed a circle around Orlando, who had slithered out of Degon's grip. Degon roared in fury.

"Degon! Stop!" Prymaw yelled.

"Who the hell are they?" Tim muttered.

"Meet my friends. You are still fresh to this new world, Warriors, so I'll let you into a little secret. Many years ago, gods ruled the world. It's true! This was before humans sucked the life out of existence with their so-called intellect and reasoning. When I was exploring the world of gods, I met a beautiful woman. She was intoxicating and I had to make her mine. One day, we were discovered making love by her father, Phorcys. He was incensed that his daughter, Medusa, had broken her vow of celibacy. He drew his sword to slay us both, but I took her with me into my pod to escape. When Mequitha, my Piscean ally, brought us out, Medusa had taken on some of my powers. I took her back in many times, and that is how she came to grow snakes in her hair."

He stroked the head of one of the women and trailed his hand over the mighty serpent she carried.

"After that, I experimented with other humans."

"You mean that by entering the pod, we can take on the power of the Warrior?" Lily touched her hand to the bumps that had grown on her head.

Prymaw shook his head. "This is nonsense!"

"You want proof?"

Orlando nodded to his attendants. The women lifted the snakes above their heads and gave them a command. The snakes slid out of their hands to the floor and towards the humans.

"Stand behind us!" Degon shouted.

The Warriors jumped to alert, and the humans leapt up, backing away from the serpents. Teres and Plaadio were ready to strike. Prymaw's horns vibrated, as did Fyon's tail. But the snake handlers shouted again, and the snakes ceased and slunk back to the women.

"So you see. My attendants have my powers."

"Enough of this exhibition, Ophiuchus. Bring us the Pisceans."

"Wait a minute, Degon," said Plaadio. "Why have you given humans these powers, Ophi?"

"Always the practical one! I thought you'd never ask. Did you really expect us all to fit on one tiny planet which is already overrun with these weaklings?"

"Now, wait just a minute!" Tim stepped forward. "I'm sick of you freaks. You've done nothing but put us down. You are nothing without us!"

"He's right. I don't suppose you have told the humans of your plans?" Orlando said.

Lily looked at the Warriors. "What plans?"

The Warriors glanced at each other.

"Do you think we all came here to live a life on our own? Just one of a kind? We have lost our loved ones, our homes, our civilisation. The plan was always to rebuild, was it not? To reconstitute the DNA held in the pods by vast amounts of water this sweet little planet had to offer."

"Oh my God!" Stevie breathed. "You liars. You tricked us. You told us, promised us you wouldn't hurt us. Idiots, thinking you were here to save us! I knew it!"

"Wait, Stevie, that's not the whole story..." Pollux began.

"How much water do you need?" Zak asked.

"Good question. Shall I tell them?"

"We do need water, but it's not what you think," Chime said. "The water will be returned once the hatchlings, our new life, are born."

"Hatchlings? This is sounding like a freaking horror movie." Jason moved towards the door.

"How much water do you need?" Tim asked.

Orlando smiled. "More than is left on this planet. We had no way of calculating how long it would take."

"Wait a minute, Ophi. There is not enough water left to regenerate?" Plaadio asked. "You are lying. Our calculations assured us we would have enough."

"Those calculations were made on the planet 65 million years ago. Hastia, what say you? You are the hydro expert. Tell us what your currents sense."

Hastia said nothing.

"Speak!" Orlando yelled.

"There is not enough water."

"Incorrect, sister. There is enough water for one Zodiac to regenerate and for the humans to continue their population."

"My dear humans, I'm sorry to say these Zodiac Warriors have misled you. They will fight each other to gain control of this planet and you will be the victims."

"That was never what we said. We agreed that we would do no harm, Ophiuchus," Regida said.

"Then who is the one who has saved this planet from starvation and dehydration. Who has pumped water from the sea and made it potable? Who has invested in dams and irrigation? Who has catered for the good people of this planet since the dawn of time?"

"You bastards," Stevie growled. "I knew I shouldn't have trusted you. Come on Ma, Sal. We're getting out of here."

He grabbed his sister by the hand, and they edged around Orlando and his attendants and joined Jason.

"Wait, Stevie!" Castor cried out.

Stevie looked back and shook his head. "Anyone else coming?"

Mack joined them. Tim and John nodded in agreement and went too.

"Me also. I trusted you, Chime. For all those years, we talked. I thought we were friends." Astro had tears in their eyes.

Lily looked at Prymaw. She couldn't believe they had been tricked, an alien invasion by stealth.

"Lily?" Zak said, as he too moved towards the door.

She was rooted to the spot. Her heart was human, yet she felt another part of her was now Arian. She looked at Zakary and felt torn. There was something that wanted to surrender to the charge she felt inside. It was a rising power that felt better than anything she had experienced; love, sex, drugs.

"Wait!" she said. "Prymaw, is it true?"

"We came here to rebuild, to live in our constellations. Like I told you, it is written in the stars, Lily. We need Earth to do that but..."

"So you came to rape our planet for your own ends? To kill us off?"

"No, we need you, as much as you need us."

"So you are using us! That's no better."

"Lily, your planet is dying. If humans were to save it, they would have done so by now."

"That's not true! There are thousands of people working towards a healthy planet."

"Thousands? Out of eight billion?"

"No, no, there's more."

"For once, I agree with Prymaw," Orlando said. "Earth is on a fast trajectory to death. I've watched it happen over 100 million years, give or take a few millennia. That's why I have invested in it, to save it."

The humans headed for the door.

"Before you leave, you may want to hear this. Prymaw was correct. They did need you to actualize them from their pods, or medallions, as you so quaintly call them. But what they haven't told you is..."

"Ophiuchus don't..." Xincon warned.

"My name is Orlando!" he yelled at them so loud the glass panes that protected them from the sheer drop into the valley shuddered. He turned to the group, who were desperate to leave. "What they didn't tell you is that you have the power to de-actualize the Zodiac Warriors back into their pods."

The humans looked at the Warriors.

"How?"

"Why didn't you tell us?" Astro asked, another flood of disillusion bringing tears to their eyes.

"Because we didn't know, for sure," Chime said.

"Truth is..." Amrez stepped towards the humans. "We didn't know if you would use the power wisely. It put us at risk."

"It could put you at risk too." Prymaw joined Amrez.

He looked imploringly at them. "Orlando is lying! How do you know he won't use the water to regenerate?"

"Because I can't regenerate on my own. You know as well as I that we need our combined knowledge to build our new planets. Humans barely have the technology to explore outer space, let alone build there."

"And why would we trust you?" Stevie spat.

"As I said, I have watched you humans destroy this planet. I have dedicated my time to ensuring it is saved. I own enough water to rebuild my own planet and save yours. Without these Warriors, you and I can all survive. But with them all rebuilding..." he opened his hands up. "We all die."

He left the statement in the air. Stevie plunged his hand into his pocket and pulled out his medallion. He held it out in front of him and pointed at Castor and Pollux.

"Go back in! Retreat, liars!"

The twins had no time to react, but disappeared into beams of yellow light.

"Well played, young man."

"Wait, Orlando, let's discuss this," Chime said.

Fyon, Degon and Teres glanced at each other and leapt toward Orlando. But his attendants and their snakes jumped into defend their master and deflected the three Warriors.

"What about Maroda and Mequitha?" Hastia spoke for the first time.

"As I said, they are my allies. I will ensure they are taken care of."

"We need to hear that from them."

"Then you will have to dig them out of 25 metres of ice. Be my guest."

"I knew they were in there! I told you!"

"Beside the point, dear Amrez. Not even Degon could have melted that far down," he sneered. "Enough of this. Do you deny that to reconstitute the DNA and rebuild our planets, we need more water that exists on Earth?"

"Hastia?" Sal said. "If anyone knows, it's you."

Hastia contained a storm of waves that broke out all over her body. She rippled up to Orlando and surrounded his body in a whirlpool.

"You think you can control me? You think you own me? I do not bow down to anyone but Horos." The words emanated from her swirling body. Orlando wavered in the strong current. He commanded a word which released a snake. It launched itself in with Hastia. The snake and the river tangled up. The mass writhed and splashed.

"Hastia! Retreat to your pod!" Sal's voice had never been so loud. Within half a second, the snake fell onto the floor with a thud as a flow of turquoise light sped into the flask.

"Teres, I thought we were friends. Tell me this isn't true?"

"Of course, we came to save ourselves but not at your expense."

John shook his head. "How could it ever have not been at our expense?"

He held out his medallion and recalled the mighty bull. Mack and Tammy withdrew Fyon and Xincon. Jason took great pleasure in aiming his at Plaadio.

"Guys, you've got his all wrong, he's tricking..." Amrez disappeared in a purple flare.

Degon and Chime soon followed.

"Lily, you know me better than anyone. Please, you are making a big mistake," Prymaw, the second last Warrior pleaded.

"Is there enough water on earth to rebuild all your planets and keep us alive? Yes or no."

All Lily could hear was her ragged breath and a terrible roar in her head that she'd made a big mistake.

Prymaw dropped his head. "No but..."

"Prymaw, retreat!"

He was gone. Lily held the medallion to her heart as tears fell, hitting the hand that held it.

"And then there was one. It seems the queen of self-sufficiency didn't feel the need for a guardian. Feeling lonely?" Orlando moved towards Regida. "But of course, you're never lonely with your faithful boyfriend by your side."

He pointed at Tim, where a snake had slithered to his feet and was now winding its way up his legs. Tim shrieked and the others leapt away from him. A cluster of snakes circled the group.

"Now, be a good girl and disappear or lover boy here will be gone forever."

"Ophiuchus. We can sort this out. We can save ourselves and the humans."

He grasped Regida's chin in his fingers. "My name is Orlando," he said between his teeth. "You left me to die!" he shouted in her face and pushed her to the floor. Tim cried out, but the snake tightened its grip.

"There was a time when I was doing all this for you! I planned to gather all the water we needed and rebuild our galaxy. But when I saw the look in the Piscean's eyes when I found them, I knew you all hated me. They were never my allies; they are my slaves! These

humans have shown me kindness and friendship despite their weak-
nesses. I'd rather share my existence with them than with the traitors
of Horoscopia. Now, retreat!"

Regida looked at the humans, at Tim. With rare tears in her eyes,
shook her head and flowed into herself in a green stream of light and
her medallion dropped to the floor.

"Lovely," Orlando said. He picked it up and went to the back
wall and dropped it in one of the tanks. "You have just saved your
race. I congratulate you! Now, I will keep the pods safe. Please..."

Orlando motioned to one of the attendants to collect the medallions from the humans and he dropped each one into the tank of a
deadly snake.

"Apologies for my strong-arm tactics, my friends. It's all for the
best. We can now work together to bring harmony and water back to
this planet."

He sighed with a warm, satisfied smile. "Ah! Forgive me! Sophia,
stand down."

The snake hugging Tim unwound and slid across to her master.
The other snakes backed off.

"I think I can hear your lift arriving. Quick, quick, you don't want
to miss it. I'll be in touch, and rest assured you and your families will
be well recompensed for your traumatic experience and rewarded for
saving your race."

They moved as a group to the door and put on their jackets in the
anteroom. There was shocked silence but a hurried chaos as they
were eager to leave. The door glided open, and Orlando waved them
off like old friends who had enjoyed a leisurely lunch.

"What the hell just happened in there?"

"I don't know. Was it for good or bad?"

"I'm so confused. What the... who the hell is that guy?"

"The snakes..."

"AND his 'attendants'."

"Army more like. How many of them has he, he trained?"

"Quick, I can hear the helicopters."

They rushed up the side of the volcano. The helicopters were landing on the crested ridge and they ran to it. Lily paused at the side of the lake. She took something out of her pocket.

"Come on, Lily!"

"Let's get the hell out of here!"

They called out, but she didn't move.

"What on earth is she doing?"

Suddenly, the centre of the lake whipped up and a sea green lightning bolt flew out of the water into Lily's hand. She turned and ran to the helicopter and scrambled in.

"Go, go," she shouted breathlessly, and they lifted off the icy white ground into a clear blue sky.

The helicopter lifted away along with the tension of being in the presence of Orlando Focus. They all felt a release, as if they were at last disengaged from a magnet.

Mack let out a sigh. "Didn't know I was signing up for this when I met you in that bar in Nome."

"Yeah, sorry about that, Mack," Tammy said, and they both laughed in a slightly hysterical way.

"What were you doing down there, Lily?" Zak asked. "I thought you were staying there for a moment."

"What was the flash that came out of the lake?" Jason asked.

Lily opened her hand up and there on her palm sat the Pisces medallion. If it weren't for the blades of the chopper, they could have heard the clouds floating by.

Eventually, Jason spoke. "How did you bloody well get that?"

"When Degon pounced on Orlando, he dropped the medallion. I managed to pick it up when Hastia attacked him."

"And you called the Pisceans back into their pod at the lake. You are a genius, girl!" Tammy exclaimed.

John scratched his head. "But how? You're Aries. You shouldn't be able to control the Pisces medallion."

"My birthday is 21st March. I am Aries, but I'm also on the cusp of Pisces. Jase, remember the day at 17 Mile Falls? I couldn't actualize Prymaw. Sometimes I can and sometimes I can't, depending on where my Sun is. Luckily, today was a Pisces day."

"Do you think we made a mistake leaving the Zodiac Warriors with Orlando?" Tammy asked.

"I don't trust him."

"Me neither."

"Nor me."

"Who does?"

"He's a complete nutter!"

No one spoke.

"But the Warriors did lie to us."

"Well, they didn't tell us the whole truth."

"So what do we do?"

Nobody had an answer. But everybody was relieved to see the roofs of Reykjavik appear in the distance.

Back in the city, the night-time sun bathed the streets in a milky glow. Tourists teemed to one of the few places on Earth that wasn't drying out. They poked around in the shops and crowded into noisy bars. The ragged Zodiac discoverers all yearned for that innocence, the peace of ignorance.

"So, we've had some time to think. Do we walk away, and hope Orlando Focus has our best interests at heart, or do we go and undo what we did and free the Warriors?"

"I don't think 'heart' and 'Orlando Focus' belong in the same sentence," Sal said.

"We need to talk to the Piscean sisters. Let's go back to my room and bring them out before my Sun passes back to Aries."

They battled against the tourists as they walked back to the hotel room. They locked the door and Lily held the medallion in her hand.

A weak green light bled from it. Slowly, the image of two women curled over each other appeared on the floor. Their bodies ended in fish tails, one a deep sea green, the other sapphire blue. One had deep russet hair, the other jet black, which intertwined over their collapsed bodies.

"Wow, they really are mermaids!" Zak breathed.

"They don't look well." Lily crouched down and brushed the hair aside. "Hello. Hey, are you OK?"

The redhead lifted her face and looked around her.

"Where is he?" Her voice was reedy.

"We have rescued you from Orlando. We need to talk to you."

"My sister is weak. She has been frozen for longer than I."

"What can we do?"

"Give me the medallion. We need its power. The short time we had inside is not enough."

"I'm afraid we don't have much time. Orlando will know by now the medallion is missing."

"Speak to me. I will hold it to Maroda. It will help," said Mequitha, reaching for the medallion.

"Before we do, tell us... are you Orlando's allies?"

Mequitha's laugh rang out like a bell.

"He has enslaved us, used us, separated us, threatened us for thousands and thousands of years. No, we are not his allies." She looked at her sister, who barely breathed. "We want him dead."

The humans each felt shame for falling for Orlando's words. It was as if he had hypnotised them in his house and made them turn against the Warriors and their own better judgement. They told the Piscean sisters everything that had happened.

"He will use you now. When he begins to rebuild, he will need the knowledge of the Zodiac Warriors. We swore to do no harm so he will threaten you so the Warriors will do his bidding."

"But he has helped humans by securing the water supply," John said.

"He has been part of the problem, don't you see? He is controlling the water, so he has enough for himself. We do not know if there will be enough for the human race."

"So, we need to go back in and rescue the medallions from the snake tanks and bring Orlando down."

Maroda stirred. "She is coming back. We need as much time as possible in our pod."

"But what if I can't bring you out again?"

"It's a risk we have to take. If we do not return to our pod, she will die and if she dies, then I will too."

"We need a plan," Jason said. "We have no room for error. What is your power?"

"We have our song."

"Your song?"

"When we sing, we hypnotise. It immobilises."

"But not Orlando?"

"No. We just give the other Zodiac Warriors a headache."

"So how did you use it on your planet?"

"To sing our babies to sleep, of course!"

"Are you saying your superpower here on Earth had no power on your own planet?"

"Pisces was a peaceful place. There was no need for force. The only thing that upset us was our tired children!"

"Have you been singing here on Earth?" Tim asked.

"Yes, trying to reach someone. We've been trapped for so long."

"The migraines!"

They looked at Tim.

"What are you talking about?"

"Jill, er Regida, she used to get terrible migraines. She said it was like a high-pitched sound in her head."

Mack had been rubbing his chin, thinking. "There's a story where I come from about the mermaids. They say their song can break the ice of winter. These songs," he said, "you reckon they're strong enough to break glass?"

❄

They allowed Mequitha and Maroda to return to the medallion.

"If we go in via the valley, we can track along the gorge until positioned under Orlando's house."

"Then bring out the mermaids."

"Their song will shatter the house and the snake tanks..."

"Bringing the medallions down the mountain side..."

"And the snakes," Jason gulped. "We need weapons."

"Where are we gonna get guns from?"

"And not get crushed by the glass?"

"That's if Lily can even actualize the Piscean sisters."

"This is a crazy plan."

Ten sets of shoulders slumped around the room.

Suddenly, the door slammed open. A tall black woman stood in the doorway, pointing a gun at them.

"Nobody move!"

Tim and Mack jumped up and the gun tracked them. The others looked on wide eyed.

"Sandra?"

Caught off guard, she lowered her gun a little and looked across the room.

"Zakary? What the...?"

"What are you doing here?"

Zakary stood up and walked towards her.

"Don't come any closer!"

"Whoa, Sandra. It's OK."

"Who the hell is this?" Mack growled.

"This is my cousin Sandra," Zakary smiled. "Haven't seen you for, wow, long time. I can't believe this! What brings you here?" Zakary slowed down as he registered the gun. "Work?"

"Still sharp as a machete, I see cuz. You know I always planned to work for the CIA. Well, triple bingo with ice-cream on top, that's what I do. So, from now on I'm asking the questions. What in your sweet mother's name are you doing here?"

"OK lady. Touching family reunion and all that, but we got a situation on our hands," Mack said.

"Sandra, do you know what you're dealing with here?" Zakary asked.

"Yes, I know! It's an extra-terrestrial invasion!"

"Now, hang on, whoever you are!" Lily butted in. "This is not an invasion."

"Oh really? Did you see what that scorpion bitch did?"

"Yes, but she was protecting herself. You would have done the same."

"You got to listen. If the government seizes us, we'll not be able to free the Zodiac Warriors."

"Can't argue with that, kind of the point of my mission. You must be Lily. Given us quite the chase. Props."

"They are here to help us, not destroy us."

"I'm not here to argue with you. I'm here to take you in. In about one minute, those gorgeous Iceland police boys will be here to bring you in. You can do all the talking you want then. Until then, put your hands on your head."

Zakary gave Lily a sideways glance and then to the medallion that sat on the table.

"Wait, Sandy. Trust me. You got to give us that minute..."

Lily struck her hand out and grabbed it. Shimmering beams of jade and grey green light flooded the room. Sandra pointed her gun at the emerging bodies.

"It is too soon!" Mequitha said. She adjusted Maroda's head to rest on her fish tail lap.

"I'm sorry, but there's been a development," Lily said. "Can you tell this woman about Ophiuchus?"

Mequitha looked at Sandra with eyes filled with an ocean of tears.

"He is angry. And powerful. He has gained control of the water. He will destroy mankind so he can rebuild his race and live here."

"Who are you talking about?"

"Ophiuchus, he's the thirteenth Zodiac, an outcast," Lily said.

"We didn't mean to outcast him. His people were Horoscopians. We were friends."

"And what about you and the others? You will all take over the planet for yourselves," Sandra said.

"No. We came to do no harm. It seems that humans are a danger to themselves without any help," Mequitha said. "Our plan was to rebuild in our constellation with the help of planet Earth. Not to inhabit it."

"So, you are telling me that these aliens are not invading us, but here to help us and save themselves?"

"Yes!" everyone said.

"Sandra, we have spent the last few weeks with the Zodiac Warriors. If they were going to destroy humans, they would have done so by now," Zakary implored.

"Please, hold off the police."

"Help us. We don't have much time. Orlando Focus has probably already started cutting off the world from their water supply."

"Orlando Focus? Of NuDelta?"

"Yes, he is the Horoscopian Ophiuchus."

A realisation dawned on Sandra. The answer to that uneasy feeling she's had about Mr Focus became clear. His eyes. He had the same silver circle in his iris that the aliens had, including the Pisceans she was looking at now.

"I knew there was something about him. This is bad. This is very bad." She put her gun in her holster and took out her phone and requested the police to stand down.

"We don't have much time," Lily said. "Orlando knows we have got the Piscean medallion, but he doesn't know they are back in it or that I can actualize them. But he will be preparing for his final move to gain control over humankind."

"OK. What's the plan and what do you need?"

They told her their plan. She called her contact in the Viking Squad. He would provide her with guns and also back up if this whole set up was what they said it was. She wondered if she could trust anyone back at the CIA. As loyal as she was to her job, something felt right about going along with this rag-taggle bunch of people.

The choppers landed six kilometres from the volcano overlooking Orlando's house. They dropped down into the gorge dressed in army fatigues and moved along the valley. After two hours, they recognized the waterfall Hastia had frolicked in the day before. They looked up and saw the glass house jutting out of the rock face. Hiding behind bushes and rocks, they positioned themselves along the bank of the river. Lily advanced until she was directly below the house. She pulled out the medallion and willed the Pisceans to actualize. Nothing.

"God dammit," she muttered. She willed it again. A movement above her made her glance up. Orlando stood at the window, looking down.

"Shit!"

She shook the medallion. "Shit, shit, shit! Not now, please!"

She backed away and joined Sandra.

"What's happening?"

"I can't get them out. We're done for. We need to get out of here."

"What do you mean? They came out for you before."

"It's complicated, we haven't got time."

"Hackshinduibfo osinfop."

Lily and Sandra turned around.

"Hackshinvuibfo oshinfop."

"Astro?"

"Yackshinvuibfo oshinfop."

The medallion in Lily's hand vibrated, emitting the incandescent green light.

"How did you...?"

"Chime taught me the words, but I didn't know if I remembered them, or even if they worked."

"You're a genius!" Lily kissed Astro on their cheek.

As she turned back, the mermaids were now whole and Maroda was sitting up next to Mequitha. She looked plumper, brighter.

There was movement on the path cut into the cliff above them.

"He's seen us."

Lily raised her hands in the air. It was the signal for everyone to put their earplugs in their ears. She did the same.

"Sing! Now!"

Mequitha and Maroda opened their mouths and sang. As they did, they raised in the air and floated, their tail fins flowing with the melody. The humans put their hands over their ears as the shrill notes seemed to penetrate the earplugs, sending holes into their brains.

Suddenly, a shot rang out. Lily and Sandra pulled their eyes off the Pisceans and dived behind a boulder. More shots were fired from the pathway leading down from the house. It seemed like an army was pouring out of a cave in the mountainside and lining up.

"They're going to shoot the Pisceans!"

But Mequitha and Maroda dived under the water, keeping up their piercing song. Rubble fell from the cliff face. The glass of the house shimmered. The human's teeth rattled as the song reached a higher pitch again, and the armed people on the path put their hands to their ears as the song echoed off the walls of the valley, increasing its force with each pulse. All the humans scrunched up their faces and dropped to their knees. The gunmen and women fled along the path, trying to escape the sound. The vast panes of glass visibly vibrated, the rocks around the foundations coming loose. Another shot rang out, its sound ricocheting around the gorge. More of Orlando's army was pouring out of another exit near the house.

But as the song reached their ears, they dropped to their knees, clutching their heads. The glass walls shuddered but held fast. Then Orlando was out of the building. A sea of snakes slunk around his ankles. A command took them down the cliff face towards the humans below.

"Oh no," Jason murmured, "The snakes. Why aren't they running away from the sound?"

"Snakes can't hear the song. They don't have ears," Tammy said. "Get ready to shoot 'em." She drew the pistol up and scanned the ground. She shot at a movement out of the corner of her eye and the body of a serpent flicked in the air. Jason shrieked and fumbled for his weapon as he saw another heading towards him. Tammy shot. More snakes tumbled down the incline. Tim and Zakary leapt onto a boulder and shot at the approaching serpents. Mack, Stevie and John followed suit. Sal screamed, but couldn't bring herself to fire.

Orlando was yelling at his army, kicking the men and women crouched on the ground with their hands on their ears. Lily, Sandra and Astro watched the pantomime above them, unable to hear the gunfire happening behind them, only hearing the high-pitched siren that leaked around their earplugs. They saw Orlando bring a machine gun around to his front. The notes increased to a higher pitch yet. The windowed walls of the house shuddered now, loosening more rocks. Orlando lifted the machine gun and aimed it at Tammy, John and the others who were intent on not being bitten by his snakes. The windows cracked at the edges. Orlando pulled the trigger and as bullets splayed across the valley, the glass house exploded into the void.

Lily, Sandra and Astro dived into the ice-cold river. John, Tim, Mack, Tammy, Stevie and Zak were blown aside with the tremors that ripped through the earth. Salina landed in the water. Fragments of glass shot like fireworks into the valley. Beams of steel, tables, chairs, kitchen cupboards and house contents tumbled through the air, crashing off the protruding rocks.

Suddenly, there was silence.

Lily broke the surface. Glass and rubble scattered the ground like an apocalypse aftermath.

"Oh my God!" she yelled into the deafening silence, unable to hear her own voice.

Sandra and Astro broke the surface and gasped lungfuls of air.

"Zak, Jason!" Lily cried out.

She saw bodies lying on the ground through the dust clouding the air.

"No, no, no!" Lily yelled as she scrambled over to the others.

They were lying on the ground, each wound up in a snake. Other smaller snakes, some black, some with bright yellow markings, others lime green, brown and white, slithered around the row of Lily's friends. Orlando's army scrambled down the slope, armed only with their power to command the snakes.

There was a moan and movement. Lily ran over to Zakary, but she drew up as a snake reared up and hissed at her. Another came from behind and curled itself around her legs. She screamed and kicked at the serpent, but its muscled body easily overcame her struggle and she toppled to the ground.

"Astro!" Lily yelled. "Say the words! Bring the Warriors out!"

But the snake tightened itself around her neck. Another snake entered the water and circled Astro.

"I wouldn't say a word, or the Pisceans are dead!"

Orlando was standing on the huge rocks in the middle of the water. He trembled with intense fury. His fingers held Mequitha's head by her long hair. A python was wrapped around Maroda. She gasped as it tightened its grip. Mequitha wriggled. He shook her head roughly, making her squeal.

"What do you want?" Lily hissed at Orlando through her contracted throat.

Everything was happening so fast. Her ears were still ringing from the siren song and the explosion, the dust still clouding her vision. Her scalp tingled and twitched. She did a mental inventory of her friends. Tammy and John moaned. Tim opened his eyes and screamed as he became aware of the scaly reptiles coiled around him. Stevie came to and struggled against their grip, swearing. Zak dared not move as a rattlesnake bared its fangs at him. Snakes crawled over Mack's motionless body. A shard of glass protruded from his head. Astro lay motionless, bound in a python. And Salina? There was no sign of her.

"Give me the Piscean pod," Orlando said.

"No!" Lily yelled. "Mequitha, retreat!"

Mequitha writhed in Orlando's grip.

"You think they would, wouldn't you?"

Orlando gave her head another shake.

"Retreat, NOW!" Lily tried to yell but choked as the snake squeezed her.

"I have separated them, you see. If they are not joined, they cannot go back. How do you think I've had control over them all these years?"

"But, in the ice?" Lily croaked.

"They must have made contact when I froze them. An unfortunate lapse on my part. We didn't have ice in Horoscopia. It's a little detail we had no way of foreseeing. Now, give me the pod so I can keep my fellow Warriors safe and sound in their little coffins."

"NO!"

Sandra, who had been shivering in the water, stood up.

"Looks like you got your hands full there, Mr Focus." Sandra aimed her gun at his head.

Orlando smiled. Lily relaxed a little.

"Ah! The newcomer. I believe you have been doing some work for me?"

Lily shot a look at Sandra.

"That's right. I said you could trust me," Sandra said, lowering her gun.

Orlando smiled a smile so smug Lily wanted to vomit. She could feel the lumps on her head vibrating.

"It's a pleasure to finally meet you," Sandra said to him.

"You know him?" Lily struggled against the snake as her stomach dropped.

"Sandra has been doing some work for me courtesy of the CIA."

"You're with the CIA?" Lily croaked at Orlando.

"Let's say the CIA is with me."

Mequitha writhed against Orlando's grip. "We're going to have to postpone the social niceties for now," he said, yanking the Piscean's head violently. "Sandra, get the medallion off her."

Sandra moved towards Lily.

"Sandra! What the hell are you doing?" Zakary yelled.

"My job, Zak, I'm doing my job." She swung her firearm at Zak. "Now release the medallion," she said to Lily, "or I'll shoot him."

Lily's heart lurched. She knew in that second, she would give anything for Zak. Her head quivered, the hairs pulling out of the buns she had coiled over the ever-protruding lumps. Lily freed her arm from the snake with the medallion in her hand.

In the river, Salina was face down. Today, she realised that holding her breath was a useful skill. She slowly turned her head to one side and drew in a big breath. She reached her hand down to a small mass of bubbles that was gurgling in the flow.

Lily tossed the medallion beyond Sandra. "Here, take it!" It tumbled onto the ground.

"No!" Zak and Stevie yelled.

"Get it!" Orlando screamed at Sandra.

Sandra stepped back, keeping her eyes on Zak and Lily. Staring at them so intently, her eyes widening until she could open them no further.

Suddenly, from behind Orlando, a huge wave of water crashed him off the rock. Lily could make out the form of Hastia, who fought Orlando in a frenzied whirlpool. He released Mequitha was, and she lunged at her sister. They distilled into a green light that poured into the medallion.

Salina was crouched in the water. She leapt up and tackled Sandra. Sandra shrieked as she was plunged again into the cold river.

"Stop, wait! I'm on your side!" Sandra gasped.

"Bullshit! You're working for that creep," Sal yelled.

A wave washed over them as Hastia swept Orlando into the middle of the river, tumbling them over. Sandra pulled herself onto the bank with Salina grabbing for her feet. In that second, they both saw one of the medallions. It held a bright sapphire glinting in the sunlight. Sandra went to lunge for it, but Salina got hold of her calves and pulled her back.

"I was working for the CIA, and the CIA work for him, but I thought he was corrupt. I'm with you and the Warriors!"

Sandra's fingers closed around the medallion, which vibrated in her hand. An otherworldly hue of khaki burst out of the sapphire. It formed a tall figure that stood majestic in the clear air of the fjord. She wore a long dress of silvery-white auburn hair tumbled over her shoulders. Her pale skin was like fine porcelain. Regida held a staff. She quickly assessed the situation with an impassive face. She turned to the men and women who commanded the snakes that held her friends. One by one, she penetrated their minds, which released a flood of endorphins. As Orlando's men lost grip on their senses, the snakes released their grip of the humans and slithered away in many directions. Lily jumped up and ran to Astro. Tammy waited for the snakes to clear away and knelt by Mack. As Sandra gawked at the beautiful being that stood before her, Sal yelled, "Find the other medallions!"

Sandra snapped out of her stupor and scoured the ground for the medallions. John and Tim pulled themselves together and scrabbled around the rocky earth.

Zak leapt onto Sandra. "You traitor, I can't believe you've been working for that snake!" he shouted at her. "What happened to you?"

"I was going to kill him, you idiot! Didn't you see my face? I was trying to tell you! Did you really believe I'd shoot you?"

Down the river, Orlando had commanded the upper hand and had tossed Hastia far down the valley. He roared, a green mist floating from his mouth, and more of his army emerged out of the cave in the mountainside accompanied by more snakes.

"We need to find Amrez!" Jason yelled.

It was as if John was drawn to his Warrior. He fell upon the Taurus medallion. A flash of green light delivered Teres to the scene. With a yelp of relief, Stevie chucked Leo to Tim and the mighty Degon flashed to life. He and Teres jumped to action, taking out five of Orlando's army. Lily had turned her attention to the other armed people. She felt her head explode and two muscular horns uncoiled. She willed them to lash out at the snakes. With each swipe, she gained better control. Zak caught sight, pausing in his battle. A soldier took advantage and punched him. Within a second, Lily's new limbs had the man sprawled across the ground metres away. She stood over Zak and helped him up with her outstretched arm.

"You've got horns!" Zak said in disbelief.

Lily nodded, but before she could respond, they were attacked by more of Orlando's soldiers.

Someone found Gemini and they materialized, jumping into hand fights.

Sal, sharp-eyed, scoured the ground and found Sagittarius. The medallion was sitting in the middle of a coiled rattle snake.

"Shit!"

She stood up and swore at the reptile. "Shoo! She picked up a rock and flung it. The snake rattled and raised its head threateningly.

"Goddamn it!"

She raised her pistol, shut her eyes and shot at the snake. When she squinted at it, she saw two halves of the mutilated snake draped each side of the medallion. She used her wet foot to push the guts off it.

"Zak!" She rushed over to him. "Quick, get Amrez, he can find the others!"

Zak held the medallion. The purple light flooded out and revealed not the Warrior they were used to, but the body of a horse with the torso and head of Amrez.

"You have got to be kidding me!" Amrez moaned as he twisted round to see his old Zodiac form had returned. Gunfire broke his thought. With lightning reflexes, he armed his bow and shot a woman soldier right in the heart.

"Find the other medallions!" Zak yelled as a man tackled him to the ground.

Everyone was fighting Orlando's army. Amrez fetched Prymaw, Xincon and Plaadio. Lily, Tammy and Jason released them, and they joined the fight. Tammy put her attention on Astro. She checked their pulse and gently tapped their cheek. Astro opened their eyes. Tammy helped them to their feet, but they were disorientated.

Amrez dropped Scorpio into Mack's lifeless hand before returning to Tammy and Astro. His strong arm pulled them onto his back, and he galloped off, depositing them at a safe distance along with the Libran medallion.

As Tammy stroked Astro's forehead, Chime materialized. She nodded at Tammy and knelt at Astro's side, placing her hands on their shoulders. They disappeared into the medallion and Tammy pocketed it in her dungarees.

Fyon appeared at Mack's side. She looked down at him, and then to the fight surrounding them. Her tail quivered, eager to let loose its full fury on the enemy. She dropped to one knee. A piece of glass pierced Mack's good eye. She put a hand on his heart and felt it beating weakly through his generous chest. Gently, she dislodged the shard. If he even survived, he would be blind. Degon galloped past her and leapt upon a soldier, taking him down. The battlefield was in full swing. Fyon put her hand on the blood that pulsed out of Mack's eye socket. This man was her guardian, and she was his. That was the law they had made before leaving their galaxy. That they would be guardians, protectors and guides. She lifted the slack body of Mack into her muscled arms and closed her eyes. They disappeared into the medallion.

Salina waded through the water down the valley. The force at which Orlando had flung Hastia had her explode into a million droplets. Aquamarine pieces of her lay scattered over the banks and floated in the water. As Salina got closer, the medallion she held under the water sucked up the drops one by one like mercury.

Prymaw and Degon, having dispensed with most of Orlando's army, were now taking the snake-master on. As they deflected the serpents, they got closer to him until his defences were spent. Prymaw's horns held him like a vice, and Degon shimmered over him, only just catching the licks of flame that threatened the Ophiuchus Warrior.

Teres, Xincon, the Gemini Twins, Amrez, Regida and Plaadio dispensed with their opponents and came still, breathing deeply from exertion. They surrounded Orlando.

"Traitors!" Orlando yelled.

"Hypocrite!" Teres yelled back. "How could you do this?"

"How could *I* do this? You left me to die, you left my whole planet to disappear without a trace," he spat, a green vapour pouring from his mouth.

Stevie, Tammy, Lily, Zak, John, Tim, Sandra and Jason arrived. Stevie fired at a stray snake, splattering it across the gravel.

"Where are Mack and Astro?"

Regida actualized Fyon and Chime. The Warriors placed the injured humans on the ground gently.

"What's going on?" Fyon demanded.

"He's upset we left him behind."

"We had to. If we didn't leave then, we'd all be dead. We didn't plan to..." Fyon began.

"Ay, but I wish we had now. Look at the trouble he's caused! Let's finish it now," Degon said.

He bared his teeth and growled in Orlando's face.

"You don't scare me, pussy cat. You should know I have substantial life insurance. Kill me now and you will all perish."

"He's bluffing," Teres said. "I agree with Degon, let's finish this snake."

"Wait!" Plaadio yelled. "Let him speak."

Salina released Hastia from the water. She shimmered onto the land, diminished in size but with currents running through her.

Prymaw released his grip on Orlando slightly. "What kind of insurance?"

"Under the foundations of every desalination plant I own, which is the majority of them, a snake is sleeping in a chamber. Its body is all that separates the wires that will trigger enough explosives to blow up the whole plant. If you kill me, each snake will awake from its slumber, and once it makes a move... BAM! Any hope of water for your regeneration, or to keep this pathetic race alive are gone."

"How do we know he's telling the truth?"

"I'm not willing to put it to the test."

"What do you want?" Regida asked.

"I want to be your leader."

The humans and Warriors were silent.

The distant rumble of helicopter blades chugged in the distance. "The Viking Squad."

The helicopters reached them and circled. Operatives hung off the choppers, guns aimed at the group. Sandra walked away from the others and gave a signal to hold their fire. Two more helicopters flew past, this time photographers snapped the Warriors.

"They're journalists. The games up. In half an hour, the whole world will know you exist. So what's it going to be?" Orlando said.

Nobody said a word.

"We need to be a unified force," Plaadio said.

"And bow down to this lunatic?" Fyon spat.

"You cannot be our leader," Degon said.

"Then watch me call my snakes awake."

"Then you will kill us all—humans, animals and us," Teres said.

Orlando shrugged. "I don't care. I have lived here thousands of years on other people's terms, pretending I am someone, something else. Either I rule, or we all die. You choose."

A helicopter chugged above them and landed on a flat further up the valley. Armed forces stalked towards them with raised guns.

Lily pulled away from the group.

"Stop! They're not here to harm us. Put your guns down!"

The commander raised his hand to halt his troops.

"Who are you?"

"My name is Lily Noor. I am the Guardian of Aries." She lifted the medallion. Prymaw joined her. The forces tightened their grip on their weapons.

"Retreat Prymaw!" Lily yelled.

"Lily..." Prymaw dissipated before he could protest.

Zak joined her.

"Lily, what are you doing? What will happen to Focus without the Warriors to control him?"

"It is safer for them to be inside until we speak with the UN. Orlando needs them as much as we need him. Trust me."

"I don't know. What if they take the medallions off us?"

"He won't let them. Bring Amrez back into his pod."

"Amrez! Return to the medallion!"

Amrez snapped into a thread of light that flowed to Zak's hand.

"Everyone, protect your Warriors!" Lily yelled.

As Degon withdrew, he left Orlando to drop to the ground. He scrabbled upright, dusting himself down, and strode to Lily's side.

"Good decision, young woman. Good decision." He put his arms in the air and spoke to the crowd of journalists and local armed forces that had gathered.

"Citizens! This is a new beginning. These alien beings you have witnessed here today bring us hope. Under my command, together we will build a planet that can sustain us all. No longer shall you go thirsty or hungry, no longer shall the air be polluted. The Zodiac Warriors are here to save us all!"

The President of the United States of America stood on one side of Orlando Focus. On the other, the United Nations Secretary General. Behind stood the leaders of the 192 other Member States. Twelve human guardians stood around the circular pool in front of the Secretariat Building. The roads around the United Nations' buildings had been closed off and thousands of people had gathered. The photos of the Warriors in Iceland had gone viral around the world. Cameras swept over the crowd, and large screens had been erected on two sides. The press conference was to be broadcast across the planet.

The Secretary General raised her hands to quiet the spectators.

"Ladies and gentlemen, citizens of the planet, I welcome you here today for the unprecedented introduction of life from another galaxy. As we have seen from the footage and many interviews with the guardians, we are honoured to welcome the Zodiac Warriors to Earth. Without any further ado, let us begin. Please welcome Mr Orlando Focus, a well-known businessman and philanthropist who has discovered the Zodiac guardians and brought them together."

She nodded to Orlando, who stepped up to his microphone.

"Thank you, Secretary."

Orlando waited for the crowd to quiet. "It is oft said our fate is written in the stars. Many have waved that off as superstition and nonsense. But many have also denied the existence of extra-terrestrial life. In this auspicious time, I believe that naysayers have been proved wrong on both accounts. The stars have delivered us saviours from another galaxy. Because, fellow citizens, our beloved Earth is in trouble. While I have been doing all I can to make sure each and every human being has access to water..."

The people cheered again and raised their hands in the air. Lily glanced at Zak. Jason stared at his feet. As the cameras panned across their faces, they dared not make any facial expressions.

Orlando continued after the cheers had subsided. "But one man alone cannot save an entire planet. So, I am proud to have gathered together these brave human beings who have each discovered the medallions that house the incredible Zodiac Warriors from Horoscopia."

Lily looked to Zak across the fountain, then to her left—to a new addition to the group. Her mother Abigale who was born in March. A true Piscean, a dreamer, a creative, a gentle woman who had been afflicted with an addiction, but who now stood firm next to her daughter. Today, her shaking was from nerves, not withdrawal. Lily smiled at her, giving her an assuring nod.

"Lily Noor, guardian of Aries. Please..." Orlando instructed her to commence.

Lily picked up the medallion from the plinth in front of her. Prymaw's bright red light wowed the crowd. As his huge, muscled body became solid, the people gasped. A million phones were raised. His vast horned head loomed large on the screen.

"I am Prymaw of Aries."

Lily smiled at him. He gave her a nod of his head before spinning around for the world to get a good look at him.

"Professor John Robertson, guardian of Taurus," Orlando declared.

John placed his hands over the medallion. Teres' vast body and fierce look caused the crowd to pulsate.

"Steven Rutherford, present your Zodiac Warrior of Gemini."

Stevie's belt had been removed from the medallion. He took it in his hands, bringing Castor and Pollux to life. In unison, they said their names to the watching world.

Xincon and Degon terrified the crowd as Xincon clacked his mighty claw and fire dripped off the roaring Leo.

The people cheered as Sandra and Astro actualized Regida and Chime in their more familiar human form, before Fyon and Amrez leapt onto the wall surrounding the fountain, raising their weapons in salute. Jason nervously brought Plaadio to life, who merely nodded at the audience. As Salina summoned Hastia, she played through the fountain's cascading water. The people gasped at her display.

Finally, Abigale lifted her medallion. Mequitha and Maroda shimmered into form and draped themselves over the edge of the pool to whistles and cheering.

"Citizens of Earth, please join me in welcoming our," Orlando paused, "*new* friends to our magnificent planet. The Zodiac Warriors!"

He clapped at and nodded to each of the Warriors. An orchestra erupted with sweeping music and a choir sang the Anthem of Planet Earth.

'Gainst stars that twinkle in the gloam,
Rests this blue planet we call home.
To you this Earth our spirits raise,
We offer our hearts to you in praise.
We walk together small and big,
Upon this land, we toil and dig.
This soil that feeds and air we breathe,
This water gives life and plants that weave,
Rocks that house and fire that warms,

We honour this planet in all her forms.
You are part of us, and we part of you,
And united we stand to protect and renew.
Twixt sun and moon and stars above,
Planet Earth is the home we all love.

As the last dying notes drifted over the crowd and through the airwaves and along the internet, through telegraph poles and underground lines, Pollux and Castor sent a message to Regida through their own communication channels.

"We need to take Ophiuchus down."

Regida looked at the twins and nodded.

THE END

AFTERWORD

Thank you for reading The Zodiac Warriors. Did you relate to your Zodiac characters? What will happen now Orlando Focus is in command of the Warriors? Will he maintain control over the water on Earth? For updates on when following stories are released, please join the mailing list:

https://www.subscribepage.com/zodiacwarriors

If you have enjoyed this book, please leave a review! It really helps us to promote the book.

Many thanks,

Tony